M000288793

OFF LIMITS

A STORMFINCH SECURITY NOVEL

HELENA NEWBURY
NEW YORK TIMES BESTSELLING AUTHOR

For Leo

© Copyright Helena Newbury 2022

The right of Helena Newbury to be identified as the author of this work has been asserted by her in accordance with the Copyright, Design and Patents Act 1988

This book is entirely a work of fiction. All characters, companies, organizations, products and events in this book, other than those clearly in the public domain, are fictitious or are used fictitiously and any resemblance to any real persons, living or dead, events, companies, organizations or products is purely coincidental.

This book contains adult scenes and is intended for readers 18+.

Cover by Mayhem Cover Creations

Main cover model image licensed from (and copyright remains with) Wander Aguiar Photography

Second Edition

ISBN: 978-1-914526-23-7

1

ERIN

WHEN I MET DANNY BRIGGS, I was a long way from home.

I need you to understand how unusual that is for me. I don't do so well outside of my cozy, secure little burrow and I avoid leaving it at all costs. But my brother needed me so I'd driven for thirteen hours and eight hundred miles, all the way from Vegas to a tiny town in the mountains of Colorado. Now I was sitting in a café, shivering, warming my hands on a mug of coffee and feeling way, way out of my comfort zone.

Some of it was the cold. I was used to Vegas, where *winter* meant the temperature dropping into the fifties. Up here in Colorado, everything was covered in a thick blanket of snow and the thermometer read nine degrees. I'd driven through the night, fueled by gas station coffee and gummy bears, and the heater in my car doesn't work. Halfway across Utah, with the stars overhead, I'd had to pull over, empty my suitcase at the side of the road and pull on more clothes. I'd wound up wearing two t-shirts, two shirts and a denim jacket. As I'd climbed into the mountains, it had gotten even colder and I'd stopped at a truck stop and bought a deerstalker with fluffy flaps to go over my ears but I was still freezing.

Some of it, though, was the town. Las Vegas is one giant machine, designed to separate tourists from their money, and I live right at the heart of it. I can feel the data humming through the air all around me, see a million neon lights twinkling under computer command, hear the slot machines clatter and jingle in a carefully-tuned symphony. *Heaven.* Even better, Vegas is designed to be anonymous. No one knows you, no one *wants* to know you. Someone like me can just hunker down and be ignored. But this quaint little town was the opposite. I had one bar of signal on my phone and everyone in the café seemed to know each other. I slid lower in my seat and tried to hide behind my laptop screen.

I checked the time: it was eight in the morning, still too early to call my brother and tell him I was in town. I brought up a tech jobs website and started job-hunting but the words blurred together. I took off my glasses and cleaned them but when I put them back on, I still couldn't focus properly. I was in that dozy, morning-after fug you get after staying awake all night.

That's when I noticed the guy smiling at me from across the café. I blinked and checked over my shoulder...but no, there wasn't some hot girl behind me. He was smiling at *me,* which didn't make sense. Guys don't smile at me. Guys don't *notice* me.

This one was about thirty, the same as me. But he leaned against the counter with an easy confidence I'd never have, a leather jacket open over a hoodie with the name of some band too cool for me to recognize. His smile widened as he saw me notice him: he was sort of good looking, if you went for the rough look. I felt my cheeks flare red. *Why's he smiling at me?* Did I have a milk mustache, or—

The guy collected his coffee and then strolled past me and out of the café's rear exit, turning to give me a friendly nod. When he was gone, I sat there, stunned. *This never happens.*

Deep in my chest, something flared into life. Cautious and flickering, ready to die at any second because better that it died than to have it snuffed out by someone else again. But it was there, fragile but hopeful. *Maybe I'm not so weird. Maybe he really did smile at me because he likes me. I should have smiled back. Maybe it would have been the start of something.* And my sleep-deprived brain started to fill up with daydreams: maybe the guy was a fellow nerd and techie. I imagined cuddling up and reading together, safe and warm....

Then I caught myself. What might have been didn't matter. He was gone and I was only here for a day. I'd never see him agai—

The guy burst back in through the rear door. "Help! There's a woman unconscious out here!"

For a second, I just gaped at him, caught in emotional whiplash. But my mom had drilled into my brother and me to help, if we could, and taught us basic first aid. I jumped up and ran over to him. "Where?"

He stepped aside to let me through the door. "There! Behind the dumpster!"

I raced out into the alley. The street was slick with ice: maybe the woman had slipped and hit her head. Or she could be homeless, and she'd passed out in the snow and was hypothermic...

I rounded the dumpster but there was no one there. *Where is she?!* I looked back towards the café but the guy hadn't followed me outside: probably, he was calling an ambulance. I realized there was a second dumpster, further down the alley, and raced over to it as fast as I dared on the ice—

There was no one there, either. *Cheese and crackers!* Where was she? I looked up and down the alley, desperate. *What if she dies because I can't find her?*

I took a few more steps down the alley and then stopped. Realization hit, spreading through my mind in a sickly gray cloud. *No. No, no, it can't be....*

I ran back to the café and burst in through the rear door, eyes already on the table where I'd been sitting. My laptop was gone. So was my phone. So was my backpack.

And the guy who'd smiled at me was halfway across the café, my backpack in his arms, heading for the front door.

Everything was in that bag. Not just the laptop and phone he'd shoved into it but my money, my ID, my car keys.... "Stop!" I called, but my voice was swallowed up by the noise of the café. Why couldn't I have a big, booming voice like my brother? "Somebody stop him!" I yelled. This time, a few heads turned and people frowned with concern, but it was too late: the guy was already hurrying past them.

I ran after him. I only have short legs but I put everything I had into running and, as the guy slowed to haul open the front door, I caught up. Just as he stepped out onto the street, I grabbed his shoulder. "Stop!"

He turned and scowled at me, all the warmth gone from his eyes. He shoved me in the chest and I skittered backwards, hit the door and went down hard on the sidewalk.

He smirked and his lip curled in disgust, like he couldn't believe how easily I'd been fooled. I could see it all, now. How he'd picked out his target, the geeky girl on her own. The smile, to make me feel special and put me off guard. The story about the unconscious woman that made him seem like a caring, helpful hero.

I watched, tears filling my eyes, as the guy ran towards the curb, where his buddy sat waiting on a dirt bike.

I was an idiot. Of course a guy hadn't been interested in me.

And there were no heroes.

Someone slammed into the guy, ramming him sideways like a semi-truck hitting a car at an intersection. The guy hit a wall and cried out: I thought I heard a bone snap. He crumpled and slid to the ground, dropping my backpack.

"You just stay there, sunshine," said the man standing over him.

The accent was British, but not the British of butlers and tea parties. This was rough as brick, filthy as a smokestack. It was supremely cocky, completely unafraid. In the darkest alley in the worst city in the world, that accent would tell you to *come and have a go if you think you're hard enough.*

The guy on the dirt bike paled and roared off.

The man turned, his black overcoat flaring out around him, and walked towards me. I was still awkwardly half-sitting against the door where I'd fallen. As he came closer, I had to crane my head way back to keep him in view. He was *big,* a full head taller than me, and wide in the shoulders, too, and he was wearing a black suit under the overcoat. On some guys with a lot of muscle, suits look awkward and wrong: they look like kids forced to squeeze into their Sunday best. But on this man, the suit couldn't have looked more *right*. The dark fabric flowed over his legs, flattened by the breeze against thickly-muscled thighs. The shirt was as white as the snow around us and beautifully tailored, following the vee-shape of his upper body and then skimming a hard, flat stomach. The black tie drew a perfect line between the broad swells of his chest, the tip pointing cheekily down towards his groin.

I craned my head further back and saw black hair cut short, the wind tousling it just a little, as if nature herself couldn't resist him. Hard cheekbones and a strong jaw. Dangerously sexy lips, wide and full, the corners lifted into a permanent little smile, as if he didn't take anything in life completely seriously.

And then I saw his eyes.

They were a color I'd never seen. Absinthe green, glittering and intoxicating. They were clear, honest: they didn't play games or try to pretend he was something he wasn't. They didn't promise anything except a wild, filthy ride.

He looked down at me and his smile widened, turning into a full-on grin. His eyes sparkled and something in my chest just *lit up* and went *ding ding ding,* like a pinball machine hitting a super bonus multiplier.

He offered his hand to pull me up. I reached for it and saw that my palm was scraped from the sidewalk. The man noticed, too, and his eyes narrowed: a quiet, dangerous rage. He looked over his shoulder at the guy who'd stolen my bag and the guy shrank back against the wall. It was like a warm blanket was being wrapped around me: I'd never felt so protected.

The man took my hand in his big, warm one and hauled me to my feet. I'd been wrong before. He was *over* a foot taller than me: my eyes were level with his pecs.

"I'm Danny," he told me in that deliciously rough London accent. "And who are *you?*"

2

DANNY
ONE MINUTE EARLIER

THE SKY overhead was eggshell blue and a bright sun made the snow drifts sparkle like they'd been dusted with diamonds. It was bitterly cold outside but I had the Jaguar's heater set *just so* and as I swung the car around each corner, I had a big, stupid grin on my face. It was a beautiful day and I was doing my favorite thing in the world. Who could ask for anything more?

It was my first day off in months. The private military team I worked for, Stormfinch Security, only needed us for jobs a few times a month, but between the jobs there was planning and scouting and lots and lots of training. My best mate JD, a big Texan who commanded our motley crew, had us doing five mile runs before the sun was even up and skulking through the local forests doing night training long after dark. When I wasn't training, I'd been helping Kian, the Irishman who handled all the admin and got us our missions, to turn a derelict factory into our base.

Today, though, JD and Kian were both in Washington, answering questions about what we'd been getting up to. Kian had told JD he had to wear a suit and it had been so long since he'd worn one, I'd had to help him tie his tie. "Wasn't what I signed up for," he'd grumbled. "Sitting in a meeting all day being grilled by pencil-necks. Why can't you do it? You *love* wearing a damn suit!"

"I'm not the leader of this merry band, though, am I?" I'd told him, adjusting the knot. Something I was eternally grateful for. I'm no leader. I couldn't take that responsibility, couldn't make those judgment calls that decided whether someone came home alive or in a box. I've always been the light-hearted one, the joker. Maybe that's why we work so well together: I'm the Robin to his Batman.

JD had looked so miserable, when he was dressed, that Kian had sighed and said he could wear his Stetson, and that had cheered him up. I shook my head, chuckling. I loved the big doofus.

I flicked the wheel and slid the car around the corner onto Main Street, letting the back end slide just a little on the ice. I love the throb of a big V8: primitive and simple, like me. I had the Jag tuned exactly the way I wanted it and it felt alive, *ready*...all I was doing today was cruising but I could feel it begging me to let loose, it *wanted* to go fast. I patted the steering wheel lovingly. *Good girl. Maybe later.*

A plan started to take shape in my head. First, I'd stop at the little café down the street for a cup of coffee. I'm a Brit so I mainly drink tea but I've spent enough time in the US that I've come around to having one big, steaming mug of joe in the morning and this place did the best in town.

I'd get my coffee, cruise around a little more, then there was an engine I wanted to work on. This afternoon, I might call Jackie. Or Stephanie. Or that dental receptionist...Hannah? I'd got myself a nice little list of booty calls around Mount Mercy, women who melted when they heard my accent in a bar and liked it even more when I was on top of them, whispering in their ear as I spread their legs and told them all the filthy things I was going to do to them.

Okay, maybe driving is my *second* favorite thing.

I made sure the women knew upfront that it was just fun, that it wasn't going to turn into anything, and they always nodded eagerly: *that's all I want, too.* But I knew that after a few months, they'd start to get attached and I'd have to gently push them away. I hated doing it, but it was the only way. I couldn't give them what they needed.

I couldn't love them.

Back to the plan. After the booty call I'd grab a bite to eat and then in the evening, when JD got back, I had to take him out for a drink. It was going to be a tough night for him: the anniversary. Of course, JD being JD, he wouldn't talk about it, but I could at least sit in a bar with him and make sure the poor guy wasn't on his own.

I pulled up in front of the café, turned off the engine and stepped out. I caught a glimpse of my reflection in the café's windows. *Looking sharp.*

"Somebody stop him!"

The yell came from inside the café but it took me a second to find the speaker. She was small and slender built and she was drowned in all these layers of clothes that made her seem even smaller, but it was more than that. She sort of...hid, like she didn't want anyone to notice her.

I followed her eyes. A guy was running towards the café's door, a cherry-colored backpack in his arms with a laptop sticking out of the top. It didn't take a genius to figure out what was going on.

The woman raced across the café and caught up with the guy just as he got through the door. "Stop!" she pleaded.

The guy turned to her and straight-armed her back into the door. She smacked into it and went down hard.

Something swelled in my chest, scalding and powerful, expanding to fill my whole body. I ran at the guy. He didn't notice me, focused on getting to his buddy who was waiting for him at the curb on a dirt bike.

I'm built for strength, not speed, but I was powered by raw, primal rage and I was accelerating with every step, coming at him like a freight train. Five strides away, four, three...the guy finally heard me coming and turned to look but, by now, it was far too late. I slammed into him and rammed him up against a wall. *See how you like it.* Admittedly, I might have done it a little harder than he'd done it to the woman. I heard a rib break. *Good.*

He slid down the wall and slumped on the sidewalk. "You just stay there, sunshine," I told him. I glanced at the guy on the dirt bike to let him know he was next, and he went sheet-white and roared off.

I marched over to the woman. For a moment, all I could see was the deerstalker she was wearing and then she looked up at me and—

Something happened. That feeling I'd had when I saw her being shoved, that protective need, came back even stronger. She was just so small, so...vulnerable. Her eyes were big and innocent and they were this very pale shade of blue that I could imagine on a butterfly's wing. They peered out at me from behind big, gold-framed glasses. And how many layers was she wearing?! There was an old denim jacket, covered in sew-on patches, then a soft cotton shirt, then *another* shirt, then a t-shirt and I could see the collar of *another* t-shirt peeking out from beneath that. It was like she was trying to keep warm, but she hadn't any cold-weather clothes to put on. *She's not from around here.*

I could feel myself smiling. Not my usual flirty smirk, more like the stupid smile I got when I was driving, that good feeling that bubbles up from down in your chest when you're having fun. I'd never had it with a woman before. But then she wasn't like any of the women I normally met. They were all confidence, perfume and hair flicks: they knew what they wanted and they knew how to play the game. This woman...I wasn't sure she even knew what the game *was.* She reminded me of some small animal, nose twitching the air nervously.

She was...*cute.* Adorable, in fact. And I didn't go for *adorable,* but...

I put out my hand to help her up. She reached and I saw that her palms were scraped and red from hitting the sidewalk. Hot rage blossomed in my chest again and I twisted and glared at the guy I'd taken down. He shrank back, his Adam's apple bobbing as he gulped.

I took her hand gently in mine and hauled her up to standing. God, she was just a little thing. Even smaller because she wore sneakers: I was used to women in heels.

I said what I always say. "I'm Danny. And who are *you?*"

But it came out differently. I barely recognized my own voice. I'd been using that line since high school and every other time I'd used it, what I'd really been asking was, "What do I need to do to get your panties off?"

This time, I actually wanted to know who she was. *What's going on?!*

"Erin," she said, uncertain. There was something in her voice, an accent, but it was difficult to catch from just one word.

She frowned, her blonde brows knitting, and pulled off the deerstalker. Underneath was ash-blonde hair pulled back into a long braid: it fell down her back, swinging. She rubbed at the back of her head, wincing a little: she must have bumped it, when she went down. And as I looked down at her in that unguarded moment, I realized...she was beautiful.

I hadn't seen it immediately, I'd been fooled by how cute she was. But she had that kind of beauty that crept up on you and then hit you all at once, and once you saw it.... She had high, delicate cheekbones and her lips were blush-pink and looked so, so soft...

She was lovely. She just *hid.*

"Are you okay, Erin?" I asked. "Are you hurt?"

"No," she said. "Yes." She frowned again, pushed her glasses up her nose and shook her head. "No, I'm not hurt, yes, I'm okay."

Her awkwardness put her back into adorable mode. But it didn't matter because I was equally fascinated by both sides of her, now. Her accent was deeply country, soothing and gentle, like a warm shaft of sunshine in the middle of all the cold and snow.

I heard something in the background, an ugly *blarrrt.* But I didn't pay it any attention because at that moment, Erin turned a little, reached back and rubbed her rump where she'd fallen on it and...she had this perfect peach of an ass, the soft denim stretched tight over it. As she twisted, all those layers she was wearing pulled tight across her chest and I saw the twin hillocks of what looked like perfect little perky, upthrust breasts. I could feel myself getting hard in my pants. But when she turned back to me, her expression was completely innocent. She was oblivious to what she was doing to me...which only made her hotter.

I felt myself shuffle an inch closer to her. I wanted to know her better. I wanted to know everything. I couldn't understand what she was doing to me: *I don't go for adorable.* But there was something about her... She looked up at me warily and I thought of an animal again, ears pricked up for any sign of danger. But there was a determination in her eyes, too: she'd chased after that guy even though he was bigger than her.

That *blart* sound again, closer, this time. But I'd become aware that I still had hold of her hand and even though I knew it was high time I let it go, I really didn't want to. In fact, I—

Wait, no, don't, you'll scare her away.

But it was too late, I was already doing it. Couldn't stop myself. Just a little squeeze of her hand.

She looked down at our joined hands in shock. Looked up at me, worried. But she must have seen something in my face because she softened. Could she see how confused I was?

We looked into each other's eyes and—

That ugly noise became a roar and I suddenly realized what it was. A dirt bike engine. The guy on the bike had ridden all the way around the block and now, seeing us distracted, he skidded up to the curb. The guy I'd taken down climbed to his feet, wincing, grabbed the backpack from the sidewalk and jumped on the back of the bike. And the two of them roared off down the street.

"Oh, you little bastards," I muttered. Now I was *really* mad. I dropped Erin's hand, ran to the Jag and jumped in. I threw open the passenger door. "Get in!" I yelled to Erin.

But she just stood there, uncertain. I realized I was still a complete stranger. We stared at each other for one, two, three seconds as she nervously bit her lip....

And then she ran to the car and jumped in beside me.

3

ERIN

THE INSTANT my ass hit the seat, we were moving. It felt like Danny didn't so much hit the gas as let the car off the leash: it leapt forward with an angry roar and I was pinned in the big leather seat by the acceleration. The dirt bike, which had been disappearing into the distance, began to creep closer. I grabbed the seatbelt and fastened myself in. *What am I doing?! I'm in a car chase. With a stranger!*

His accent reminded me of one of the characters in my favorite book series, *The Throne of Night*. In my head, everyone in medieval-y, fantasy worlds have British accents. Danny didn't sound like one of the princes. More like the rough warrior from the backstreets who winds up saving the kingdom. I'd never heard an accent like it in person. All the men I'd known had had southern accents, calming and mellow as a cold beer on a hot day. Each time Danny spoke, it was like a shot of whiskey, rough and fiery and completely intoxicating. The words burned into my brain and soaked down through my body, leaving me heady.

The car was British, too, an old Jaguar, full of character and attitude. The chrome had been polished until it gleamed and someone must have been busy under the hood, too, because the engine sounded like a choir of angels yelling a vengeful war cry.

The dirt bike was threading its way through the morning traffic, darting through gaps and dodging down alleys. We were thundering after it, a bull chasing a dragonfly. We skidded around a corner and I slid across the leather seat until I was wedged against the door. *Ulp.*

We straightened out and accelerated, the buildings becoming a terrifying blur. I felt my stomach knot. I'd never gone this fast in a car: I'm always the one getting honked at for being too cautious at intersections. I found the grab-handle above me and clung on for dear life. *Maybe if I close my eyes.* I tried it. *Nope. Nope, that's worse.*

I opened my eyes and focused on Danny, instead. That was better. God, he was *gorgeous*: sinful lips pressed into a tight line of concentration, gleaming green eyes flicking over the road ahead. He drove like no one I'd ever seen, his hands and feet moving in a complex, coordinated dance as he shifted through the gears, his hands dancing on the wheel as we slewed around a corner. It didn't feel like he was driving...more like he was silently communicating with the car, guiding it the way a good horseman guides his horse. I could smell his cologne and it was amazing: citrus and vanilla, light and clean, *playful*...but there was a twist of some dark spice, too, sophisticated and rawly sexual. I wanted to bury my nose in his shirt collar.

"Short cut," announced Danny, and whipped the wheel to the left. A building filled the windshield and I screamed—

We shot through an open doorway and suddenly we were *indoors*, blasting through an abandoned warehouse, missing stacks of crates by inches. He spun the wheel again and the car seemed to float. I stared out of my window as the world rushed towards me. *Oh my God, we're going sideways...*

We shot back out onto the street again. Danny effortlessly flicked us out of the skid and now we were right behind the dirt bike. I saw the rider look over his shoulder in disbelief and fear.

We stayed right on the bike's tail as it roared out of town and up into the hills. It finally came to a stop at an abandoned sawmill halfway up a hillside. There were a bunch of other dirt bikes there, and a van with peeling brown paint. Ten or twelve people were standing around, most of them warming themselves by a bonfire. Music was playing on a wireless speaker and a bottle of vodka was being passed round. A woman sat cross-legged on a blanket, a phone in her hands and a credit card in the other. In front of her, more credit cards formed a gleaming, rainbow pile. As I watched, she tossed the card she was holding over her shoulder and picked up another at random, her fingers tapping the phone screen too fast to follow. Another guy had a whole bunch of phones in front of him, together with some laptops and a few cameras. He seemed to be taking photos of them.

It all fell into place: they were a gang. They traveled to a new area and set up camp, then pairs of them rode out on dirt bikes and stole bags, phones and laptops. Then they came back here, where the stolen credit cards would be maxed out before their owners could cancel them and the electronics could be photographed and auctioned online. Just as the local police realized they had a problem, the gang would move on to another town.

Ahead of us, the pair on the dirt bike jumped off and ran towards the group. As we got out, everyone at the bonfire turned to look at us. *Maybe this wasn't such a good idea.*

But Danny just straightened his tie, told me to *wait here,* and marched straight towards them. I've never seen someone so confident.

The guys from the dirt bike ran straight up to a big guy in a leather jacket—their leader, at a guess—and muttered something, pointing fearfully at Danny. The leader nodded and swaggered forward, waving the two guys behind him. He was wide and stocky, his black hair shaved down to sandpaper and his face flat and sour. The wind was stronger, up here in the hills, and it was bitterly cold, but his leather jacket was open and he was only wearing a t-shirt underneath.

Danny and the gang leader stopped when they were six feet apart and the two men faced off. The gang leader stepped his feet apart and puffed his chest out, all sneering intimidation. But Danny just stood there, calm and collected and utterly at ease. It was like watching a playground bully face off against a grown up.

"You hurt one of my boys," the gang leader said, his voice cigarette-raspy. He smiled as he said it, like he welcomed any excuse to take Danny apart.

But Danny just lifted his chin a fraction of an inch and stared back, unafraid. "He hit a lady," Danny told him. "And took her stuff."

I couldn't remember the last time someone had called me a lady —my brother, probably. Men think of me as a geek, when they think of me at all: I wear jeans and sneakers, not dresses and heels. But there was something about the way Danny said *lady* that made a warm bomb go off in my chest, however ridiculous it was. He sounded genuine. He sounded...*gallant.*

The gang leader started to crack his knuckles one by one. He had thick, meaty hands, the backs of them covered in tattoos. He nodded at Danny's Jag. "Tell you what: give me the car and I'll only break your arm."

My stomach tightened into a cold, hard knot. I didn't want Danny to get hurt.

But Danny just looked at the frozen ground for a second and gave a long-suffering sigh. Then he looked the gang leader dead in the eye and spoke, his voice low. "I don't want to embarrass you. Just give the lady her stuff back and we'll be gone."

The gang leader gave a disbelieving little chuckle. He stepped forward and swung for Danny's face...

Things happened very quickly.

Danny swayed to the side and the punch sailed harmlessly past him. He drove his fist into the leader's stomach, doubling him up, then brought his elbow up under the man's chin, lifting him almost off his feet. As the gang leader staggered back, Danny whirled and kicked the man's legs out from under him, and he went crashing to the ground.

The whole thing was over in less than five seconds. I stood there staring in disbelief: Danny wasn't even breathing hard. *Where the hell did he learn to fight like that?!*

Danny adjusted his tie and then walked towards the two men we'd been chasing. Behind him, the gang leader clambered slowly to his feet, blood streaming from his nose. He pulled a butterfly knife from his pocket and flicked out the blade. "Danny!" I yelled in panic.

Danny turned, caught the leader's wrist and twisted, quick and brutal. I heard a bone snap and the leader screamed and dropped the knife. Danny caught it and slammed it down hard—

The leader cried out again, cursing and wailing. The knife was buried to the hilt in the toe of his boot, pinning his foot to the ground. "Now *stay,*" Danny told him. He looked towards me and gave me a nod of thanks. Then for the second time, he turned to the pair we'd been chasing.

The whole group fled. The pair who'd robbed me bolted for the closest dirt bike, pushing its owner out of their way. Danny broke into a run and I chased after him.

The two guys reached the bike just as Danny caught up to them. In desperation, the thief hurled my backpack high into the air, knowing we'd have to choose between catching it and catching them. They roared away as Danny skidded to a stop and lifted his arms, shuffling left and right to try to get under the backpack. It reached the top of its arc and started to fall towards him but, to my horror, my laptop slipped free and tumbled separately, falling towards me.

"Catch it!" yelled Danny.

My chest tightened. Suddenly, I was back in high school, kids screaming at me as the softball dropped towards me. The laptop spun through the air, glossy and fragile, the lid half-open. I heard the soft *wump* as my backpack landed in Danny's arms. *C'mon, Erin, you can do this—*

I shuffled forward, shuffled back, grabbed...and my fingers brushed smooth plastic. *I've got it!*

The laptop slid through my hands and slammed into the ground with a sickening crack.

I screwed my eyes shut, not wanting to look. *Maybe it's not that bad,* I told myself. *Maybe it's tougher than I think, maybe I'll open my eyes and it'll be fine, just a couple of scratches....*

I opened my eyes. It wasn't fine.

The laptop had come open as it flew through the air and it had landed facedown, snapping the hinge. As I gingerly turned it over, chunks of glass fell from the shattered screen. The case had cracked open and circuit boards and wiring were spilling out.

The wind was getting up and an icy gust blew through me, leaving me shivering uncontrollably. I felt myself crumble, about to break. I was exhausted, freezing cold, out of work, I'd just lost the laptop I needed to job hunt and I was in the backwoods of Colorado, almost a thousand miles from Vegas. My instincts kicked in: I wanted to be somewhere warm, somewhere safe. I wanted to be *home*.

Then I remembered what happened, what was waiting for me when I got back to Vegas. I didn't *have* a home anymore.

I'd never felt so adrift, so alone. I felt my eyes going hot—

And then suddenly, the wind stopped. I looked up.

Danny was standing in front of me, sheltering me, his overcoat billowing out around him like a cape. His green eyes were burning with such a fierce, protective need that it took my breath away.

I wasn't alone. And even though I was far from my burrow, I felt safe and warm in a way I couldn't explain, in a way I'd been searching for my whole life. I took a slow breath, staring into his eyes, transfixed. *Who is this guy?*

He slowly leaned closer, almost as if he didn't realize he was doing it. In that moment, he dropped his guard: he was so busy worrying about me, he let his mask of cocky confidence slip and I thought I glimpsed something underneath.

Pain. Unbelievable pain.

4

DANNY

I STOOD there staring at her, drinking in every detail of her face. Her eyelashes were so blonde, they almost disappeared and she looked innocent. Then she'd turn her head just a little, the light would catch them and she'd look sexy as fuck. My eyes kept going back to one particular spot at the back of her jaw, just below her ear. The skin there looked incredibly soft and with all her hair drawn back into that golden braid, that place looked...naked. And very, very kissable.

I couldn't understand it. I'm a pretty simple guy: I like cars, beer and the sort of sex that makes the neighbors push angry notes under your door the next morning. I don't do relationships, I don't get...*interested* in someone in that way. I fuck and move on. And yet Erin had come out of nowhere and in the space of fifteen minutes, I was fascinated.

The women I usually go for are like female versions of me: flirty and confident. Erin was totally *unlike* me but for some reason her shyness drew me in. And underneath the awkwardness, she was *gorgeous,* gorgeous in a way that turned me into a panting, pawing animal. I wanted to peel off all those layers of clothing and see those perky breasts for myself. I wanted to grab hold of that tight, heart-shaped ass, lift her off the ground and press her to my chest. I wanted to tilt her head back and look down into those big blue eyes, watching her expression as I slowly slid up into her...

But there was something else, too. She looked so small and lost, standing there in the snow, that I just wanted to pull her tight to my chest and wrap my overcoat protectively around her. And that urge led to another one.

Deep inside, there's a part of me that doesn't work anymore. I think of it like cogs that have melted together from brutal, savage heat, so they won't mesh and turn. They cooled like that, and eventually stayed still so long the whole ruined mess froze. Years later, it's buried so deep in ice, I'd almost forgotten it ever worked.

But just then, for a second, as I watched Erin's golden braid bounce against her back in the wind...I wanted to kiss her. Not just my usual kind of kiss, open-mouthed and panting with my hands in her hair. I wanted to kiss her slowly, gently, my lips just brushing hers.

And I felt that frozen metal *ache,* straining, trying to come back to life. All of the pain that had melted it together, the stuff I keep pushed down deep, rushed up into my mind—

She was looking at me, curious and worried. *Shit.*

I looked away, shaken. *What was that?!* I crammed the memories back down into their pit and only then did I turn back to her.

She was turning the laptop over in her hands. "I can fix this," she muttered. She did that a lot, mumbling or muttering. Like she was worried someone might notice her if she made too much noise.

I stared at the circuit boards poking out through the cracked case, at the spiderwebbed screen. "Really?!"

Her eyes flicked up to look at me and for a second, she looked wounded. She thought I was doubting her. Had people done that in the past, because she was a woman? The thought made a fresh wave of protective anger slam through me.

I shook my head quickly. "I just meant..that's incredible."

She blinked and then her cheeks bloomed pink in a way that was absolutely adorable. She spoke to her shoes. "It's what I do. I've got tools in my car. A couple of spare screens." She sighed and looked around at the windswept hillside. "But I can't do anything until I get some place I can work. Let me message my brother."

She dug in her backpack, found her phone and typed furiously. A moment later, there was a chime as a message came back. "*Sugar!*"

Sugar? She must have been raised not to curse. I felt myself grin. She just kept getting more and more adorable. "What?"

"He's out of town. I sort of...didn't tell him I was coming. He's back later today. I don't want to tell him I'm here and make him rush back." She looked around at the freezing hillside and then down the slope to the town.

"I've got a place you could work," I blurted. "You could fix your laptop while you wait for your brother to get back."

"Oh, no, I couldn't—Thank you, but—If you could just give me a ride back to the café, I'll stay there, I can just—" She glanced down at the smashed laptop and broke off, her shoulders slumping: with her laptop gone, she had nothing to do. "I'll be fine."

I stared down into those big blue eyes, thinking fast. A feeling was forming, hard to put into words but...it felt like the day I went for selection for the army, my only shot at staying out of jail. Like something really important was in front of me, something I only had one shot at.

If I dropped her at the café, I'd never see her again.

"My place," I said, "is a garage. It has this big workbench...*really* big, so you can spread out" I mimed the width of it with my hands. "And it has really good light."

It was like her ears pricked up. We might be very different, I might work with socket sets and spark plugs instead of a soldering iron and circuit boards, but we both appreciated a good workspace. She looked tempted. But then she bit her lip again, just like she had when I told her to get into my car. She didn't know if she could trust me.

Hot rage bubbled up inside me and I sucked in a lungful of freezing air to try to cool myself. I wanted to kill all the men who'd left her feeling that way.

I searched for the right words. I needed her to know that this wasn't about getting into her panties, however much I liked her. I just...didn't want to leave her alone in a strange town. "Seriously," I said, "I've got this engine I was going to work on and I could do with the company."

And weirdly, I realized I actually could. I'd never minded being on my own but right then, the idea of spending the day alone when I could have *her* lighting up the room with that adorable awkwardness felt miserable. And maybe because I was telling the truth, she started to look like she was coming round to the idea.

"There'll be terrible coffee," I told her. "Or really good tea."

She nodded. And I felt something swell in my chest: Jesus, I was excited as a teenager.

I drove her back to the café to pick up her car and then we drove in convoy to my place. She was a nervous driver so I went super slow, checking my mirror to make sure I didn't leave her behind.

I stole my first car at fifteen, with a couple of mates. The idea was just to screech around for a while to impress the girls, then dump the car and set fire to it. But as soon as I got behind the wheel, it was like someone had thrown a switch in my brain: for the first time in my life, I was in control. We drove to a deserted parking lot and I just drove around and around, getting to know the car. I was a lousy driver, back then, but it didn't matter: I was in love.

I went out the next night and stole another one and it became my life for the next few years. I spent every night tearing around the streets of London, most of it with the police on my tail. I must have stolen over five hundred cars by the time I was seventeen. Each night, I got a little better, until I could balance a car perfectly through each corner, until it felt like flying. I never got tired of that feeling of being in control, the opposite of how I felt at home.

I'd always dreamed of having somewhere to work on cars but I'd never had a workshop of my own until I moved to Mount Mercy to join Stormfinch. It's one big room with two bays for cars, a huge workbench and big roller doors. What it doesn't have is any living space, but it has a sort of gallery overlooking the workshop, and I'd put a bed up there. I loved it. Most women probably wouldn't be so keen on the idea of sleeping in the same room as a bunch of greasy, half-disassembled engines but when I brought them back there the lights were off. And the next morning...well, I'd never see them again, so who cared what they thought?

As I opened the door for Erin, though, I was weirdly nervous. It was the first time I'd shown a woman my place with the lights *on* and for some reason, I did care what *she* thought.

She ventured slowly inside, her nose wrinkling at the smell of gasoline and rubber. She walked over to the engine I'd been working on and examined it curiously, standing on tiptoe to look down inside it. I happened to glance up and noticed a pair of panties dangling from one of the overhead lights. *Oops.* I snatched them before Erin saw. They must be Lauren's, from the night before. No, wait...I remembered that color. They were Bree's, from three nights ago: I'd undressed her upstairs, but I remember tossing her panties over my shoulder. I stuffed them quickly into my pocket.

Erin was on the move: she was squirrely, never staying in one place for more than a moment. She looked at the tool rack, the tire inflation gear, and finally arrived at the workbench. I turned on the lights for her and the whole length of it lit up nice and bright. "This *is* a good workspace," she mumbled.

"As promised," I told her. I put the kettle on and, by the time I'd made two steaming mugs of tea and changed into coveralls, she'd brought tools and spare parts from her car and arranged them on the workbench around the remains of the laptop. She pulled out a stool and hopped up onto it: she was so small that her feet dangled well clear of the floor. She nodded her thanks for the tea, picked up her soldering iron and pushed her glasses up her nose....

"What?" she asked, sounding worried.

I blinked and realized I'd been staring at her again. "Nothing."

I picked up a socket wrench, turned to the engine and we both went to work. But I kept looking at her reflection in the engine's polished metal. Now that she was working on something, all that nervous energy was gone and she sat stock still, utterly absorbed. I couldn't figure her out at all. One moment, when she wrinkled her nose as she thought, or blinked at the circuitry from behind her glasses, she looked adorably cute. But the next, she'd adjust her position on the stool and that gorgeous ass would rock back and forth, and I'd feel my cock getting hard.

"So what happened in the café?" I asked gently.

She told me about how the guy had fooled her into leaving her stuff. "I'm an idiot," she said, her face reddening.

"You were trying to help!" I told her firmly. "That's more than most people would do."

Her shoulders relaxed a little and she gave a quick little nod of thanks.

We worked in companionable silence for a full hour. I couldn't imagine doing that with any of the women I normally went for: they were all talkers. At last, I took a break and swiveled around on my stool to see what she was doing.

She was peering through a magnifying glass at the circuit board she was repairing. I shook my head in wonder: the intricacies of it were amazing. Golden wires that criss-crossed and switched back in a map more complex than any city I'd ever driven around. Lights that pulsed cherry red and lime green. Shining blobs of solder like liquid silver. Her hands were so small and quick, they made mine feel huge and clumsy. She reminded me of a medieval monk, toiling away on one of those huge, elaborate letters at the start of a bible.

She'd brought in a machine from her car and it was whirring and moving: I watched as a tiny plastic part took shape, layer by layer, like coral being laid down on a reef. A 3D printer: I'd never seen one up close. "What is it you do?" I asked.

"I work in Las Vegas," she said. "For a company that installs security systems for casinos. Lasers, motion sensors, radio tags to keep track of money carts." She paused and her voice grew tight. "Or...that's what I *did*." She swallowed. "What do you do?"

I hesitated. I was still processing what she'd just told me. So she'd lost her job, somehow, but she clearly didn't want to talk about it. And now I had to decide what to tell her about me. The sort of women I usually went for would lap up the idea that I worked for a private military team. But someone like Erin...wouldn't they run a mile? It was so completely outside her safe little world.

"I tune cars," I told her. I hated lying to her. But I didn't want to lose her, either.

I'd turned on the heating when we arrived and as the workshop warmed up, she started to slowly shed layers of clothes. I watched, enthralled, as the denim jacket with all the patches came off. Then one shirt, then the next...then, finally, the extra t-shirt, leaving her in just a black one. It wasn't even low cut but, somehow, just seeing her in a t-shirt was far sexier than seeing Katie or Bree in their lingerie and stockings or, hell, even naked.

That got me thinking about seeing Erin naked. That golden braid swishing back and forth as she bounced on top of me. Those perky little breasts thrusting up towards the ceiling as she arched her back....

I coughed and pointed to one of the circular sew-on patches on the denim jacket she'd taken off. "What's that?" The patch showed a red dragon with text in gold letters around the edge.

"Oh!" she flushed. "It's from a book. *Throne of Night.*"

I'd never heard of it: I'm not much of a reader. But if she was interested in it, I wanted to know more. "What's it about?"

And so, as we worked, she told me. She described the world it was set in, sort of medieval but with magic. There were dragons and elves and crystals that could capture a person's soul. She was hesitant at first: she kept giving me *do you really want to hear this* looks. But I was enthralled and, as I kept nodding her on, her shyness dropped away and she came alive. She didn't just tell me about the book, she told me about why she loved it so much, how it transported her away. I'd never known a book could do that. "I'm going to have to read it," I told her.

She gave me a doubtful look. I guess she could tell I'm not the reading type.

"I mean it," I said. "I want to try it."

And when she realized I was serious, she gave me a shy little smile that made something lift and tug inside me.

We worked away, talking happily for hours and it was only when my stomach rumbled that I realized it was lunchtime. We stopped to get takeout sandwiches from the café, slab-like BLTs with crispy bacon, juicy tomatoes and just the right amount of mayo.

We went back to it, talking and working. The engine gradually came together and so did the laptop: by mid-afternoon, she had the circuit boards fixed and was working on the screen. She was a certified genius. And I was...I didn't know what to call it. *Smitten?*

Stupid. I didn't feel things like that.

Hooked, then. I was hooked. It made no sense because she was so utterly different to me. She was small, shy and smart; I was a big cocky idiot who only really knew how to sink beers, drive fast and shoot straight. But I loved spending time with Erin.

Maybe it was *because* we were so different. Everything in my life has always been physical, real. Fights in the dirt-poor neighborhood where I grew up, fists smacking faces, blood running down knuckles. Then my time in the army, the clump of my boots hitting the ground in endless marches, the rush of cold night air against my face as I jumped out of a plane. Then the SAS and later Delta, with JD: the feel of mud soaking through my uniform as I belly-crawled through the dirt, the comfort of a wall against your back when you finally find cover, the feel of JD's hand in mine as one of us pulled the other to their feet. Even the stuff I did for fun was physical: screeching round a corner in a car, tires smoking, fitting an engine together, drinking, fucking....

But Erin was different. Sure, she worked with her hands, but the wires and solder was just the beginning. All the magic happened in the power that flowed through the wires, the data that shuttled back and forth as radio waves. A whole invisible world that the rest of us didn't understand but that she worked in as naturally as our world of dirt, blood and bullets.

And for fun, she lost herself in a world that didn't exist, where dragons flew. I'd never done that, never imagined a place so intensely that I felt like I was there. I wasn't sure I could. But Erin made me want to find out.

Both of us reached a tricky bit in our work and we stopped talking and lapsed into a comfortable silence. But after a while, as I tinkered with the engine, I started to hear something. A soft mumbling, made even softer by that gentle country accent.

She was talking to herself.

I didn't turn around because I didn't want to spook her. I just worked away for a full hour, listening to her tell wires and circuits that *you need to go to the RAID controller* and *we'll bring you round here and get you hooked up to the CPU*. She clearly didn't realize she was doing it and it was the cutest thing I'd ever heard. I could have listened to it all day.

It hit me that I'd been sitting here with a woman for most of a day and I hadn't made a single move. Usually by now we'd have fucked, eaten ice cream and be starting round two. *What did that mean?*

Without thinking, I looked at her and she glanced up and saw me looking. Her mumbling stopped and she flushed red down to the roots of that golden hair.

"Why are you embarrassed?" I asked sincerely. "I do it too. Especially when I've got an engine that won't turn over."

She looked away. Looked back at me, frowning, as if trying to figure out if I was for real. She bit her lip.

I swallowed and stared right back at her. My chest went tight and the room went so quiet, I could hear my heart beating...

She turned abruptly back to her work, her golden braid swinging. I stared at it, my heart thumping.

What is this?

I didn't know. But I really, really liked it.

5

ERIN

I TRIED to focus on fixing the new laptop screen in place but my hands were shaking and my chest had gone light and fluttery. As I angled the screen to put it in, I saw the reflection of his glittering green eyes: they were burning right into me like lasers. My breathing went tight. Guys *never* looked at me.

Very slowly, I tilted the screen. His mouth crept into view. God, that jaw...strong, confident: I remembered how he'd lifted his chin a little, when he'd faced off against the gang leader. And then those sinful lips, soft but hard in just the right way. If the rest of him disappeared, Cheshire Cat style, that cocky, flirty grin alone could make a woman wet.

I tilted the screen again and stared at my own confused face. I was giddy and happy: happier than I had been in a long time. I liked him a lot but he was nothing like me. I went through life trying to blend into the background. Danny walked down the street with his cocky confidence and sharp suit and everyone turned to look. And he was brave in a way I could never be. He wasn't afraid of anything. I'm afraid of *everything*.

Something else... He was calm and controlled, friendly: when we'd gone to the café to get sandwiches, he'd laughed and joked with the people behind the counter. But there was this aura of quiet menace, something in the way he held himself, the way he scanned the room when he walked in. An unspoken promise that if you hurt someone he cared about, he'd break every bone in your body. It should have scared me but it made me feel safe. *Protected.*

He was mysterious, too. He said he was a mechanic but I'd seen the way he'd taken down the gang leader: quick and brutal, with no showiness or wasted movement. Like he'd been trained.

I tiptoed through life. Danny tore through it like a cannonball. He was so physical, so *real,* he made my world seem floaty and unsubstantial. And that made me want to...

I felt my cheeks go hot. It made me want to be grabbed, to feel those big hands all over me, squeezing my ass, running up my sides, cupping my breasts. I wanted to be scooped up and hoisted into the air, his lips on my neck as I tangled my fingers in those soft, black locks. I wanted to be tossed on a bed, to feel his muscled weight pressing me down into it. I wanted to be spread. *Filled.*

I tipped the screen slightly, trying to see his face again and—

He wasn't looking at the back of my head, anymore. His eyes met mine in the reflection.

I fumbled the screen, dropped it and only just caught it in time. I got on with the job of fitting it, deliberately keeping it angled away from him.

This man had me fantasizing and crushing my legs together. And yet, when we'd been deep in our work, I'd started talking to myself, something I never, ever do unless I'm alone. He was gorgeous, exciting...but he was also just really easy to be with. And he didn't tease me for being weird.

I finished gluing the new screen in place, connected the last wire and that was it: the laptop was fixed. I put down my tools and, as I stretched my neck, I saw the sky outside was dark. God, had I really spent the whole day here?

My brother would be home by now. I quickly messaged him to tell him I was in town and he said he'd pick me up. I gave him the address and looked around at my tools: I needed to start packing everything away.

And that's when I realized it was over. In a few minutes, my brother would arrive and I'd go to his place. Tomorrow, I'd be back in Vegas and I'd never see Danny again.

It hit me right in the chest. An ache like I'd never felt, childishly stubborn. *But I don't want to go!*

I glanced over my shoulder at Danny and the ache tightened. *Don't be stupid. You've known him less than a day.* I'd only met him by pure chance. The plan was always to see my brother for one night, then tomorrow get back to my life in Vegas.

And suddenly, the memories I'd been holding back all day rushed in, my ex-boyfriend's words stinging like slaps. Hot tears of humiliation prickled at my eyes.

I didn't *have* a life in Vegas. Not anymore.

I slid off my stool and hurried towards the back of the garage, plunging into a maze formed by tool racks and stacks of tires. I could feel tears running down my cheeks and I wiped at them desperately, trying to get myself under control.

How could I have lost my boyfriend, my friends and my job, all in one go?!

"Erin?" Danny's voice, worried. Then his footsteps, getting closer.

"I'm okay," I insisted, in a voice that clearly wasn't. I blundered deeper into the maze.

I turned a corner and came to a dead end. I turned around but it was too late: I could hear Danny around the bend. I blinked furiously and tried to swallow down the pain. *He'll think I'm pathetic.* I didn't want that to be the last memory he had of me.

Danny strode around the corner, his big shoulders almost brushing the shelves. I kept my eyes on the floor, afraid to look at him. I saw his feet stop in front of me and braced myself for his questions: *why are you crying? What happened in Vegas? How did you lose your job?*

But he didn't speak. When I finally worked up the courage to look at him, the concern in his eyes made me melt. I could see he wanted to ask...but he knew it would break me. Instead, he just lifted one brow very slightly. *You okay?* I'd never known a man be so subtle. How the hell was he so good with women?

I swallowed. "Just..." I croaked, then started again. "Just looking around."

He nodded, his voice gentle and infinitely patient. "You look all you want."

I nodded gratefully and turned to stare at a socket set while I willed my face to cool. The memories retreated, scared away by Danny's presence. There was something about the way he looked at me...I felt safe, even from the past.

I took a deep breath, back in control but feeling stupid. And then I saw something in the shadows behind Danny that made me forget everything. I frowned. "Is that...?"

I walked towards it and Danny backed up to let me through. As I got closer, my jaw dropped. I crouched in front of it, running a hand over the glass top. "Oh my *God!*"

It was a jukebox. A proper, old-fashioned jukebox with vinyl records. I crouched, put both hands on the glass and pressed my nose to it, entranced. "I *love* these things," I breathed. Retro tech is art, to me. I have a whole collection of tape decks, big CRT TVs and neon signs. "That's the arm that picks up the record," I mumbled to myself. I craned my neck to peer at the mechanism. "*That* must flip it so you can have the A side or the B side...." Then I remembered I wasn't just talking to myself. I looked up at Danny, embarrassed for geeking out. But he wasn't sneering or rolling his eyes. He was grinning almost... adoringly. I flushed.

"Do you want to put something on?" he asked.

I jumped to my feet so fast I got room spin. "You mean it *works?!*"

"'Course it does. It's what I use to play tunes when I'm working on cars." He used his toe to flick a switch on the back and the jukebox came to life, bathing us in orange, red and yellow lights. Danny dug in his pocket and passed me a quarter.

I flicked through the printed tracklists. I was self-conscious about my lousy taste in music: it was one of the many things people had picked me apart for in college. Eventually, I gave up trying to be cool and picked an old rock track I liked. I watched, transfixed, as the mechanism shuffled through the stack of records and swung one over to the turntable.

"Oh, I love this one," said Danny, sounding surprised.

"Really?"

He nodded, a big, honest grin spreading across his face as he hummed along. I giggled, not something I do very often. He was always so cool but, just then, he looked unguarded, almost goofy. Like he didn't care what anyone thought of him. Maybe that was *part* of being cool?

Then he offered me his hand.

Dance? Memories from college unfurled in my mind, hotly humiliating: being asked to dance by some guy, only to find out later that his buddies had dared him to ask the dorky girl. Those moments had slashed insecurities into my mind and then what happened in Vegas had opened those narrow cuts into yawning canyons. Danny was too cool, too gorgeous, he couldn't actually want to—

But then I looked up into his eyes. I'd never known that green could be so warm.

"I don't really know how to dance," I mumbled.

His voice was gentle. "C'mon. You'll be fine."

I gave him my hand. As soon as his fingers closed around mine, it was as if we'd completed a circuit, all the electrons in my body racing down my arm and into him, and then he took my other hand and all of *his* electrons rushed into *me,* forceful and male, scattering mine. The two sets twisted together, forming something new that surged around and around our loop, leaving me breathless. I saw his chest fill as he slowly inhaled and his grip tightened. *He feels it too.*

He began to rock and sway to the beat and I shuffled and tried to follow, stiff-limbed and awkward. He gently pulled me closer and moved one hand to my waist, his palm throbbing warmth through my t-shirt, and then we were moving together, rocking and spinning. I could feel myself breathing faster, getting drunk on the vanilla and spice scent of him, the feel of his hands on me. We stepped back, stepped forward... My foot came down on his toe but he just laughed. Then he lifted my hand and twirled me around, and I stumbled and stepped sideways onto his *other* foot.

"You really *don't* know how to dance, do you?" That voice: London-rough and laced with filthy charm, but with a warm, affectionate chuckle underneath, laughing with me and not at me.

"Sorry. I told you."

The hand on my waist slid around to my back and his fingers spread, controlling me with gentle presses of his fingertips. He let go of my other hand and held my shoulder, and now we were even closer, my breasts a half inch from his chest. I stretched up and put my hand on *his* shoulder, and the other one on his back. The size of him, the muscled solidness of him, was overwhelming, this close, and it was making my brain fog and my whole body go trembly and hypersensitive.

I realized the music had stopped. The garage was so quiet, I could hear my breathing. Time seemed to go syrupy slow but, at the same time, my eyes were flicking everywhere, taking in every detail of his face.

His hand pressed on my back and now my breasts *did* touch his chest, just a gentle little double kiss. He was like warm rock and the feel of him, brushing against my nipples through a thin layer of cloth, sent a wave of heat down my body to detonate in my groin.

His cocky smirk was gone. His eyes were hooded and when he spoke, his voice was ragged with need. "Erin..." he began. His hand came off my shoulder and cupped my cheek—

A metallic *boom-boom-boom* reverberated through the room and we flew apart, turning to look. The big roller door at the front of the garage was shaking. I blinked my way back to awareness. "That'll be my brother," I told Danny, and hurried to the front of the garage. My mind was spinning, my lips still tingling in anticipation of the kiss that almost was.

I reached the front door and checked through the door viewer: *yep,* it was my brother. And he looked mad, which explained why he'd banged on the roller door instead of just knocking on this one. But why would he be mad?

I opened the door and he stepped inside, accompanied by a flurry of snow. I wasn't used to seeing him in a suit, or to seeing those gorgeous, soulful blue eyes so full of anger. But one thing was familiar: he still had his beloved cream Stetson on his head.

"Danny," I said, "this is my brother, JD."

6

DANNY

MY BODY HAD MOVED to the door but my caveman brain was still back by the jukebox, tangled in feelings it wasn't used to. She was quirky and adorable and sexy all at the same time and she smelled like peaches and Christmas, and I was just about to kiss her—

And then suddenly, JD was there.

I frowned, eager to get back to the kiss. Why was JD there?

My brother, Erin's mouth said.

Her brother.

HER BROTHER.

JD IS ERIN'S BROTHER.

Oh FUCK.

"What are you doing here?" JD was speaking to Erin but he was looking at me and there was an edge to his voice I'd never heard before, a protective fury so cold it burned. *What's my little sister doing in your love nest?* JD knew my reputation. *Everyone* knew my reputation.

Erin told him how I'd saved her outside the café and helped her get her stuff back. Her gorgeous country accent was so obviously Texan now. But on her it was so soft and gentle...that's why I hadn't made the connection with JD's rough growl. She looked between the two of us, confused by the tension. "How do you two know each other?" she asked.

"Danny's one of the team," JD told her.

"Oh." Erin looked at me, her nose wrinkling in confusion. Then she looked down at her feet and I saw the disappointment in her face. I felt like someone had punched me in the guts. *Fuck.* Why had I lied to her?

"I've known him for years," JD said, still staring at me. "He's my best friend. I trust him like a brother." And his eyes flicked up to the balcony that overlooked the workshop and the messy bed there.

I gave him a quick shake of my head. *No. Absolutely not. Of course not! Like I'd do something with your little sister!*

The little sister who I'd been about to kiss. Who set off a whole fireworks display of confusing feelings every time I looked at her.

I held JD's gaze and my poker face must have been better than I thought, because his scowl slowly faded and, at last, he looked away. When he looked at me again, he looked sheepish. "Thanks," he said. "For looking after her."

I smiled and nodded, my stomach twisting with guilt.

I helped them carry Erin's tools and equipment out to her car. As they climbed in, Erin gave me one last look over her shoulder and the look in her eyes matched the ache in my chest. They drove off and I watched until their tail lights disappeared into the whirling snow.

How can she be his little sister, I wondered as I walked slowly back inside. She must be ten years younger than him. I remembered JD saying he had a sister, back when we first met, but he'd barely mentioned her since. How come I'd never met her, in all the years I'd known him?

The workshop seemed weirdly empty and quiet without Erin there. I leaned against the door, putting things together in my mind. Erin had come to Mount Mercy to visit JD. She must not have told him she was coming, or he would have told her he'd be away in Washington....

She was here for the anniversary. To look after JD, just as I'd been planning to do. That's why she'd made it a surprise visit, so he couldn't put her off. She'd driven all the way from Vegas, up into the frozen mountains, to make sure he was okay. It made me like her even more, and I liked her *a lot*.

Then I thought about the look in JD's eyes. God, if he knew, if he even *suspected* that we'd nearly kissed, or the thoughts I'd been having about her perky breasts and that ripe peach of an ass.... An icy shudder went through me, the kind you get when you forget to check your mirror and a semi-truck misses you by inches. What would JD have walked in on, if he'd been a few minutes later?

I found a bottle of bourbon, poured a shot and knocked it back. That chased the shudder away but, as it burned its way down my throat, the new reality took shape in my mind, cold and gray as rainswept concrete.

I couldn't be with her. Ever. JD would never allow it, not with my reputation. And if we sneaked around and he found out—and he *would* find out—I'd lose him. That was something I couldn't risk. He was the closest friend I'd ever had and he'd saved my life more times than I could count. JD made me feel like I wasn't out there on my own. I'd never had that with anyone.

Except...

I walked over to the workbench, where Erin had sat. The scent of her was still in the air and I gently breathed her in.

I didn't know what it was, between me and Erin. It was only just getting started but there was something there, something that was about more than sex...

I snorted and turned away from the workbench. *Stupid.* I couldn't feel that stuff, the deep stuff. That part of me broke a long time ago. All I was good for was talking women's panties off, some filthy, no limits fucking and a quick goodbye kiss in the morning. And that was fine with the sort of women I hooked up with: they knew exactly what I was. But Erin was an innocent little thing. She deserved better than that. If I messed around with her, I'd hurt her *and* I'd lose my best friend.

Erin was off limits.

I sighed. I had no idea what to do with myself: my plan had been to spend the evening with JD but he was with Erin, now.

The bar, then. Beer, flirting and fucking: that's what I needed to make everything feel normal.

Ten minutes later, I walked into Krüger's Tavern, the town's bar. It's a beautiful old wood-built place with a German beer cellar theme: soft fur throws on the seats, a roaring fire and really good beers on tap. It's popular with the tourists, so there are new women every night, all in a thrill-seeking, holiday mood.

I headed straight for the bar, where two women were chatting and giggling as they waited to order. One had straight black hair cut into sharp bangs and was in a silver sequined top and short skirt. The other was pale and curvy, with long walnut tresses and a bottle-green dress. I slid in next to the black-haired one. She turned and found herself looking right into my eyes. I gave her a Danny Special, a grin that's one-third warm and friendly, one-third cocky and teasing and one-third *I want to do wicked things to you.* Her lips parted. Her throat bobbed as she swallowed.

"I'm Danny," I told her. "And who are *you?*"

Five minutes later, the three of us were sitting on bar stools, me in the middle, and each of them had a bare thigh pressed against my leg. I'd learned that Terri (black hair and sequins) was here on a much-needed girls' getaway with her BFF Vanessa (pale and curvy). They were both from Seattle: Terri, a flight attendant, had wangled them cheap flights and their mission was to help Vanessa, a wedding planner, forget a painful breakup. We were doing flaming shots, they were getting me to say things in my London accent and, from the way Terri was looking at me, all wide-eyed and urgent, she was debating whether to be a good friend and let the shy, broken-hearted Vanessa have me or take me for herself. Another half hour and I reckoned I could gently introduce the idea that maybe *both* of them could be happy.

But something was wrong. They were gorgeous, confident, flirty... everything I look for in a woman. So why, when I looked at Terri's tanned, bare thigh and the soft cleavage revealed by Vanessa's dress, did my mind keep going back to Erin, taking off her layers? To that golden braid swishing back and forth like a cat's tail as she walked, drawing my eyes down to that heart-shaped ass?

These women were fun and friendly, they were *like me*...but only on that surface level. They were like the Danny that everyone knew. Erin...she was like the real me. Her love for electronics was like my love for engines. We'd both happily tinker away all day. And where she *was* different to me: shy where I was confident, innocent where I was experienced...I liked those differences. Terri and Vanessa were familiar and comforting. But Erin made me want to grow, to be smart like her, to try new things. And her nose twitched like a rabbit's. And she talked to herself, when she was deep in her work....

I knocked back one more shot with Terri and Vanessa and then made my excuses and left. Outside, the snow had turned to a miserable sleet. *Great.* I stalked home with it pelting my neck and trickling under my collar. It was the first time I could remember walking back to my place alone.

What's going on? This whole thing made no sense. I couldn't have Erin. Even if she wasn't JD's little sister, the whole thing would be doomed from the start. I don't *do* relationships: I can't. And she deserved better than a one-night stand. I knew all of this.

So why couldn't I get her out of my mind?

7

ERIN

As long as I can remember, I've been trying to fit in.

I wasn't planned. Our mom thought she was long past the age when she could get pregnant but then suddenly, ten years after JD was born, there I was. Even so, she and my pop and JD all made room for me in their lives and I should have been just another South Texas girl growing up on a small ranch.

Except right from the start, I was different. While the rest of my family seemed to be genetically wired to crave the outdoors, all I wanted to do as a kid was stay inside and build with my Lego bricks. JD and my folks are tall and look like they could wrestle bulls but I capped out at 5'2" and can be dragged around by a medium-sized dog. And while they all had 20/20 vision, I needed glasses by the time I was eight.

When I was two and JD was twelve, our pop was thrown from a horse and broke his back, leaving him bedridden for months and in a wheelchair for the rest of his life. JD took on a lot of the ranch work and a good slice of my parenting. I sometimes wonder if that's why he wound up as a leader, helping shape younger soldiers. I know it gave us an unbreakable bond: I love my folks but there's no one I'm closer to than JD.

I was determined to do my part. I'd stagger around the ranch carrying hay bales that were almost as big as me and spent an entire summer building a fence around the property, with me holding the stakes and JD patiently whacking them into the ground with a sledgehammer. I wanted to fit in but it became obvious when we had relatives over that I was some sort of misfit. Everyone else talked in big, room-filling voices while I sat timidly looking up at them with big eyes. It was only much later that I realized that my family talked non-stop about the weather, or sports, or who was dating whom, but they never talked about the important stuff, like feelings. Especially the men. My pop never talked about how hard it was for him, being confined to a wheelchair after being a rancher his entire life. And years later, when JD lost his wife and child, he never talked about it, either. He'd learned from his pop that you just man up and get on with it.

JD tried patiently to teach me to ride but I just didn't have that way with animals everyone else in our community seemed to have. He'd effortlessly swing himself up into the saddle and instantly bond with the horse; I'd struggle to get on, cling on too tight and make the horse skittish. All the other kids in my school had learned to ride as soon as they were walking so it was another thing that made me stand out as the quiet, weird kid. Add in that I was more interested in math and science than boys and dresses and I was mercilessly bullied by the other girls.

By the time I was twelve, I was so desperate to fit in that I got up before anyone else one morning, snuck out to the stables and saddled up a pony, determined to learn to ride and not wanting to take any more of JD's time. I barely got out of the stall before I came off and broke my leg in three places. While I was at home healing, my mom bought me a gift to cheer me up: an electronics kit.

It was like she'd shown me a secret door, right there in my bedroom, to a world I never knew existed. I fell in love with the puzzle of building circuits, using logic and rules to make power and light and information flow in intricate, synchronized dances. Finally, there was something my weird brain was good at. Within days, I'd gone far beyond the simple circuits the kit was made for and started devouring books on electronics from the local library. By the time I was thirteen, I was bringing in extra money for the family repairing people's phones and laptops.

By this point, JD was off serving his country, but he came home after each tour to help on the ranch and spend time with me and our bond stayed as strong as ever. High school turned out to be a repeat of middle school, with crueler bullies. I hid out in the library, losing myself in books. JD got fiercely protective when it came to boys—the few that were interested in the science nerd were scared away by him glowering at them.

I managed to get a scholarship to UCLA to study electronic engineering, supporting myself by doing electronics repairs in the evenings. I thought that finally, I'd be somewhere I'd fit in. But the other students all balked at my "hick" accent and country ways. While they were out partying and falling in love, I hunkered down in my dorm room and studied, feeling lost and alone.

I graduated and landed a job with a tech startup in Las Vegas making security systems for casinos. Like most startups, the money was bad and the hours were long but for the first time, I felt like I'd found somewhere I belonged. There were just six of us, all geeks from places like MIT and UCLA. We became friends, bonding over video games and weekly *Dungeons & Dragons* sessions. The CEO was a guy from LA called Toby. He had long, curly blond hair that gave him a romantic look and gorgeous, pale blue eyes.

I'd never been to Vegas before and when I first arrived, I was childishly excited about it: I had this stupid fantasy about putting on a cocktail dress and walking around on the arm of some gorgeous guy in a tuxedo, even though getting dressed up wasn't normally my thing. Then I saw the casinos for the first time and they were nothing like they were in the movies: it was all grandmas playing slots and drunks hitting on waitresses. But the work was pure heaven and after a few months, I went to Toby with an idea for a new product: poker chips with tiny wireless transmitters that let the casino track them wherever they went in the casino, eliminating theft, fraud and fake chips. When we showed the casinos a prototype, they went nuts for it. And at the party to celebrate our first contract, on a balcony surrounded by fairy lights, Toby gently turned me to face him, leaned in and kissed me.

I should have known getting together with my boss was a bad idea. But it didn't *feel* like that: we were all friends, putting in long hours together to get the company off the ground. After three months, I moved into his apartment and it was the perfect home for a couple of geeks: a cozy burrow full of books, computers and little statues of dragons. We snuggled up under a blanket and watched TV together, we played video games together, we read to each other. I thought I was in heaven.

Six months later, it was Christmas. Toby refused to travel to Texas to meet my family. I was disappointed but I thought that maybe he just wasn't ready, yet. It was fine: we'd have Christmas together in our apartment and it would be the best Christmas *ever*. I told JD and my folks I wouldn't be coming home this year and started hanging tinsel and candy canes. On Christmas Eve, we threw a party and, as the first guests arrived, I was flushed and giddy with excitement, running around with bottles and plates of snacks. I'd found somewhere I fitted, I had someone who loved me and I had a cozy burrow to share with them.

Then I pushed open a door and found Toby kissing Bridgette, one of our co-workers.

I stood there frozen in the doorway, waiting for him to tell me that it was a joke, a one-time thing, a moment of madness. But he seemed almost frustrated with me. "It's been going on for months," he said. "We didn't know how to tell you."

More of our co-workers arrived and found me standing there, red-faced and sobbing. They exchanged looks with Toby and I realized... they *all knew*. I'd been the only one who hadn't.

I couldn't stay there. I grabbed a few things and just ran. I couldn't face going home to Texas and telling JD and my folks what had happened so I spent my Christmas Day crying my eyes out in a Vegas hotel, eating cold turkey legs in congealing gravy with other sad and lonely people. The hardest part was calling my family and telling them how great everything was, because I didn't want to ruin their Christmas.

Then it got worse.

On the first day back after the Christmas break, I walked into the office to find everyone waiting for me in the conference room. Toby made a speech with a lot of phrases like, "given what's happened," and "because of how things have worked out." As if all this was because of some external event and not because he'd cheated on me with one of my friends.

Toby was good with people in a way I wasn't. While I'd spent Christmas sobbing alone, he'd been getting everyone on his side. They were about to take a vote to kick me out of the company.

Toby and his new girlfriend raised their hands viciously fast. Some of the others looked uncomfortable, some wouldn't meet my eyes, but they all followed Toby's lead. I stared at the forest of hands, then turned and ran from the room, tears filling my eyes.

I found a cheap apartment and scraped by repairing electronics for people while I hunted for another job. JD eventually got the truth out of me on a phone call a few weeks later. He tried to persuade me to move back in with our folks but I knew that if I ran home now, I'd never want to leave again.

I figured I'd feel better with time, but I didn't. My confidence was shot and I barely left the apartment for two months. Then, one morning, I realized that the next day was the anniversary of JD's wife and child dying. I couldn't let him be alone. So I got in my car and drove through the night to Colorado.

JD only lived a few streets away from Danny's garage, but it took us almost twenty minutes to drive there. The streets had been plowed but fresh snow was falling fast, dusting the road ahead like powdered sugar, and I'd never driven on snow before. So we crawled along with me sneaking sideways glances at JD as I drove, trying to gauge his mood. He sat there silent and brooding, the hard lines of his face etched in red from the taillights of the car in front.

Why had he been so mad when he found me with Danny? Yes, we'd been about to kiss but JD didn't know that! Shouldn't he have been happy that I'd spent the day warm and safe with his best friend? A warm glow spread through my chest as I remembered Danny calling me a lady. The guy was a gentleman, in a rough, filthy, blue collar kind of a way.

I shook my head. It didn't matter. I was only in town for a day: I probably wouldn't even see Danny again before I left. What mattered was JD, and getting him through tonight. How was he doing?

Twelve years ago, when JD was home on leave, helping out around our family ranch in Texas, he met Jillian. She was like a female JD, as gorgeous as he is handsome, with long blonde hair and curves that made men stare, and that same toughness and no-nonsense attitude. She had the country gene that I'd somehow missed out on. Not long after they started dating, she arrived at our ranch with a dead coyote that she'd shot from horseback while on her way home from digging a well. But despite us being so different, she was always warm and welcoming, becoming like a big sister to me. She always acted sweet and demure when my folks were around, but she had a filthy sense of humor and was refreshingly open about sex— It was her I went to with all my sex questions.

Right from the start, we all knew she was The One. JD *doted* on her, going after her with the same unshakeable determination he goes about anything. A little over a year after they met, he popped the question and six months after *that,* they were married in a beautiful, outdoor ceremony. When JD kissed her, I remember thinking I'd never seen my brother happier.

A couple of years later, they had Max, a baby boy with Jillian's shining blonde hair but JD's thick curls. He had JD's pale blue eyes, too, and with the blonde curls he looked like a choirboy. Pretty young, he discovered he could get away with most anything if he turned those eyes on you. *But it wasn't me who let the chickens out, Aunt Erin!* I loved the l'il rascal and spoiled him rotten.

And then, not long after Max's fifth birthday, my mom got a frantic call from JD, saying she needed to get to his place *right now*. My mom arrived to find the street filled with police cars.

Jillian and Max were dead.

JD was overseas, on an op. He'd been on the phone to them when an intruder broke into their house and he'd had to listen from a thousand miles away as they were killed, unable to do anything to help.

Their deaths broke him. He quit the army, which had always been the core of his life, and sank into a deep depression for years. Then, six months ago, his best friend had managed to persuade him to come and lead this team in Colorado—

Wait. His *best friend*? JD had never mentioned his name but I was sure now that he'd been talking about Danny. Danny was the one who'd pulled him out of that dark pit, maybe even saved his life. But if the two of them were so close, how come JD had never introduced us?

"There," said JD from the passenger seat. "On the left."

I pulled up next to an apartment building and we stepped out into the snow. JD took my suitcase—it wasn't heavy but I knew it was useless to argue—and led the way upstairs. He unlocked the door and I got my first look at where he'd been staying,

I felt my chest close up. *Oh, JD!*

The bed was stripped, the blankets folded and piled up neatly at one end. Everything was spotlessly clean but there were no photos, no personal effects...*nothing*.

This wasn't a home. This was accommodation, army style. I'd hoped Colorado would have given him a fresh start but he wasn't building a life here in Mount Mercy. The job was keeping him going but it was obvious that he hadn't moved on, hadn't healed.

"You want something to eat?" asked JD. "I got some, uh..." He opened the refrigerator and I winced. All that was inside was a neat stack of microwave meals. Fuel, not food. He probably would have lived off army ration packs if he could. "Maybe we should go get a pizza," he muttered.

"JD," I said quietly.

He turned and saw my expression. He knew what I was going to say because I'd said it before: that he needed to talk about losing them, that he needed to rebuild his life and find somebody new. Before I could even speak, he cut me off with a curt shake of his head. He was being the stoic tough guy, just like our pop.

But I wasn't giving up. He'd done so much for me: practically raised me, helped pay for college. Now he needed my help. "JD, I think you need to talk about—"

He fixed me with a look and shook his head again. That's when I saw the pain in his eyes. The pleading not to push it.

It was much worse than I'd thought. The loss was an open wound inside him, still leaking poison. He *did* need help. But it wasn't just that he didn't want to talk about it. He *couldn't* talk about it. What he needed was to meet someone, someone who'd help him open up and heal and build a new life. It was so unfair: JD was the kindest, most loyal guy I'd ever known and he had a heart the size of Texas. Plus, he was drop-dead gorgeous, with those big blue eyes. There were a million women out there who'd love to meet him. But as long as he was hurting like this, he'd just keep pushing them all away.

JD looked away, scowling, and I knew he was beating himself up for being weak—as in, actually having feelings. I loved my pop but sometimes I hated him for raising JD this way.

I put my hand on JD's arm. "Okay," I said gently. "Let's go get a pizza."

He met my eyes and I nodded reassuringly. *Okay. We won't talk about it.* I saw his shoulders slump in relief.

If I couldn't help him, I could at least distract him.

So we set off on foot, crunching through the snow towards Main Street, talking about my mom's pecan pie and how my car wasn't going to last too much longer and how the Cowboys did last season. Anything except Jillian and Max.

We were halfway to the pizza place when I tentatively said, "So... Danny seems nice."

JD grimaced, like he'd been expecting this. Then he sighed and nodded. "He is. He's a great guy." I could hear the warmth and respect in his voice. He loved the guy. So why....?

He saw my expression and sighed again. Then he pointed at the window of a bar we were passing. I followed his finger.

Danny was sitting at the bar, mouthwateringly gorgeous in his suit. His head was thrown back in laughter, his chest pushing his snow-white shirt out in two broad, curving slabs. A woman with long dark hair and perfect legs was cuddled up to one side of him and another, with brown hair, was pressed up tight to the other. Both of them were touching his arms and flicking their hair: they were doing everything except unzipping their dresses and saying *take me.*

"Danny doesn't do relationships," JD said gently. "He's more into...." He indicated the scene.

I nodded quickly and looked away. I was the dumbest person in the world. This was why Danny was so good with women. And now I understood why JD had never mentioned him, when they were in Delta together, or when Danny got him to lead the team. JD had been keeping me away from him. He was still protecting me, just like in high school.

I felt like an idiot. Danny was just a horndog who fucked anything that moved and I was his best friend's dorky little sister who'd gotten a crush on him.

I told myself I'd dodged a bullet. If he'd fucked me and dropped me then I'm not sure I could have taken it, after Toby. I should be happy.

So why, each time I remembered how far from home I was, did I keep thinking about dancing with Danny, and how safe and warmly protected I'd felt?

I sighed. *Idiot.* Right now, he was probably back at the garage with one or both of those women. I needed to forget about him because one thing was for sure: he'd already forgotten about me.

8

DANNY

I HAD one of Erin's breasts in my hand, squeezing it in slow rhythm as I rammed into her from behind. My thighs slapped against that tight, heart-shaped ass, every stroke drawing a high little cry from her.

I fell back on my knees, tugging her with me so that she wound up sitting in my lap, and she yelped as my cock went even deeper inside her. I gripped her hips and started to ease her up and down on me, and she trembled and moaned, her fingers searching out mine and knitting together. I kissed her throat and she threw back her head, her braid silky against my neck—

The wail of an electric guitar split the room and suddenly I was blinking and thrashing and—

Waking. I was alone, tangled in sheets, my cock was rock hard and—

An electric guitar solo of *The Star-Spangled Banner* was coming from my phone. The ringtone I have set for JD—he has *Rule Britannia* for me. I stared at my phone, still panting from the dream sex. *How did he know?!* Did he have big brother radar?!

I hit the *answer* button and tried to sound innocent. "Yeah?"

"Need you to come in," said JD in that bass Texas growl. "Got a mission."

"On my way." I hung up, then rubbed my face with my hand. "Fuck," I whispered, looking down at the tent in my jockey shorts. Now I was *dreaming* about her?!

I took a cold shower, dressed and headed down Main Street. One of the things I love about Mount Mercy is that it's small enough that you can walk everywhere. It was barely eight in the morning and the town was just coming to life.

I passed the town's little bookstore. It had weird opening times and it was the first time I'd ever seen it open, since I moved here. Further down the street, I met Earl, the head of the town's tiny police force, coming the other way on his beat. I waved and he gave me the *I'm watching you* sign, but he was grinning as he did it. He's ticketed me for speeding a few times, up in the hills, but he knows I keep it down wherever there's people.

A moment later I stopped, turned around, and looked back at the bookstore. I was thinking of Erin, and the book she'd talked about. I'd said I'd read it.

It was stupid. I knew I couldn't be with her. And the last book I'd read was back in school, some story about life in the Victorian Age that my English teacher had made us all read. I hadn't really paid attention, more interested in checking out her ass.

But the way Erin had talked about that book, as if it was a magical experience...I was curious, and I wanted to understand her. And I didn't like the idea of breaking my word.

I marched back up the street and into the bookstore. At first, I thought the power was out: the place was so dark, I was worried I was going to trip over something. Then I realized there *were* lights, high overhead. The owner apparently just liked it this way. I wrinkled my nose: there was a weird smell, too, one I'd never smelled before.

As my eyes adjusted to the gloom, I made out towering shelves of books all around me. I turned a slow circle, stunned. There was a whole world here that I hadn't ever been part of. How did geeks find time to read all this stuff?

As I finished my circle, I saw a woman standing behind a counter, eyeing me with suspicion. Maybe she could tell I wasn't the reading type. "Do you have, er…"—*wait, what was it called?* "Dark…castle?" The woman looked blank. "Palace of Night?" I tried. She still looked blank. "It's got dragons in it."

"Ah, *Throne of Night*." She ducked down, retrieved a book and dropped it on the counter with a *whud* of satisfaction. Jesus, the thing was about a billion pages long. But at least I'd have something to do on the flight to wherever we were going. I bought it, then realized I had nowhere to put it. *How are you supposed to carry these things?* I wound up tucking it under my arm, which made me feel like a school kid.

A little while later, in the hills just outside town, I arrived at our base. We'd nicknamed it *The Factory*, because that's what it used to be. When the team first formed, the place was derelict, with no windows and a leaking roof. But five months and a lot of hard graft later, it was starting to approach respectable. The rooms had been cleared of machinery and painted, the roof was fixed, the windows replaced and the heating worked. We even had a discreet metal plaque by the front door saying *Stormfinch Security.*

I found JD in the kitchen, waiting for the coffee pot to heat up. I put my mug next to his, threw in a teabag and poured on boiling water. And as the tea brewed, I thought about how I'd met him.

After years of stealing cars with the gang, the police finally caught up to me. I was eighteen and the judge gave me an ultimatum: prison or join the army. I was smart enough to know that the army was my only chance for something better so I signed up and went for it, eventually passing selection for the Parachute Regiment. The training was hell but I refused to quit, even when it was four in the morning and I was covered in freezing mud and someone was making me bawl *Yes Sir* at the top of my voice. My commanding officer said I had guts: I thought I was just bloody stubborn. But I made it through and found that I loved being in a unit. It felt like a family, even more so than the gang.

I liked the guys I was with but I didn't make those deep, lifelong friendships that the others did. I couldn't and I knew why: I was broken.

I was itching to drive again but it was a long time before I got the chance. In Afghanistan, our unit was riding in the back of a truck when we came under fire and three of us, including the driver, were shot. I jumped behind the wheel and managed to get us past three roadblocks and back to base in time to save the injured. After that, I became my unit's go-to driver.

Fast forward a little while and I'd made it into the British Special Forces, the SAS, who needed someone who was handy with a gun and good behind the wheel. And a little while after *that,* on a joint mission with Delta Force, I met JD.

It was one of those missions where everything went to hell. We were in Yemen to snatch a terrorist leader who was behind a whole series of attacks on US bases. It should have been a quick in and out but the intelligence was bad. Our helicopter was shot down on the way in and crashed into the mansion we were meant to be raiding. I got separated from the rest of the SAS and wound up outnumbered and pinned down in the middle of a ballroom as fire spread through the mansion. And there, hunkered behind an upturned table, I met JD, the leader of the Delta Team, also separated from his men. Together, we managed to shoot our way out of there, rescue the rest of the lads and get everyone down to the basement garage, where I hotwired a Range Rover and got us out of there. JD said that Delta could use a guy like me and pulled some strings to get me seconded to them, and so it began.

We couldn't be more different: the party-loving, womanizing Brit and the boy scout, stoic cowboy but, for some reason, it worked. I balanced JD, helped him unwind and have a little fun. And JD was like the big brother I'd never had, responsible and always there for me. For the first time in my life, I felt that deep connection that other people seem to make so easily. JD became my best friend and the only really close friend I'd ever had. For years, we fought side by side: The Middle East, anti-terrorist and protection work in Europe, Africa and Asia and countless secret missions in places the US and UK has never officially sent troops to.

I'd die for JD. I'd taken a bullet for him more than once, and he'd done the same for me. But I couldn't protect him from the thing that destroyed him: losing his wife and kid. I'd watched, helpless, as he quit the military and withdrew to a dark, dark place. That was when I got out of the army, too: I didn't want to carry on without him. I did private security work for a few years, mostly driving VIPs around. Then, when Kian O'Harra recruited me for the team, I saw a chance to get my best mate out of the pit he was in. I told Kian I'd join...but only if he recruited JD to be the team's leader. The team had been good for him so far but I was still worried. JD was as good a leader as ever, the best I'd ever seen, but he still wasn't the guy he'd been before his wife and kid died. There'd been a lightness to him back then and I wasn't sure he'd ever get it back. Last night, the anniversary, must have been hell for him.

I threw my teabag at the trash can and scored a direct hit, then glanced across at JD. "How are you doing?"

JD started to shrug but I pinned him with a look. He sighed. "I'm okay," he said at last. Then, "It was good to have Erin there."

I added milk to my tea. "She okay?"

JD didn't answer. When I looked up, he was glaring at me suspiciously.

I spread my hands wide. "She told me she lost her job in Vegas. Just wanted to check she was okay." It actually *had* been an innocent question. But now I could feel my face blooming with heat: it was like being a kid in school, when someone realizes you like some girl. *What's going on?* I never normally had a problem playing it cool.

JD crossed his arms, muscles bulging, and pushed out that heavy jaw. "Danny..." he growled.

"JD, I swear, nothing happened. We sat in my garage. She fixed her laptop."

"Yeah?"

"Yeah!"

"Because she asked about you."

In the SAS, they train you to resist interrogation. I'd learned how to remain a rock, even when I'm being waterboarded. But when JD told me *that,* my poker face disintegrated. I leaned forward, helpless. "Yeah?"

JD slammed his coffee down, spilling it. "Goddammit, Danny! Just for once, *for once*—She's my little sister!"

"It's not...." I trailed off. *It's not like that,* I was going to say, but how could I explain what it *was* like, when I didn't even understand it myself?

"You want to know what happened in Vegas?" JD was in full rant, now. "Fine."

And he told me about how her bastard boyfriend, Toby, had cheated on her, kicked her out of the company and taken her friends. When he got to the part about her spending Christmas day alone, I was shaking with rage. *If I jump in the Jag right now, I can be in Vegas by tonight....* I was going to find this Toby guy and fucking *annihilate* him.

But then I saw the way JD was looking at me. He was just as mad, just as protective. But he wanted to protect Erin from *me.* That's why he'd never introduced us.

"She's just had her heart broken," he told me. "I'm not going to let you do it all over again."

I searched for words. I wanted to tell him that it wouldn't be like that, but—

"You don't *do* relationships," he reminded me.

And that made me stop and think. He was right, I didn't. Because I knew I couldn't. Things felt different with Erin, but what if I was wrong? JD was right, she was fragile. If I slept with her and then it didn't work out, it could destroy her.

JD stepped closer, his voice ragged. "Danny, I love you, pal. But if you go near Erin, I *swear,* I will beat the crap out of you. You and me, we'll be *done.*"

It was like a slap to the face. He and I have tussled a few times, all best friends have, usually when I'm about to get into a drunken bar brawl. But this was different: he was a papa bear, protecting family. He really *would* hit me. And far worse, that last part: we'd be done. I swallowed. A life without JD was unthinkable. "Okay," I said, and I could hear the rawness in my voice: this was from the heart. "I promise."

He studied me for a second, cautious, but the mood was already shifting. He nodded...and then he suddenly pulled me into a big JD bear hug, crushing me close and patting my back. "Thank you," he whispered.

I squeezed him back, hard. I felt like I was waking up from a dream. Of *course* I couldn't put this at risk. What had I been thinking?!

Footsteps and voices from the hallway. We unwound just as Cal walked in, ducking his head to miss the door frame. The sniper's nickname in the Marines was *Bigfoot* and it fitted: he was huge, quiet, and more at home in nature than around people.

Cal was debating fishing lures with Colton, our other country guy. Colton didn't have Cal's height but he made up for it in lean muscle. He bounty hunted between Stormfinch jobs and he was quickly getting his own little fan club around the town. I'd be flirting with some woman in the bar and then Colton would stroll in, hungry for a beer after bringing down some criminal, and he'd dump all his chains and cuffs on the bar. The woman would whisper *who's that?* I'd tell her about how he tussles the bad guys to the ground, ties them, tosses them over his shoulder, and carries them off. Some of the women recoiled in fear but some of them went big-eyed and breathy, and asked me to slip him their phone number.

As Cal and Colton started pouring coffees, Irish voices filled the hallway. Kian O'Harra, the former Secret Service guy who'd put the team together and Bradan, his brother. "You can't keep putting it off," Bradan said as they walked in.

"Keep putting what off?" I asked.

Kian gave Bradan a long-suffering look: *now look what you've started.* But his younger brother just nodded for him to answer and Kian sighed and looked at the ceiling. "Asking Emily's dad if I can marry her. I'm not *putting it off.* I just haven't found the right moment."

Everyone looked at him skeptically.

"I was all ready to ask him when he was *former* President Matthews. Then he got into the re-election campaign and it was impossible to get a minute alone with him. Then he *won* and now he's the bloody president again, and you don't just walk up to the president and ask—" He sighed. "Look, can we get onto the mission?"

People grabbed coffee and we all trooped through to the briefing room. It had a long table, comfy chairs and a huge, fancy screen at one end that none of us could figure out how to hook up. Gabriel, the smooth-talking former thief, was kicked back in a chair, feet up on the table. JD gave him a look and he sighed good-naturedly and put them down.

We all sat down and I leaned forward in anticipation. Going on a mission was just what I needed. I'd be away from Erin, away from temptation.

"So where are we going?" asked JD.

"Berlin," said Kian. "The CIA got a tip that someone's traveling from New York to sell military secrets and they're meeting the buyer tonight, in a parking garage in Berlin. They want us to identify the seller, then grab him after he's made the sale and get him out of Germany."

"Why don't the CIA just ask the Germans to handle it?" asked Bradan.

"They don't want it getting out that someone's stolen US secrets. The Germans can never know we were there. We'll go in on fake, civilian passports. I've got fresh ones coming from Lily."

"Tell her not to give me a name that sounds like a dentist, this time," said Colton. *"Harold?"*

"All you've got to do is stake out the meet and take some photos," Kian told us. "Then grab the guy—Colton, that'll be your job—and bring him home.

"We'll have guns but only as a last resort," said Kian. "This one'll be quick and simple: you'll be home by tomorrow. Everyone good?"

We all nodded.

"Okay. Wheels up at noon."

9

ERIN

I'D COME to The Factory to see JD off. He introduced me to the team: the huge but quiet Cal, the charismatic Gabriel, Kian and Bradan, the two Irish brothers, and Colton, the heavyset, bearded guy from Missouri. They were a friendly bunch and I took to them immediately. But one person was missing. *Where's Danny?*

I knew he'd probably just been flirting with me in the garage like he flirted with everyone. I knew that the nearly-kiss hadn't even happened and maybe it wouldn't have meant anything if it had. I knew that I was just the geeky little sister with a crush on her brother's best friend. But I still wanted to say goodbye to him before he went off into danger.

Other women started arriving to see their men off. First a woman who Gabriel introduced as Olivia, his girlfriend. Like me, she hadn't adjusted to Colorado winters, yet: she was in a hugely thick green winter coat, woolly hat and gloves, and a scarf was wrapped over her mouth. I wondered if she was from somewhere warm, too. "You remember what I taught you?" she asked nervously from behind the scarf.

"Olivia's been giving us first aid lessons," Gabriel explained. He gently unwound the scarf from her face, then kissed her tenderly, and I saw her calm a little. "We remember."

There was a bark and then a blur of fluff shot past my legs. A huge German Shepherd leapt up at Cal, pawing at his chest and demanding ear scratches. Everyone started fussing over it. A woman with long black hair followed behind the dog and, without words, she cuddled up to Cal's side and put her head on his shoulder.

Next, a woman in a business suit, all energy and efficiency. She marched up to Bradan. "We've got everything planned for the party, when you come home," she told him, adjusting his jacket. "Bethany's cooking, Emily's decorating, I'm getting the booze, Olivia's baking cookies—"

I saw Colton's head jerk up at the mention of cookies.

"So..." The woman adjusted his jacket again. She was breathing fast, like she was trying not to cry. "So just...don't be late, okay?"

Bradan smoothly captured her hands and held them in his. "Okay," he said softly.

Another woman quietly entered, accompanied by a couple of guys in dark suits who took up positions by the door. *Emily Matthews!* The President's daughter. She hugged the other women in turn and then went over to Kian and squeezed his hand.

"I wish I was going with them," I heard him mutter under his breath.

Emily glanced up at him and then looked around at the other women. I could see the conflict on her face: relief that he was staying here but guilt, too, that she'd be the only woman not worried sick for the next twenty-four hours. She squeezed his hand again.

I looked at the clock. JD had said the team was heading out at noon and it was ten to, but there was no sign of Danny. And no women had shown up to say goodbye to him. What about the two from the bar the night before? There should be a whole crowd of women waving him off.

Unless...he hadn't told any of those women he was going. If he really did keep it just sex, never getting attached... He'd have no one to say goodbye to, no one to worry about him while he was away. *That's so lonely!*

A woman strolled in from the kitchen in torn jeans and a hoodie snacking on a bag of chocolate-covered raisins. "Can't believe you're flying commercial," she said. "I could have flown you, you know."

"This is Gina, our helicopter pilot," Gabriel told me. "I didn't know you could fly fixed-wing."

Gina gave him a look. "I can fly *anything*. Don't come crying to me when some kid drops ice cream down your neck and they run out of peanuts."

As she moved away, Gabriel took me to one side. He gave me a wolfish smile and I flushed a little. JD had told me about his background and, looking into those hazel eyes, glittering with intelligence, I could *absolutely* imagine him masterminding some daring heist. He reminded me of a highwayman: not evil or violent, more romantic scoundrel. Supposedly he was reformed, now, but there was still something about him that was seductively wicked. "You grew up with JD, right?" he asked.

I nodded.

"So you must know what his real name is," said Gabriel, grinning. "I've got a book going."

Colton joined our huddle. He was equally hot, but in a very different way. Where Gabriel was all smooth sophistication, Colton was all about power, his muscles stretching out the shoulders and chest of his red plaid shirt, and there was a brutish, primal authority about him. Danny had told me about the Colton Fan Club and I could believe it. "I'm in for twenty dollars on *Josiah Dallas*," Colton told me. "So come on, spill!"

I opened my mouth...and then saw JD watching me from across the room. I know how he feels about his name: there's a reason he always introduces himself as *JD*. "Sorry. It's a secret."

Gabriel and Colton grumbled. Behind them, I saw Kian glance at the clock. *They're about to head out!* "Hey, have you seen Danny?" I asked urgently.

"He was lifting weights," said Colton. "He's probably taking a shower."

I thanked him and hurried off in the direction he pointed. When I heard the sound of water running, I homed in on it. There was an open doorway up ahead and I could glimpse tiles inside.

I peeked around the door uncertainly. I could see lockers and showers, but no Danny. *Should I call out?* I opened my mouth—

Danny suddenly strode into view from behind the row of lockers. He was topless, a towel around his waist, and....

He looked like he'd been chiseled out of a block of marble by a master sculptor. His abs were gorgeous hard ridges with softly rounded ends, like the feathers on an angel's wing, and they shone with little jewels of water. Higher up, his body widened and flowed into full, wide pecs that made me think of a heavyweight boxer, loaded with brute power. There was that special spot, the one I'd fantasized about, where my cheek would rest against his pec. it looked even better, without the shirt. Above that, his body widened again to broad shoulders, the smooth spheres of muscle gleaming wetly. Then the bulges of his biceps, huge and solid: I hadn't realized how *big* he was, under his suit. His forearms were thickly-muscled, too, and like his biceps, they were completely free of tattoos. In fact, I couldn't see a single tattoo anywhere on his body, which only made him look more like some classical work of art.

Then he turned and my chest tightened in pain.

His back should have been as breathtakingly perfect as his front: the tight waist, the broad, strong lats, the spheres of his shoulders.... But someone had destroyed it.

Vicious, thick scars lay across his back, the skin raised where it had been split open and then left to heal. I saw the ones that ran across his shoulders, first. Then my eyes roamed lower and I saw the ones on his upper back. I started praying under my breath that the next scar would be the last one, but they went on and on, slashing across his lower back in cruel efficiency, as if the person who'd left them hadn't wanted to leave an inch untouched. They only stopped an inch above where the towel clung to the hard cheeks of his ass.

I stared in shock. *Who would do this?! How could someone....* The more I looked, the more sadistic details I saw. The scars were layered, wound on top of wound, criss-crossing. This wasn't just one event, this was time after time. And at the end of some of the scars, there were extra marks where something had cut in deeper, something square. The buckle of a belt.

He carried this with him, hidden under his suit, cloaked by that cocky grin. *Danny!* I just wanted to put my arms around him and hug him close.

He dressed slowly and then looked at the clock on the wall. It was nearly ten a.m. but Danny didn't move. In fact, he sighed and leaned back against a locker.

I suddenly realized that he wasn't running late. He was deliberately killing time in here, waiting until the last possible minute before he went through to where everyone was gathered. He was avoiding someone. But that didn't make sense, he was one of the team, he saw these guys every day—

My stomach lurched. He was avoiding *me.* He'd just been flirting in the garage, and now he didn't want to run into the geeky girl who'd read too much into it.

I stepped back to leave but, at that second, he glanced around and saw me. Those glittering green eyes locked with mine and—

It was an animal reaction, before thoughts could get in the way. A wave of raw heat that shot through the air and slammed right into me. I felt like I'd been pushed right out of my clothes and pinned, naked and wriggling, against the far wall, his mouth on my neck. The heat flooded my body, filling me up, leaving me gasping. He wanted me. Here. Now. Up against the lockers or on the tiled floor.

He took a step towards me as if pulled, his eyes narrowed with lust.

My whole body had gone trembly and weak and the blood was thundering in my ears. I swallowed, feeling drunk.

Then he faltered and stopped. He looked away for a second and, when he looked back, the lust was contained, just barely. And with it was a longing that made my chest go tight.

He hadn't been avoiding me because he didn't like me. He'd been avoiding me because he *did*. But why?

A holler from down the hall. "*Erin!*" JD's voice.

Danny looked towards the voice, then gave me a look I'll never forget. A very British look, a little shake of his head and a helpless grin, humor mixed with pain.

JD had warned him off me. He had to stay away from me...or he'd lose his best friend.

An ache began in my chest, cutting right through to my core. *No!*

But I slowly nodded. I'd never forgive myself if I came between them.

"*Erin!*" JD hollered again.

I turned and scurried back to where everyone was gathered. People were saying their final goodbyes. Gabriel had one hand on Olivia's cheek and was talking to her in a voice too low for me to hear, but whatever he was saying, she was transfixed, doing little nods and gulps as if on the verge of tears. Cal was staring down intently at his girlfriend, whose lip was starting to tremble, too, but he didn't seem to know what to say to make her feel better. So he put both hands on her waist and just lifted her right off the ground. She yelped and then shrieked and then, as he laid her across his massive shoulders and spun around and around like a helicopter, she started laughing hysterically. Only then did he bring her down and hug her close.

JD held his arms out. I didn't hesitate for a second. I was aching inside, frustrated, but I knew he was just trying to protect me and he was my brother. I threw my arms around him and pressed my face deep into his plaid shirt. "Be safe," I pleaded.

He smoothed my hair and kissed the top of my head. "Always."

As I grudgingly released him, Stacey was hugging Bradan and I saw Emily take Kian's hand again, anchoring him in Colorado, just in case he got any ideas. Only Danny and Colton didn't have someone to say goodbye to.

One by one, the team trooped outside into the cold, heading for a huge black SUV. Danny was the last to leave and, as the door closed behind him, I felt this soul-deep tug. I knew I had to stay away. I couldn't come between him and JD. But this didn't feel right. What if something happened to him? I walked over to the window and watched him walking away and with every step he took, the pull got stronger. He was halfway to the SUV....

I bolted out the door and ran to him. He must have heard me at the last second because he turned just in time for me to *whump* into his chest. I squeezed him hard. "Come back safe, okay?" I whispered.

I quickly stepped back before anyone saw. Danny gazed down at me, the conflict raging on his face. His eyes flicked to my lips. His hand crushed the leather handles of his travel bag and then loosened, as if he was about to just drop it on the ground and grab me instead.

Then he gave me a quick little nod, turned and walked towards the SUV. I stood there with the icy wind whipping around me, feeling more alone than I'd ever felt.

10

DANNY

"I COULD GET USED TO THIS," said JD, as he was handed a drink by a flight attendant. "Sure beats a military transport."

"Could use a little more leg room," muttered Cal from the seat next door. The poor guy was scrunched up like a pretzel.

Colton disagreed, too. A kid in the seat behind him was kicking his seat. They'd been doing it since we took off and they didn't show any signs of stopping. "Gina had a point," he muttered.

I was silent, lost in thought. When I'd seen Erin at the base, all the feelings I'd been suppressing had come rushing back. I knew I couldn't be with her. But there was something I could do. I could try her world a little.

I dug in my bag for the book and then looked at it uncertainly. The last thing I'd read had been the service manual for a '93 BMW. This thing was intimidating. Not only was it thick enough to beat someone to death with, it had a big map in the front full of places with no vowels. *Am I really going to do this?*

I took a deep breath and plunged in. It was hard going at first: I wasn't sure how to pronounce anything and there was a lot of stuff about legends and prophecies that made my brain hurt. But then it got into a battle and that was something I understood. I started following this woman called Vessia, who was an elf with pointy ears who wore a sort of leather corset that sounded pretty hot. And she was a scullery maid, but she had eyes that were eerily similar to the king's, so I wondered if maybe he was her real dad. And then she got caught up in a war and was racing across a battlefield to unleash some magical creature and killing everyone who got in her way and—

"Ladies and gentlemen, in around ten minutes we'll be starting our descent into Berlin...."

Already? I realized I'd read about a fifth of the massive book. Suddenly, I could see why Erin was into this stuff. I wanted to talk to her about it, about whether the archer and the squire were going to get together and whether my theory about the heroine being in line for the throne was right.

Only I couldn't. I had to stay away. And I wasn't ready for how much that hurt.

Some hours later, I was in the driver's seat of a parked van, trying to keep warm. It was three in the morning and a bitter wind was whistling straight through the open sides of the concrete parking garage, turning it as cold as a meat locker. We couldn't run the heater or it would kill the van's battery and we couldn't start the engine because we wanted people to think the van was empty.

The parking bay where the meet was supposed to happen was directly behind us. Colton, Bradan and Gabriel were in the back of the van, watching through spy holes, Gabriel ready with a camera. We had Cal on top of a building across the street, keeping watch. JD was in the passenger seat watching his side and my job was to watch my side.

But my mind kept wandering back to Erin. *Why her?* I'd gone my entire life without feeling that connection. Why did the one woman I had it with have to be JD's little sister?

"Got a car coming in," said Cal over the radio.

We waited silently while the car crept slowly through the garage... and then pulled into the bay we'd been watching. Everyone inhaled: this was it.

A moment later, another car arrived, a big black Mercedes. It pulled into the bay next to the first car. As a guy climbed out of the first car, Gabriel started snapping pictures. The man was stocky, short and carried a cardboard file. "There's our seller," whispered JD.

A guy climbed out of the Mercedes. He was older, fifties, maybe, with a silver beard and wearing a suit and black leather gloves. There was a....*hardness* about him. He was all muscle, but it went beyond that. His scowl was so deep set, it looked like he'd never smiled. And his eyes were weapons: he didn't look at things with curiosity and joy, like Erin did. He stared at them as if he was extracting every useful scrap of information from them before discarding them. It felt like he'd been cast from iron, cold and utterly unyielding.

The man with the beard held out a thick brown envelope. "He must be the buyer," I muttered. I was supposed to be watching my side but my eyes were glued to the mirror, watching it play out.

"That can't be right," muttered Gabriel to himself.

I twisted around in my seat to look. Gabriel had moved the camera away from his eye and was looking at the last photo he'd taken on the screen. "That writing on the front of that file's in Cyrillic," he said, confused. "And it's got the Hammer and Sickle in the corner. He's not selling US secrets, he's selling old Soviet ones."

Behind us, the stocky guy checked the money and then handed over the file. And then—

It happened so fast. The bearded guy stepped close to the seller and made a sudden, quick movement: at first, I thought he'd punched him in the chest. But then the seller was collapsing to the floor, clutching at his stomach as blood welled between his fingers.

"Oh, *shit!*" hissed Gabriel. We all looked at each other in horror. We'd just witnessed a murder and the guy we were supposed to grab was dead. I stared at the man with the silver beard. He tossed the knife beside the body, then looked down at his suit, inspecting it for any trace of blood.

"Okay, everybody just sit tight," whispered JD. "We'll wait until he's gone, then leave. Let the CIA figure out what the hell this was."

There was a knock on the window, about an inch from my head. I jerked around in panic and stared right into the face of a gray-haired man in a security uniform. I gawped at him. *How is he there? How did he get right up beside us without me seeing?*

Because I'd been too busy watching what was going on behind us, when I should have been doing my job.

The guy asked me a question in German. I waved frantically for him to shut up, before the murderer behind us heard him. But it was too late.

In my mirror, I saw the bearded guy spot the security guard and pull a gun. I opened my mouth to shout a warning but then the shot rang out and the guard fell to the floor. I stared down at him in shock. Just a sweet old guy working the graveyard shift, he'd wandered over to ask what we were doing there and now he was dead.

And now the murderer knew someone was in the van. He started shooting and we all ducked down as bullets sprayed through the van. We could hear him snapping out orders into a radio, his voice calm and clinically efficient.

"Get us out of here!" JD yelled.

I started the engine...but it wouldn't turn over. One of the bullets must have hit something vital in the engine..

"Got another SUV coming in fast," reported Cal over the radio. *Shit.* The guy had called in backup.

"Out the back!" yelled JD. We scrambled out of the rear doors of the van but gunfire chased us, forcing us to duck behind a parked car. Whoever he was, this guy was a good shot.

Bradan had a radio tuned to the police frequency and it suddenly squawked. He listened to it for a second. "Someone just called in shots fired," he said. "Police'll be here in five."

We started shooting back at the bearded guy and pushing towards the exit. But just as we neared it, an SUV screeched into the garage and six guys with automatic weapons jumped out. The murderer yelled orders to them and we were forced back under a hail of gunfire. We were outnumbered and outgunned and these guys knew what they were doing: Special Forces, maybe. Who *was* this guy, that he had special forces backing him up?

Then Colton cried out and clutched his leg. A bullet must have clipped him. Gabriel got an arm under his shoulders and helped him limp along. We were cut off from the exit: the only way to go was up to the next level. As we retreated up the ramp, Gabriel shook his head. "This isn't good. The next floor's the roof and that's a dead end."

We took cover behind another parked car. With our backs pressed against the icy metal, Bradan ripped open a package of gauze and pressed it onto Colton's wound to slow the bleeding. I was suddenly glad Olivia had given us those first aid lessons. The windows of the car shattered, showering us with safety glass. Bradan sneaked a peek around the corner. "They're coming!"

We were pinned down and about to be overrun. We all looked at each other, panicked and shaken. *How did this go so bad, so fast?*

JD frowned, thinking hard. Then he grabbed my arm. "Get them home."

I blinked at him. "What?"

He gripped my arm even harder. "And take care of Erin. Promise me, Danny!"

I stared at him. "Yeah, I promise but—"

Too late: he jumped up and ran, heading for the ramp that led up to the roof. We all cursed and gave him covering fire, forcing the bad guys to duck down behind cover for a few seconds. When they poked their heads out again, they all looked towards the ramp and started moving that way. They thought we'd all followed JD upstairs. *Oh God, that was his plan: to lead them away, so the rest of us could escape.*

The special forces guys moved past us and disappeared up the ramp. We crouched there panting. "What do we do?" asked Gabriel.

My mind was spinning. All my instincts as a friend said *go up there. Fight it out. Try to rescue him.* But we were outnumbered, Colton was hurt and the police would be here any minute. JD's words echoed in my head. *Get them home.*

"We have to go," I croaked.

They all went pale at the idea of leaving him. I knew how they felt because my guts were twisting, too. But if we didn't go now, JD would have sacrificed himself for nothing.

I led them downstairs. Above us, there were long bursts of gunfire from the bad guys as they closed in, then the sound of JD's lone gun trying to hold them off. He was making a last stand. My chest went so tight I could barely breathe. *JD!*

We burst out of the parking garage and ran across the street, ducking down behind some bushes just as police cars pulled up outside the exit. We'd made it out by seconds.

Cal climbed silently down a fire escape and dropped to the ground beside us. "Where's JD?"

I turned to him, my voice ragged with emotion. "They got him."

11

DANNY

WHEN WE ARRIVED HOME, Bethany, Olivia and Stacey were waiting for us. As their men climbed out, the couples all silently embraced. No one knew what to say. We'd never come home a man down, before.

Inside, the tables were set up for the big homecoming dinner Stacey had organized, but the fairy lights had been switched off and the food put back in the refrigerator. As Olivia took Colton off to take a look at his leg, the rest of us walked into the briefing room.

Kian was on a video call on his laptop. Emily was sitting beside him, just out of view of the camera. On the screen was Roberta, our contact at the CIA. She was about sixty and, normally, she was a model of cool control. Right now, she looked frazzled. "You were just supposed to take pictures and quietly grab the guy!" she snapped. "You got into a firefight!"

"Your intel was bad!" yelled Kian. His Irish accent got stronger when he was upset and right now, it was the strongest I'd ever heard it. "We walked in on someone selling old Soviet files and getting killed by the buyer!"

Roberta turned away for a second as someone off-screen handed her a document. Her eyes flicked over it. "Your man's alive," she announced..

We all slumped in relief. Roberta visibly relaxed, too. Some of her anger had been down to guilt, I realized. "What do you know?" I asked.

"We had a satellite over the area. The gunfight on the roof ended with your guy being captured and bundled into an SUV. That's the good news."

"What's the bad news?" asked Kian.

"We ran the photos you took through our computers. We can't identify the seller, but the buyer's name is Otto Becker." An image of the guy with the silver beard appeared next to her on the screen, and even in photo form, his eyes gave me the creeps. Roberta paused, looking worried.

"So who is he?" Kian asked. "Mafia? An arms dealer?"

Roberta took a deep breath. "He's the head of Special Operations at the BND."

"*What?!*" The BND is Germany's CIA. "So the German government has JD?"

Roberta shook her head. "If they did, they'd be getting the American ambassador out of bed and demanding to know what we were doing over there. Becker must be running some sort of rogue operation and you walked into it. He's captured JD but he's kept it off the books. He's probably finding out what he knows. And then..."

She didn't say it but we could all finish the sentence in our heads. *And then he'll kill him.* "Well then we've got to get him back," I said, my voice tight with fear. "Tell the Germans what happened, tell them this Becker guy is dirty and he's holding one of our people!"

Roberta sighed. "No."

"*No?*" Kian leaned closer to the screen. "What do you mean, *no?*"

"It can't come out that we were running an op in Germany," said Roberta. "We can't get involved. We have to disavow JD, claim we don't know him. I'm sorry."

Kian stared at the screen, speechless, then stabbed the *end call* button so hard he almost broke the keyboard. We all sat there fuming. I'd always known this was a possibility, if something went wrong. This is why the government used people like us, because we were deniable. But I hadn't thought it would ever actually happen.

"I'll call the Sisters of Invidia," said Kian. "See if they can find out where this Becker guy is holding JD." The Sisters were an all-female hacking group he knew, the best in the business. One of them, Lily, was also the person who supplied all our fake passports. Kian stood up. "And when they find him, I'm going with you to get him back."

"What?" asked Emily.

He turned to her. "We're a man down."

She looked terrified. "But—"

"I stayed here last time and look what happened!" he snapped.

"That's not your fault!"

"I'm going and that's the end of it." He looked at me and jerked his head for me to follow him, then marched out of the room.

I hurried after him and caught him out in the hallway. He was looking back towards the briefing room, his face troubled. Probably regretting snapping at Emily. Then he turned to me. "We need a new field leader," he told me.

It took a second before I realized he meant *me*. "But I'm—Wait, no, I'm not...." I knew how to drive and how to party and that was it. "You're coming along, *you* do it!"

"I've been out of the field too long. You know these guys, you've fought beside them."

I stared at him. I was reliving that moment when I'd given the order to leave JD behind. The toughest moment of my life...and now Kian wanted me to take over, to make decisions like that all the time. "I can't."

Kian put his hand on my shoulder. "You have to," he said gently.

I sucked in a deep breath and let it out. Then I forced myself to nod.

He squeezed my shoulder. "I'll be back in a bit," he said. "I need to go tell Erin."

Erin. She didn't know, yet. When we'd called Kian from Berlin, we'd agreed someone should tell her in person, and Kian had been waiting until he knew more.

"I'll do it," I said. Kian looked uncertain but I gave him a firm nod. I'd promised JD I'd look after her. It was my job.

It was the middle of the night and bitterly cold. I set off walking, scrunching through the snow, but now I was alone with my thoughts, everything started boiling up inside me and the energy had to escape somehow. I broke into a jog, then a run.

This was my fault. I was meant to have been watching the front. I should have seen the security guard. I could have intercepted him, sweet-talked him, bribed him....I could have knocked him out, if I'd had to. The old guy should be waking up with a bump on his head or a crisp hundred Euro note in his pocket and instead he was lying on a slab. And JD was God-knows where, probably being tortured for information. And Erin....

Erin was about to find out her brother wasn't coming home. Maybe ever.

I reached JD's apartment building and stared at the buzzer for his apartment. *Ah, Jesus.* Every soldier thinks about this moment, someone opening a door to be told their loved one is lost. I knew it wouldn't ever happen with me because I didn't have anyone who'd be waiting for me. But I never thought it would be me giving the bad news.

I pressed the buzzer. Told her it was me. She buzzed me up and by the time I'd raced up the stairs, she was standing at the door of the apartment. When she saw my expression, her face went sheet-white. "Oh God," she whispered. "No, no, no—"

"He's alive," I said quickly. "But they've got him."

She just crumpled. And I couldn't stop myself: I pulled her into my arms.

12

ERIN

HE CRUSHED me to him and, as big, hot sobs geysered up inside me, I wrapped my arms around his back and hung on for dear life. *What if this is it? What if I never see him again?* A huge void was forming in my mind, as big as JD and stretching on for the rest of my life. I had things I needed to do with him, things I needed to say to him....

The sobs shook my chest and my tears soaked his shirt but Danny just hugged me closer. I clung to him like I would a rock, preventing the thoughts from dragging me away to oblivion. And gradually, the crying stopped. He kept holding me and now I could feel the tension in his arms: he needed JD back as much as I did.

I slowly released my grip and he let me step back. He looked down at me, his jaw set like iron. "I promise you," he told me, his voice ragged, "I *promise* you, I will bring him back to you."

I gulped down the last of the sobs and nodded. I wouldn't have believed it from anyone else, but I believed it from Danny. And now I became aware that I was standing there in just a thin pink nightshirt, and that I'd been pressed against him like that, with no bra. But it hadn't been sexual, in the moment. Just caring and very, very protective.

"I have to go," he said. "We've got to find him and start planning a rescue."

"I'm coming with you," I told him instantly. There was no way I was staying in JD's apartment by myself, unable to sleep. I pulled on jeans, sneakers and a sweater and we went.

Even though it was the middle of the night, the men were all still at the base, sitting tense and worried around the briefing room table. I'd braced myself to argue when they told me to go home, but Kian just gave me a little nod of sympathy: he understood why I had to be there.

At that moment, Kian's laptop screen lit up with an incoming video call. The caller ID said *Lily.* A woman with olive skin and long dark hair appeared, her face lit by the glow of computer screens. "We found him," she said.

Everyone leaned forward. "Where?" asked Kian.

"Siberia."

13

DANNY

WHAT?!

The woman on screen brought up some photos and narrated over them. "We used traffic cameras to track the SUV with JD in it to this military base just outside Berlin. Ten minutes later, a helicopter flew him to this place."

She showed us an ugly, concrete structure built into the side of a cliff, with sloping walls and no windows. "It used to be a gulag, back in the Soviet era," she told us. "These days, the Germans use it as a black site."

"What's a black site?" asked Erin.

I grimaced and turned to her. I'd forgotten that she didn't live in our world. "Sometimes, the intelligence services catch terror suspects, and they want to question them in a way that's not legal in their own country—"

"Call it what it is," growled Cal. "They want to torture them."

I nodded grimly. "So they take people to secret prisons in other countries where they can get away with it. Germany must have done a deal with the Russians to use this old Soviet prison in Siberia. This guy who captured JD, Otto Becker, is high up in German intelligence.

He probably sends prisoners there all the time. It wouldn't be hard for him to stash JD there while he figures out what to do with him."

"Lily, can you show us where this place is?" asked Kian.

A map of Europe appeared on the screen. It zoomed in on Moscow and then started panning north.

And it kept going.

And going.

The cities stopped. The towns stopped. Then the roads stopped and there was just...*nothing*. Just snow and forests. And still the camera kept moving. One by one, the team reacted, cursing and groaning. Even Cal, who'd spent years living in the wilderness.

The camera finally reached a black dot: the prison. Kian was tapping on his phone, his face grim. "Just to give you a sense of scale," he said, "See that dark blob, south of the prison? That's a lake. It's *the size of Belgium.*"

We all stared at the screen, slack-jawed. This place was hundreds of miles from civilization.

"It's minus twenty degrees there," Kian told us, "and that's during the day. At night, it can get down to minus *thirty* Fahrenheit."

For the next three hours, we studied photos of the prison. The place was a fortress, guarded by heavily-armed German soldiers, in the middle of a frozen hell. Getting JD out was going to be near impossible. And everyone was exhausted: we'd been on the go for two days straight. I shook my head. "Let's pick this up tomorrow."

At that moment, we were bathed in blue light. The big screen at one end of the table, the one we'd never managed to get hooked up, was glowing. Erin stood up from where she'd been kneeling behind it. "It works now," she told us shyly.

I walked Erin home. At the door, she turned back to look at me and the sight of her there, small and vulnerable and so alone, made me want to just pick her up and hug her. She'd lost everything, thanks to me. I had to look after her. I promised JD I would. But as that protective need welled up, it brought all the other emotions with it.

I forced myself to step back into the cold darkness. "I'll let you know as soon as we have a plan," I told her. And trudged away into the snow.

When I hit Main Street, I stopped and looked longingly at the lights of Krüger's Tavern. A beer or two would help me unwind...

Then I shook my head and turned towards the garage. *Not until JD is safe home.* I was the leader, now, God help me. I suddenly had a whole new appreciation of what JD did. I was going to have to make decisions, send people into danger. What if, this time, someone died? How many lives should I risk, for a shot at getting JD back?

I couldn't sleep, so I started going through the information the Sisters of Invidia had found on Otto Becker. It wasn't good news.

The rest of the intelligence community were terrified of this man. Most spies are carefully-spoken diplomats from top colleges who sit in meetings and tap at computers all day. Becker was something utterly different, a German Special Forces veteran who still swam a mile every morning and was a black belt in four martial arts. But it wasn't just his physical toughness that scared everyone.

Becker was fifty-five. He'd grown up in a different world: East Berlin, when it was a police state controlled by the Soviets. His dad had been high up in the *Stasi,* the secret police, and little Otto had grown up thinking it was normal for the authorities to have absolute power, normal for civilians to be threatened or tortured or just *disappear* because there was a suspicion they were disloyal to the party. There'd been all sorts of allegations against him since he joined the BND: beating suspects, water torture, even threatening their wives and girlfriends with rape. But nothing had ever been substantiated: my guess was, no one was brave enough to come forward as a witness. And because he got results, he'd risen fast, to the top levels of the BND. Now he had his own hand-picked military team and he reported directly to the German Chancellor. We couldn't have picked a worse enemy.

I fell into bed, exhausted and alone. When I finally slept, I had nightmares: ones where I screwed up again and watched the whole team die in front of me.

The next morning, I was the first to arrive. Hazy from lack of sleep, I stared at the keys for The Factory, trying to remember which one fit which door. JD had given me a set but I'd never had to use them: I'd never been the first one in, before. I made tea in the kitchen and my eyes kept falling on JD's mug, sitting unused on the drying rack.

Kian walked in, his phone to his ear. "It's the CIA," he told me. "Roberta, I'm putting you on speaker."

He did and Roberta's voice filled the room. "We intercepted a call an hour ago between Otto Becker and the guy who runs the prison in Siberia, a guy called Werner Kraus." She played a recording and two German voices filled the room. One was quick and brutally clinical: *Becker,* I decided. The other was nervous: I could almost hear him sweating. *Kraus.*

Roberta spoke over the voices, translating for us. "Kraus is saying that the German authorities are coming to inspect the prison in three days. *So I need to clear out those personal effects I'm looking after.* Becker asks him to delay, Kraus says he can't. Kraus says *Arrive by nine and you can have one last listen to your records, then we'll have to throw them in the trash.*"

"They're talking about JD," said Kian. "They can't have the authorities ask why an American's being held there. So Becker's going to go there and interrogate JD one last time and then they're going to kill him and get rid of the body before the prison inspectors arrive." He turned to me. "We only have three days to get him out of there."

Three hours later, I was sitting at the big table in the briefing room, wired from too much coffee but glad that I hadn't drunk the night before. Kian had left to go and chase up some lead while the rest of us planned. "Okay, let's go over it," I said. "Remember, we've got to do this without killing anyone: it's German soldiers guarding this place, they're not our enemies. Plus, if we kill one, the whole of Europe is going to be hunting us as terrorists and we'll never get home."

"We fly commercial to Latvia," said Gabriel. "The CIA won't help us officially but Roberta's letting us use one of their safehouses to prep. I'll use my contacts to get us guns and uniforms."

"We rent a chopper and I fly us over the border into Russia and all the way to the prison," said Gina.

"We'll use tranquilizer darts on the guards," said Colton. "They'll be out for an hour."

"We find JD's cell and I pick the lock," said Gabriel.

"We put a virus the Sisters are sending in the prison's computer and it wipes the cameras," said Bradan.

It sounded like we had a plan. But then Kian marched in. "We have a problem," he said, and threw something on the table. We all stared: it was a thick metal ring with a box attached to the side.

"It's an ankle bracelet," Kian told us bitterly. "The prisoners all wear one. If JD leaves his cell with that on, the alarms go off."

"So we'll get the Sisters to hack it," said Gabriel. "They can hack anything."

"They can hack anything *connected to the internet*," said Kian. "This is old Soviet tech, from the eighties, when the prison was built. No one's ever been able to get one of these off. Some MIT guys tried for a challenge but they got nowhere. The circuitry's insanely complex." He shook his head. "We're fucked."

I picked up the ankle bracelet and turned it over in my hands, thinking. "Maybe not."

14

ERIN

I'D BEEN GOING out of my mind, pacing JD's apartment. I'd wanted to go to the base again but I hadn't wanted to be in the way. So when the door buzzer sounded, I leapt across the room, desperate for news. Danny was standing there, eyes downcast. He stared at his shoes for a second before taking a deep breath and looking me in the eye.

Instantly, all the feelings were back. The attraction, deep and raw, heating the air between us. The tug towards him, the need to just press myself to that strong chest and feel safe again. And he was looking at me the exact same way, both of us leaning forward a half inch.

He looked away for a moment and took a deep breath. When he looked at me again, his green eyes were burning but he was under control: *just.* "We need your help," he told me. He showed me the ankle bracelet and told me what it did. "Can you make something that'll open it?"

I took the thing and turned it over in my hands. Finally, a way I could help! And this was *what I did:* within a few weeks, I was sure that—

"We need it today," he added. "We need a day to prep and a day to get there, and we only have three days."

I looked up at him. "What happens in three days?"

He told me and my stomach lurched. If I didn't figure this thing out quickly, JD was dead. "Get in here." I told him.

It took me half an hour just to figure out how to get the casing open. *"Cheese and crackers!"* I muttered when I saw the contents.

I felt Danny looking at me and glanced up. He was giving me this look of shock that softened into a *you're adorable* look. I blushed. It's just the way JD and my folks raised me.

I showed him what was inside the bracelet: a mass of tiny circuit boards joined by a jungle of tiny wires as thin as angel hair. It was the most complicated thing I'd ever seen.

I started to trace the wiring but it was too delicate to run my fingers along. I had to get out my laser pointer and use its thin green beam to follow the wires instead. Even then, I couldn't make sense of it. There was nothing to guide me, no way in. It was like trying to figure out the plot of a book that's written in a foreign language. After four hours, I slumped in my chair and put my head in my hands.

Danny came up behind me and laid his hands on my shoulders, gently massaging them. "You'll get it," he told me.

I shook my head, on the edge of tears. "What if I *don't?* What if I can't and—" I couldn't say it.

His hands squeezed. "You will," he said. His voice was rough granite. "Because you're amazing."

I looked up. He gazed down at me, upside down, his green eyes molten. "You're amazing," he said again, more quietly.

I swallowed. Nodded. And got back to work.

I *could* do this. I had to be able to because if I didn't, my brother wasn't coming home. I told myself it was just a puzzle, like the ones I'd done when I was a kid, and all puzzles can be solved. I put myself in the mind of the engineer who'd designed this. "What were you thinking, Boris?" I muttered.

For hours, I traced wires and made notes and, at last, I saw a pattern. "How many floors does the prison have?" I asked.

Danny studied the photos they'd found. "Five."

I'd found a series of tiny switches that seemed to be for setting which cell the prisoner was assigned to. Twelve cells per block, three blocks per floor and *five floors!* I was right! And once I understood that, it was like finding the Rosetta Stone.

It took the entire afternoon and into the evening, first figuring out the bracelet and then building the key that would open it. Danny stayed with me the entire time, fetching me water and ordering pizza to keep me going. It was past ten in the evening when I finally put down my soldering iron.

Danny had fallen asleep, slumped sideways on the couch. I crept over to him. I knew I needed to wake him but he looked so peaceful, asleep, and it was the first time I'd been able to just drink him in, without him looking at *me*. God, he was gorgeous. I went closer, gazing at him from a foot away, and now I could smell that delicious vanilla and spice scent of him. I tilted my head sideways to match his: it felt like we were lying in bed together, and the idea felt so warm and comforting it made me ache.

Danny's eyes opened. I jumped back and fell on my ass.

"What were you doing?" he asked sleepily.

"Nothing!" I flushed. "Coming to wake you up. I did it."

15

DANNY

WE RAN TOWARDS THE FACTORY, fresh snow crunching under our feet. *How did I fall asleep?* I've spent enough time on watch, in the forces, that I'm good at staying awake. There was just something about Erin's presence that really relaxed me.

She suddenly slipped on the snow and went headfirst towards the sidewalk. I lunged and grabbed her hand just in time, jerking her to a stop. Then I hauled her upright and both of us just stood there for a moment, panting and shaky with adrenaline. "Thanks," she managed.

Her little hand throbbed, a block of ice wrapped in my big, warm palm. I told myself to let go but my hand wouldn't listen.

She'd found an old winter jacket of JD's and it was way too big for her. Her face peeked out of the fur-trimmed hood like she was looking out of the mouth of a cave, those delicate blue eyes blinking up at me and she was just so adorable...and then I looked down at those soft lips and they were so damn kissable. The snow was falling around us, deadening all sound and isolating us in a private, black void. No one was watching. I could just lean down and—

I squeezed her hand...and then made myself let it go. "Come on."

Moments later, we arrived at The Factory. Everyone was still there: no one was interested in going home until we had a working plan to get JD.

Erin showed everyone the key she'd made, a six-inch rod of metal with circuitry glued to it, some batteries and a single red button. "You just put the tip next to the bracelet," she said, demonstrating, "press the button and—"

The bracelet clicked open. Everyone cheered.

Kian tore open a cardboard carton. "I managed to get hold of a second one," he said, digging through the packaging. He put another ankle bracelet down beside the first one.

Erin passed the key to me. "You try it."

I nodded and held the key like she had. Pressed the button....

Nothing happened. "Am I doing it wrong?" I asked.

Erin slipped under my arm and pressed in close against my side, so she could see. I could feel the warmth of her body, smell the subtle peach scent of her shampoo. "No..." She took out her tool roll and opened up the second bracelet. After just a few seconds, she gave a moan of horror. "The circuit boards are different."

"Can you make a key that opens this one, too?" I asked.

"Yeah, but that'll only open these two." She slumped against the table and closed her eyes. "The prison was open for decades back in the Soviet days and they must have kept updating the design. I can't make a key that opens them all, not without a sample of every one and there could be hundreds."

She opened her eyes and looked up at me and I knew what she was thinking because I was thinking it, too. There was no way to get the bracelet off JD. And that meant there was no way to get him out.

JD was going to die.

16

ERIN

I felt myself breaking inside. *JD!* It couldn't end like this. I couldn't lose him!

I looked around at the team. Kian was hunched over the table, knuckles white where he gripped the edge. As the leader, he'd carry this for the rest of his life. And the others, they were in pieces, too. But no one looked worse than Danny. He was about to lose his best friend.

I moved away from the others and started to pace, unable to keep still. I racked my brains. There had to be some way to make a key that would open every type of bracelet. But there just wasn't. It was so ironic: if I was there in person, I could just take apart JD's bracelet and hack it manually, but making a key that did that automatically was impossible.

I stopped. *If I was there in person.*

The thought was utterly terrifying. *Me?! I'm not a soldier!*

I started pacing again, the fear driving me. I tried to lock the idea out of my mind. But the thought of JD never coming home ate away at my defenses until it crept back in. I came to a stop, my chest tight with panic.

I couldn't!

But I couldn't lose JD, either.

I turned to the others. "I could hotwire it," I blurted.

They all turned to look at me.

"But I'd have to be there," I said. "I'd have to come with you."

17

DANNY

For a second, I just gaped at her. Then, "No. *No!* No, no fucking way!"

"It's our only chance," said Erin.

"Do you know how dangerous this is going to be? You're a civilian, you're not a—Jesus, you're not even a cop, you've never used a gun or —" I turned to the others for support. "She could get killed or captured or...Jesus, *we'll* be lucky to make it back alive, never mind —" I shook my head. "No. Just no. We'll leave the bracelet on him and take our chances."

"We take him out of his cell with that bracelet on, all the alarms go off and the place goes into lockdown," said Kian quietly. "There must be a hundred guards in that place, all with automatic weapons. There's no way we're getting out alive."

"*No!*" I snapped, and stormed out of the room.

I marched down the hallway and up the stairs to the roof. You can see right across Mount Mercy from there and it's the place we all go when we need to calm down. I stood there shaking with anger and fear, letting the snowflakes cool my cheeks.

Kian found me there a few moments later.

"She can't go," I said immediately. "Jesus, have you looked at her? She's just a little—she has no training—she's—" I turned to him. "*I promised him, Kian!* I promised JD I'd take care of her! That was the last thing I said to him!"

Kian nodded. "It's you who has to lead the mission. This should be your decision." He paused, letting me cool off. "But...honestly, if we don't get that bracelet off him...do you think we can get him out?"

I looked away and stared out at the lights of Mount Mercy. "No," I said at last. "No, I don't."

Kian patted me on the arm and went back downstairs, leaving me with my thoughts.

What the hell am I meant to do?! I'd promised JD I'd protect her. But now the only way to save him was to put her in danger.

Just the thought of something happening to her was enough to make that protective instinct surge in me, fierce and overwhelming. It wasn't just what I'd told JD. It was that need I'd felt ever since I first saw her outside the café. I *had* to keep her safe.

I couldn't let her come with us.

But if she didn't, JD was dead. My best friend, my *only* close friend. And that meant Erin would lose her brother. She'd never forgive me for stopping her from going. She'd blame herself for not persuading me, when really this was all *my* fault, for not spotting that security guard. And even if we could get JD out with the bracelet still on him, it would mean getting into a firefight. What if Colton died, or Gabriel, or Cal? How did I weigh their lives against hers?

Jesus, how does JD do this?! How was I meant to make a decision like this? I had no idea what to do. *I'm not meant to be a leader!*

I filled my lungs with freezing air and yelled into the night. And then, as I stood there panting, a kind of clarity came over me. There was only one option that had even a chance of letting everything work out okay.

I went back down the stairs and into the briefing room. Everyone looked up as I walked in, but I ignored them, focused only on Erin. "Do you really want to do this?" I asked.

She looked at the floor for a moment, debating. She looked so small, so vulnerable, that I almost changed my mind.

Then she looked up at me and nodded. Small, but brave beyond words.

"Okay then," I said, my voice rough with emotion. "Let's do this."

18

ERIN

THE NEXT MORNING, everyone was at The Factory soon after dawn. We had one day to give me a crash course in how to be a soldier...or, at least, how to not get everyone killed.

The men—including Kian—put on combat gear and loaded their guns, and we all trooped over to what they called The Killing House, a cavernous building that they'd filled with partition walls and pop-up targets. "We've got to move fast," Danny told me. "But quiet. We want to get in and out before they know we're there. If one guard raises the alarm, we'll have an army to fight."

We went inside and, immediately, I was out of my depth. It was as dark and disorienting as a haunted house and the team moved *fast,* flowing effortlessly along hallways and up stairs. For the first minute, I managed to keep up with them. Then they suddenly stopped and, in the dark, I wound up right behind the massive Colton. He backed up, tripped over me and we went down in a heap on the floor. Someone turned on a flashlight and I looked up into a circle of worried faces.

"Sorry," I said sheepishly.

Danny reached down, took my hand in his and hauled me to his feet. "It's alright," he said gently. "We'll just go again."

We went back to the entrance and crept into the building again. This time, I only made it thirty seconds before I turned the wrong way in the darkness and got separated from the team. I stepped out into a hallway and heard someone whirl around in the blackness next to me—

"*Jesus Christ!*" a strong Irish accent rang through the building. A flashlight went on again and I saw Bradan three feet away, his gun pointed right at me and his face pale with fear. "What are you *doing?*"

"I'm sorry!"

"I nearly shot you!" snapped Bradan.

I stared down the barrel of the gun, my stomach churning. "I know, I'm sorry!"

"Easy, mate," Danny said quietly.

Bradan sighed, nodded and gave me an apologetic look. I got it: I knew he was just shaky and scared from nearly shooting me. But it didn't make me feel any better.

We reset and went again. This time, I did fine...right up until I fumbled my roll of tools and screwdrivers went clattering across the metal floor, a noise that would have woken every guard in the prison. No one had to say anything: I turned and stalked out of The Killing House, tears rising in my chest.

I stopped outside, snowflakes melting on my burning cheeks. I heard running footsteps crunching through the snow and then a strong hand on my arm spun me around. I looked up into Danny's face. "Hey. *Hey!*" he said when he saw my expression. "You're doing fine."

"I'm *not!*" It wasn't just the humiliation of being clumsy dead weight. It was the *fear:* it was sinking in that this was real. The guards would have guns. One mistake like I'd just made and—"I'm going to get us all killed!"

He put his hands on my shoulders. "No you're not," he told me, and that London accent was rough steel. "You're just new to all this. You'll get it." He gazed down at me, and those absinthe eyes were steady and firm.

Against all the evidence, he really believed I could do this. I hiccoughed and managed to gulp the tears back down.

"We're going to go back in there and do it again," he told me. He took one of my hands in both of his...and for a second, he just stopped, staring at it, the warmth of his big hands throbbing into my small, cold one. Then he took a shaky breath, shook his head sternly and continued. "I want you to stay right behind me." He turned half-around and guided my hand to the middle of his back. "And keep your hand right there."

I nodded, not trusting my voice.

We went back to the others and started the exercise again. I kept my hand pressed against Danny's back and it was exactly what I needed: I could feel when he stopped or moved off, knew where I was meant to be and the feel of that warm solidness under my palm calmed my panic.

Slowly, I began to make progress.

We trained solidly all morning. After a few hours, my hamstrings and quads were screaming from going up and down stairs but I grimly kept at it.

At noon, Danny called a break and everyone trooped outside into the light, panting and cursing with relief. I leaned against the wall, sucking in big lungfuls of freezing air. I was perversely pleased when I glanced up and saw that one other person looked almost as exhausted as me: Kian was doubled over, scowling and panting, and when he sensed me looking at him, he shook his head grimly. "I've been behind a desk too long."

All of us were soaked in sweat. The men pulled off their heavy combat gear and let the cold air bathe their bodies. Danny stripped down to a t-shirt and it was hard not to stare: the tight cotton hugged the hard contours of his chest and his biceps and thickly-corded forearms gleamed. Then he turned to talk to Cal and—

The t-shirt was thin enough that I could make out the criss-crossing scars that covered his back. I felt my chest constrict again. *What happened to him?*

Danny turned around and I didn't look away quickly enough. He nodded in understanding and moved closer, so he could speak just to me. "I got captured," he said. "In Iraq. One of the blokes who was holding me went to work on me with a belt." His voice was warm, cocky, reassuring. *It's okay that you saw. It's no big deal.*

I nodded. But as he moved away, I watched him go, my eyes locked on his back.

I'm lousy with people. But I'd spent so much time with Danny, over the last few days, that I heard that rough London voice even in my dreams.

And I was pretty sure he was lying about his scars.

We trained relentlessly. I learned the hand signals that meant *stop* and *go* and *I see an enemy.* I copied how the team moved: that quick, half-crouching prowl, until I could do it almost as quietly as them. By mid-afternoon, the team trusted me enough not to walk in front of someone that they loaded up their guns and we ran live-fire exercises, to get me used to what it would be like if there was actually a firefight. It was nothing like how it was in the movies. The roar of gunfire was like someone hammering an iron bar into my eardrums. The muzzle flashes blinded me and the air filled with gun smoke that caught in my throat. It was scary and disorienting and this was with the team shooting at wooden targets that didn't fire back. I pressed my palm hard against Danny's back and squeezed my eyes shut. *How do they all stay so calm?*

Whenever we took a break, I pulled out my roll of tools and one of the ankle bracelets and practiced hot-wiring it with just a flashlight for light. I got it down to four minutes but would that be fast enough?

It would have to be. Danny checked his watch and called time. I wasn't ready. I wasn't *nearly* ready. But it was time to go.

19

ERIN

For the second time in a few days, the women had to say goodbye to their men.

Stacey was all tight efficiency, as before. "I made you something," she told Bradan, and pressed a small package into his hand.

"Do you have enough layers?" Olivia was asking Gabriel. "Face protection? It's thirty below there. You need to watch out for frostbite."

Gabriel pulled her close. "We'll only be outside for a few minutes." He buried his nose in her hair and inhaled, running his hands up and down her back as if memorizing the feel of her.

Rufus was making a low, keening whine. Cal squatted in front of him and ruffled his head. "I know, I know. I didn't think I'd be going away again so soon," Cal told him. "I'm sorry. But I gotta do this." He was speaking to Rufus but it felt like the words were meant for Bethany.

"Just hurry back," she whispered.

Danny had told me how Kian had snapped at Emily, but he must have apologized because the two of them stood with their foreheads touching, as securely together as two people can be. Kian leaned forward and kissed the top of Emily's head. "It's going to be okay," he told her, and she nodded. But then she pressed herself to him and clung on like a limpet.

And me? This time, I wasn't saying goodbye to anyone. This time, I was going. I swallowed and tried to fight down the rising panic. Danny caught my eye from across the room and gave me a nod: *you've got this.*

I gave him a weak smile but inside, my stomach was twisting. *No I don't.*

At the airport, we were just getting our bags out of the car when red and blue lights lit up the night. Secret Service agents in black suits poured out of a big black SUV, led by a guy with close-cropped, graying hair.

"*Miller?*" asked Kian in disbelief.

"Can't let you go," said Miller. "You're dating the President's daughter. If you got caught breaking into a German facility...."

Kian got in his face. "One of my guys is missing, *I'm bringing him back!*"

Miller sighed, pulled out a phone and dialed. Then he held it out to Kian.

Kian took the phone and listened. "Yes, Mr. President," he said at last. "I got it, Sir." He passed the phone back to Miller. "Either I stay here," he grated, "or we can't go at all."

Danny put his hand on Kian's shoulder. "We'll be okay," he told him, but he sounded shaken. We hadn't even left yet, and we were already a man down.

The day was a blur.

First, the fifteen hour flight to Latvia. Then the sick tension of standing at the Immigration desk while a Latvian official checked my fake passport.

Next, we went to a house in Riga owned by the CIA, where bundles of clothes and weapons were waiting for us. The clothes were military fatigues: white, to blend in with the snow. Mine were way too big for me. Gabriel, who'd arranged all the gear, winced. "Sorry. That was the smallest size they had."

"Gimme a minute," muttered Colton, and disappeared with my clothes. Fifteen minutes later, they fit.

Gabriel stared at the big, bearded brute. "You can *sew?*"

Colton shrugged. "Didn't have a whole lot of money growing up. Everything I had was hand-me-downs. Got pretty good at making stuff fit."

Then it was time to go to the airfield. As we climbed into the helicopter, Danny looked around at the peeling paint and oil stains. "Bloody hell, how old *is* this thing?"

"Old." said Gina from the cockpit, frowning at the Cyrillic labels on the controls. "What matters is, it's the same type they use to ferry staff to the prison so it won't arouse suspicion. Just don't expect it to be fast."

It was a long flight to Siberia. The helicopter was dark, noisy and very, very cold but despite that, most of the team dozed off. I realized that to them, this was all normal. As we neared the prison, people started to wake up and check their weapons. Bradan sat there sharpening a knife. That's when it started to feel real, and the panic came back. *What am I doing here?* This was all a mistake. *I'm not a soldier!* I didn't have a gun, or even a knife. I had a tool roll.

A warm hand covered mine. I looked up to see Danny leaning over to me from across the aisle. *You'll be fine*, he mouthed over the noise of the helicopter.

I nodded, but the panic didn't ease. In just a few minutes, people would be trying to kill us.

Danny leaned closer, until his mouth was only an inch from my ear and I could smell the amazing, sweet-but-sexy scent of him. When he spoke, each syllable was a hot little rush of air against my skin and that rough, London accent was unshakeable. "I know you're scared," he said. "But you just stick with me and you'll be okay. I won't let anything happen to you."

He drew back and gazed into my eyes, watching my reaction. His green eyes looked even brighter, against the all-white uniform. I swallowed and nodded, feeling better.

He was still holding my hand. The heat of him soaked into me, calming me. And as I calmed, I felt that connection again. That *pull.* He gripped my hand more firmly and his fingers stroked the back of my hand. I saw his eyes change, flaring and heating with need.

Then pain crossed his face and he squeezed my hand and released it, sitting back in his seat. He'd remembered that we couldn't, and why. *JD.*

"Showtime," yelled Gina.

We were there.

20

DANNY

THE HELICOPTER DESCENDED, there was a bump and we were down. Bradan slid open the door and the wind rushed in, plastering us with snow and making everyone curse and cry out in shock. We'd known it was going to be cold but none of us had realized what minus thirty would actually feel like. It was *unbelievably* cold: each time I inhaled, it felt like the inside of my throat was freezing over and, when we moved, any exposed skin burned and ached. We all pulled our hats down low over our ears, but that didn't protect our faces. Olivia had been right: we really could get frostbite. Thank God it was only a few minutes to the prison.

We climbed out and stood in a huddle, shivering, the wind whipping around us. Everyone looked at each other: we could all feel it, the hole where JD should be.

Then they all looked at me and my stomach dropped. *Oh yeah. I'm the leader now.* They wanted the little pep talk JD always gave before we went into action. They needed it now more than ever. But I wasn't JD. *What should I say?*

I closed my eyes for a second, took a deep breath and just said what I was feeling. "None of us expected this," I said. "We should be at home right now, sleeping off the homecoming party. Instead, we're freezing our arses off, about to try to break into a fortress. JD's not here. We all miss him. I know I do." I looked around at their despondent faces. "But you know what? We're going to pull this off. We're going to do it for JD. He brought all of us together and made us a team." I looked at Bradan and Gabriel. "He gave us second chances. He believed in us. So let's make him proud. Let's go get our boy back."

To my surprise, everyone nodded and straightened up. "Gabriel, you take the lead," I said. "Colton, you watch our backs."

"You got it, chief," said Colton. He always called JD *boss*. Maybe only JD could be *boss*.

We started crunching through the snow towards the prison. I glanced across at Erin and the panic suddenly hit me, full-on and brutal. *Oh God, what was I thinking, letting her come?* She was half the size of everyone else. She looked adorable, bravely marching through the snow with her glasses dusted with snowflakes. But this was no place for adorable. My chest was tight: I'd never felt this kind of fear before. I'd never had someone to feel it for.

We'd arrived on the same sort of helicopter the prison staff used and we were wearing the same military uniforms. We'd hoped that would let us get close before anyone suspected anything and, as we approached the huge, concrete entrance, it seemed like it was working. The guards even got the door open ready for us. I guessed they were worried about prison riots and breakouts: they never dreamed someone would try to break *in*.

Gabriel, ever the conman, raised his hands and greeted them warmly in German. He got within six feet of them before he pulled out his pistol and fired a tranquilizer dart into each of them. We grabbed them as they fell and pulled them into the guardhouse so they wouldn't freeze to death.

Inside, the prison was dark and quiet. Three more guards sat at a control desk, watching surveillance cameras. Cal, Gabriel and I shot one each and we dragged their sleeping bodies out of sight. So far, it had gone like clockwork. But now came the hard part.

Bradan uploaded the virus that would wipe the cameras after we'd gone. Gabriel searched the computer. "Got him," he whispered a moment later. "Cell 308." Then he cursed. "Right over on the far side."

He pointed the way and I stared at the darkened hallway. We'd have to creep right through the prison. If *one* guard saw us and raised the alarm...

I turned to Erin. "Stay behind me," I reminded her.

She nodded and I felt her hand press between my shoulder blades. It was comforting but also terrifying, a reminder of the fragile prize I was going to have to protect.

I told Bradan to lead the way: he could sneak like no one else. "Okay, this is it," I whispered. "Not a sound from now on." I took a deep breath. "Let's go."

21

ERIN

THE PRISON WAS DARK, damp and horribly cold, the bare concrete walls like ice. As we crept down the hallway, the howl of the wind outside fell away and the sounds of the prison surrounded us. We could hear the footsteps of patrolling guards, the mutterings of prisoners as they half-woke and fell back to sleep.

I could feel the hairs on the back of my neck rising, the tension almost unbearable. The place felt like a trap that could spring shut at any second. The prison had been dug into a cliff so there were no other exits, not even a window. If anything went wrong, the only way out was the entrance we'd come in by and we were getting further and further from that with each step. The warm pressure of Danny's back under my hand was the only thing that kept me going.

The team seemed different, now. Around the base, they'd been just a bunch of big, friendly guys, hugging their girlfriends and goofing off. But now they were soldiers, ultra-focused and alert, working together with smooth efficiency, and it was amazing to watch.

The hallway had doors on both sides and we had to stop before each one so that Bradan could peek through the window and check for guards. The rest of the team were quiet but he was like a ghost: I could see why Danny had put him up front.

We began to pass cells. Gabriel glanced at the metal bars and grimaced. I caught his eye and frowned, curious. *Bad memories,* he mouthed.

As we got deeper into the prison, we started to come across guards on patrol. Bradan would suddenly raise his fist in the air and we'd freeze, waiting for the guard to cross the junction. Sometimes, we'd have to wait for a minute or more, until the guard was out of earshot. Twice, we had to backtrack and take a different route because there was a guard in front of us. We couldn't just tranquilize them all: someone would notice they were missing. But I could see Danny checking his watch: we couldn't take too long, either, or the guards we had tranquilized would wake up.

We were passing a cell when I heard a rustle of fabric. I turned and—

A prisoner was sitting up in his bunk, staring right at me.

I stopped dead. Danny, feeling my hand lift from his back, stopped too, and then the rest of the team.

The prisoner and I stared at each other. It was hard to see his face, in the darkness, but he was small and looked young, only about the same age as me. In desperation, I put my finger to my lips, pleading with my eyes.

He stared at me silently for another few seconds...and then nodded. I guess he figured that whoever we were, we weren't on the side of the guards and that was good enough for him. We all let out a silent breath of relief and Danny nodded to me: *good job!*

We crept on. Bradan pointed to the junction up ahead. *Next one.* We were almost at JD's cell!

There were no guards nearby and some of the lights were broken here, leaving most of the hallway in deep shadow that would help to hide us. We picked up the pace a little, moving as fast as we could while staying quiet. We were only ten feet from the junction when there was a creak of metal from beside us. I felt Danny falter and try to stop but then something rammed into us, sending us stumbling.

We'd completely missed a door in the darkness. A guard had come out of it just as we were passing and had literally walked into us. For a second, he just gaped at me. Then he pulled out his gun and raised it to fire.

22

DANNY

TIME SEEMED TO SLOW DOWN.

When the guard had rammed into me, I'd gone staggering sideways. I was trying to regain my footing and at the same time turn around to get the tranquilizer pistol pointed at the guard, but it felt like I was wading through syrup. The guard was looking right at Erin and he was bringing his gun up to shoot.

I wasn't going to be able to get a shot off in time.

Erin locked eyes with me, her mouth open in a silent scream. I've never in my life felt more helpless. My chest contracted, waiting for the shot to ring out....

An arm like a tree trunk cinched tight around the guard's throat and he was lifted clean off his feet. He kicked and pawed wildly at the arm but it wasn't letting go. *Colton!*

The guard's movements slowed and he went limp. My heart started beating again. *Whew.*

Then the gun slipped from the guard's fingers. It fell towards the floor and Colton had his hands full. We all tensed for the crash of metal—

Cal dived and caught the gun just before it hit. Everyone slumped in relief.

As Colton hid the unconscious guard in the shadows, I went over to Erin. My legs were shaky and I felt like I'd aged ten years. I wished I could talk to her properly, but I had to somehow do it silently. *Are you okay?* I mouthed.

She just stared, panting with fear. I wanted to just scoop her up into my arms and carry her the hell out of there. But the best I could do was to put my hands on her shoulders and look into her eyes, letting her know I was there. *You're okay,* I mouthed. *You're okay.*

And gradually, I felt her breathing slow. She tentatively nodded. *I'm okay.*

I squeezed her shoulders, overcome with emotion. She was just a little thing but she was turning out to be braver than any of us could have imagined.

We moved on and when we reached the next junction, we could see JD's cell in front of us. But there was a problem. A guard was patrolling in a circuit around the block of cells. Bradan timed him twice around and then showed us his watch: we only had a three minute window when he couldn't see JD's cell. If we weren't out of there before he got back....

As soon as the guard had disappeared around the corner, we hurried over to the cell. Gabriel picked the lock in seconds and we slipped inside.

I slapped a hand over JD's mouth and he jerked awake, then relaxed when he saw who it was. I lifted my hand and motioned for him to stay still, then pointed to the ankle bracelet. JD nodded and lay back on his bunk.

Then Erin stepped out of the shadows and JD sat bolt upright. There was terror in his eyes, but as he looked at me it turned to anger. He'd trusted me to look after her. *Why?!* his eyes demanded.

I lifted my chin and stared right back at him, unrepentant. *Because I wasn't going to let you die.*

JD's glare faltered, faded...and he reluctantly lay back down.

Erin went to work. She had the bracelet's casing off in seconds. She teased out the bird's nest of wires and tiny circuit boards and I shone my flashlight at the shining tangle so she could see what she was doing.

Bradan showed me his watch. We had two minutes left. I nodded curtly, feeling icy sweat trickling down my spine. If they caught us, we'd go to jail for the rest of our lives. That thought was bad enough but the thought of Erin huddled in some cell was much, much worse.

She was deep into it, now, completely absorbed. I could see her face moving in the gloom and realized she was silently talking to herself.

Bradan showed me his watch again. One minute left. I scowled at him: *not helping!* I imagined the guard strolling along the cells. *Maybe he's getting tired. Maybe he'll walk a bit slower. C'mon, just a little bit? Please?* And then I didn't have to imagine because I could hear his footsteps. We had maybe ten seconds. Eight. Five.

The bracelet sprang open. The whole team moved like a well-oiled machine: Erin slipped the bracelet off JD's ankle, I grabbed Erin's tools, JD jumped up off the bed, Gabriel put JD's pillow on the bunk, and Bradan and Colton laid the blanket over the pillow. Soundlessly, the six of us crept out of the cell and round the corner into the next hallway, making it out of sight just in time. The guard glanced into the cell, saw the mound under the blanket and continued on his patrol.

Everyone slumped in relief. I wanted to hug Erin and tell her what a great job she'd done, but I had to settle for squeezing her hand in the darkness. "Let's get you the hell out of here," I whispered to JD.

It was easier, on the way out, because we were retracing our steps. I could see JD glancing at Erin: I could tell there was so much he wanted to say but he couldn't, yet.

When we reached the entrance, we stopped. Of the three guards we'd tranquilized, two were stirring. We'd taken too long: they were waking up! I looked helplessly at Colton. He looked at the tranquilizer pistol in his hand, rubbed at his beard, then shook his head. "We can't dose 'em again. It could kill 'em."

We couldn't risk that. We'd just have to get out fast and hope we were gone before they raised the alarm.

We hurried past the guards, hauled open the door....and stopped, our hands up in front of our eyes. For a second, I thought the prison had been surrounded by soldiers and they were shining searchlights in our faces. Then my eyes adjusted. Dawn had broken while we were inside and the sun was gleaming off an endless white landscape, overpoweringly bright.

We raced towards the helicopter. It was the first time we'd seen the landscape in the light and it was so huge, so barren, that it made my stomach twist uneasily. In every direction it was just snow-covered hills and frozen forest. There wasn't a road or even a power line anywhere.

Gina started the engines as soon as she saw us coming. We all started to pile aboard, while Cal hung back and watched the prison entrance through his rifle's scope.

JD grabbed Erin by the shoulders and turned her to face him. He stared down at her, and I could see anger and love battling for control. Then he sighed and hugged her. "Thank you," he said.

Erin squeezed him tight. I smiled, but I felt a sudden stab of jagged pain, too. Seeing her hugging JD brought it home: *I'll never hold her again. Never so much as touch her again.* "C'mon," I told them both. "Time for that once we're safe."

They jumped aboard and strapped in and I followed. Cal came last of all, leaving the sliding door open so he could keep watching the prison entrance.

"Gina, get us out—" JD broke off awkwardly, looking at me. He gave me a sheepish nod, acknowledging that I was the one in charge.

It meant a lot to me. But I shook my head and grinned at him. "You can have it, mate," I said with feeling. I'd had my fill of being the leader. "Welcome back." Then I grabbed hold of him and hugged him, touching my forehead to his.

JD crushed me against him, slapping my back. "Thank you," he whispered.

A big swell of emotion filled me, sending out fresh waves of guilt.

I loved this guy. How could I ever even contemplate risking this friendship?

"Get us out of here," JD called to Gina, and we lifted into the air. Colton glared disapprovingly at the still-open door and I saw his hands grip his harness a little tighter as the ground dropped away. The poor guy really didn't like heights.

I felt myself start to relax. A long, cold flight back to Latvia, an even longer flight back to the US and then things could start getting back to normal. Erin would go back to Vegas, I'd go on a bender of tequila and filthy sex for a week or so and—

"Someone's awake!" yelled Cal, his eye pressed to the scope of his rifle.

We all looked down at the prison through the open door, but all we could make out were a couple of black ants moving outside the entrance. Then an alarm started to blare, echoing off the snowy hillsides below.

"Hurry," I told Gina.

The chopper rose slowly. "One of the guard's just picked up a guided missile launcher," reported Cal.

Now we were *all* yelling at Gina. "Go! Go, go, go!" But the chopper lumbered forward with horrible slowness.

"Can you hit him from here?" JD asked Cal.

"Yeah," mumbled Cal. "But I can't be sure I'd only wound him."

"Don't risk it," JD said immediately. "If we kill someone, this whole thing goes south."

"*Missile in the air!*" yelled Cal.

We all reacted instinctively, grabbing hold of something. But both JD and I did something else: our heads snapped round to look at Erin. I quickly looked away before JD saw.

"Evade!" yelled JD.

"This thing's not exactly nimble," muttered Gina.

We could see the missile rising towards us, now, a serpent made of white smoke, stretching up from the ground to strike us. The chopper rolled on one side but it wasn't enough. There was an ear-splitting bang and a jolt as if a freight train had hit us. I could see flames from just outside the door and thick black smoke billowed into the cabin, choking us. "We lost an engine," yelled Gina. We started to drop sickeningly. An alarm blared in the cockpit and an automated Russian voice repeated the same phrase over and over. "Yeah, yeah," Gina snapped, "I *know* we're crashing!"

Then it got worse. The burning engine broke free and fell from the chopper, ripping fuel lines as it went. Burning jet fuel sprayed into the cabin, setting fire to the wall right above where Erin was sitting.

She screamed and tugged at her harness but the buckle was jammed. Burning drops of fuel were falling like rain onto her shoulders and chest, and she frantically swatted at them. Meanwhile, the fire was spreading downwards: it was almost at her hair. She was going to be burned alive and it was my fault, I got her into this.

JD started to unbuckle his harness to help her, but I was closer. I got mine open and took a step towards Erin but, at that moment, the chopper started to spin. I stumbled forward, fighting for balance. Through the open door, I could see the ground rushing past, worryingly close.

I reached Erin and pounded on her belt buckle until it popped open, then pulled her away from the flames.

We were even lower, now, barely clearing the tops of hills as we passed over them. I started to haul Erin back to my seat so I could strap her in. But the chopper tilted, our feet skittered sideways...

And we fell straight out of the open door.

23

ERIN

ONE SECOND, there was metal under my feet. The next, I was tumbling with just freezing air on all sides of me, flailing for something, *anything* to grab onto. Danny was next to me for a second but then he was gone and...

Oh God I'm falling. I could feel the air rushing past my face but all I could see below me was white: there were no features, nothing to gauge distance. *Oh Jesus—*

There was a thump that knocked the air out of me and then I was rolling, seeing sky and then snow, sky and then snow. Finally, I slowed and stopped.

I climbed to my feet, groggy and unstable. Everything was blurry but I could see a massive mound of white in front of me. A hill. I'd landed on top of a hill and rolled down it. I could hear the chopper high above and searched the sky for it. *There:* a black dot, trailing black smoke. Small and getting smaller. The noise receded and then there was nothing but the whisper of the wind. The realization hit me and I wanted to throw up: *I'm on my own!*

I looked around. *Why is everything so blurry?* I felt my eyes and gave a groan of horror. *My glasses!* I spun around and then looked back up the hill. They could have come off as I fell, or as I rolled: they could be anywhere, buried under the snow. I was alone and I was half blind.

Where's Danny? Hadn't he fallen from the chopper too? "Danny!" My voice was horribly small in the emptiness. I waited: nothing. "Danny! *Danny!*"

But there was no reply.

24

DANNY

I BLINKED. Focused. I was looking at glittering snow from an inch away.

My head throbbed and I rubbed at it. It definitely felt like I'd taken a knock, and maybe blacked out. I was bruised but nothing seemed to be broken. When I managed to roll over onto my back, I was looking up at walls of snow. Maybe eight feet above me, I could see the sky. I'd landed in a massive snowdrift.

I trampled down the snow until I had a slope I could climb up, then clambered out into the icy air and looked around. The chopper was nowhere in sight and I was at the base of a huge hill. *Erin! Where's Erin?!*

At that moment, I heard her yelling but it was muffled, distant. *Shit! She must be on the other side of the hill!* I ran, my boots sinking deep into the snow. She yelled again and again but I couldn't answer: I was too out of breath and I needed to home in on her voice before she stopped. I came around a corner and—

The instant I saw her, something huge and warm just *lifted* in my chest. She looked so tiny in the huge landscape, so vulnerable. I ran towards her and she jerked back, scared. *She's not wearing her glasses!*

She was squinting, mole-like and absurdly cute. "It's okay!" I told her. "It's me, it's Danny!"

She gave a strangled groan of relief and threw her arms around me. I hugged her back and all those feelings I'd been pushing back for days flooded through me. They broke against my resolve like a wave and it weakened and cracked.

"What are we going to do?" asked Erin in a tiny voice.

It was the first time I'd had a chance to think about it. I tried my radio but got nothing but static. Either JD and the others were out of range or....

"You think they crashed?" asked Erin. "Are they...?"

I shook my head firmly. "No. Not with Gina flying. Maybe it was a rough landing but she'll have got them down safe."

"So what do we do?"

I took a deep breath. "We go to the emergency rendezvous point," I told her with a confidence I didn't feel.

Erin looked around, utterly lost. I tried to imagine how frightening it was for her, not being able to see. "Wait there," I told her, and started slowly climbing the hill, following the trail of broken snow where she'd rolled down. I was nearly at the top when I saw something reflecting the light.

Back at the bottom, I shook the snow from her glasses and pressed them into her hands. She moaned in relief as she slid them onto her face. "Thank you!"

We both looked around and, as I gazed out at the featureless, frozen terrain, my stomach knotted. I'd done survival training but that just meant I knew how hard it would be to last more than a few hours out here. It was brutally cold during the day and at night we'd die if we hadn't found shelter. There were virtually no plants we could eat or animals we could hunt, no food of any kind. I looked towards the prison. The soldiers knew we were here and they'd be coming after us. It was just about the worst situation possible, far worse than anything in my training. And in training, I wasn't doing it with a civilian in tow. A civilian I was crazy about.

"Are we going to be okay?" asked Erin.

"'Course," I told her. "But we should get moving."

And we set off across the snow.

25

BECKER

WE ARRIVED to interrogate the American, only to find the prison in uproar. I marched inside with my men, pushed my way through the chaos and found Werner, the prison warden, in his office with his second-in-command and five guards. We'd served together, back in our Special Forces days. But while I'd kept myself in shape, Werner had let himself run to fat.

He rushed out from behind his desk when he saw me, wringing his hands. "They got him, Otto. The American you were keeping here, they took him." I could see the sweat glistening on his forehead. *Disgusting.* "The government already knows something happened: when the alarm went off, that sent them an alert. And the inspectors will be arriving in an hour. We have to come clean, Otto. Tell them everything."

I looked around. "These are the guards who saw the intruders?"

Werner nodded. "We don't know much. They were in military gear, well trained. They used tranquilizer darts and choked another guard unconscious. No one's hurt, thank God. We hit their helicopter and we think it crashed a few miles away."

I nodded absently, thinking. It was safe to assume these were the same Americans I'd run into in Berlin, trying to rescue their friend.

This might actually be a blessing in disguise. Maybe I could still salvage the plan, if I kept the situation under control. "This is *everyone* who saw what happened?" I asked.

Werner nodded. "Yes, everyone."

I drew my gun and shot him in the head. Turning, I killed the five guards with five quick, clean shots. They were poorly trained: even the last one had barely begun to reach for his weapon. *Sloppy.*

I turned to Werner's second-in-command. "When the authorities arrive, you will tell them how the Americans broke in here and killed these men."

The man stared at me, panting in shock and anger. Then he looked down at my gun. It wasn't pointed at him, exactly, but it wasn't pointing away from him, either. A warning.

"Yes," he croaked at last. "What about the American we were holding here?"

"We weren't holding any American here. They attacked the prison for reasons unknown and killed these men. Tell the government that I'm taking my team in pursuit."

26

ERIN

THE PRISON LAY at one end of a shallow valley so the first thing we had to do was climb out of it. The slopes wouldn't have been a problem if we'd been walking on grass, but the snow was deep enough that it felt like wading and the ground underneath was smooth rock that was as slippery as ice. As it got steeper, Danny turned around and took my hand, acting as my anchor when I began to slide back and giving me an extra boost when I needed it. We marched in silence, too out of breath to talk, but every now and again he'd squeeze my hand: *you okay?* And I'd squeeze back, *I'm okay.*

Then we reached the rim of the valley and in front of us....

It was like nothing I'd ever seen, nothing I'd even known existed. From horizon to horizon, there was just a sea of rolling white hills, some bare and some covered in thick, snow-covered forest. Ahead of us, the land rose sharply to form a towering peak, the top covered in clouds.

Just looking at the landscape made my stomach sink to my feet and I couldn't figure out why, at first. Then I realized it was because of what I *couldn't* see. There wasn't a building in sight. There wasn't a road or a power line, there were no planes in the sky...there was no trace of mankind. At night, there wouldn't even be any lights. I looked down at the ground: the snow was completely unbroken in front of us. We were probably the first people to walk this way in weeks, maybe months. *If we die out here, they might never find the bodies.*

The panic rose in me, filling me until I could barely breathe. I'd never felt so alone. So tiny. I spun to face Danny—

He put his hands on my shoulders. "Stop. Just breathe. *Breathe.*"

I stared up into those deep green, glittering eyes. I *wasn't* alone. My breathing eased a little.

"Now listen. Here's what's going to happen. You and me, we're gonna hike over there," he pointed off beyond the peak, "about fourteen miles. We're gonna meet up with JD and the others. And we're gonna get ourselves to the border, back into Latvia and back home to Mount Mercy. Okay?"

He sounded so confident. So completely certain. The landscape was huge but Danny, somehow, was bigger. I nodded.

But then I looked again at what we had to cross. *Fourteen miles.* No way we could cover that in a day, not in this terrain. And we had no supplies. We didn't even have a tent. We'd have to climb the peak and the higher we got, the colder it would get. I felt the panic rise again—

Then Danny's hand was on my cheek, turning me to look at him. He'd slipped off his glove and his palm was gloriously warm against my skin. "You and me, together. We're going to pull this off." His voice was unshakeable. He believed it.

And that meant I believed it, too. I swallowed...and nodded.

Danny gave me one of those huge grins, the ones that made my brain light up like a pinball table. He looked so proud that I just melted. And then, underneath the pride, I saw something else. That fierce, burning need. His hand tensed on my cheek just a little. I saw his eyes flick down to my lips...

Then he took hold of my hand instead and squeezed. When he spoke, I could hear the strain in his voice. He was keeping that need restrained...just barely. "C'mon," he said. "Let's go."

And we set off into the wilderness.

27

DANNY

As we climbed the foothills of the mountain, it got colder and colder. It began to snow, just a few flakes at first and then heavier and heavier, deadening all sound and wrapping us in a silent white world.

I shouldn't be here, I grumbled to myself. *I don't know anything about the wilderness, I'm from bloody London.* If Cal was there, he'd carve a cabin out of a tree and whip up a banquet out of a squirrel and a pine cone.

But there was someone who belonged here even less than me. I looked across at Erin. If something happened to her....

That protective urge again, stronger than ever. And right on its heels, all the other feelings. That *pull* towards her, an ache that throbbed through me: the closer I got to her, the stronger it was. Being on the mission with her had been hard enough. Now the snow was falling in silent white curtains all around us, creating a tiny, isolated space where only the two of us existed.

Why does it have to be her? Why does the one woman I feel like this about have to be JD's little sister?

Every time I glanced at her, my eyes locked on her lips and wouldn't let go. Even when I forced myself to keep my eyes forward, I could smell that peaches and Christmas scent of her, hear her soft breathing....

There was no one else for miles. If something happened out here, no one would know.

I pushed that thought away. They call it being crazy about someone and it was true, she was making me crazy. If something happened, *I'd* know. And inevitably, JD would find out and that would be the end of our friendship.

We marched on but the mountain didn't seem to be getting any closer. We started to talk and, just like at the garage, she was easy to talk to. It wasn't like when I was flirting, where each line was like a move in an elaborate dance. It felt natural. *Real.*

We talked about cars and the garage and engineering. I told her how I'd always wanted to drive a Nissan GTR and she told me about always wanting to fix up an old pinball table. We talked about life in Mount Mercy and somehow, we got onto Krüger's Tavern and what I did there in the evenings. "Is it always just one night with them?" she asked. Her cheeks colored in a way that was utterly adorable and the words rushed out. "Just...roll around in bed for a few hours and go?"

She held my gaze for a split second and then quickly looked away.

I stumbled a little and tried to pretend I'd slipped in the snow. *Oh God.* I'd gone rock hard in my pants. Her shyness was the sweetest thing in the world but then there'd been that little look, that reminder that under all the awkwardness, she had needs of her own. She just needed someone to coax her out of her shell and set her free. My mind started to fill with thoughts of how that tight, heart-shaped ass would feel as I squeezed it, of the noises she'd make as I took one of those pert little breasts in my mouth and tongued the hell out of it.

I realized I hadn't answered her question, yet. I nodded and focused on the mountain ahead, not trusting myself to look at her.

"Why?" she asked, her voice tender.

I thought about it. The answer was simple: I couldn't have anything longer than a quick fling because I wasn't capable of it. That part of me was broken. I couldn't make those deep connections.

Except...I glanced across at her and there it was, surging up inside me.

I turned away. "Just wired that way, I s'pose. What about you?" I tensed, wincing. The last three words had just slipped out. I'd been trying to turn the spotlight off me but I suddenly realized I didn't *want* to know about all her past boyfriends. The thought of her with someone else made me crazy. *You idiot, she's not yours!* I braced myself...

But it was so much worse than I expected.

"Me?" She gave a little laugh and it was the single most painful sound I'd ever heard: cold and jagged, like it was made from frozen tears.

I spun to face her, shocked.

She lowered her head and, if we'd been back in Colorado, I think she'd have left it there. But then she glanced around at the silent emptiness: we were the only two people for miles. I knew how she felt: the quiet pulled secrets out of you. "Who'd want *me*, even for one night?" she asked tightly.

She stared at me, challenging me to say something, but I just gaped. This was *me*, I'm never lost for words with women. But I couldn't process what she was saying. *That's really how she thinks of herself?* And when I didn't answer, she lowered her head again and marched on.

My arm shot out and blocked her path, my hand closing on her shoulder. I couldn't find the words but I wasn't going to let her walk on with *that* toxic crap in her head. She glanced up at me, her eyes liquid.

I looked her right in the eye. "Anyone."

She swallowed hard. "But I don't have big boobs and I'm not confident and I like *books,* not partying...what is there to like about me?"

My hand tightened on her shoulder. *"Everything."*

She stared stubbornly up at me, denying it. But I just gazed down at her, burning straight through, and saw her weaken and then melt.

And as the anger and hurt collapsed, I saw her eyes light up with hope.

Now *I* swallowed. My hand was still on her shoulder. All I had to do was tug her forward for my kiss. And oh God, I wanted to. More than I'd ever wanted anything in my life. My fingers tightened...

But then I thought of the anger in JD's voice, back in the kitchen. He hadn't been kidding. If anything happened with Erin, I'd lose him forever.

"Now you listen to me," I told her. "You. Are. Amazing. And you're going to be someone's whole world. Their everything. They're going to love you without question and fuck you without mercy."

I stared down into those delicate blue eyes until I was sure she knew that I wished it could be me. She flushed and nodded...and we walked on.

As we continued to climb, the wind picked up, whipping around the side of the peak. We were up above the tree line, now, with nothing to shelter us. The noise rose from a low howl to a piercing shriek that drilled into brains and made it impossible to talk. We hunched our shoulders and pulled our heads in like turtles, sheltering our mouths behind our jacket collars and only exposing them to snatch a breath.

We marched on for hour after hour. The silence should have made it easier but it just made everything I'd said go round and round in my head. With each step I took through the snow, the *pull* towards her got stronger. She was the one woman I could maybe have something real with and she was the one woman I could never have. I wanted to scream in fury.

Just get through this. Get her back to JD like a good friend.

The temperature dropped fast. I could see Erin shivering and I pressed tight against her to try to keep her warm, my arm around her waist and my hip rubbing hers. The *pull* became unbearable. She was all wrapped up in military clothes and a beanie hat but, to me, she was the sexiest woman alive. I had to keep my eyes on the mountain because if I so much as glanced at her, I was just going to grab her and kiss her.

The snow was blown sideways by the wind and plastered us, making our limbs heavy. Visibility shrank and shrank until we couldn't see anything beyond ten feet. The snowdrifts got deeper and deeper: I was soon up to my knees and Erin was up to her thighs. We trudged on, forcing our way through, bent over against the wind. I could feel my face going numb and that triggered a memory. I spun Erin to face me and put my face close to hers.

Shit. Her nose and ears were already turning red. "We've got to wrap ourselves up," I yelled over the wind. "Or we're going to get frostbite."

I dug around in my pack looking for something to use and finally thought of the bandages in the first aid kit. I wrapped them around Erin's head, protecting her ears and nose, going down to where the high collar of her jacket protected her mouth. She looked like a mummy, just her eyes showing....

I stopped.

Her eyes were so bloody beautiful. That gorgeous shade of pale blue, so vulnerable that I just wanted to hug her and yet so brave that it left me awestruck. There was concern there, too, concern for *me,* even though it was meant to be me looking after her. And that aching need, nervous and twitchy but overwhelming....

I was crouching in front of her, my hand on her shoulder. I slid it up over her bandaged cheek and stared at her, rubbing my thumb across her cheekbone. The cold had weakened me. I felt my willpower crumbling.

She tilted her head back, moving her mouth out from behind the shelter of the jacket's collar and took a shaky breath. I looked at her lips.

I couldn't stop looking at her lips.

And then I was leaning forward to kiss her.

28

ERIN

HIS HEAD DIPPED. I drew in my breath, my lips parted....

At the last moment, he closed his eyes and frowned. He stayed there, eyes closed and brow furrowed, for three beats of my racing heart. *JD.* He was thinking of JD.

Danny straightened up and, as he rose away from me, it was like a physical pain. He started wrapping his own face with bandages, his movements stiff and robotic.

I could see how hard this was for him. And if he was struggling with it this much...that meant he really did feel something for me. *Why did it have to be him? Why couldn't JD's best friend have been Colton or Cal or Gabriel?*

We marched on. The wind was so strong, now, that Danny had to walk in front of me, shielding me from the worst of it. We battled on in silence: even if he'd wanted to talk, there was no chance of us hearing each other over the wind. I was staggering through snow that was almost hip-deep now, and even in thick boots and two pairs of socks, my feet started to go numb. Soon, I couldn't feel them at all.

My legs began to feel heavier and heavier. I looked up and realized that I'd started to fall behind. I lengthened my stride, even though it made my thighs ache—

And then I put my numb foot down on a slippery rock, skidded and went flat on my face.

I lay there for a second, stunned, then looked up to see Danny disappearing into the blizzard. I tried to yell for him but the air had been knocked out of me and I couldn't do more than wheeze.

I struggled to my feet. By now, Danny was completely gone from sight. I could see maybe six feet in any direction and everything looked the same. I took two steps forward and then hesitated. *Is this the right way?* I thought it was, but I'd twisted around as I got up and I couldn't be sure.

Footprints. I can tell by our footprints. But when I looked down, the ground was a chaotic mess where I'd fallen and further out, our footprints had already been covered by the snow.

I finally got enough air into my lungs to yell. *"Danny!"* But the wind seemed to snatch my voice away. I wasn't sure he'd be able to hear me.

I was on my own.

29

DANNY

I MARCHED ON, brooding. I was glad of the deafening wind, it meant I had an excuse not to talk. I didn't even look back: looking at her was too difficult. I'd so nearly kissed her.

What the hell am I going to do?

Nothing. That's what I was going to do. I was going to keep on bloody marching until I reached JD and the others. Once he was with us, nothing could happen. I just had to hold out until then. A day or so. I could do that, right?

I wasn't sure. *God, what's wrong with me?* I was guiltily aware that some women had fallen for *me,* however much I'd tried to stop that happening, but I'd never come close to falling for someone. Not until Erin.

My steps were getting slower. I was getting tired, which meant that poor Erin, with her shorter legs, was probably exhausted. I glanced over my shoulder. *Maybe we should—*

She wasn't there.

I froze, staring into the blank whiteness. *No. No, it's okay. She just fell behind a little.* Any second, she'd step out of the snow and everything would be fine.

But she didn't.

Oh God. I'd never felt fear like it. *I've lost her!*

I'd been pushing my feelings down deep, trying to keep up that tough, cocky, exterior. Now it was like I'd been split open with an ax. "Erin!" I shouted, terrified. "*Erin!*"

I listened. Was that a voice? I stripped the bandages from my ears because *fuck frostbite*, I had to find her. But between the howling wind and the echoes from the hills around us, I couldn't be sure I was hearing anything, and there was no hope of figuring out a direction. I tried to retrace my steps but my footprints were gone. *I'll never find her!*

This was all my fault. How long had I marched on, not talking to her or even looking at her, because I was trying to hide how I felt? I thought of her lost and alone, gradually succumbing to cold and exhaustion. She'd collapse and the falling snow would cover her in minutes as her heart slowed and finally stopped.

No! I staggered through the snow, frantic. "Erin! *ERIN!*" But there was nothing, just the howling blizzard in every direction. My heart was hammering, my breath coming in big, panicked gulps. "*ERIN!*"

Then something swept across my vision, a green glow. It took me a moment to figure out what I was looking at: her laser pointer. It didn't look much like a beam of light, in the blizzard: the snow made it fade and spread until it was a thick wedge. But I could see where it was coming from and that was all that mattered. I started forward—

The light disappeared and I stumbled to a stop. I realized she must be rotating on the spot like a lighthouse. I could only see it when she was facing me. It came round again and I ran, not stopping, this time, sprinting headlong into the snow—

And suddenly, there she was in front of me, huddled and shivering. I lifted her clear off the ground and hugged her to my chest, arms locked around her like I was never going to let her go.

30

ERIN

His voice was rough and shaky with adrenaline. "From now on," he rasped, "you stay right beside me. *Right beside me!*"

The relief of being back with him and the fiercely protective growl in his voice made me go weak. I nodded against his chest and it was a long time before he grudgingly put me down.

We pressed on through the rest of the day, this time staying side by side. The ground leveled out and then began to slope down and I realized we'd done it: we were over the highest part of the peak.

As we started to descend, the snow stopped and we could see properly again. A few hours later, we made it to the tree line. But the forest wasn't like any forest I'd ever seen. The trees were bare trunks, like something evil had stripped them of everything. Normally, when you walk through a forest, you can sense it growing. It's in the smell of sap in the air, the creak of branches, the sound of twigs falling to the ground as trees shed the old parts and grow new ones. The trees are *breathing,* just in slow motion compared to us. But here, it was so cold and the days were so short, nothing was growing. The forest was frozen in time and everything felt brittle and fragile.

And we had a new problem: it was getting dark and, now that the snow clouds had moved off, it was a clear night. The temperature was dropping moment by moment. It was so cold, my head began to ache. "We've got to make some shelter," said Danny. "Or we're going to freeze to death."

We found a clearing and Danny dug out a tarpaulin and some rope from the bottom of his backpack. He tied the tarp between two trees so that it hung down in an arc, making a wall and a floor. It wasn't much but it would keep the wind off us.

We needed a fire but there were only a few twigs lying on the ground. We'd have to cut down a tree but we didn't have a chainsaw or even an axe. Danny opened up his survival tin, a tiny thing no bigger than a box of breath mints, and showed me a thin, curled-up ribbon of metal with jagged teeth. "That's all we've got," he told me.

We unrolled it, poked sticks through the holes at each end to use as handles and faced each other, like old style lumberjacks. Then we laid the saw against the trunk of a tree and started to scrape it back and forth. It was ridiculously hard going: the stick-handles kept breaking and every time the saw got stuck in the tree, we had to painstakingly work it free: if the saw snapped, we were dead. After sawing for ten minutes, we'd barely made it through the bark.

But gradually, we got into a rhythm and began to see progress. We sawed until our shoulders and backs burned and our arms were limp noodles and finally the tree crashed to the ground. We looked at each other with a weak smile of victory, too tired to even high-five.

We gave ourselves a five minute rest and then started sawing the tree into logs. By the time we'd finished, the sky was pitch black and the stars were diamond-bright above us. It was *breathtakingly* cold.

We needed kindling but everything in the forest was damp from the snow. Danny thought for a while and then pulled a thick, blocky *something* from his backpack. I squinted in the moonlight and then blinked in amazement when I saw the dragon on the front. "You bought it?!"

Despite everything, he cracked a grin. "I said I would."

I just stared at him in wonder, warmth expanding in my chest and stealing my words.

He tore off the cover and crumpled it into a ball. "Don't worry," he told me seriously. "I'm about two hundred pages in."

I helped him build the fire. "So Vessia's met Thassius?"

"Oh, I'm well past that. She's already tricked the prince into bringing his army across the river. I'm at the bit where Thassius—"

"*Teaches her how to go invisible!*" we said together. I was beyond amazed. He hadn't just bought it and read it, he was enjoying it. We got the fire going and started to build it up while we talked about the book. The cold, the night, the soldiers looking for us...all of it receded, for a while. I read a lot, but it had been a long time since I'd been able to *share* a book. "Wait till you meet Vessia's sister," I told him.

"When does that happen?"

"Not until book seven."

"Book *seven?*" He weighed the book in his hand. "How many of these *are* there?"

"Twenty-three, but she's still writing."

Danny rubbed at his chin, his stubble rasping. "I've got a lot of reading to do," he mumbled thoughtfully.

We got the fire roaring and, huddled next to it, we gradually began to thaw out. Danny dug a ration pack out of his backpack. "I've only got one," he said sadly. "I only brought *that* from force of habit. We were only meant to be out of the chopper for half an hour. But it's something."

There was a sachet of beef stew and a sachet with some sort of peach cobbler. We heated them over the fire and shared them, and I felt the hot food start to warm me from the inside out. I was ravenous: the last time I'd eaten had been on the flight, over twenty-four hours before.

When we were done, we lay down on the tarp. The fire bathed my front in heat. Then Danny spooned me from behind, using his body heat to keep my back warm.

Immediately, the tension started building. As I lay there staring into the fire. I could feel his eyes on the soft skin at the back of my neck, feel his breath stirring the tiny hairs there. *What if I just turned over, right now, and faced him? What would happen?* My chest was tight with anticipation. *Do it, do it, do it!*

But I couldn't. JD would never forgive him. Both of them would lose their best friend and I couldn't do that to them.

I didn't think I'd be able to sleep: not out in the open, not with soldiers searching for us. Then Danny wrapped his arms around me and it was like everything bad in the world was being shut out. I was thousands of miles from my burrow in Vegas, but it was the safest I'd ever felt. I relaxed, the exhaustion rolled over me in a wave, and I slept.

31

BECKER

WE'D BEEN SEARCHING all day, scouring the hills for any sign of them. It was bitterly cold but my men knew better than to complain.

Me? I welcomed the cold. It reminded me of swimming with my father. He'd take me down to the river each morning, even when it was so late in the year that the sky was still black and there was snow on the rocks. The cold stripped away your weaknesses and you came out pared down and iron hard.

One of the two-man search teams radioed in. "We've found tracks coming down from the peak and into the forest. Two men, one smaller than the other. We can go after them at first light."

"We can go after them *now*," I hissed. I ordered my men to gather at that location. If the Americans stopped to rest for the night, we could be on them by morning.

32

DANNY

I'D BEEN DREAMING about her again. We'd been somewhere hot, Italy, maybe, with the sun streaming through gauzy curtains that flapped in the breeze. Erin was in a sundress made of thin, cream cotton and the sun was shining right through that, too, silhouetting the jutting softness of her breasts and the slender grace of her legs. I grabbed her and pulled her back against me, kissing her neck as my cock hardened against her ass.

Dawn light, bright through my eyelids, brought me grudgingly back to consciousness. I grumbled, woke, and—

The dream was real!

I was pressed against Erin's back, my arms around her. My lips were brushing the back of her neck and I could feel that golden braid lying across my cheek. My half-awake brain struggled to make sense of it. Were we in Italy after all? Had we just had sex?

Then a gust of freezing air blew against my face and it all came back to me: we were in Siberia, separated from the others, on the run...and the woman I was crazy about was off limits. It felt like Colton had just sucker-punched me in the chest.

And now I had a new problem. *I* knew I couldn't have her, but my cock didn't. It was still rock hard against Erin's perfect, heart-shaped ass. And it wouldn't listen to my grumpy orders to stand down.

Erin stirred in her sleep: the dawn was close to waking her, too. Her ass stroked against my cock and that made things even worse. Any second, she was going to wake up and feel what was pressed against her.

I opened my eyes. The fire had burned down to embers but it was still putting out enough warmth to make things comfortable. With tiny movements, I eased myself away from Erin but, just as I managed it, I looked down at her sleeping face. And suddenly, all the feelings rose up inside me, overwhelming.

She had her glasses gripped protectively in one hand. She wore them so much that she looked naked without them...naked and just a little less innocent, the balance tipped from *adorable* to *hot as fuck*. She was frowning slightly, as if she was working on a difficult problem, her lower lip pouting. I lay there propped up on one arm, staring down at that lower lip, at the way it trembled when she exhaled. I could imagine how silkily soft it would feel against mine, how her lips would part as I kissed her....

She opened her eyes and I quickly pulled away, turning so she couldn't see the bulge in my pants. "'Morning," I said with forced lightness.

She gave a soft little yawn, like something a dormouse would make, and my chest lifted and swelled. I had to clamp down on the feeling, hard. *Fuck.* I'd never in my life found someone so cute and lusted after them so hard, at the same time. "There was coffee in the ration pack," I told her. "Do you want it before we go?"

She sat up and rubbed her face. "Let's save it. It can be a mid-morning reward."

I nodded, kicked snow over the fire and then stopped, looking through the trees ahead of us. The sun was just creeping over the horizon, bathing the forest in rich orange light. Above that, the orange faded to a warm yellow and then it blended into a cool blue. There was no sound at all, not even birdsong, like the whole world was holding its breath to watch the sunrise. It was one of the most beautiful things I'd ever seen.

I felt Erin's fingers slip into mine and, without words, we squeezed hands. We stood there just watching for a few moments before we started to walk.

We'd been crunching through the snow for maybe a mile when I grabbed Erin's arm. I'd seen a tree ahead of us twitch. I dropped to a crouch and readied my rifle. Had they found us and circled ahead of us?

The tree twitched again. Then a wolf pushed its way out from under the branches and straightened up, looking right at us, its thick brown and white coat dusted with snow.

Shit. "Don't panic," I told Erin. "They're only dangerous in packs."

Erin seemed to hear something and glanced behind us. Then she silently plucked at my sleeve. I looked back to see two more wolves there. Then another one, in the trees off to our left. They started to slink closer and now I could see how thin they were. We were in the depths of winter, when pickings were thin: they probably hadn't eaten in weeks. And now they'd found us.

I brought my rifle up and went to take the safety off. *"Fuck."*

"What?" asked Erin.

"The rifle must have been too far from the fire, last night," I told her. "It's frozen solid."

33

ERIN

THE WOLF ahead of us started forward. It was bigger than the rest, and bolder. Danny pointed the useless rifle at it and the wolf froze. "Yeah, you know what a gun is, don't you?" said Danny. "Smart boy. Just stay there."

From behind us, the soft crunch of paws on snow. Danny spun around to point the rifle at the two wolves who were creeping forward. But now the one to our side was closing in, and the one in front had started moving again. By switching rapidly between them, Danny managed to keep them at bay. But how long would they stay scared of the rifle, if he couldn't actually fire?

Even as I thought it, the wolves started to edge forward. "We're going to have to push through," Danny said. "Stay right beside me."

I pressed tight to his side. He began to walk straight towards the big wolf in front of us, forcing it to make a choice: stand its ground or let us through. As we got closer, it began to growl. It wanted *us* to stop, so we'd stay inside the closing circle. My legs were going shaky with fear: it could cover the distance between us in a few seconds and it was easily big enough to take us down if it pounced.

Danny squared his shoulders and lifted his chin. "Get out," he snapped at the wolf. "Away!"

The wolf stayed where it was. The growl deepened. We were close enough that I could see the saliva dripping from its jaws. I imagined them closing on my throat.

"*Move!*" snapped Danny, still edging forward. The wolf bared its teeth and my stomach lurched. I could hear the other wolves following behind us, waiting to see what happened.

Danny pointed the frozen rifle right between the wolf's eyes. And with every bit of that cocky, swaggering confidence, he told it, "I will end you, you bastard, if you don't get out of my way."

The wolf growled, glared...and backed away.

We slid past it, turning and walking backwards so that Danny could keep the rifle trained on it. I could see now how close the other wolves had been behind us, just feet away. They joined their leader and stayed there, watching us, as we retreated.

We walked a half mile like that, watching the trees for any sign they were following. When we reached a clearing and everything was still quiet, we finally allowed ourselves to relax. I let out a long groan and leaned against a tree. I was soaked with sweat. Danny's shoulders slumped in relief and he chuckled. "When we get back, I've got to tell Cal that—"

A shot rang out and Danny fell to the ground.

34

DANNY

WHITE-HOT PAIN EXPLODED in my thigh and my leg crumpled under me. I crashed to the snow, grabbing at my thigh, and saw the white fabric turning red under my fingers.

Through the trees, I could see figures moving in the distance. Soldiers, and their uniforms didn't match the guards at the prison. Then I glimpsed the silver beard on one of them. *Becker.* He was here with his special ops guys and that was very, very bad news.

I scrambled to my feet but, as soon as I put any weight on my leg, the pain exploded and I nearly fell again. I couldn't even hobble until I got the pain under control. "Go!" I yelled to Erin. "Run!"

But instead, she ran over to me. She hooked my arm around her neck and then got her shoulder under mine and tried to lever me up to standing.

"No!" I snapped. Another shot rang out and I heard the bullet hiss past us. "Leave me!"

"Don't be an idiot," she told me, and grunted as she pushed me up to standing. I was comically lop-sided because she was a foot shorter than me, but I was up. With her supporting me, I managed to limp to the edge of the clearing and into the trees. I didn't have time to figure out which direction we were going, I was just trying to put distance between us and them. But after only a few minutes of stumbling along, I checked over my shoulder and shook my head. "Stop," I panted. "Stop."

She stopped and I pointed behind us. We were leaving a trail of bright red splotches in the pure white snow. "We've got to bandage it, or we'll never throw them off."

She lay me down in the snow and pulled out the first aid kit. Wincing, I managed to shove my pants down to my knees. The wound didn't look bad: the bullet had just clipped me, leaving a shallow slash. While Erin wrapped bandages around it, I pulled out one of the prefilled morphine syringes and plunged it into my leg. By the time I'd got my pants back up, the pain was dropping away: it still hurt, but it felt like it was happening to someone else. *Good.* I struggled to my feet and almost fell over because my head was so floaty. *Not so good.*

We could move faster now. But the soldiers had closed the gap and they were gaining on us. The fear grew in my chest. If we'd been caught by the prison guards, Erin might have spent the rest of her life in a cell. But Becker had been planning to execute JD to cover up whatever scheme we'd stumbled onto.. He'd do the same to us, if they caught up.

I forced myself to limp faster. We broke through the trees and—
Oh *shit.*

Ahead of us, the ground fell away in a sheer cliff. A hundred feet below, a river crashed and foamed along the bottom of the rock face. I looked left, right...but the cliff continued. We were trapped.

Shouts from behind us, getting closer. "What do we do?" asked Erin in a strangled voice.

I walked to the very edge of the cliff and looked down. "There's only one thing we can do," I told her.

35

BECKER

I was the first to reach the cliff edge, bursting out of the trees with my gun leveled. But they were nowhere in sight.

As my men arrived behind me, I motioned for them to fan out and search, just in case they'd hidden behind a tree or a rock. But they returned shaking their heads: *nothing.*

I stalked towards the edge and glanced down at the river. *Idiots.* The fall had probably killed them and the shock of the freezing water certainly would. I kicked a rock over the edge and watched it arc down towards the water, then sighed. It rankled, not catching my prey after hours of chasing, but dead was dead and I was a practical man. There were still four more to find. "Get the prison on the radio," I ordered. "Find out if they've found the helicopter yet."

36

DANNY

Don't think about it.

I had my eyes screwed shut and I was trying to breathe slow and steady. To concentrate on the feel of Erin's body against me. To not think about the—

Don't. Don't think about it, Danny.

—the *drop.*

I opened my eyes.

We were on a ledge, about three feet below the edge of the cliff. It was partially hidden from the top because the cliff had a bit of an overhang. To see it, you had to walk right to the very edge, like I'd done. And fortunately, Becker hadn't gone close enough. Now all we had to do was wait until he left.

Except...the ledge was too small.

The problem wasn't the length. It was only five feet long, which meant my ankles and feet were hanging over the end, but I could live with that. No, the problem was the *width.*

It was only a foot wide. Erin was lying on her side, facing the cliff, and she was pressing herself against the rock as tightly as possible. But however much she squished in, there was still only about two inches of ledge for me to lie on. What made it worse was that there was nothing to grip onto: the cliff face was just smooth rock. I just had to balance there precariously, spooning her and trying not to roll back, with a hundred foot drop behind me.

I closed my eyes again and inhaled, drinking in Erin's scent. My nose was buried in the blonde hair at the back of her neck and I thought about how silky it felt, not how most of me was hanging over the edge. *Any second*, I told myself, *any second now, they're going to leave and we can climb up.*

Then we heard an electronic trilling. I recognized the sound because the team's satellite phone made the same noise. *Becker's getting a phone call.*

He answered in German. Then he yelled something that must have meant *go on ahead, I'll follow,* because we heard the rest of the soldiers moving off. But we could hear Becker still pacing around on the cliff edge, a few feet above us. *He's going to take it here!*

I felt Erin tense against me. She was trying to breathe shallowly, both to stay quiet and because the deeper she breathed, the more her back pressed against me, forcing me off the ledge. I was trying to do the same, for the same reason, but it was hard not to take big panic breaths when I could feel the open air behind me. My leg wound throbbed and I gritted my teeth.

Becker switched to English. "No," he was saying, "But we'll acquire it in the next few days."

All of my weight was on one narrow strip of rock and it was grinding into my shoulder and ribs, compressing the nerves and sending my muscles to sleep. I could feel myself weakening and starting to tip backwards. It didn't help that the morphine was making me spacey.

"I assure you we can deliver as planned," Becker told the caller.

I started to tremble from the effort of holding myself in place. Then my chest began to lift from Erin's back. *I'm going....*

"Make sure the money's ready to transfer," Becker said. He hung up...and then we heard his footsteps moving away from the cliff edge.

I knew that we should wait a while to make sure he was definitely gone but I couldn't hold on any longer. I wormed my way along the ledge, reached up...and gripped the edge of the cliff. Just having a handhold sent the relief slamming through me and I wilted, just hanging there for a second. Then I clambered up onto the cliff, wincing whenever I had to use my injured leg. Becker was gone. I reached down, helped Erin up off the ledge and then we both just lay there on the ground, utterly spent.

We needed to make sure Becker and his men were well clear before we risked going back into the forest, so we stayed there a while, finally having that mid-morning reward coffee we'd planned. It was freeze-dried instant with powdered creamer, sipped from a mess tin, but it tasted better than anything a fancy barista could whip up. There was an oat bar, too, and we wolfed it down. But that was everything in the ration pack and we were still a long way from the rendezvous point at the village. At least we had plenty of snow to melt into water.

Erin helped me to my feet and I tested my leg. The pain had dropped down to something manageable. I wasn't going to be winning any races, but I could walk.

We headed back into the forest and used the sun to figure out the direction to the village. The route took us downhill: we were dropping down the far side of the peak now, and as we descended, it got a little warmer. About two hours later, we emerged from the trees. Ahead of us was an endless white plain, completely flat. It went right to the horizon and the only feature was a tiny, rectangular *something,* a little structure of some kind, at the edge of the plain maybe five miles away. It was the first sign of civilization we'd seen since we left the prison.

"The village should be just over there," I said, pointing. The route would take us across one corner of the vast plain. "I reckon we can be there by tomorrow morning." The sky was clear, the plain looked like it would make for easy walking and with Becker no longer hunting us, it actually sounded doable.

As we stepped onto the plain, Erin frowned, looking around. "Why does nothing grow here?"

She was right. There wasn't even a single tree, just crisp, even snow. The ground felt iron-hard under my boots. "Maybe the soil never thaws here, and plants can't put down roots?"

A memory scratched at the back of my mind but I was still foggy from the morphine and I couldn't quite get hold of it. "C'mon," I said. "Let's go."

And we set off across the plain.

37

ERIN

WE WALKED ALL AFTERNOON. We were only crossing one small corner of the plain but it was so vast that it took forever. All we could see was the flat whiteness stretching on for miles: our only sense of scale came from the tiny building in the distance. The temperature had risen now that we were on lower ground. It was still probably minus ten but, compared to what we'd experienced in the snowstorm, that seemed almost warm.

We talked non-stop: he was so easy to talk to, and he didn't make me feel weird for liking geeky stuff. I told him about getting dressed up as comic book characters at conventions, and running around with rubber axes at live action role-playing events. He told me about balancing the weight of the car through a bend and how to get the most air through a supercharger. I realized he was much smarter than he gave himself credit for: he knew a lot of physics and engineering, he just understood it on an instinctual level that probably hadn't been picked up by his teachers.

I told him about growing up on our little ranch in South Texas: country-early starts, trying to keep my eyes open while I staggered around with a bucket feeding the animals, and the sunrises that made it worth it. My dad checking my history homework and wheeling himself over to the dinner table, saran-wrapping the whole surface so he could walk me through Gettysburg with marker pen maps until I got it. My mom's pot roast and the legendary sandwiches she made from the leftovers. Simple stuff. I was almost embarrassed, telling him because growing up in London must have been way cooler. But he looked entranced. And when I'd finished, he looked off at the horizon, his jaw tight, and I saw that unspeakable pain in his eyes again.

The sun was close to going down when we finally reached the tiny building. It really was small, a tiny hut big enough for maybe one or two people to sit inside. We were curious, but we didn't have time to stop and look. It would be night soon and we needed to get off the plain and into some trees so we could find firewood to get us through the night.

The sun kissed the horizon as we were about halfway across the plain. We were walking west so it was dead in front of us and there were no hills or buildings to block it so we could watch as it slid slowly down. It turned deep orange and then crimson, throwing out a fan of color until it felt like we were walking across a red carpet towards a glowing red doorway. Without meaning to, I reached for Danny's hand and curled my fingers around his.

His hand towed me to a stop. I turned and found him looking at our joined hands. Then he looked at me and *God,* the battle in his eyes. He'd been enjoying talking as much as I had, but now that *friendly* had tipped over into *romantic,* he'd remembered that we couldn't have this.

And he wanted it. I could see it in his face. He wanted it *so bad.* "Erin..." His voice was strained and when his fingers squeezed mine, I could feel the tension running through his body. "I never..." He glanced away for a second, then looked back at me and those green eyes were blazing. "I never met anyone I wanted to be with as much as you." he said in a rush.

I lit up inside like someone had thrown the Christmas lights switch. Deeper down, the fragile silver wires that Toby had stamped into a crumpled mess at the bottom of my soul unfolded and straightened, almost pretty again. But as I felt myself start to lift, I clamped down hard on the feelings. I knew what was coming next.

"But I can't be with you." He said the words as if they tasted bitter. This went against everything he was: he never let anyone stop him doing anything. He never cared about the rules.

But he cared about JD.

I nodded that I understood and went to drop his hand. But he squeezed mine, not letting go. "You promise me something," he ordered. "Promise me that when we get back, you'll find some guy who'll kiss you awake and tell you *every day* how gorgeous you are. Who'll hold you tight when the movie gets scary. Who'll put love notes under your pillow. Who'll fuck you so hard you can feel it the next day. Who'll annihilate anyone who tries to hurt you and who will never, ever break your heart. Because you're a princess and you don't settle for anything but a *fucking prince*. Got it?"

I pressed my lips together very, very hard to stop them trembling and managed to nod.

He dropped my hand and I marched off towards the sunset so he couldn't see the tears filling my eyes. We were nearly at the village. We'd meet up with JD and the others, we'd get back to the US, I'd go back to Vegas....

And I would never, ever, find anyone like Danny again. I knew it like I knew my own name.

It would have been okay if I'd never known he existed. But the universe had tossed us together just long enough for me to be *sure*. Danny Briggs was the one. And we'd never be together.

Something cracked under my foot and I looked down, thinking it was a stick, but there was just snow. I took another step and there was another crack, this one as loud as a gunshot.

The ground shifted. And as realization hit, my stomach dropped through my feet.

I knew now why the land was so flat, why nothing grew here. There was no soil beneath us, just deep, black water.

We weren't on a plain, we were on a gigantic frozen lake. And the ice was cracking.

38

DANNY

THE CRACKS ZIGZAGGED OUTWARD from where Erin was standing, the snow shifting and dipping as they passed, as if sea serpents were moving beneath us. They reached me and I felt the ice move sickeningly under my boots. *You bloody idiot, Danny!* This was the same lake I'd seen on the map. How could I have forgotten?

Erin had started to run towards me. I held up my hand. "No! Don't bunch up! We have to spread our weight!" I pointed. "Get to shore!"

I was further out than she was, which meant I was probably on thinner ice. But she was between me and the shore and I didn't want to risk moving any closer to her. So I stayed where I was, listening to the ice fracture and snap around me, while she ran for the edge.

She was quick, but I could see the ice moving each time her foot came down, the cracking noises getting louder and louder. *She's not going to make it.* "Stop!" I yelled. "Drop to the ground!"

Both of us dropped to our bellies and starfished, spreading our weight. The cracking noises under Erin stopped. But they kept going under me: I was heavier.

"Your pack!" yelled Erin.

I hadn't thought of that. Panting, I shrugged out of the straps, then grunted and hurled my backpack as far away from me as I could. It slid across the ice, spinning around and finally coming to rest a hundred feet away. The ice there must have been thinner because I saw the backpack drop a little and the snow turned to slush as water soaked through from underneath. The backpack didn't fall through but it was going to, any minute. My stomach twisted. *That could be me.*

We lay there panting, waiting. I'd knocked the snow aside when I fell to the ground and I could see straight through the ice to the black water beneath it.

The cracking slowed...and stopped.

I waited until the lake was completely silent. Then, "Erin, very slowly, start to slither to shore."

She took a deep breath and then began to slide on her belly. The ice held. But when she was almost to shore, she realized I hadn't moved. "Come on!" she yelled.

Reluctantly, I began to slither forward. But as soon as I moved, the cracking started again. I was heavier and the ice under me was thinner. It sagged under me and then freezing water welled up through the cracks and soaked my clothes.

I went stock-still and the cracking stopped again. "If I move, the whole thing will go," I yelled. "You have to leave me."

39

ERIN

No. No way was I leaving him. "I'll pull you in to shore!"

"You can't reach me," he yelled. "If you come close we'll both go in."

I thought hard. "There's rope in your backpack!"

"No!" he snapped. "The ice is too thin!"

I wasn't going to let him die. I looked towards the backpack. It was about a hundred feet away from me. *Only a hundred feet.* I turned away from shore and started to slide on my belly towards it.

"Erin!" yelled Danny, "No!"

I ignored him. The first thirty feet were okay. Then, as the ice thinned out, I started to hear cracking under me. I went slower, trying to make every movement syrupy smooth. *Ice is strong, ice is strong.* I thought of ice crystals, the water molecules locking together, icebergs punching through the steel hulls of ships, ice floes supporting polar bears. But as I felt the ice shift under me, other thoughts started to creep in. I started to think about the vibrations each movement was sending through the brittle ice, hairline cracks spiderwebbing outwards. About the weight of my body pressing down, splitting those cracks open further. About the heat of me soaking into the ice and melting it. *Just a few more minutes,* I prayed. *Just hold together a few more minutes.*

The backpack didn't seem to be getting any closer. I couldn't go fast or I'd fall through the ice but I couldn't go too slow or the ice would break under Danny before I could get back to him. I took a deep breath and sped up, wincing as the cracking got louder.

When I reached the backpack, it was close to going through. The ice all around it was awash with freezing water.

"Erin!" yelled Danny. "Stop!"

I stretched out...but couldn't reach the backpack. I shuffled a few inches closer and felt the ice sink under me.

"Erin!"

I strained, plucking the air with my fingertips...and just managed to hook one of the straps with a finger. I gritted my teeth and hauled the soaking backpack towards me until I could get a grip, then backed away from the thin ice, pulling it with me. I turned towards shore and belly-crawled until the ice was thicker, then got to my feet and ran. The ice here had split into car-sized islands that moved and tilted under me. I jumped over the gaps and finally made it to shore, not far from the little wooden building. Feeling grass under my feet was glorious but there was no time to enjoy it. I was safe, but now I had to save Danny.

40

DANNY

I WATCHED her scamper over the floating ice islands, nimble as a squirrel. She passed the rope around the trunk of a tree, then picked up the end and started twirling it around her head, like a cowgirl with a lasso. Some of that Texas upbringing must have rubbed off on her because when she threw, the end of the rope landed within three feet of me.

Gingerly, I slithered across the ice and grabbed it. The sun was almost down, now, the water beneath the ice inky black. I started to pull myself along the rope but even that small movement was enough to start the ice cracking again, and I froze. I was going to have to just lie there, a dead weight, and let Erin pull me in.

She hauled on the rope and I began to slide. The ice snapped and sagged under me and I held my breath...but it held, as long as I stayed still.

Erin was walking backwards from the tree, moving along the edge of the lake as she pulled me in. The ice gradually stopped cracking and started to feel more solid. And then I was at the edge. I let out a long, shaky sigh and crawled onto the shore. *Safe!*

Erin had walked so far backwards, as she pulled me in, that she'd actually drifted onto the ice, but only the thick stuff close to the edge.

She grinned at me and started walking back towards me, coiling the rope as she went.

But her next step took her onto one of the floating ice islands and her weight was too close to the edge. The slab of ice tipped almost vertical. She had time to cry out...and then she plunged into the black water and was gone.

41

ERIN

I HIT the water face first and it was so cold that it didn't even feel like liquid, more like falling through a tank of knives. Then I choked on water and that was even more painful, like my chest was filling with razor-sharp shards of ice. I flailed frantically, kicking and grabbing. The cold made me forget how to swim, how to think, everything except the pain.

The water was pitch black. My hand scraped something solid. Was I upside down? Had I gotten turned around and I was clawing at the bottom of the lake?

I squinted...and saw a faint orange glow. The sunset. I *was* at the surface, but between me and the sun was—

I was under the ice! The ice island that had tipped me off had righted itself, filling the hole I'd fallen through.

I was trapped.

42

DANNY

I'D RUN to where I saw her go under and was on my knees, staring down through the ice. I saw her hand press against the underside of the ice island. *Erin!*

I scrambled to the edge of the island. Maybe I could guide her over to the gap between islands. But they were too closely packed: there was barely an inch gap between them and I couldn't even stick my hand through.

I crawled back to where I saw her hand. It had disappeared, and I felt my heart stop. Then I saw a flash of skin: she was scrabbling at the ice, running out of air....

I brought my fist down on the ice but it didn't even crack. Then I remembered the rifle on my back. It hadn't gone into the water and it had been warmed by my body all day. I jumped up, pointed the gun at the ice a few feet from where I'd seen Erin, and worked the safety. *Please have unfrozen....*

The safety catch clicked off. I fired, holding down the trigger and chewing up the ice until I broke through. Then I dropped to my stomach, shoved both arms through the freezing soup of shards and water and fished around until—

Freezing fingers brushed mine. I grabbed her hand and pulled, rolling over on my side as I hauled her up onto the ice.

She coughed up water and then flopped on her side, shivering.

"Erin? Erin!"

She didn't answer.

I picked her up and hugged her to my chest. "Erin?"

Her head lolled and her eyes closed. Then her shivering stopped and I knew that was very, very bad. She was hypothermic, fading fast. She was already too cold and her soaking clothes were sucking every last scrap of heat out of her body.

I looked around frantically. We weren't far from the tiny wooden building and now that I knew it was on the edge of a lake, I realized what it was: a fisherman's hut. I had to hope it had some way of keeping warm. "Hold on, Erin," I muttered, and ran, snatching up my backpack as I passed it.

The hut was only about four feet square and just tall enough for me to stand up in. There was a narrow wooden bench around the edge so that a couple of fisherman could sit while they waited for a snowstorm to pass. But what I cared about was in the middle: a stove someone had cobbled together from an old oil drum and a metal pipe. Following some sort of fisherman's code, the last person to use the hut had left the stove stacked with dry wood and some balled-up Russian newspaper for kindling. I lit it, then sat on the bench with the semi-conscious Erin on my knee.

I had to get the wet clothes off her. I stripped off her sopping wet camouflage gear, her boots and socks and then the thermals and bra she had on underneath. I didn't register that she was naked, just that her skin was like ice and I had to get her warm. I turned her to face me, took off her glasses and used the street clothes in my backpack as towels to dry her off. Then I rubbed her back and arms, trying to get the blood flowing again. "C'mon Erin," I muttered, frantic. "C'mon." But she showed no signs of waking up.

The small room was toasty warm now, thanks to the stove, but I still had to warm her up *fast*. I stripped off my clothes, wrapped my arms around her and hugged her to my chest, letting my body heat soak into her. But she still wouldn't wake. She lay like a ragdoll in my arms, her head on my shoulder. I rubbed my hands up and down her back. "Come on," I begged. "Come back to me."

I was losing hope when she twitched in my arms. "Erin?"

She muttered sleepily. Then she opened her eyes and peered blearily at me like a small animal waking from hibernation. "Where are my glasses?" she mumbled.

I wanted to sob with relief. And the relief released everything I'd been holding back, everything I'd been fighting against over the last few days. I looked down at her, cute and sexy and vulnerable and tough all at the same time, and I just fucking lost it.

I leaned down and kissed her.

43

ERIN

I'D BEEN WAITING for that kiss for days. It felt like I'd been waiting my entire life.

His lips explored me gently, almost reverently, as if he'd been imagining it for so long that he couldn't believe it was really happening. Then he growled low in his chest and pressed harder against me: this was real, he had me, and he could finally show me everything he'd been feeling. He was kissing down into me but it felt like the kiss was lifting me up, the room spinning as I spiraled towards the ceiling. The kiss was soft, loving, but it was like the delicate, foamy surf that caresses the beach just before the big waves thunder in. I could feel all the pent-up tension in him: in the hard swells of his biceps, in the way his chest filled and pressed against my breasts, in the way his hands gripped my back. He was forcing himself to go slow but that wouldn't last for long and the idea made me go heady.

He pulled me harder to him and I felt my breasts pillow against his chest. That's when it sank in that I was naked and I had a sudden twinge of panic: this was the first time he'd seen my body and it was all happening in a rush. I wasn't all lusciously curvy, like some women. What if he didn't—

His lips lifted from mine and he kissed a scorching trail across my cheek and down my throat. He was kissing the warmth back into me, heat blossoming and spreading everywhere his lips touched.

He suddenly grabbed my wrists and tipped me so that I was leaning back, supported by my arms, opening up space between us so he could kiss lower. His mouth reached my breasts but before his lips or his tongue, I felt his words, scalding little rushes of air against my sensitive flesh that made me squirm in his lap. "Jesus, girl, you've got the nicest breasts I've ever seen. 'Been thinking about 'em since the garage."

He used his grip on my wrists to lower me a little more. I had my eyes closed but I could feel him gazing at me, hungrily devouring me. "Bloody perfect," he breathed. The words sank into my brain, heated chunks of rough London granite that crushed my insecurities into dust.

He lifted me a little closer. My wrists felt deliciously small in his grip and I could feel the raw strength of him as he lifted me like I weighed nothing. There was something wonderful about being so effortlessly handled.

Then his mouth engulfed one breast and I cried out in delicious shock, arching my back as his tongue slathered the soft underside, then swept over my nipple. My nipples were hard from the cold but now, as his mouth pumped a slow, steady, drumbeat of heat into my body, they stiffened more, into throbbing, sensitive peaks. Each swipe of his tongue sent crackling, silver ribbons of pleasure straight down to my groin and I started to pant and groan.

It sank in that *he* was naked, too. I opened my eyes and gazed at him: leaning back and looking up at him like this, he looked even bigger. The tan swells of his shoulders and biceps were standing out huge and hard as he supported me and his soft black hair brushed my chin as he licked at me. He must have felt me looking at him because he lifted his mouth from me, leaving my breast wetly shining, and raised his head to look at me. Those absinthe eyes sparkled, his lids heavy with lust. "God, you're incredible," he said.

I swallowed. No one had ever called me *incredible* before.

"Come here, girl," he muttered, and he tugged on my wrists to pull me up. I gave a little squeal that got higher when I felt him let go of my wrists. But he caught me before gravity could pull me back again, his big hands cradling my back and crushing me to his chest.

When I was securely snug against him, he cupped my chin in one hand and kissed me long and deep. I moaned and twisted, my ass grinding against his thighs. For the first time, my hands were free to explore him and I slid them over the huge, hard spheres of his shoulders, then rollercoastered them down over the bulges of his biceps and along the inside of his forearms, going a little weak at the veined strength of them.

The kiss was changing, now, soft and gentle giving way to hard and urgent. His lips demanded entrance and I flowered open under him, my fingertips skating along the backs of his arms as his tongue sought me out and owned me. Our bodies flexed in rhythm, the hard slabs of his chest rubbing against my spit-wet breasts until I was grabbing hard at his shoulders just to contain the pleasure.

He broke the kiss and gently pushed me back. I opened my eyes slowly, feeling almost drunk. "Stand up," he told me.

I stepped carefully down to the floor. There wasn't a lot of room in the little hut, but there was just space for me to stand facing him, if he spread his knees wide and I stood between them. The stove was throwing out a lot of heat and with it only a foot from my back, I was blissfully warm.

Danny sat there gazing up at me for a moment, then reached up and fingered my braid. "*This.*" He inhaled, a long, throaty sound. "The way it's all gathered up and *tight*. The way it swishes when you walk."

It swishes when I walk?

He ran his hand down the length of it and made a noise that started as "*Mmm,*" and ended as a low rumble in his chest.

Apparently, he liked my braid. I flushed, confused but pleased.

He ran his hands down my back and I yelped as they squeezed my naked ass. He drew me closer, bent forward and—

My eyes went wide and I sucked in a huge, trembling gulp of air as his tongue traced along the line of my lips and flicked against my clit. My hands found his shoulders and my fingers began to knead as his tongue outlined the shape of me and then pressed in, gently opening me.

He began a slow, steady rhythm, alternating between firmly tasting me and feathering my clit with a touch as light as a butterfly's wing. Molten scarlet pleasure, silver-edged and uncontainable, spiraled outward from my groin and tightened into a spinning spiral that brought me up onto my tiptoes.

His hands slid from my ass to the backs of my thighs and he gently but firmly spread my legs. I let out a strangled cry as his tongue speared up into me. His upper lip rubbed in soft circles on my clit and my eyes rolled back in my head, my hands climbing his neck to tangle in his soft, dark hair. I panted and gasped, head thrown back and eyes closed, as the pleasure spiraled faster and faster. It wasn't just what his tongue and lips were doing to me. It was the way he was breathing, in quick, animal pants, the way he gave little growls of lust. He was enjoying it at least as much as me.

The pleasure became a cyclone, spinning my mind until I couldn't think. I forgot about Siberia, about the soldiers and the mission, about everything except how it felt. I *let go* in a way I'd never done before, in a way maybe I'd never dared to before, and when the pleasure finally exploded into a blazing white starburst, it was so strong that I staggered against him, legs wilting as I jerked and spasmed.

He chuckled low in his throat as he held me up. Then, as the orgasm ebbed away and I went floaty and pink, he gathered me into his arms and pulled me onto his lap again. I fell against him, panting, and put my head against that perfect, safe spot on his pec that I'd stared at for so long. It was just as snug and warmly comforting as I'd imagined.

He ran his hands up and down my back, calming me, comforting me, while I drifted down. Only when my brain had started working again did his touch start to shift, smoothing over my ass and hips, his thumbs gliding along the soft sides of my breasts. I shifted in his lap and felt his cock, rock hard and standing vertically against his stomach. I tilted my head back so that I could look up at him.

He looked me straight in the eye and gave me a smirk that was so filthy and cocky, I felt my cheeks heat despite everything we'd just done.

His backpack was on the bench beside us. He rooted in a pocket and brought out—

"You take condoms on missions?" I asked in disbelief. Then I remembered that this was *Danny*.

He gripped my waist and slid me back a little on his thighs and I went melty: the way he moved me around so easily tripped some primitive switch in my brain, making me feel all small and feminine. Then I looked down at his cock and went melty for a whole different reason. His cock, like the rest of his body, had been carved by some master sculptor. The head was a beautiful purple-pink, engorged and glossy, and it balanced at the top of a shaft as thick and strong and perfectly straight as any flagpole. It twitched with each breath he took, stiff and *ready*.

Even his cock looked cocky.

He rolled on the condom, then slid his hands under my ass and lifted me. I looked down, watching, a little nervous but also weirdly hypnotized, as he lowered me down.

Then the first brush of him, the arrow-shaped warmth of him parting me and—my fingers played a piano scale up his arm—*filling* me in one slow, silken push. He slid his hands up my sides and cupped my breasts, squeezing and stroking, while I got used to the size of him. Then he guided me gradually lower, my toes dancing on the floor as I sank down on him. I closed my eyes, my lips forming silent half-words as I took him. Every millimeter sent a new ribbon of silver pleasure rippling to my core, where they started to twirl into a glowing, incandescent ball. The heat of him inside me, the satiny stretch of him...it woke something in me, an ache I'd never known before. Part of me, still nervous, wanted to go slow. The rest of me wanted *all of him. Right. Now.*

I straightened my legs and rose a little. Sank again, throwing my head back and gasping as I took more of him. He let me take my time, leaning back and watching me. The third time I sank, my groin kissed his and I knew he was in me to the root.

My eyes fluttered open and I looked straight into scalding, lust-filled green. It felt unbelievably good: just the throb of him was making the silver ribbons of pleasure shiver and dance. And every breath we took pulled those ribbons tighter, drawing more heat and pressure into the glowing ball at my core. I wanted it. But I knew how inexperienced I was, compared to him. I traced my fingers along the tops of his shoulders and looked imploringly at him. *Please?*

He understood. And, with his hands on my hips, he guided me. He showed me how to lift and sink in just the right rhythm to keep us both teetering on the edge. He showed me how to twist my hips ever so slightly to make him groan and growl. He showed me how to rock, when he was buried in me, so the base of him ground against my clit just right.

I began to explore, growing gradually bolder, until I was riding him, my braid bouncing and slapping against my sweat-covered back, my breasts dancing against his lips and tongue. Our pants and moans filled the little hut, our bodies slapping together as the pleasure tightened and tightened, becoming too dense, too hot, to possibly contain. I felt his hands on my ass, driving me harder and harder, and then all thought ceased and there was only the feeling of him plunging into me, stretching me, faster and faster.

Just as I reached my peak, he grabbed my ass with both hands and *pulled,* impaling me, grinding up into me, and my world exploded, the waves of pleasure rolling through me again and again until all I could do was cling onto him, panting into his ear as he unleashed in long hot streams inside me.

We sat like that for a long time, my head resting on his shoulder. Then he lifted me and rearranged us, so that he was sitting lengthwise on the bench, half-reclining with his backpack as a pillow, and me lying on top of him. Outside, the wind had picked up and we could hear it blowing snow against the walls. But inside, with my head cradled on his chest, I was warmly snug and more secure than I'd ever felt. I closed my eyes...and slept.

44

DANNY

I'D SLEPT half-sitting on a wooden bench with my backpack as a pillow yet somehow, when the dawn light coming through the cracks in the walls woke me, I'd had the best night's sleep of my life. I looked down at Erin, dozing on top of me, and knew why. Sleep had never felt like that with any of the other women I'd slept with. Maybe I'd never fully relaxed with them.

The sex had been incredible, too. Just the memory of her bouncing on top of me made my cock rise. It had *never* been that good. Even with Elodie, in Paris, and she'd done things that even *I'd* thought were kinky.

I stroked Erin's hair and felt my chest tighten. Maybe it was because I hadn't cared about the others.

Erin mumbled something and started to slowly come awake. I watched as she frowned, grumbled, and put her glasses on. She was extra adorable when she was sleepy. She finally managed to blink herself awake and focus, then looked up at me. "Hi," she said shyly.

I ran my hand over her naked back. "Hi yourself."

She looked around the hut and I could sense everything sinking in. What we'd done. I felt her tense against me, her breath tightening. "What's wrong?" I asked.

She put her head down on my chest and stared at the stove. "I just..." She paused. Took a deep breath, then another. "I want you to know that if that was just a one-night thing, that that's okay. I mean, I'll be okay."

I took her chin in my hands and gently made her face me. She looked me in the eye, her jaw set, determined to convince me. But I could see the fear in her eyes. "No," I said firmly. "No, it wouldn't be okay. And it wasn't just a one night thing." I went to tell her how I felt about her: happy and bonded and, oddly, *secure,* like I could trust her with anything. But I couldn't figure out the words. That threw me. This was *me,* talking to women was what I *did.* So why was saying this so hard?

Maybe because, for once, it wasn't just jokes and flirting. It meant something.

Erin was still looking up at me, worried. So I told her the one thing I knew with cast-iron certainty. "You're my girl, now." No one was ever taking her away from me.

She flushed, nodded, and the grin she gave me lifted me right up through the ceiling. I wrapped my arms around her, she cuddled into my chest and all was right with the world.

After a while, though, my soldier brain started to kick in, infuriatingly practical. It started to think about how today we'd reach the rendezvous point at the village. And what would happen when we got there.

I just fucked JD's little sister. Not after a month of careful dating but within a week of meeting her. My stomach twisted. JD was going to be... *Mad* didn't even begin to cover it. *But he'll get over it. Right?*

I'd put Erin's clothes on the stove and they'd dried overnight. We dressed and then opened the door to find everything covered in a blanket of pristine white snow. The sky was clear again and we were feeling pretty good, aside from being achingly hungry.

Before we left, we gathered some branches from the edge of the forest and filled up the stove for the next person. Then we set off for the village, holding hands.

Two hours later, I saw smoke rising from behind a hill. Another hour and I was lying on my stomach, peeking over the brow of the hill with Erin beside me. Becker thought we were dead, but what if he'd caught up with the others and was waiting here for us? It didn't hurt to be cautious.

Through the scope of my rifle, I saw several huts, an old truck and a few people who looked like locals, but there was no sign of the team.

A crunch of snow behind me. I whirled around, bringing my rifle up...and found myself looking right into Colton's bearded face. Both of us lowered our rifles with sighs of relief. I wanted to hug him. Then, fuck it, I *did* hug him. It had been a long few days.

Colton thumped me on the back. "Thought you were dead, when you fell outta the chopper. See, *this* is why I don't like flying."

Poor fella. Colton hadn't been a fan of heights before this. We'd probably scared him off flying for life.

We followed Colton down into the village and over to one of the huts. He pulled open the door and I let out a groan of relief. Bradan, Cal, Gabriel, JD and Gina were all sitting inside, all okay.

JD and Erin ran to each other and hugged. "You alright?" asked JD urgently. "You okay?"

Erin nodded and I saw JD relax. It must have been a sleepless few nights for him. He looked at me over her shoulder. "Thanks."

I nodded. *Not here.* I wasn't going to tell him here, with everyone around. I'd wait until we were alone. "What happened to you?" I asked.

"Gina got us down okay but we were a few miles from where you fell out and the prison guards were between you and us. We had to circle around to the village and hope you could make it here." He looked between Erin and me. "How was it for you two?"

I looked at Erin. "Cold." Then, to change the subject, "Is there anything to eat?"

"The locals have got some stew on the stove," said Gabriel. "Should be done by now." He led the way outside and we all followed. But JD waved for me to hold back for a moment. Erin threw me a look as she left and I nodded. This was a good moment to tell him.

I went to speak but JD got there first. "I wanted to say thanks," he said. "For getting me out of there. For taking care of Erin."

I looked at my boots. "You would've done the same for me."

"Sure. But I was an asshole, back home, about Erin."

I looked up, shocked, my chest filling with hope. *He's going to say it's okay if I date her!*

"I should have known you wouldn't try to bang her," said JD. "I mean, she's my *little sister.* But..." He sighed. "Y'know, you got a reputation."

I'd never minded my reputation. It had always been a joke between JD and me that I'd sweet talk every woman we met into bed. But I minded it now. I hadn't realized I'd been slowly building something that would put Erin off limits to me forever. I suddenly regretted every one of those one-night stands. What if, back when JD and I had first met, I *hadn't* been like that? Maybe he would have let me meet Erin back then. Maybe he would have even introduced us deliberately.

JD stepped closer. "I knew I'd never forgive you if you *did* sleep with her. That's why I got mad. Because I can't lose you. I love you, pal."

He pulled me into an embrace. I closed my eyes and patted his back. Things were different with Erin. I had real feelings for her. But how could I ever make JD believe that, when he'd had years of knowing me as a horndog who never hung around the morning after? And when I told him I'd already slept with Erin, after he told me not to, that would be *it:* like he said, he'd never forgive me. I'd lose him forever: like he'd warned me in Mount Mercy, we'd be *done.* And if he hated me, that would poison his relationship with Erin. *Both* of us would lose him. And that would leave JD on his own, right when he needed people who cared about him. It could send him back to that dark place I'd pulled him out of.

I knew what I had to do.

45

ERIN

THE LOCALS WERE reindeer herders and they lived out here, six of them alone in all this vastness, with just a supply run every three months to break the monotony. They introduced us to the reindeer, which were incredibly sweet and gentle. I'd thought of reindeer almost as fantasy creatures, harnessed to sleighs. Having them nuzzle feed from my palm, feeling the velvety softness of their noses...I was a long way from my burrow, a long way from everything I knew. But I was seeing things I never normally would.

Danny and JD rejoined us. I was desperate to know what had happened, but I'd have to wait until I got Danny alone. The locals handed out bowls of rich, dark stew and we ate while we talked.

"We need to get to a town so we can find a plane and get out of the country," said JD. "But it's too far to walk. And the satellite phone didn't survive the crash, so we can't call Kian for help."

"What about the truck?" asked Danny, pointing. It was ancient, with faded olive paint and a tarp covering the back.

"Hasn't worked in months," said JD. "They'll sell it to us but it's no good unless we can get it going. We took a look before you showed up and the electrics are shot."

I nodded. "Danny and I will take a look."

The two of us walked over to the truck and popped the hood. "Well?" I asked. "How did he take it?"

Danny didn't answer and my heart sank. *He didn't tell him.*

Then he looked at me and I realized it was worse than that.

My stomach tightened down to a cold, hard ball as he told me what JD had said. "If we're together," he said bitterly, "I'll lose him."

I bent low over the engine, staring at it without really seeing it. The anger boiling up was darkly hot and indignant. *But it's not fair!* People might not understand it but we had something together, against all the odds, we *worked.* He got my weirdness and I saw that he was more than his reputation. *We should just tell JD and the hell with the consequences!*

I could feel Danny watching me. I glanced up and, when I saw the pain in his eyes, I softened. He was terrified that he was going to lose his best friend. But I could see the concern there too. He really cared about me. Enough that he'd lose JD, if I asked him to.

I couldn't do that. I could see the way the two of them felt about each other. Military men form unbreakable bonds, stronger than brothers, and they'd served together for years. And I couldn't do it to JD, either. He'd lost his wife and child, he needed Danny at least as much as Danny needed JD.

An endless gray emptiness opened up inside me and it made me flail and panic, a last-minute urge to grab him and cling onto all that warm solidness. *I can't lose him!*

Stupid, I told myself, furious. *You've only known him a few days. Grow up!*

I nodded, letting him know that I agreed. That it was *our* decision, not just his. Then I turned back to the engine. "Looks like the starter motor isn't getting any power," I said, my voice raspy. I could feel that wonderful feeling of safety I'd had in his arms dissolving like smoke and when it was gone, it ached so bad I couldn't speak for a moment. I was suddenly alone again, naked and vulnerable in this immense world, and it was so much worse now that I knew what I was missing. Without looking up, I held out my hand. "Can you pass me the big flathead screwdriver?"

A moment later, I felt the plastic handle press into my palm. But when I took the screwdriver, it wouldn't move. He was keeping hold of it until I looked at him.

I reluctantly looked up and saw the question in his eyes. *Are you okay?*

No! I wanted to run up to the top of the hill and holler it so loud they could hear it in Texas. *No, I'm not okay!* I needed him. I needed him in my life, I needed him to kiss me and touch me and make me feel safe and I needed him to fuck me. And that need that had pulled me to him so hard was now flipped around and turned into something brutal and jagged. Being near him *hurt,* now, and it would hurt all the way back to Latvia and then on the plane all the way back to the US. And then when I went back to Vegas and never saw him again, I knew it would hurt in a whole different way because then I'd have to face a future without him in it.

I forced myself to nod. I could see he didn't believe it, but he grudgingly released the screwdriver and I went to work. I focused on cleaning connections and swapping fuses and not on how much it hurt.

"Try it now," I said in a tight little voice. Danny went and got behind the wheel. As soon as he was out of sight, safely hidden behind the raised hood, I felt my self control slip away. My head came forward, my eyes closed and the first silent sob shook my body.

Danny turned the key and the engine roared to life. The truck belched out a cloud of thick, black smoke that enveloped us, then settled down to an idle.

Danny jumped down and ran around to where I was standing. I turned away, but not before he saw the shining tears running down my cheeks. "Erin?"

I walked away. "It's the smoke," I managed.

46

DANNY

THE TRUCK WAS without a doubt the slowest thing I'd ever driven and it was a long way to the nearest town. That gave me plenty of time to brood.

What was I thinking?! I'd hurt Erin and that was the last thing I'd wanted to do. Why hadn't I just stayed clear of her?

I glanced over my shoulder. Erin was in the back with the others, trying to doze as we bounced along pitted, unpaved logging roads. Being this close to her but not being able to be with her was hell. *Another day, and we'll be home.* Then she'd go back to Vegas and everything would be okay. Things would go back to normal.

Except.... My knuckles turned white on the steering wheel. Everything *wouldn't* be okay. I didn't *want* things to go back to normal. The idea of going back to Krüger's Tavern and flirting with random women felt flimsy and fake, like I'd been pushing paper doll cutouts around on a table my whole life, making the guy in the sharp suit go home with the woman in the tight dress, playing at romance without knowing what it really was.

It took almost fifteen hours before we finally reached a town and another four before we reached one that had an airfield. By that point, I was a wreck, aching and worn-out from driving. We changed back into our street clothes and Gabriel sweet-talked the owner of an air freight company. After some negotiation, some vodka shots and a thick wad of US currency, the guy agreed to smuggle us into Latvia. We piled into the back of a plane, squeezed in between some mail bags and a stack of cages containing live chickens. and I was asleep before we left the runway. I dreamed of Erin, kept reaching for her and finding she wasn't there.

The next day—or maybe it was the same day, we crossed so many time zones I lost track—we touched down at a small airfield outside Riga, Latvia and were through the fence and onto the streets before the authorities knew we were there. For the first time since the helicopter crashed, we were back on track. We could go to the CIA safehouse, dump the guns and other equipment and pick up our civilian luggage, then get a commercial flight back to the US. I'd changed the dressing on my leg wound and it was feeling better—staying off my feet for a day had helped.

As the sun came up, we wandered towards the center of Riga, everyone yawning and jet-lagged. Erin was at the front of the group, talking to JD, and it was hard not to look at her. I wanted to drink in every detail of her face before I lost her forever. But I couldn't let anyone suspect what had happened. I turned to Cal. "How's Bethany doing in med school?" I asked.

"Great," said Cal. "Acing it. It sucks that she's away in Boulder so much but she's home on weekends and it ain't forever." He got a secret little smile on his face and I could tell he was thinking of her. "I'm making her something. A surprise." He shrugged, embarrassed. "She likes watching the sun come up. We used to do it back in Idaho, in the cabin. So I'm making a bench for the porch. A bench, but with rockers, like a rocking chair for two—well, three, with Rufus. Figured we could all sit there under a blanket."

I nodded. "That sounds nice." I meant it. I couldn't stop myself glancing at Erin again, imagining a life like that with her. *Fuck!*

Gina pointed to a street sign. "Nearly there." She sighed in relief. "I don't even care about having to fly commercial. I'm gonna get on board, order a *big* glass of red and—"

We turned the corner and stopped dead. The street was packed with firefighters, their hoses aimed at the window of an apartment block. Flames roared from inside. I counted windows and floors, praying I was wrong. "That's...."

"...the safehouse," finished Gabriel.

"What happened?" asked Gina. "Someone attacked it?"

Cal shook his head. "It's burning too cleanly. Look how intense the flames are, but they're not spreading to the other apartments." He turned to scowl at us. "CIA safehouses are rigged so they can be burned with just a couple of minutes' notice. They're getting rid of any evidence we were there. They're cutting us loose, just like they did with JD."

"*Why?*" I asked. "We did it! We got JD back, we got back to Latvia. Job done!"

"I don't know, but we should get out of here," muttered JD. We slunk around the corner and into the next street. That's when Erin gave a choked cry and pointed to a TV screen in a shop window.

It was showing JD's face. I didn't speak Latvian but I could figure out what the big red banner across the top of the screen meant. A manhunt was underway for us. Gabriel's face appeared on screen, then Bradan's.

"How did they get our photos?" demanded Gabriel. "We wiped the cameras at the prison."

"Why are they hunting us?" asked JD. "Becker was holding me off the books. The German government should be investigating *him,* not—"

The screen changed to show a German politician, reading a statement in English. "We are in full co-operation with our colleagues across Europe and NATO," he was saying, "to ensure that the terrorists behind this senseless, tragic attack are brought to justice."

"Tragic," croaked Gina. "He said *tragic.* Why would he—"

"Our thoughts are with the families of the seven brave members of our armed forces who gave their lives at the prison," continued the politician.

I buried my hands in my hair. "Oh Jesus." I felt physically sick.

"This is Becker. He must have killed some of the guards at the prison and pinned it on us. He's got the whole of Europe searching for us. The police'll either shoot us or throw us in jail: either way, he gets rid of us."

We all stared at each other in horror. I looked at Erin and my stomach knotted. She'd go to jail with the rest of us.

Then I noticed a woman watching us from across the street. She was laden with heavy shopping bags, but she'd stopped mid-stride and was looking between us and the TV screen in the window, which had gone back to showing our faces.

I nudged the others and we walked away, trying to look calm and casual. But when I checked behind us, the woman had run over to a policeman. "*Run!*" I told the others.

We ran down an alley and into another street. But within a minute, we started to hear sirens.

JD turned to me. "Danny, we're going to need a car. Gabriel, I need a phone."

We both nodded. I found a parked minivan and started working on the lock. Meanwhile, Gabriel sauntered off down the street to find someone to bump into. A moment later, I had the doors open and everyone was piling in. Two minutes and I had the engine started. Gabriel jumped in and we sped off down the street.

Gabriel passed JD the phone he'd stolen. JD dialed Kian, then put the phone on speaker. "It's us. We're all okay."

Kian gave a long groan of relief. "What the *feck* happened in Siberia? They're saying you killed seven people!"

"We didn't kill anyone," said JD. "This is Becker, he's framed us so the police will hunt us down for him."

"Yeah, well, it's working," said Kian. "You just made the top of Interpol's most-wanted list."

We all looked at each other. This was real. We were fugitives.

"We'll call you when we figure something out," said JD.

"Be safe," Kian told us.

JD hung up and tossed the phone out of the window. We drove in silence for a moment until I quietly asked, "Where should I head?"

JD turned to me and shook his head. *I don't know.* Then he glanced in the rear view mirror. I followed his gaze to Erin, who was in the rear seat, looking ridiculously small between Cal and Colton. I wished I could let him know that I was terrified for her, too. "Alright, options?" he asked.

"We can't get a commercial flight," said Bradan. "They'll have the airports locked down. They know our faces."

"Can't charter a plane for the same reason," said Gina.

"What about one of your buddies?" Colton asked, turning to Gabriel. "Smuggle us back to the US, the same way we got back to Latvia."

"When I bribed the guy to fly us back to Latvia, no one was looking for us. The Germans must have started the manhunt while we were in the air. We're too hot for any smuggler to touch, now," said Gabriel.

"It's worse than that," muttered JD. We all looked at him. "Even if we did make it back to the US...what then? As soon as we show our faces, they'll extradite us to Germany and we'll go to jail for seven murders."

We all went quiet as it sunk in. We couldn't go home. *Ever.*

We drove for another ten miles in brooding silence. Then Gabriel suddenly said, "Becker."

Everyone turned to look at him. He had that look in his eyes: you could almost see the cogs spinning as that scarily sharp mind came up with a plan.

"Becker's involved in something shady. We got in the middle of it when we saw him buy that file in Berlin and kill the seller. That's why he took JD prisoner, he was going to interrogate him to find out what he knew. And that's why he's framed us, he wants us discredited in case we tell anyone that he's dirty. No one's going to believe a bunch of fugitives. The only way out of this is to find out what Becker's up to and expose him." He looked at us one by one. "We have to go to Berlin."

Colton stared at him. "You want to go to Germany? You realize it's the Germans who are after us, right?"

JD thought for a while. "Gabriel's right," he said at last. "We've got to go on the offensive. It's the only way to clear our names." He looked across at me. "Danny: get us to Berlin."

Latvia to Germany. Eight hundred miles through four countries. Fortunately, driving was *what I did.* "No problem," I told him, and turned towards the highway.

~

Eight hours later, we were in a forest in Poland. It was bitterly cold but I'd stopped the car so everyone could stretch and I could pace around and wake myself up for the next stretch. The sun was going down, bathing the trunks of the trees in gold.

I was watching Erin as she slept in the back seat, her head resting on the window. She'd spent the journey getting to know the rest of the team better. I could tell it hadn't been easy for her: she was shy at the best of times and the guys are big and pretty intimidating: in the rear-view mirror, she'd looked like a mouse in a car full of gorillas. But she'd asked them about the favorite places they'd lived before coming to Colorado and the answers kept us occupied for most of the drive. Colton had told her about the boat he'd lived on in Missouri. Gabriel had described an apartment he'd had in Paris while he was casing the Louvre. Even the notoriously quiet Cal had told us all about the little cabin he'd lived in, deep in the woods of Idaho.

Gina had launched into a colorful story about a little place she'd had in Argentina and the tango-dancing guy she'd had a fling with there. The story had gradually gotten steamier and steamier until Gina finally remembered that Erin wasn't the only one listening and told her she'd tell her the rest later and all of us chorused *aww.*

It felt like Erin was becoming part of our weird little family. I stood there watching her sleep. A few strands of ash-blonde hair had come loose from her braid and were being blown back and forth by her breath, flashing gold as the sunset caught them—

"Holy shit," said Gabriel. "You slept with Erin."

I whirled around. He'd gotten out to stretch, and so he could trade seats with Gina, since no one wanted to be in the tight back row for long. I hadn't realized he'd been watching me. *How did he....* "Don't be stupid," I told him. But I could feel my face heating and this was *Gabriel,* he was an expert at reading people. The game was up.

Gabriel moved closer and shook his head, nodding to where JD dozed next to Erin. "You really can't keep it in your pants, can you?" He shook his head, halfway between shocked and impressed. "It was minus twenty, how did you even find a place to—God, JD is gonna *kill you!*"

"Don't tell him," I said quickly.

"Don't tell who what?" said Gina, emerging from the trees.

"Danny slept with Erin," Gabriel told her.

Gina stared at me. "Are you *insane?!* She's his little sister! JD is gonna kill you!"

"That's what I said," said Gabriel.

Gina shook her head. "I knew you were a horndog, but *wow!*"

"It's not like that!" I told them. "I really like her."

Gina and Gabriel's jaws both dropped. "Oh *shit,*" whispered Gina. She looked from me to Erin to JD. "That's way worse."

"We should get going," I told them both, and got back into the car. For this stretch, Bradan had the passenger seat. He was opening the gift Stacey had given him just before we left. "What is it?" I asked, glad of any excuse to change the subject.

He showed me: it was a tiny MP3 player and a set of headphones. A thoughtful gift, given that there are always long stretches of waiting around on missions, and we often have to leave our phones at home so they don't get tracked. It was wrapped in a handwritten note and he read it, then said, "She's filled it with all the best music I missed when I was in the cult." He showed me the handwritten tracklist and it was a thing of beauty: Stacey had drawn tiny hearts and cars and fireworks to illustrate the different songs. Bradan shook his head in wonder, a smile touching his lips.

Good. The poor guy deserved to be happy, after what he'd been through. Separated from his brothers for years. Raised by a cult to be an assassin. Then being rescued by Kian and his other brothers and finding out his whole life was a lie. Sometimes, when you looked at him, you could see the weight of all the stuff he'd done weighing down on him, and he still had moments when he just froze, reliving some memory of his cult days. I was glad he'd met someone who could make him smile. "How's Stacey doing?" I asked as I put the car into gear.

"She's still trying to figure out what she's going to do in Mount Mercy," said Bradan. "She had a whole business in LA, a whole chain of bakeries to run. And you know Stacey, she has this energy...she walks into a room and when she comes out, everything's alphabetized. She needs to be *doing* something. She can't just be sitting around, waiting for us to come home."

I nodded. And found my eyes going to Erin in the rear view mirror. I'd never been one to write love letters, or make mixtapes, or anything hand-crafted and romantic like that. But seeing Stacey's gift made me want to do those things for Erin. And thinking about Stacey waiting at home for Bradan made me think about how it would be to have Erin waiting at home for me.

I forced my eyes back to the road before someone noticed. Gabriel and Gina were right, JD would kill me. For the good of all three of us, I had to forget about Erin.

Ten hours later, we entered the outskirts of Berlin. Everyone was a burned-out, grumpy mess. We'd changed cars five times, had one near miss sneaking across the German border and were running on snacks and energy drinks from vending machines because we didn't dare walk into a store or even show our faces at a drive-thru. But we'd made it.

"We're going to need somewhere to stay," said JD. "Anyone know anybody in Berlin?"

"I knew a guy," said Colton. "But he moved to Frankfurt."

"I know someone," said Gabriel. "But he's doing time."

JD turned to me. "What about Katharina?"

I froze. *Yes,* she was still in Berlin. And *yes,* she'd help us. But I couldn't go there. Not *now.* Not with.... I glanced in the rear view mirror at Erin, who was dozing in the back row.

But we didn't have a choice. "Okay," I muttered.

And I turned towards Katharina's apartment.

47

DANNY

It was three in the morning when we arrived at Katharina's apartment block. We didn't want to stand around in the street while we buzzed her and hoped she was home, so Gabriel picked the lock and we slipped inside.

I led the way up the big stone staircase to the top floor. Memories started unfurling as soon as I felt the cold metal banister under my palm and they only got stronger when I smelled the flowers that Katharina's elderly neighbor grew in pots in the hallway. *I can't believe I'm back here.*

We reached Katharina's door. I smoothed out my hair, took a deep breath...and knocked.

No answer.

We couldn't just wait for her to come back, not with our faces on TV. Gabriel stepped forward to pick the lock but I put my hand on his chest. There was an old metal light fitting above Katharina's door and I fished around on top. Yes, she still kept a key there.

I opened the door and we crept inside in the dark, letting out sighs of relief. For the first time since Latvia, it felt like we were out of sight.

Someone stepped out of the shadows to my right and I felt the muzzle of a gun press against the side of my head. I grabbed the arm and pushed them back, trying to ram them against the wall, but they ducked and pulled and suddenly I was airborne, judo-flipped over their shoulder. I crashed to the floor on my back.

The light switched on. Katharina was standing over me in a bathrobe, pointing a gun at my head. She blinked as she saw my face. *"Danny?!"*

I gave her a sheepish grin. "Alright, luv?"

She gave a strangled groan of relief, fell to her knees and kissed me deep.

48

ERIN

I STOOD THERE STARING. The woman was almost as tall as Danny, with treacle-colored, shoulder-length hair that hung in a perfect, glossy bob. She was straddling Danny's chest, one hand still gripping the gun, the other around the back of his head to pull her to him. Her scarlet bathrobe had come loose and, as she leaned forward, it was obvious that she was busty.

The shock was melted away by a scalding flash of anger. I wanted to run forward and shove her off him, screaming in her face that he was *mine*.

Then I remembered that he wasn't, anymore. That he never would be again. The jealousy turned in on itself and became a sharp-edged ball of pain.

Danny finally managed to pull himself free of the kiss. I felt myself frown: there was something in the way he looked at her: tender but sad. My mind raced to catch up and I was almost there when he turned to us and said, "Everyone, this is Katharina. My ex."

Katharina. Even her name was sexy.

She punched Danny in the arm. "What are you doing breaking in here? I could have killed you!" Her German accent was strong enough that it sounded like *killt you.*

Danny rubbed his arm. "I did knock. You didn't answer."

"I have a camera in the hall. When I see a group of big guys outside my door at three in the morning, I assume they're here to kill me." For the first time, she looked around at the rest of us. "My God..you're the ones everyone's looking for." She looked at Danny. "What did you get yourself into?!"

"It wasn't us," Danny said quickly. "We're being framed."

"And you came *here?*" Katharina climbed off him and stood. Her robe was still gaping open at the front and I could see the men trying to avert their eyes, with varying degrees of success. "I'm still with the BND! My boss has us all looking for you!"

Danny got to his feet and gave her another sheepish grin. "It's worse than that," he said. "Your boss, Becker...he's the one framing us."

Katharina closed her eyes and ran a hand through her hair. "*Scheisse.*"

Danny put a hand on her arm. "Kat, I know this is a big ask. If you need us to go, we can leave."

Katharina took a deep breath, then opened her eyes and looked at Danny. "You really think I'd throw you out?" They gazed at each other for a moment and the pain in their eyes made my chest ache in sympathy. There'd been something there, once, something more than sex.

They both looked away. "All of you get some sleep," Katharina told us. "You look ready to drop. We can talk in the morning."

She fetched blankets and cushions and we all collapsed on armchairs and couches. I wound up lying head-to-toe with Gina on a big, squishy couch and after two nights of only sleeping in cars, trucks, and planes, I was asleep the second my eyes closed.

We all slept until mid-morning. Katharina organized a production line to get us all showered and fed. We handed over our clothes so she could put them through the wash, then lined up in towels to go into one of her two bathrooms. We showered, picked up a mug and had it filled with coffee, then passed by the kitchen to pick up a plate of sausage, potato and eggs. By the time we'd all finished eating, our clothes were dry. Clean, fed and in fresh clothes, I felt better than I had since the mission started.

Then I looked at the TV and my stomach dropped. The main story on the news was the continuing, Europe-wide hunt for us.

Katharina, who'd called BND headquarters to say she was following up a lead and would be in later, gestured at the screen with her mug of coffee. "You and Danny are the mystery men. Why is that?"

I frowned. "What?"

She nodded for me to keep watching. The news report cycled through pictures of JD, Gabriel, Bradan, Cal, Colton, Gina...but that was it. "Two more men are thought to be traveling with the group," Katharina translated for us.

They didn't even know I was a woman. "Why don't they have pictures of Danny and me?"

"Better question," said Gabriel. "How did they get pictures of the rest of us? We wiped the cameras at the prison."

"I didn't even go *into* the damn prison," grunted Gina.

"It must have been when we were separated," said Danny. "After the helicopter crash, before we met up at the village."

Katharina squinted at the photos. "There are trees in the background...." She thumped the table, rattling the plates. "Trail cameras, in the forest. They use them to study wildlife. You must have walked right past one. Becker must have collected the footage from all of them and got lucky."

"Next question," said JD, "what do we do now? What can you tell us about Becker?"

Katharina leaned back against a bookcase, nursing her coffee. She was wearing a black blouse and gray suit that made the most of her curves. She was almost a foot taller than me and all of it seemed to be in her legs: now that she was in heels, she was actually slightly taller than Danny. A tall, curvy, ass-kicking spy. Could his ex have been any more intimidating?

Katharina shook her head. "I've seen some bad stuff..."—she exchanged glances with Danny—"but Becker's one of the few people who really scares me. He came up through the military. Special Forces. Then he went into the BND and he moved up *fast*. So fast that people didn't realize, at first, that there was something wrong with him."

Colton leaned back in his chair. "Wrong with him, how?"

Katharina put her mug down. She looked at the floor and wrapped her arms around herself, as if shielding herself from a bad memory. "Not long after I started at the BND, I was on a mission with him. We were talking to this woman, a Chinese national who'd been living in Berlin for a few years. She was having an affair with an executive from one of the big aerospace companies and we suspected she was spying for the Chinese. But she wouldn't admit anything, even under interrogation. Absolutely *would. Not. Crack.* So Becker puts her in a car and drives us to a kindergarten. Turned out, it was the one her child went to."

I saw JD lean forward, that powerful, fatherly concern kicking in.

"Becker pulls the child out of class. It's a little girl, six years old. He takes us all to this dam, where there's a road across the top. Stops the car in the middle, pulls the girl out of the car...." Katharina stopped speaking and just breathed for a few seconds, building up the courage to continue. "He goes to the edge and..." She pressed her lips together. "He holds the girl over the edge and *dangles* her. Two hundred feet up."

JD's face was thunderous. The rest of the team were muttering curses, their faces pale.

"The girl's screaming," grated Katharina. "But what I'm never going to get out of my head is the woman's screams. She was absolutely hysterical. She confessed everything, straight away. She promised him anything, everything, because she knew he wasn't bluffing." Katharina lifted her head and looked at us. "He would have dropped her daughter, if she hadn't broken. That's the sort of person he is."

"Didn't you report him?" asked Gina.

"Of course. And an investigation was launched. But then his higher-ups quietly closed it down. Becker was just too good: he got results and that was all they cared about. By the time they realized what he was, he'd used his power at the BND to gather blackmail information on most of the politicians in Germany. Now everyone's too scared to take him on." She looked around at us. "Why does he want *you?*"

We told her about the mission in Berlin that ended with JD being captured. Gabriel showed her the photo of the guy who'd sold Becker the old Soviet document. "Becker killed him as soon as the deal was done," he told her.

"I know this guy," said Katharina. "Gennady Stasevich. He's Russian mafia. Flew in from New York a week ago with the Malakovs."

"Who?" asked JD.

"Russian mafia family, Vasiliy, his son Luka, Luka's girlfriend, plus some bodyguards and your man Gennady - he's one of Luka's underlings. We're keeping an eye on them while they're in Berlin but it seems like they're just on vacation. Gennady must have tried to do a deal while they were here."

"This guy Luka might know what was in the file that Becker bought," said Gabriel.

"Getting to speak to him won't be easy," said Katharina. "He's surrounded by bodyguards and they're going to be on high alert since Gennady was killed." She thought for a moment. "Luka's taking his girlfriend to the ballet tonight. Someone could try to intercept him there."

"I'll do it," said Danny quietly. Everyone looked at him. "I'm the only one whose photo isn't on the news."

Katharina looked worried. "Everyone else there will be in couples. A man, on his own, trying to get close to Luka...that's exactly what his bodyguards will be looking out for. Especially because you're all..." She hunched her shoulders and grunted and everyone laughed. But she was right: Danny, like all the men, had that hulking former military look. They even walked like soldiers. "You won't even get close," said Katharina.

An idea flickered into life in my head. The fear hit me an instant later, turning my blood to ice water. This was *me*, I couldn't do something like that!

But if I didn't, we wouldn't get to talk to Luka. We'd be at a dead end. The team needed me.

I blurted it out before I could change my mind. "I could go with him." I looked at Katharina. "You said everyone would be in couples."

"*No*," said JD and Danny simultaneously.

Katharina stared at me, amazed. Then she nodded reluctantly. "That *would* help," she allowed.

"No way," said Danny. "This guy's Russian Mafia."

JD nodded. "You're not going anywhere near him." He looked at Katharina. "You're trained. *You* could go with Danny."

Katharina shook her head. "We pulled Luka in for questioning last year. He knows I'm BND, I wouldn't get within twenty meters."

I reached across the table and took JD's hands in mine. As a kid, I'd watched him go off to war so many times, risking himself for his country. It was my turn to put my neck on the line. "Let me do this."

JD scowled. "You shouldn't even be here!"

"But I *am* here," I said. I looked around at the team. Just a few days ago, I'd been so intimidated by them all. But after all that time traveling together, we'd bonded. "And this guy, Becker...he's going to find us, or the police will. We need to throw everything we have at this...including me."

The team slowly turned to look at JD.

JD glowered and huffed and finally sighed in defeat. He looked at Danny. "Can you keep her safe?"

Danny looked at me and I could see the battle going on in his eyes. He wanted to say *no*, he didn't like this plan any more than JD did. But he knew I was right, too. This was our only chance. "'Course," he said at last. "I won't let anything happen to her."

"I need to get to work," said Katharina. "I'll bring you both back something to wear. Erin, I'll need your dress size. She looked at Danny. "I still remember your measurements." Then she smirked. "You may have put on an inch or two on the waist."

"*Oi!*" said Danny.

Katharina was gone for the rest of the day. I imagined her at work, brazenly pretending to search for the fugitives who were holed up in her apartment. How could she do that?! I'd crack in five minutes under the pressure.

I spent the time reading up on Berlin. I'd seen footage of the wall being sledgehammered but I hadn't known much about the city itself, or how bad life had been in East Germany during the Cold War. The more I read, the more ill I started to feel. The Stasi—the secret police —had arrested *a quarter of a million people* as political prisoners. Every apartment block had a designated police informer and they reported everything, even who had stayed the night in someone else's apartment. Anyone found to have "incorrect attitudes" had their home bugged and their career and personal life ruined. And Becker had been raised by someone high up in this organization? No wonder he was so ruthless.

That evening, Katharina arrived home with two garment bags. She gave one to Danny, along with a phone. "Picked you up a burner phone," she told him, as casually as if it was a pint of milk. Then she nodded for me to follow her. "Let me show you what I got you."

She showed me through to her bedroom. It was painted deep red, with an old, free-standing gold-framed mirror and a big skylight that would let you look up from the bed and see the stars above. I was surprised by how romantic it was, for an ass-kicking spy.

She unzipped the garment bag and held up a dress. It was the deep, rich blue of the sky an hour after the sun has gone down. It was a ruched tube that would leave my shoulders bare and hug me from chest to midway down my thighs. Then she showed me the shoes she'd found to go with it: sparkling silver pumps with a four inch heel. I looked down at myself helplessly. I was used to jeans and sneakers. "It'll wear *me,*" I told her.

Katharina shook her head. "You just need a little help."

She sat me down at her dressing table and picked up a pair of hair straighteners, then lifted one eyebrow questioningly. I looked uncertain: I never wore my hair any way but in a braid.

"Do you trust me?" she asked.

I nodded.

She carefully unfastened my braid and went to work. I managed to hold back until she'd made three passes with the tongs and then I asked what I'd been longing to ask since we arrived. "How long were you with Danny for?"

The straighteners paused, then continued. "Three months. Not very long really, but for Danny...."

I nodded. For Danny, it was an eternity. "How did you meet?"

The straighteners swept through my hair for three more strokes before she answered. "We were in Syria together. Germany didn't get involved officially, but the BND was there and Danny was over there with the SAS. We met in a bar, he was..."—she smiled, her eyes distant—" ...charming.``

She saw me looking at her in the mirror and shook her head dismissively. "It wasn't love," she said firmly. "It was...convenient. Just sex. It was a warzone, we were seeing atrocities every day. You seek out any comfort you can."

I said nothing. There are some things even a spy can't hide. After another few swipes with the hair straighteners, she finally met my eyes in the mirror.

"He never loved *me,*" she said. Her German accent made the confession sound even more brutal. "He cared for me. But he never loved me. I didn't think he was capable of love." She looked away. "Then I saw the way he looks at you."

I felt my face flood with heat, embarrassed and thrilled and awkward.

"You'd be good for him," said Katharina. "I want him to be happy." And I believed her. But I could hear the twinge of pain in her voice, too. This woman I'd been so intimidated by...she was envious of *me.*

I shook my head. "We already ended it." I told her about JD and what he'd been through, and the strong bond between him and Danny. "I can't make Danny choose," I told her.

"There's going to come a time when he has to," she said. She lifted the straighteners from my hair. "There."

I hadn't really been paying attention to what she'd been doing. My hair had become a golden waterfall that went most of the way down my back: I couldn't get over how *long* it was, straight. Then Katharina mounted a two-handed attack on it with sprays and it became glossy and flowing, like something out of a shampoo commercial.

I stared at my reflection, stunned, and when she asked if I wanted some help with my make-up, I nodded: I was in good hands, here. She gently took off my glasses, then brought out eye shadow and lipsticks and a whole range of incredibly soft brushes she used to dust color onto my face. "There," she said again. She gave me my glasses back and turned me to the mirror.

How did she do that?! My eyes looked bigger and my *lips,* my lips looked so full and soft. I had cheekbones! *Where did they come from?*

She helped me wiggle into the dress and strap on the shoes. I took an experimental step and teetered sideways. Katharina grabbed me before I fell. "You'll be fine. A little practice."

She showed me over to the full-length mirror. The heels really did incredible things to me: my legs looked endless and the dress's straight neckline made even my small boobs look good. "Thank you," I told her seriously.

She rested a hand between my shoulder blades and said nothing for a moment. Then, "Be good to him." And she marched out of the room before I could see her face.

I was still practicing walking in heels when there was a soft knock at the door. I looked up just as Danny pushed it open.

My heart forgot how to beat.

Danny always looked good in a suit: the smooth fabric next to that rough, working-class charm, the stylishness perfectly complimenting his cockiness. But Danny in a *tuxedo?* That was something else.

Katharina really had known his measurements because the dress shirt hugged the broad curves of his pecs perfectly, turning them into smooth, snow-covered ski slopes I wanted to slalom my hands down. The pants and jacket were so deeply, richly black, they looked as if they'd been cut from pure night. The jacket emphasized the width of his shoulders and strong back and how his upper body tapered down to that tight, powerful core. The pants skimmed his quads and thighs just right, hinting at the brute power of him, and smoothly caressed the hard cheeks of his ass. With his black hair soft and just a little tousled and those deep green eyes glittering and molten....

He looked *rakish,* like he'd lean over the baccarat table and offer a bet for someone's wife. He looked like a rough James Bond. He looked *amazing.*

"*Wow,*" I breathed.

He said nothing and I realized that while I'd been looking at him, he'd been looking at me.

He took a step towards me, then another. On the third step, I realized he wasn't going to stop. I instinctively backed up. By now, he was close enough that I had to look up to look into his eyes and when I did...it felt like I was looking over the rim of a volcano, my whole body bathed in a heat that was primitive and raw. I felt myself respond, the heat soaking through me and waking me, bringing every millimeter of me to trembling awareness. I backed up another step and my calves touched the bed. And then he was touching me, his jacket flaring out to surround me like a cape, his pecs like warm rock against my breasts.

He stared down into my eyes from inches away. I could feel him wrestling for control, his whole body straining under the tuxedo. I stared back, my brain frantically trying to catch up. This was *me,* doing this to him?!

His eyes flicked over my hair, my face, my neck, my breasts... We were so close that I could feel his chest move with every breath he took and he was so on a knife edge that I was almost afraid to breathe. If my chest swelled and my breasts pressed against him a little more, would he just grab me?

I started to say *we can't,* but the second my lips parted on the *w,* his eyes locked onto them and I felt his whole body tense, an animal about to spring. I froze. Not because I didn't want him to kiss me, because I wanted it more than anything else in the world. But if it happened, that would be the end of him and JD. I stood there motionless and pleaded with my eyes.

His nostrils quivered as he slowly inhaled, trying to calm himself. I didn't dare glance away but I knew his hands were making fists.

His chest filled, pressing harder and harder against me. I took a shuddering breath. I was trying to stand firm, to be iron, but the heat of him was melting me, making me buckle and run like butter. He was pressed against me so hard, I was leaning back a little and with the edge of the bed against my calves, I was almost losing my balance. *I could just fall back onto the bed.* That's all it would take. Just let myself fall.

"Your car's here." Katharina's voice from the doorway, carefully neutral.

Danny stared at me for a second longer...then he closed his eyes and slowly exhaled. He took a step back, paused, and only then did he open his eyes. In control again...but only just. He held out his hand.

When I'd volunteered to go with him, I'd been thinking about the mission, the team, helping to get us home. I hadn't thought about the fact we'd be dressed like this, holding hands....

I took his hand and we headed downstairs to the car. The instant his fingers curled around mine, I could feel that connection, the cocky, confident spirit of him throbbing into me, and me flowing into him. With every second we were in contact, the ache in my chest grew.

How were we meant to stay apart when we had to pretend to be together?

49

BECKER

I WAS ALMOST ALONE in the BND headquarters. The others had gone home to wives and husbands, except for a small number who worked directly under me and knew better than to dare to leave before I did.

I was trying to identify the man I'd glimpsed in Siberia, one of the two Americans we hadn't got photos of. I'd only seen his face for a split second when I shot at him, but it was burned into my mind. It wasn't enough to create a photofit, but I'd know him if I saw him. So I was going through photos of former US special forces soldiers of roughly the right age and height. There were thousands, but I could look at one photo every five seconds. I'd been at it for four hours but I wasn't quitting. My father had sometimes done this for entire days, searching for the face of a traitor he'd glimpsed.

And then, quite suddenly, his face filled the screen. British, but seconded to Delta Force. *Danny Briggs.*

I picked up the phone and organized a flash alert. In ten minutes, every police force in Europe would have the photo. Then the online news sites would pick it up, then the TV news. The best part was, he thought he was still anonymous. He didn't know we were coming.

50

ERIN

WE PULLED up outside an imposing building with towering stone columns. Danny stepped out first and offered his hand.

I put my hand in his and his warm fingers curled around mine in a strong, safe grip. I used it to haul myself up out of the car and his arm didn't shift at all, even when I suddenly wobbled in my heels. The brute strength of him made me go weak. For a second, I just wanted to throw myself at him and cling to him, wrap myself around him and feel utterly safe again, like I had in the fisherman's hut. I'd been missing that feeling ever since.

I forced the feelings down inside. *We can't.*

Danny offered me his arm and we joined the flow of people heading up the red-carpeted stairs towards the massive entrance doors. Katharina had been right: everyone was in couples. As we followed the staircase around the bend and joined the crowd waiting to step through the doors, I started to hang back, my eyes darting around nervously. The other women strutted around confidently, like they'd been born in heels. They were tall and elegant and *beautiful* and suddenly it was like prom all over again: I needed to find a corner to stand in, with the other geeks.

Danny looked at me. "Erin?" he asked softly.

I said nothing, embarrassed.

He followed my gaze to the other women and then looked back at me. He blinked, as if surprised.

And then his eyes narrowed and his jaw set. Like he wouldn't allow *anyone* to make me feel bad...even me. He put his finger under my chin and lifted it so that I had to look at him. His eyes flared, the green going from cool to scalding.

"You," he said, "are the most beautiful woman here by a long, *long* way."

My brain rebelled and tried to push the words aside. But they were granite, immovable, and my insecurities crumbled against them. I felt myself stand a little taller. I nodded: *thank you.* And at the same time, a big, hot ache rose inside me. No one had ever made me feel like Danny made me feel. And I'd lost him forever: tonight was just a cruel reminder of what I could never have.

He took my arm again and we moved through the door and into a huge, high-ceilinged lobby with a massive, curving staircase and a glittering chandelier overhead. Waiters were handing out flutes of champagne and it was just like my fantasies of Vegas had been, before I'd found out what it was really like: arm-in-arm with a gorgeous guy in a tuxedo, surrounded by glamour. The ache got worse. *Why can't it be real?* I couldn't stop myself from cinching my arm a little tighter around Danny's. And then his arm pulled a little tighter around mine. For a second, I caught his eye and the look I saw there made the ache ten times worse.

He felt the same way.

He looked away. "Let's find this Malakov guy."

I nodded quickly. We'd both taken a good look at some photos before we left so that we could recognize him. I started searching the faces of the men in the crowd but none of them were him. Meanwhile, Danny was looking the other way. "Anything?" I asked after a minute.

"No." He glanced at the staircase, worried. Some couples were already making their way upstairs, where attendants in red and gold uniforms were checking their tickets. We didn't have tickets. If Malakov had already gone in, we were screwed.

Suddenly, a hush went through the crowd. We turned and saw that three men in suits had entered behind us. They had the same muscled, quietly efficient look as Danny and his team and they took up positions in a fan around the doorway, protecting whoever was following them. The doors opened again and—

I hadn't needed to look at the photos. I would have known the man was Luka Malakov immediately. There was an energy coming from him, cold and brutal and immensely strong: you could feel it in your chest as soon as he walked into the room. I felt like a peasant meeting a king and it wasn't to do with the money, even though supposedly Malakov had billions. It was the power. I wanted to lower my eyes so he didn't notice me because I knew, in my soul, that this man could decide on a whim whether I lived or died. At the same time, I couldn't look away. Danny's cocky smile and green eyes had my heart, but I couldn't deny Luka was gorgeous. He had high cheekbones, a strong, stubble-dusted jaw and eyes that reminded me of the sky back in Siberia, so coldly blue it hurt.

Next to him was a woman with pecan-colored hair in an updo, wearing a bottle-green dress. She didn't look as strongly Russian as him...or even Eastern European, really.

A man followed just behind the couple. He was older than Luka, with a scar running along one side of his face. His eyes scanned the crowd and I heard him mutter an order in Russian to one of the other men in suits. *He must be the head bodyguard.*

The three of them started to move towards the stairs. Danny waited a second so as not to make it too obvious and then began to follow. We had to pass one of the men in suits and his head snapped round as we approached.

We tried to stroll casually but it felt too formal, too fake. "Put your arm around my waist," I whispered.

Danny let go of my arm and slid his arm around my waist, then snugged me into him. My body crushed against him from shoulder to thigh. "Like that?" he asked.

I looked up at him and, despite everything, he gave me one of those cocky Danny grins, and I felt myself light up like a pinball table, just like the first time. I smiled back, and *he* smiled more and—*God, I want this to be real! Why can't this be real?* I wanted it so much.

I suddenly remembered the bodyguard we were meant to be fooling, and realized we were already past him. We'd done it.

We closed in on Luka and his girlfriend. We were halfway up the stairs, now, dangerously close to the point where we'd lose them. Danny walked a little faster and we caught up, but the head bodyguard was still between us and them. Danny accelerated around him and tried to come in from the side—

But the head bodyguard took two quick steps and suddenly he was there, blocking Danny's path. He was big, up close: not as big as Danny and much older, but he had that wiry, tough look, like he'd been fighting wars when Danny was still in diapers. He gave a tiny shake of his head.

Danny put up his hands: *okay, you got me.* "I just want a quick word with your boss."

"Is busy," the head bodyguard told us. His Russian accent carved the words into rough-edged blocks of ice, the *s*'s becoming *z*'s. "With his girlfriend." He nodded at me. "Maybe you should be with *your* girlfriend. Ballet is no place for business."

Meanwhile, Luka and his girlfriend had continued up the stairs. I exchanged panicked looks with Danny. We were going to lose them!

Danny frowned. Filled his lungs and bellowed—

"*OI!*"

The shout bounced off the stone pillars and marble statues. It set the crystals in the chandelier tinkling. Every single person in the lobby turned around, appalled by the blue-collar, uniquely British sound. They stared at Danny as if he'd ripped open his tuxedo and revealed a janitor's uniform underneath.

But it worked. Luka stopped dead and turned around, buying us a few seconds. He glanced at us, then at the head bodyguard. "Yuri?" he asked. *What is this?*

The head bodyguard—Yuri, apparently—scowled at us, clearly

not happy that we'd caused a scene. He grabbed Danny's lapels and started to muscle him back down the stairs. The other three bodyguards were rushing up from below. It was all smoothly practiced and professional: Yuri turned and nodded curtly to Luka: *don't worry, we've got this.*

Except...he hadn't reckoned on Danny. As Yuri turned back to him, Danny punched him in the face, fast and brutal. Yuri staggered back and Danny charged up the stairs after Luka with me by his side.

Luka whirled around to face us and stepped protectively in front of his girlfriend. However evil he was, apparently he really cared about her.

We reached him just as the three bodyguards from downstairs grabbed Danny. But now we were close enough to be heard. "I know who killed your boy Gennady," Danny told him.

Yuri stalked up the stairs, his white shirt soaked with blood from a broken nose. He grabbed one of Danny's arms and wrenched it up behind his back. "*Outside!*" he snapped.

Luka held up his hand: *wait.* "*Who?*" he barked.

Danny didn't flinch. He just gave one of those cocky grins. "Ah, well, see, I need something from you, too," he told Luka.

"Is not negotiation!" thundered Luka. "Gennady was a friend. Tell me or Yuri will break arm."

Yuri hitched Danny's arm higher and Danny grunted in pain, starting to sweat. But he still wouldn't back down. "Yeah, well I've got mates, too. And they're in trouble and the only way I can get 'em out of it is with your help. So how about we go somewhere and talk?"

Luka leaned in until their faces were a foot apart The two men glared at each other, the air almost crackling between them, neither one willing to back down. And despite how scared I was for him, I felt that *pull* again, stronger than ever. The way Danny stood up to the universe, cockily confident even when everything was against him...

Luka's expression softened slightly, becoming a look of grudging respect. He said something in Russian and Danny was hustled down the stairs and along a hallway, with the rest of us following behind. I found myself walking next to Luka's girlfriend, who gave me a shy smile and a kind of awkward half shrug. She didn't seem like a mobster's girlfriend, who I'd always imagined as having three-inch nails and leopard skin skirts.

We followed Danny and Yuri through a door and into a big, black-and-white tiled room with marble statues. It was so ornate, it wasn't until I saw a urinal that I realized this was the men's room. One of the bodyguards leaned against the door to stop anyone coming in.

"Now talk!" snapped Luka.

Danny nodded. He showed Luka the photos from the parking garage in Berlin. "Your mate Gennady sold a file to this bloke. As soon as he had the file, he murdered Gennady. His name's Otto Becker. He's after me and my mates. He's BND."

"A spy," said Luka in disgust. He thought for a moment. "You and your friends...you are the ones on TV?"

Danny nodded slowly. "But we didn't kill those German soldiers. Becker framed us. You and me, we're on the same side."

Luka scowled at him. "I am not sure about that." He thought for a while. "But I am not sure you are enemy, either."

"What was in that file?" asked Danny softly.

Luka sighed. Then he turned to his girlfriend and talked in rapid-fire Russian.

She stepped forward and translated effortlessly. Her accent was American, soft and gentle: the Midwest, maybe. "Gennady went to collect on a gambling debt in New York. The man couldn't pay but he was a collector of Cold War antiques. He had something he said was valuable, a file lost in a plane crash years ago, information that was still valuable today. The names of some Soviet generals and the names of women."

"Women they'd had affairs with?" I asked.

Luka's girlfriend translated and Luka nodded. "We assume so," his girlfriend told us.

"Do you have a copy of the file?" Danny asked.

Luka sent a photo of a printed document to Danny's phone.

Danny nodded his thanks. "Look, me and my mates are up against it, here. We both want Becker. We could do with a hand."

"You are wanted as terrorists," said Luka. "I am not in business of going up against governments." He studied Danny for a while, then sighed. "But I am not in business of letting the murder of a friend go unpunished, either." He said something to Yuri. Yuri, still bleeding, pulled out an expensive-looking cream business card and gave it to me. There was no name, just a number. "My direct line," said Luka.

We nodded gratefully and the Russians withdrew. Danny and I looked at each other and sighed in relief. We'd done it!

We slipped out of the men's room and down the hallway. We walked into the lobby arm in arm...and stopped dead.

Four German police officers were standing there, talking to one of the ticket attendants. She was talking and gesticulating, pointing upstairs to where Danny had punched Yuri. One of the police officers showed her a printed picture and asked her something. We didn't need to speak German to catch the meaning. *Are you sure it was him?*

The picture was of Danny.

At that second, one of the cops glanced our way. His eyes widened when he saw Danny. "*Halt!*" he yelled, pulling his gun.

Danny grabbed my hand. "*Run!*"

51

DANNY

I'D JUST STARTED to relax after our run-in with Luka Malakov. I could feel my pulse slowing...and then suddenly, there was a gun pointed at us and the adrenaline was slamming through my system again. My brain took a while to get turned around but the rest of me knew what to do. I'd told Erin to run, grabbed her hand and we were moving while my brain was still thinking about how tempting her bare shoulders were in that dress.

When my brain finally got into gear, it started figuring out where to go. Up the stairs? We didn't have tickets but I could muscle us past the ticket attendants. But then what? There was no way out, up there, and the police would run us down eventually. The exits were all down here, but they'd have security guards on them. We needed another option, an exit not for the public.

We raced down the hallway, the police still yelling at us to *Halt!* I saw a door that said *Nur für Personal* which sounded like somewhere we weren't supposed to go. It was locked. I kicked it and the lock gave way with the sound of splintering wood. Some sort of office area: everyone looked up in shock as we burst in. We ran straight through and into another hallway, with staff schedules pinned to the wall: we were definitely where the public wasn't supposed to be. Behind us, I could hear the police sprinting through the office. We burst through another door—

A castle thundered across my view, painted stonework a foot from my face. I skidded to a stop and then had to pull Erin tight up against me as a house swept by right where she'd been standing. We were backstage, and they were moving the scenery. We ran again, towards a dark, quiet area. I was panting, now, and Erin was really struggling in her heels.

We ran into the dark and then I suddenly slowed: I'd thought this part of backstage was empty but suddenly I realized there were people there, ballerinas waiting silently in the darkness. A few of them hissed at us in German, furious.

Then music started to play and light broke across my feet, gradually rising up my legs. I looked to the left and saw a huge velvet curtain rising. We were *on the stage!*

We ran on, clearing the stage just as the curtain finished coming up. We burst through a curtain, then another one—

Women sitting at mirrors, others being helped into costumes, some of them half-dressed. They shrieked and tried to cover themselves as they saw me. We kept running, our lungs burning, now. Behind us, confused laughter from the audience: the police must be running across the stage.

We burst out into another hallway and there, at the end, was what I'd been looking for: an unguarded fire exit. We crashed through it, stumbled out into the darkness and pouring rain. An alleyway. Perfect. Now we just needed to—

There was the metal click of a gun being cocked. I looked round to see a cop, his gun up and ready to fire.

He was pointing it right at Erin.

My heart froze in a split second, like someone had just switched my veins to pumping ice water. "No no no!" I threw my hands in the air and Erin did the same.

The cop looked barely old enough to shave. His hands were trembling, the muzzle of the gun dancing around Erin's chest. His radio was squawking a non-stop barrage of orders. He was overloaded, panicked. He was going to fire.

I imagined the bullet punching into Erin's body, the bloodstain spreading across the blue dress. I'd never known fear like it. "*No!*" I jumped in front of her. "*No!*"

The cop's arms tensed and I winced. What if the bullet went through me and hit her?

Nothing happened.

The cop and I both stared at each other. I saw him pull the trigger a second time. Nothing.

The safety catch. The poor kid had probably never fired his gun since the academy. We both realized at the same time but I was a second faster. I lunged forward and punched him, then pulled the gun from his slack fingers and threw it away into the darkness.

Police sirens were wailing towards us. Erin took a second to finally unstrap the heels and pull them off her feet, then I grabbed her hand and we ran. I thought the fear would ease but the ice around my heart constricted, crushing it. The scene wouldn't stop replaying in my head, the muzzle of the gun pointing right at Erin—

We ran down the alley and turned into another, water soaking our legs as we splashed through puddles. Another turn. Another. The wail of the sirens dropped away behind us....

We stumbled to a stop, both of us doubled over and panting. But before I'd even gotten my breath back, I was grabbing Erin and pushing her back against the wall. The fear had me, tightening in brutal, cold throbs until my whole chest ached. "You're okay," I panted, tracing my hands along her waist. "You're okay, you're okay." I wasn't asking so much as reassuring myself. But when she nodded, the relief buckled my knees. *What's wrong with me?* I'd been in bad situations before, I'd even been in danger *with her* before—

But never like that. I'd never seen her life nearly snuffed out in a second before, saved by dumb luck. My hands moved up to her cheeks and I held her face between my hands. "You're okay." I kept repeating it, a mantra. "You're okay."

I'd almost lost her. And that moment was like a flash of lightning in the dark, lighting up everything that had been hiding in stark, clean detail.

I stood there panting, staring at her. She stared up at me, tired and shivering and brave and wonderful.

It was impossible. That part of me was broken, had been since I was a kid. But it had happened anyway. I didn't just care for her or like her or want to protect her.

I was in love with her.

52

ERIN

BAREFOOT, I was *much* smaller than him and he hulked over me protectively, little jewels of rain falling from his wet hair. He cupped my face in his hands, panting, and I'd never felt so protected. But this was more than him wanting to look after me. This was way beyond lust. He looked helpless.

I understood because I felt the same way. I stared up at him, *hoping...*

But then he closed his eyes and turned away. "They'll be sealing off the area," he said. "Come on, we need some wheels."

We hurried on, both of us soaked through and shivering. The next alley led onto a quiet street. Danny found an aging Mercedes and went to work on the lock. Less than twenty seconds and the door was open. We jumped in...but, as soon as the doors were closed, it was awkwardly quiet and private. Just the two of us, sitting a foot apart. I saw his eyes go to my bare legs: my dress had ridden up a little as I jumped in. He looked up and caught my eye and we stared at each other.

Since Siberia, the pull was a thousand times stronger. I knew, now, exactly how he'd touch me. I wanted his hands on my hips, his fingers digging into my ass and squeezing just right. I knew how his kisses would feel, on my lips and my neck and my inner thighs. I knew the sounds he'd make and the sounds *I'd* make. I needed him. But I could fight all that. I could push it down inside.

What I couldn't handle was when he looked at me like he'd looked at me in the alley. When he made me feel special. When he looked so fiercely protective. Because those instants were snapshots from a future we could never have, Polaroids with razor-sharp edges that cut me to the bone every time I looked at them...and I couldn't *stop* looking at them.

This time, it was me who turned away. I couldn't bear to look into those absinthe eyes any longer. "How did you get so good at stealing cars?" I asked, trying to keep my voice light.

He reached under the steering wheel and started cracking open the plastic so he could get at the wiring. I dug in my purse, pulled out a flashlight and shone it for him and he nodded in thanks. He told me about growing up poor in London, about the gang he'd been part of. "Probably sounds stupid, now," he muttered as he stripped wires. "But nicking cars, driving them fast...that's all we had. It let me be part of something."

His voice tightened on the last few words. Barely perceptible, I only noticed it because we'd spent so much time talking over the last week. Being part of something was important to him, more than he wanted to admit.

There was a spark and the engine roared into life. Danny hit the gas, speeding through the dark streets as fast as he could without attracting attention, heading out of the city center. We turned the next corner and joined slow-moving traffic. Up ahead, a police van was stopped by the side of the road. Two officers were unloading barricades from it, ready to block the road.

The traffic ahead slowed. "Come on, come on," whispered Danny.

But the cars moved slower, slower.... The police officers had the barricades in their arms, now, and were just waiting for a gap in the traffic to set them up. As the traffic slowed to a crawl, I saw one officer look at the other: *Now?*

"No no no, *please,*" I whispered.

The traffic sped up and we slid past the police. They stepped into the road behind us and set down the barrier, stopping the traffic. Both of us slumped in our seats in relief. I turned the heater up to max, hoping to get warm, but it was broken. *Great.*

We drove well out of the center, then pulled into a quiet side street and called the team. I could imagine them all in Katharina's apartment, huddled around the phone. "Glad you're okay," JD rumbled when we'd brought them up to speed and sent them the photo Luka gave us.

We heard Katharina typing rapidly in the background. "I'm checking the names from the file. They *were* all Soviet generals. Five of them, each one based in a different city. But the date on the file is 1981. Whatever they did with these women, it happened over forty years ago. How can Becker use this as blackmail? The generals are all dead. Who would even care that they had affairs?"

"Maybe it wasn't affairs." I recognized Bradan's Irish accent. "Maybe it was...I dunno, secret sex parties or something, and the government killed the women to stop word of it getting out. The coordinates could be where the bodies are buried. Becker's not interested in the *generals*, he wants to blackmail the person behind the murders: someone in the German government, maybe."

"We need to talk to someone," said Gabriel. "Find out what the hell this is all about."

"One of the generals was based in East Berlin," said Katharina, "back before the wall fell." The keyboard rattled again. "General Sauer. He has a son, right here in the city." She read off an address.

Danny studied the map on his phone. "That's not far from here."

"No," said JD. "It's too risky. The police know your faces, now. Come back to the apartment."

I spoke up. "We can't just huddle in the apartment forever. We need to get some answers."

JD went quiet. Danny looked across at me with something like awe, and I flushed, surprised at myself. When did *I* get all gung ho?

"Be careful," JD told us at last.

And we set off into the night.

53

ERIN

THE DOOR OPENED, but only a crack. I couldn't see much of the man, but he seemed to be dressed all in black. Silver eyebrows frowned at me. "Ja?"

Now that we weren't running around, the cold was really getting to me. It was winter, I was in a short, soaking wet dress and bare feet. "Please, I need to speak to you," I begged, hugging myself. "About your father."

A second face peeked through the crack: a woman, also with silver hair. When she saw me standing there shivering, she made the exact same cry of concern my mom would have, and opened the door wide. Then she saw Danny looming behind me and hesitated. I quickly took Danny's hand: *it's okay, we're together.*

The woman looked at Danny, then at me, then clasped her hands together and gave me an *oh, they're so sweet* smile and beckoned us in. We hurried in out of the cold and the woman showed us through to a small living room. Two children—grandchildren, from their ages— were playing on the floor and the heating must have been on full blast because it was blissfully warm. The man followed us in. He was very tall and I saw now that he was dressed in priest's robes.

The woman fussed around us, first passing us towels and then bringing a blanket to wrap around me. I told them a cut-down version of what was going on: a file had shown up with information about some generals, and we were worried someone might try to blackmail them. The man told us that the woman was his sister and that yes, General Sauer had been their father. "But what could they blackmail us about? My father was a good man."

I looked at Danny: this was going to be the delicate part. He started talking to the kids, gently distracting them while I leaned forward and showed the man and woman the photo of the file. "There's a woman's name next to your father's name. *Svetlana.*" I swallowed. I wasn't good with people but I did my best to be subtle. "Could she be someone he...knew?"

The man shook his head. "My father didn't have affairs. And he didn't visit prostitutes."

"You were close?"

The man shook his head. "Not always. He wanted me to follow him into the military." He indicated his robes. "I chose a different path. But we made peace, as he got older. He even had this made for me." He touched the crucifix that hung around his neck.

I glanced over at Danny. He was on all fours on the rug, talking to the kids about the house they were building from Lego bricks, going down on his belly to look through the windows. They didn't speak the same language but he was making himself understood by miming. He panted and made dog ears with his hands: *is there room in the house for a dog?* The kids laughed and he did a giraffe, then an elephant. The woman was watching him, too, and gave me an approving nod. *He'd make a good father, this one.*

I knew he would. It made the gray emptiness inside me ring and ache. He *would* make a great father. But it wouldn't be with me.

I looked at the woman. "Did your father ever mention a Svetlana to you?"

She shook her head...but then looked doubtful.

"Anything," I said quickly. "Even just a mention."

Danny looked round, listening intently.

The woman sighed. "He used that name once. When I was a

child. He was drunk, and I was on his knee. He said he had to take care of Svetlana, because she was his sister." She shook her head. "He didn't *have* any sisters, he was an only child." She shrugged. "He was very drunk. It's probably nothing. Svetlana is a common name."

We thanked them and left. Twenty minutes later, we were back at Katharina's apartment. We brought the others up to speed and then we all sat in a circle, trying to figure it out. The room fell silent as we racked our brains in grim silence. We were at a dead end.

A heavy knock at the door made us all jump. Katharina frowned: it was too late for visitors. She put a finger to her lips, then walked over to the door. She put her eye to the spyhole and then jerked back in shock. She turned to us in panic but before she could speak, there was another pounding on the door and a voice yelled for her to open up.

I recognized the voice from Siberia.

Otto Becker was at the door.

54

DANNY

KATHARINA POINTED TO THE WINDOW. Then she yelled through the door to Becker, trying to stall him.

We had to move fast, but we had to be silent, too. We crept over to the window and opened it, wincing at every tiny sound. Gabriel and Gina went out onto the old iron fire escape but then Gabriel started pointing urgently back inside. *What?* JD mouthed at him.

Gabriel had to mime firing a gun before we got it. All of our weapons, equipment and clothes were spread out around the apartment. If Becker searched the place and found those, he'd know we'd been there.

We started racing around grabbing bags and clothes and passing them out to Gabriel and Gina. Meanwhile, Katharina was stripping out of her clothes and pulling on a bathrobe. I realized what she'd been saying to Becker to buy time: *I was in the shower.* Becker pounded on the door again. Katharina gestured frantically for us to hurry.

We grabbed everything we could see and hurried out of the window. Blue lights were flashing in the alley below but fortunately none of the cops were looking up. As I eased the window closed, I saw Katharina pick up a glass of water and pour it over her hair to wet it. Our eyes met for a second. *I'm sorry,* I mouthed.

Go, she mouthed back.

The alley was out, so we hurried up the fire escape to the roof. A bitter wind was howling across the rooftops and everyone was shivering. But it was worst for Erin: she hadn't had a chance to change out of her cocktail dress yet and was standing in inch-deep snow in her bare feet. I whipped off my tuxedo jacket and put it around her shoulders. I looked down into those delicate blue eyes and the protective urge gripped me so tight...she was scared, and cold, and all I wanted to do was hug her to me and keep her warm. But JD was *right there.*

I wanted to scream into the night. I wanted to punch something. I had to settle for closing my eyes for a second while I gripped Erin's shoulders. When I opened my eyes, Erin nodded to me. She understood. But how much longer could we go on like this?

I crept over to JD, walking carefully—the whole roof was covered in ice. JD was kneeling next to a skylight, looking down on Katharina's living room. Becker was marching around, demanding answers. He was waving my picture so I guessed he'd somehow found out that she and I used to be together. Katharina was keeping her cool, shrugging and acting like it was no big deal. *It was years ago, I haven't seen him since.*

Becker bent and pointed to the coffee cups on the table. Katharina shrugged again, probably telling him that she'd had friends round.

Becker straightened and slapped Katharina across the face. He hit her so hard she stumbled and fell against a cabinet.

I was on my feet in a split second, reaching for my gun. Gabriel and Cal grabbed an arm each and hung onto me, then gently but firmly pulled me back down out of sight, in case Becker looked up. I crouched there, panting and seething.

Katharina clambered shakily to her feet. She was clearly denying everything, covering for us. Becker yelled loud enough that we could hear it through the skylight, calling her a bitch and a whore. Then he punched her, splitting her lip open. And still she shook her head. *Why is she doing this?*

But I knew why. Because she still had feelings for me. That's why I'd ended it, because I couldn't take the guilt of knowing that she loved me when I couldn't love her back. Years on, she was still loyal. And now I knew what it was like to love someone. I wanted Katharina to find someone who felt about her the way I felt about Erin.

Becker grabbed Katharina by the hair. That was *it*: we had to go down there and stop this. But just as I got to my feet again, one of Becker's men walked into the room carrying a magazine from one of our guns. It must have fallen out of a backpack. *Shit.*

Becker took out handcuffs and cuffed Katharina, then pushed her towards the door in her bathrobe, not even letting her get dressed. I jumped to my feet again. JD grabbed my arm. I turned and glared at him. "They'll charge her with treason!" I hissed.

JD's big blue eyes were sorrowful but, as always, he was keeping calm, *thinking* when I would have gone off half-cocked. "We can't help her if we get caught," he whispered. "The only way to clear her name is to take Becker down."

I scowled, but then my shoulders slumped. He was right. But now what would we do? We'd lost our only sanctuary *and* we'd lost Katharina's help.

I looked down through the skylight as Becker led Katharina out.

He turned to close the door, glanced up...and saw me standing there.

55

DANNY

WE RAN. The whole roof was covered with ice but we moved as fast as we dared, climbing over pipes and sliding down sloping sections of roof. We reached an air conditioning duct as tall as an SUV and Erin was too short to scramble over it. I picked her up by the waist and passed her up to JD, who helped her up and let her down on the other side.

Behind us, we could hear Becker and his men pouring out onto the fire escape and climbing up to the roof. We ran faster, slipping on the ice and staggering under the weight of our packs. I grabbed Erin's hand and hauled her along. Snow crunched underfoot and I winced as I remembered her bare feet.

Ahead of us, the apartment building ended and it was too far to jump to the next building. But some construction work was being done and Bradan and Gabriel grabbed one of the planks, using it to bridge the gap. Gina walked carefully across, then Gabriel. When it was my turn, I looked down and felt my stomach drop: we were four stories up and the plank was narrow and crusted with ice. When I took the first step over the void, my body tried to rebel: it took everything I had to keep my feet moving and when I made it to the other side, I went weak with relief.

Erin went next. JD held her hand as she got up onto the plank. I could see her feet sliding a little on the ice and my stomach lurched: her feet were probably so cold, she could barely feel them. But she managed it, and as soon as she was close enough to grab, I took her hand and steadied her from our side. JD followed, then Bradan and Cal. There was no way to do it fast: only one person could be on the plank at a time. And that meant that by the time Cal made it across, Becker and his men were almost on us.

Last to go was Colton. He put one foot on the plank, looked down...and froze.

Oh shit. I'd forgotten about Colton's fear of heights. "Come on, mate," I called, relaxed and cheery. "It's okay."

But it wasn't. Colton stared down at the drop and I could see his chest moving as he began to pant in fear. Behind him, Becker and his men were sprinting across the roof.

"Come on, pal, time to go," called JD.

Even Gina dropped her usual grumpiness and was supportive. "You got this, big guy,"

Becker was sprinting. He really *was* in good shape, moving as fast as someone in their thirties. Colton had to go *now*.

I saw the big bounty hunter's mouth moving as he silently cursed up a storm, furious with himself. Then he suddenly charged forward and shot across the plank, the wood creaking under his weight. He did it so fast, the plank rocked and twisted, and Colton jumped the last few feet, smacking into JD and me and taking us down in a heap. But it didn't matter: he was across. I patted the panting Colton on the back. "Well done, mate," I said sincerely. *I'd* been scared and I didn't have his fear of heights. That had taken real guts.

Gabriel and Bradan shoved the plank and it tumbled down into the alley, cutting Becker off just as he arrived.

Becker drew his gun and opened fire. We ducked down behind the parapet as bullets whistled over our heads, then crouch-ran to the end of the building, where we climbed down a fire escape. By the time Becker and his men got back down to the street, we'd melted into the night.

But now what? We all looked at each other, worried. We were thousands of miles from home, wanted fugitives, abandoned by our country. *All* of our faces, except Erin's, were known by the police. Worse, they knew now we were in Berlin, so they could concentrate their search. And with Katharina in custody, we had no place to hide.

We trudged through the city, keeping to the shadows, until we found a group of homeless people who'd made a camp under a railway bridge. We sat down with them, hoping we'd blend in better than if we just stood around on the street. I dug in Erin's pack and got out the military boots she'd worn in Siberia so that she could finally have something on her feet. "You okay?" I asked as she pulled them on.

She nodded. God, she was so brave. I just wanted to pull her into my arms and hug her tight. But I forced myself to keep my distance.

Gina was glowering at the ground. At first, I thought she was just frustrated: she's only really happy when she's flying and she'd been forced to be a fifth wheel ever since Siberia. But it was more than that. "This is all my fault," she muttered. "We'd have been safe home, if we hadn't crashed."

"You did everything you could," I told her firmly. "We're all alive."

"Even if we *had* got back to the US, Becker still would have killed those guards," said Gabriel. "We'd have been arrested as soon as we stepped off that flight home and we'd be in jail right now. At least we're free."

"If it's anybody's fault, it's mine," said JD. "You all got into this trying to get me out."

I looked across at JD. "If I'd spotted that security guard in the parking garage, you'd never have got captured in the first place." I was still beating myself up for that. Especially because part of the reason I'd been distracted was that I'd been brooding about Erin. *None of this would have happened if I'd just forgotten about her when JD warned me off.*

I looked at Erin...and however mad I was with myself, I knew that was impossible. I wouldn't be able to forget about her as long as I lived.

"How about we just agree it's that motherfucker Becker's fault?" grunted Colton, and everyone muttered agreement. After what we'd seen him do to Katharina, we all had a new hatred of him.

Katharina. I sighed. Now I'd put *two* innocent people in danger. This mission got worse and worse.

"God, I'm hungry," said Gabriel.

"Let me check my flight suit," said Gina. "I usually have some energy bars in the pockets."

As she started digging in her pack for it, JD turned to me. He looked as helpless as I felt. "Any ideas?" he asked.

I sighed. "We could call Luka Malakov. See if he can make any sense of this."

JD immediately shook his head. "I don't want us getting involved with the Bratva."

There was a reason why Kian had put him in charge of this bunch of reprobates. We needed someone honest, what the Americans would call a *straight shooter,* to keep us in line. But....I threw up my hands in defeat. "It's the only idea I've got."

We looked around at the rest of the team. Everyone looked broken and beaten. Even Gabriel shrugged, and he *always* had a plan. JD nodded tiredly.

I asked Erin for Luka's number and she dutifully held up the business card while I dialed. By now, Gina had found a couple of energy bars and was dividing them up. But that had attracted attention. A homeless guy in his sixties with straggly white hair shambled over and stared longingly at the energy bar. He looked as if he hadn't eaten in a week. Gina sighed and gave it to him and he backed away, nodding his thanks. That left us with one bar between eight people. Gina got out her knife and started carefully cutting it up.

Luka answered the phone. With his girlfriend acting as translator, I told him what we'd learned. "Any idea why Becker would want to blackmail long-dead generals?" I asked. "Or if there was some government cover up, back in the eighties, and they murdered those women?"

I waited while Luka's girlfriend translated. "No idea," said Luka.

I stared off into the darkness, my mind racing. *Think!* I had to figure this out. A little voice reminded me that I was just a dumb squaddie, just that kid from a poor neighborhood who failed most of his exams. I wasn't a thinker, like Gabriel. I was good for chatting up women and downing shots and that was about it.

But if I didn't work it out, we were all going to jail. *Think, you stupid bastard, think!*

"I am sorry," muttered Luka. "Is all?" I could tell he was getting ready to hang up. *Think!*

"Hey!" Gina slapped Colton's hand away from the cut-up energy bar. "That's *my* piece!"

A memory glowed at the back of my brain, something familiar but upside down.

My piece.

My sister.

The general had said Svetlana was his sister, but he didn't have any sisters. What if, what if....

"*Sisters!*" I yelled into the phone. Everyone looked up. "The five women are sisters! The general wasn't saying she was *his sister,* he was saying she was *his* sister. There were five sisters and each general was responsible for one of them, each had to take care of *his* sister!"

I sat there panting for a second. The other end of the call had gone quiet. "Luka?" I asked. "Does that mean something to you?"

There was a long pause. Then, "Tell me where you are," said Luka. "I send car for you."

"A car? Why?"

"Because..." Luka sighed. "You need to speak to my father."

56

ERIN

LESS THAN FIFTEEN MINUTES LATER, two black Mercedes pulled up to the curb. JD, Danny, Gabriel and I got into one car while the rest of the team piled into the other. Our car was driven by Yuri, the head bodyguard we'd run into at the ballet. His nose was swollen and red, and a bandage was taped across it. "Sorry about that," Danny told him. "Put some ice on it, it helps."

Yuri glared at him. "Is not my first rodeo."

The car swept us off into the night. After the homeless camp, the luxurious, soft leather interior felt otherworldly. I let out a long sigh and just...flopped. After the theater and nearly getting shot and running through alleys and the rooftops and the homeless camp, I was *done,* exhausted and cold and wet through. Danny was next to me and I laid my head on his shoulder. Immediately, the world was a better place. I slipped an arm around him and snuggled in, feeling my whole body relax.

His hand smoothed my hair...and then he gently lifted my head from him.

I glanced up at him, thinking that maybe my hair was cold and wet and I'd soaked his neck, or that he was just lifting me for a second while he got comfortable and then he was going to let me snuggle in again. But no: he was looking at me sadly. He slowly shook his head.

Oh God. I'd forgotten. I was so burned out and exhausted, I'd forgotten that I couldn't do that. I'd just seen him there, so big and warm, and he'd looked so comforting...my body had cuddled in before my brain knew anything about it. Luckily, JD was up front with Yuri, staring out of the window. I quickly pulled my arm back and sat up straight. Danny and I exchanged looks and I could see the yearning in his eyes. All he wanted to do was grab me and hold me close. God, this was torture!

And it was only going to get worse. Because I realized right then that I'd finally found the burrow I'd been hunting for my entire life, and it wasn't in Texas or Vegas. It wasn't a place at all. It was a person. If I was with Danny, I was safe. But he was the one person I couldn't be with. And so it didn't matter where I went in the world or how hard I hunted, I'd never feel that securely protected ever again.

A few moments later, we turned into an underground parking garage...one where Yuri had to show his ID before the barrier would open. The second car arrived and Yuri showed all eight of us to a private elevator guarded by two more bodyguards. They relieved the team of their guns and patted us down before allowing us into the elevator. We were whisked up to the top floor where another two bodyguards led us down a hallway to the penthouse. Luka's dad took his security seriously.

Huge double doors of polished oak opened onto a double height living room. A fire roared in an oversized fireplace, leather armchairs and couches the color of blood arranged around it, and a large bookshelf was filled with old, green-and-gold books, the titles all in Russian. The place was incredible and this wasn't even Vasiliy's main home.

Luka was reclining on a couch, his arms spread along the back. His girlfriend was sitting sideways, leaning back against him so that her head was on his chest. It looked so idyllically cozy and special that my chest ached. I *want that.*

Luka's girlfriend jumped up and hurried over to me. "God, look at you! You've been out there dressed like this?" She shook her head. "Let me see if I can find you something to wear."

Luka got up and stretched, then came over. "I take you to see father," he told us.

His broken English made me think of something and I caught Luka's girlfriend before she left. "Won't we need you to translate?"

She shook her head. "No, Vasiliy's English is excellent. And getting better." She gave Luka a sly look. "*He* has been practicing to impress his American girlfriend."

Luka marched over to her, grabbed her by the wrist and growled a question at her in Russian. I saw her chest rise as her breathing sped up. She playfully stuck her tongue out at him.

He grinned, leaned down and whispered in her ear, a long string of Russian. I caught Gina's eye. Neither of us could understand what he was saying, but we caught the tone, and when it was said in that growly voice...I felt myself flush and looked away quickly and Gina did the same. Luka's voice had the same effect on his girlfriend: I could actually see her legs weaken and her eyes go big. She hurried away and Luka chuckled, then motioned for us to follow him.

Vasiliy Malakov was in his study, sitting behind a polished wooden desk and writing what seemed to be a letter. He smoothly swept the piece of paper into a desk drawer and stood.

It was easy to see where Luka got his looks. Vasiliy was in his sixties but he was nearly as big and muscular as his son and had the same high cheekbones and strong jaw. He offered JD his hand. JD hesitated...then reluctantly shook it.

"The five sisters," Danny blurted. "Who were they? Prostitutes? A ring of spies?"

Vasiliy smiled. "A colorful notion," he said. "But no." His English really was good: heavily accented, but as smooth as malt liquor. He walked over to a side table, where a chess board was set up. "It is the winter of 1981," he told us. "Deep in the Cold War. The Soviet Government worried that NATO would launch a land invasion of the USSR." He swept the black pieces across the board with his palm.

"As a last line of defense, five nuclear bombs were given to five trusted generals, one in each of five Soviet-controlled cities." He laid five white pawns along the edge of the black ones. "The generals were given full responsibility for the bombs: if their city fell, it was their job to retrieve the bomb from its hiding place and use it on the advancing troops. Each bomb was small enough to fit in a suitcase but powerful enough to wipe out ten city blocks. The whole plan was a closely-guarded secret. Only the generals knew where their bombs were hidden, plus a few select people in the government. Each bomb was named after a woman and the plan was codenamed *Five Sisters.*"

"1989 came, the Berlin Wall fell, the USSR collapsed. It was chaos. The last thing on anyone's mind was dismantling Cold War doomsday plans. Eventually, some years ago, the Russian government quietly retrieved the bombs." Vasiliy picked up four of the white pawns, then paused dramatically. "Or at least, it retrieved *four* of them. One of the generals went to his grave without telling anyone where his bomb was hidden. And the only record of all the bombs' locations was lost years before."

"They couldn't find the one under East Berlin," I croaked. Fear had made my throat tight.

"My father told me this story years ago," said Luka. "I'd forgotten about it, until you mentioned sisters."

Vasiliy sighed and started laying out shot glasses. "The whole thing was just a rumor, a tale told by arms dealers after too much vodka. I wasn't sure it was true...until now."

JD had gone pale. "You're telling me there's been a nuclear bomb hidden under Berlin for over forty years?" he demanded. "*That's* what Becker is after? *Why?*"

"We heard him in Siberia," said Danny. "He has a buyer lined up. He's going to sell it."

Gabriel whistled. "Do you have any idea how much a suitcase nuke would be worth on the black market?"

"Twenty million," said Vasiliy, pouring vodka into the glasses.

"And when some terrorist uses it, on New York, or Paris, or London," said Danny, "Someone'll work out it was an old Soviet nuke. There's nothing to lead back to Becker. Except—"

"Except us," I said. "As soon as you saw him buying that file, we became a threat to him. That's why he's been after us all this time. That's why he wants us dead or discredited. We're the only ones who know he's involved."

"We're screwed," muttered Gina, reaching for one of the shot glasses. "The only way to prove any of this is with the nuke. But he's probably already dug it up."

I thought hard, then shook my head and turned to her. "Maybe not." Everyone looked at me and I flushed, not used to being the center of attention. "Look, when we heard him in Siberia, he was telling his buyer that he didn't have the nuke yet. But by then, he'd already had the file for days, even since he bought it. Why not dig the nuke up straight away? Unless—"

"—he couldn't find it," Danny finished for me.

"If we can find it first, we've got the proof we need," said JD. "We take a rogue nuke to the German government, we'll be heroes, not fugitives."

Vasiliy nodded. "You should go to the coordinates and see what's happening. I will lend you my cars so you can be discreet. The police are still looking for you."

JD frowned. "What's the catch?"

Vasiliy raised an eyebrow. "You do not trust me?" He didn't seem offended.

"You're *Bratva*," said JD. "And an arms dealer. Most of the time, I'm trying to stop people like you. And you said it yourself: a suitcase nuke is worth twenty million."

"You think I will double-cross you, steal the bomb and sell it myself," said Vasiliy.

"The thought had crossed my mind," rumbled JD. The two of them stared at each other: the father figure of the Malakov family and the father figure of *our* weird little family.

"You may not believe it," said Vasiliy, "but there are some things that even *people like me* won't touch. A nuclear bomb going off in a city is bad for everyone. You can have it. Take it to the police. Clear your names."

"And in return?" asked JD cautiously.

"This man, Becker," said Vasiliy. "He murdered one of ours. You put him in jail or you put him in the ground." He raised a shot glass questioningly. *Yes?*

JD picked up a shot glass. *"That,"* he said, "we can do." And he clinked glasses with Vasiliy. We all downed our shots. The vodka raced down my throat, a silky rush of fire and then a blossoming heat that warmed me from the inside out.

We were met in the living room by Luka's girlfriend. "Try these," she said, passing me a pile of clothes.

Just the idea of finally getting out of the soaked, freezing cocktail dress made me groan in relief. *"Thank you!"* I said. I went to hug her, then stopped short, not wanting to soak her. "I'm Erin."

"Arianna."

A few moments later, I was in knee-high brown boots, jeans, and a sweater and feeling much, much better. We climbed into the two cars again but, this time, Danny persuaded Yuri to let him drive. He fondled the steering wheel lovingly, then tapped the coordinates from the file into the car's GPS and fired up the engine. "Let's go!"

57

DANNY

THE MERCEDES WAS armor plated and weighed about as much as a tank so it wasn't exactly speedy. But it was a relief to be driving anything. Yuri was up front with me and in the back were JD, Gabriel...and Erin. I couldn't take my eyes off her. Arianna had given her a pair of black, figure-hugging jeans and a tight, cream turtleneck sweater that molded to those pert little breasts. Then over the top was a long gray belted coat and Arianna had found her some knee-high brown boots. She'd put her hair back into its usual braid and she looked sophisticated and cool and sexy as hell. But then she'd been sexy as hell in a deerstalker and layered shirts.

"Watch road," Yuri muttered.

Yuri didn't miss much. I tore my eyes away from Erin before JD noticed. But I could feel her presence behind me, tugging at me. I'd never wanted—never *needed*—anyone so much in my life.

Except JD. I sighed. The rock in my life, the one person who'd always been there for me. I couldn't lose him. I cursed under my breath. How had I wound up having to choose between two people I loved?

If I chose Erin, I'd have to leave the team: there was no way I'd be able to stay with JD hating me. Even if I could handle no JD and no

Stormfinch, what about the impact on Erin? JD wouldn't want to visit us, wouldn't ever sit down to dinner with her again because I'd be there. Erin would lose her brother. And what about JD? Without me *or* Erin around, he might slip back into that deep darkness, and this time he might never come out.

So I had to choose JD. I had to just get this mission done and get everyone home safe. Then Erin could go back to Vegas and I—

My knuckles whitened on the steering wheel. I could do what, exactly? Tequila shots and threesomes? That just seemed empty: colorful and fun but there was nothing to it. A cotton candy life. Erin was *real*.

The coordinates were right on the other side of Berlin and with city center traffic, the sun was coming up before we got there. But at last, the GPS said something in German and I checked the screen. "Okay, we're close. Looks like it's in that park, on the left, maybe a hundred feet in."

I slowed down to a crawl as we passed. The park was thickly covered in snow and it was still coming down, but that hadn't stopped the workers. The area was cordoned off with barricades and a construction crew of at least twenty were using pneumatic drills and pickaxes on the ground. Watching them were a handful of guys in black combat gear and one man in a suit: I recognized Becker's silver hair. Luckily, the Mercedes had blacked-out windows so he couldn't see us.

The ground was littered with abandoned holes. "They must have been digging for days," said Gabriel. "Ever since Becker bought the file."

"And they're still digging," said Erin. "So they haven't found it yet."

There was still hope. As soon as we were out of sight, I pulled over, then turned around to the others. "How could they not find it yet?" I asked, confused. "They've got the coordinates."

Erin was deep in thought. "They were using pneumatic drills," she said.

"Ground's frozen," said Gabriel.

Erin turned to him. "But the whole point of the plan was that the general could dig up the bomb quickly and use it," said Erin. "It doesn't make sense to bury it, knowing the ground freezes here. What if he needed it in winter?"

"We've been assuming the bomb was buried," I said slowly. "What if the general hid it, instead?"

"Where?" asked Yuri. "Is nothing here."

He was right: the park was just open space. There was nowhere to hide anything.

"This all happened over forty years ago," said Erin. "What if there *was* something here then? Something that was meant to be permanent, but it got moved?"

I pulled out the burner phone and started searching. It took a while, but I eventually found some photos of the park from back in the eighties. And it looked totally different. Crowds of people eating Bratwurst and drinking beer as they strolled through—

"A *funfair*," breathed Erin. She twisted around in her seat and looked through the rear window. "Look, those three trees: they're the ones in the photo, just forty years' bigger. God, it was right where they're digging!"

I squinted at the screen, trying to make sense of the German text. "It was here for over thirty years. But something happened in 1989..."

"The wall came down," said Yuri. "Whole city became a construction site."

I tapped away at the phone, following links. "God, it's still here. They just moved it." I started up the car and drove on a little way. "*There!*"

We were still alongside the park, less than half a mile from where Becker was digging. Through the trees, we could see the shape of a helter skelter and a Ferris wheel.

We parked up, called the other car and told them to wait while we checked it out. Gabriel stayed with the car and the rest of us jumped out, gasping as the cold hit us. The funfair was closed for the winter, the rides dark and silent. We hurried inside, looking around. Across the park, I could see the bright orange overalls of the construction workers and the dark blobs that were Becker and his men.

The rides had been replaced over the years. Most of them were far too new to have been in the park when the general was around. We picked our way between sausage stands and souvenir booths and then—

We all stopped as we saw the carousel. A huge, vintage thing, the heart of the funfair. The sort of tourist favorite no one would ever get rid of.

We climbed aboard. There were the classic horses to sit on but there were other animals, too, all lovingly carved from wood. In the center was the operator's cabin and the revolving spindle that powered the whole thing. JD marched straight towards it. "It's gotta be in there, somewhere."

It felt right, that it would be in the center. Romantic: *X marks the spot.* But Erin stopped him. "It's been forty years. This thing must get serviced every year. If it was in there, where all the mechanical parts are, they'd have found it years ago."

She was right. "So where is it?" I asked.

"Somewhere it wouldn't need to move," she muttered, gazing around. "Somewhere big enough to hide a suitcase."

The horses were too skinny. There was a carriage, but that was mostly empty space for kids to sit inside.

Then we saw the elephant. Bright, blue, glossily varnished, its trunk raised high in the air as if it was trumpeting. It had a big, wide body you had to straddle. And when Erin knocked on it, it was hollow.

"Look," said JD, tracing the wood with his finger. "There's a line. They must have sawed it in half and stuck it back together."

"They probably did it at night," I said. "The fair would have been closed, no one around." I looked around at the carousel. "And this thing had probably been there for twenty, thirty years even in 1981. It was a permanent attraction, they had no reason to think it would ever move. They never dreamed the Berlin Wall might come down."

We looked at each other, excited. We made a good team, JD, Erin and me. *God, why do I have to choose?!*

Yuri ran back to the car and returned with a crowbar. He was grinning, caught up in the excitement of the hunt. As I took the crowbar, I wondered why he'd be carrying it around in the trunk of his car. Then I remembered who he worked for. *Oh.*

I raised the crowbar, aiming at the spot on the elephant's head. I saw Erin wincing and I knew how she felt: it seemed wrong, to destroy something so beautiful. But we had no choice.

I brought the crowbar down and the wood cracked. Another blow and there was a hole big enough to look through. Erin put her eye to the hole and shone her flashlight inside. We held our breath while she searched. Then:

"There's a case, brown leather, down at the bottom!"

We'd found it.

58

BECKER

I STALKED around the dig site, furious. "Why aren't you digging?" I snapped at one of the construction crew.

He started to say something about being on a break. I glared at him and he reluctantly fired up his pneumatic drill and began work again. But I knew it wouldn't make any difference.

The night I'd obtained the file, as soon as I'd had the American spirited away to Siberia, I'd come here with a few trusted men. I'd dug the first hole myself, breaking the frozen soil with a pickaxe. But there'd been nothing. I'd had my men dig more holes, spreading out from the first, but there was no sign of the bomb. Eventually, I'd had to make up a story about a cache of weapons hidden by criminals and bring in a city construction crew to speed up the digging. But still, we hadn't found it.

I had to face facts: the bomb wasn't here. And I was meeting the buyer later that day.

Movement across the park caught my eye. There were people in the distance, moving around the funfair despite it being closed. "Give me your scope," I told one of my men, not bothering to look at him.

He passed me the scope from his rifle and I put it to my eye. Three men and a woman. One of them turned and—

It was the one from the photo. *Briggs!*

They were smashing open part of the old carousel. It couldn't be a coincidence that they were here. Somehow, they'd found it.

I turned to my men. "All of you, with me. Shoot to kill."

59

DANNY

WE WERE ALL WORKING TOGETHER, pulling chunks of wood off the elephant. It was bitterly cold and our fingers were going numb but nobody wanted to stop.

Finally, JD and I managed to break off the whole side of the elephant's torso and there it was, a boxy leather case, smaller than a modern briefcase but thicker, too, almost cube-shaped. I got my arms around it and tried to lift it out but it slithered through my arms and landed right on my toe. *"OW! FUCK IT!"* It hurt a lot more than it should have done. I pulled my foot out from underneath it, wincing.

"You okay?" asked Erin.

I nodded. But I wasn't: my foot was throbbing. *Why did it hurt so much?* Maybe because my foot was so cold.

The top half of the case was made to zip off but the zippers were stiff from lack of use. Erin eventually managed to get them open. She took a deep breath...and lifted the lid.

I've never seen anyone look so awed. It was exactly the sort of vintage tech she loved, all mechanical timers and chunky buttons and switches. And yet it had enough power to snuff out hundreds of thousands of lives.

She ran her hands over, mumbling to herself absently. "Some sort of key must go there," she said, brushing a circular hole.

JD and I looked at each other, grins spreading across our faces. *We did it!* Now we just had to take it to a police station, give ourselves up and tell our story. With the nuke as proof, they'd have to believe us. Becker would go to jail, Katharina would be released...

Yuri suddenly shouted in alarm. We looked up to see Becker and his men running towards us, guns drawn. "Shit," I said. "Let's get out of here."

Erin quickly zipped up the case. I grabbed it and—

"*Christ!*" It felt like someone had nailed the thing to the floor for a joke. How could something so small weigh this much? "Why's it so bloody heavy?"

"Shielding," said Erin. "It's probably mostly lead."

"'Least we know it's not irradiating us," muttered JD.

I gritted my teeth, heaved and managed to get the thing up into my arms. "Go," I panted.

We ran. Or at least, everyone else ran. I did the best I could but the thing must have weighed two hundred pounds. It was like carrying a fully grown man, but not draped over my shoulders, concentrated into one small, awkward mass that I had to clutch to my chest. Now I knew why it hurt when I dropped it on my foot. I'd probably broken a toe and that didn't help with the running, either.

Becker was halfway to us, now. And he didn't have to catch us, he just had to be close enough to get a good shot. The others were nearly at the car but I was well behind, struggling and panting.

JD dropped back and grabbed my arm. "You okay?"

I nodded grimly. I knew he wanted to help but the case was too small, there just wasn't room for two people to get their hands around it and carry it together. And we didn't have time for me to pass it off to him. "Go," I grunted. "Get her safe."

He sped up, grabbed Erin by the hand and pulled her towards the car. She was looking back over her shoulder at me, worried. I gave her a nod. *I'm fine, go!*

I kept running. Falling snow was pelting me in the face but it did nothing to cool me down: my breathing was getting ragged and I was soaked with sweat.

The others reached the snowy bank that led up to the road and clambered up it. A shot rang out. It missed me, but it made me put everything I had into one final sprint, despite the pain in my foot. I pounded through the snow to the bank...

And found I couldn't get up it. It was too steep and the snow was too slippery. I needed to use my hands, like JD, Erin and Yuri had done, and I couldn't.

JD took a step towards me. But then another shot rang out, this one aimed at him, and he had to duck for cover. He still had Erin's hand and she pulled against his grip. "We have to go back!" she yelled. JD pulled her towards the car and I recognized the protective need in his eyes because I felt the same thing. *Yes,* I willed her. *Go with JD!*

But Erin slipped free of his grip and raced down the bank to me. She grabbed my arm and started to help me up, ignoring my protests.

JD started towards us again but gunfire suddenly erupted from behind us, cutting across the ground between JD and us. I pulled Erin down behind a raised flower bed. JD had to duck behind the door of the car.

There was a screech of tires and the other car arrived. The rest of the team jumped out and started to return fire. But we were still pinned down in the middle of it all and Becker and his men were creeping closer.

That's when I saw the steps leading down, just twenty feet away. The park had its own metro entrance. I struggled to my feet, nodded towards it and Erin and I ran.

I staggered down the stairs, wincing in pain, my legs weakening: at least gravity was on my side, now.

We could see a train waiting to leave but it was right down at the other end of the platform. I stumbled on but I was running out of steam and I could hear footsteps behind us.

Erin stayed by my side, her arm hooked in mine, towing me along. Sweat was running into my eyes and my lungs felt like they were going to explode. My foot throbbed and the bomb was just too heavy.

I could hear someone behind us. I assumed it was Becker but I couldn't spare the energy to look. The only reason he hadn't shot us yet was that there were a few passengers, further along the platform. But he was going to catch us, any second.

I *pushed*. Harder than I'd ever pushed in my life, lifting each leg through what felt like wet concrete and then slamming it down even though it made my muscles scream. But six feet from the train, my legs gave out and I fell to my knees. The bomb hit the floor, cracking some of the tiles.

"*Get up!*" Erin yelled. She grabbed my hand and tried to pull me up but I shook my head. There was no time.

I pushed the bomb towards her. "Take it," I rasped. "You gotta leave me and get it on the train." It was only six feet to the doors and if she slid it across the tiles, she wouldn't have to pick it up.

Erin looked at the bomb. Looked at me.

Then she grabbed my arms and hauled me onto the train, leaving the bomb on the platform. The sliding doors hissed closed.

Becker ran up to the doors and slammed his fist against the glass. The handful of other passengers jumped, shocked. And then the train pulled away.

I lay there sprawled on my back, too exhausted to get up, staring at Becker as he shrank into the distance. "Oh Christ," I said weakly. My chest was on fire and I could barely get the words out. "Oh Christ, Erin, what did you *do?*" She was crouched next to me and I twisted to look at her. "He has the *bomb!*" I searched her face. "Why did you do that?"

There were tears in her eyes. "Because I love you!"

The words broke across me and sank deep into my soul. It felt like she'd spoken some spell from the fantasy book we'd read together, one that set the cursed man free. Hearing she felt the same way made my own feelings real. Everything I'd been holding back broke loose and it picked me up and carried me like a wave. I needed her and I couldn't not have her anymore.

I grabbed the front of her coat, pulled her down on top of me and kissed her long and hard.

60

ERIN

Siberia had been about lust. This was about love, each press of his lips an explosion that sent everything he felt for me earthquaking through my body. The tremors went right to my core and all I could do was cling to him as they made me go floaty and light. I was vaguely aware that the other passengers were whooping and cheering and I didn't care.

Our lips parted for a second and he growled against my neck, his voice raw with emotion. "I love you, too. And nobody's keeping me away from you. Not anymore."

Then he wrapped his arms around me and hugged me to him, full-length on the floor, his arms like steel. And for the first time since the fisherman's hut, I felt truly safe. *This* is what I'd needed. I slipped my arms around him, buried my head in his shoulder and cuddled in. It was a long time before he loosened his arms and looked at me. But when he did, the look in his eyes made me melt. Cocky and confident, as always, ferociously hot, like in Siberia. But there was something new, too. There was a joy there I'd never seen before, like he'd been set free.

Danny called JD and told him Becker had the bomb, and that we were okay. The rest of the team had managed to escape intact, too. We agreed we'd all meet back at Vasiliy's place. I helped Danny to his feet and we found a couple of seats. When I looked around the carriage for the first time and saw everyone looking at us, my heart nearly stopped: what if someone recognized Danny from his photo on the news? But people didn't look scared or suspicious: they were smiling adoringly at us. We didn't look like fugitives. We looked like a couple in love.

Danny took my hand in his and he didn't let go of it the entire journey. We were still holding hands when we walked into Vasiliy's apartment. The metro was way faster than battling through Berlin's traffic in a car, so we were back before the rest of the team.

I helped Danny carefully ease his shoes off. Two of his toes were badly bruised, possibly broken. We strapped them with tape and he sighed with relief as the pain eased. Then he took my hand again and led me through the apartment, hobbling a little, glancing into each room as we passed it. I was about to ask him what he was looking for when Luka wandered out of a room ahead of us.

"Bedroom?" asked Danny breezily.

Luka looked at our joined hands, then grinned approvingly and pointed to the end of the hall. Danny nodded his thanks and towed me towards the door with me flushing down to my roots.

Like the rest of Vasiliy's apartment, it was sumptuous and classical. There were oil paintings of landscapes on the walls and a desk and chair that looked like they were antique. But the main feature was a four poster bed carved from glossily dark mahogany and hung with long, green velvet drapes. Outside, the snow was being whipped past the window by the wind. But there was a fire burning in the grate and the room was cozy and warm.

As soon as we were inside, Danny pushed the door shut. We were alone....and we didn't have to hold back. Danny let out a groan, pulled me to him and kissed me, gentle presses that immediately started to build into something hotter, deeper. His tongue teased my lips and I moaned and molded myself to him. But as his hands started to trace down my body, I forced myself to pull away.

"Wait," I panted. "What about JD?" I didn't want him to pull away again afterwards. I couldn't take that.

Danny took my head between his hands. "JD's just going to have to live with it because I'm not giving you up for anyone."

I melted. My hands came up to stroke his shoulders and I gave myself up to the kiss. It was gentle at first, his lips tasting me, exploring me, as his thumbs stroked my cheeks. But then I felt his muscles start to harden under my hands. Each kiss became stronger, until he was pressing me back a half-step with each one, his breath coming faster and faster. Then I felt the post of the four poster bed against my back and he pinned me there, the kiss becoming a circling, grinding, open-mouthed tussle, both of us out of control.

He broke the kiss. Looked down at me, his eyes absolutely *burning*. Then he grabbed my waist with both hands and—

I yelped as my feet left the ground. There was a second of weightlessness and then I landed on my back in the middle of the bed, my glasses askew. He put one knee on the bed, looked down at me and—

He shook his head and grinned. "How do you do that?"

I adjusted my glasses. "Do what?"

"Be so cute and so sexy at the same time," he growled.

I didn't have an answer but I wouldn't have had time to give one anyway because he sprang at me, flattening me to the bed and kissing me: deep, hot, hungry kisses that made me flex and writhe against him. He rolled us sideways so that we were on our sides, his hands smoothing up and down my back. Then I was on top, my hair hanging down like a curtain around our faces. His hands stroked all the way down my back and I arched like a cat.

He pushed me gently back, breaking the kiss. I opened my eyes slowly, my head a little foggy: I was almost drunk on him. Then I blinked down at him. *Why are you stopping? Is something wrong?*

He gazed up at me. "I just had to look at you," he told me.

I half-smiled, not quite getting the joke. Then I saw the way he was looking at me and realized he meant it, and my heart filled and soared, carrying me right up to the ceiling. It was the single nicest thing anyone had ever said to me.

"I want to read the rest of those books with you," he blurted. "And I want to go away somewhere with you." He glanced at the snow outside the window. "Somewhere *hot*. Swim in the sea with you. And I want to show you Britain."

I listened, delighted. But then I remembered what had just happened and my stomach knotted. "But we lost the bomb. We can't go home—"

He shook his head and took hold of both my hands. "I don't care."

That stopped my worrying like a brick wall. I blinked down at him and he stared up at me, stubbornly defiant, as cocky as ever. "We'll work it out," he told me. "We'll get out of this and go home. You know why? Because I *have to be with you* and no fucking German spook is going to stop me."

His confidence made me melt, and wish I was like that. And then I realized that maybe I could be. Maybe I just needed something I believed in: and I believed in *us*.

"I want to go to the ballet again," I said tentatively. "Or the opera. Somewhere you can wear a tux. Only actually stay for the show, this time."

He nodded approvingly and I relaxed even more.

"And I want to make something for you. Bake something. I'm not very good at baking, but I'll learn." I'd never had someone to bake for, before. Then something occurred to me. "Oh my God, will you come to CEE with me?"

He frowned. *What's that?*

"It's the Consumer Electronics Expo, it's where they have all the latest gadgets, it's completely geeky, I'll be staring at circuit boards all day, I always wanted to go but I never had anyone to go with, please say yes!" I was almost bouncing up and down on him, by now.

He chuckled, a rich, warm sound. "*Yes*. 'Course I will."

I squealed with joy and he pulled me down and kissed me again, light and joyous, a teenage kiss, both so eager we clacked our teeth together. He rolled us so that he was on top again. "I'm going to drive us somewhere pretty: Scotland, maybe, and we can camp." The words came faster and faster. "And we're going to dance, in my garage, to the jukebox. We're going to do that a *lot.*" It was spilling out of him, like he couldn't get the ideas out fast enough, and I realized that he'd never had anyone to do this with, before. He'd never been in love.

He gazed down at me and his eyes narrowed, going molten with lust. "And I want to get you one of those leather corsets, like Vessia wears in the book. And I'm going to fuck you in the back of my car." His voice slowed down. "Some country road, moonlight coming in through the window, skirt up around your thighs, panties off... And I'm going to go down on you again, oh, for *so long,* this time, till you squeeze my head with your thighs, 'till you don't think you can possibly come again. And I'm going to fuck you from behind. That perfect little ass in my hands, driving into you, you looking back at me over your shoulder while I go *deep.*"

Hearing it all in that rough, London accent unleashed something in me. With each word, my insecurities and hang ups dropped away. I gulped, flushed, and nodded. *"Uh-huh!*

He let out a low growl, leaned down and kissed the side of my neck, quickly discovering that doing that turned me into a helpless, writhing mess. Then he started nipping gently with his teeth between kisses and I became a hot pool of goo.

Danny rolled me on top and scooped my borrowed coat off my shoulders and down my arms. Then his hands were roving under my sweater and vest top and I groaned at how good they felt: big and strong and warm as they skimmed up my sides and toyed with the straps of my bra, his thumbs brushing the sides of my breasts. They moved down over my jeans, stroking my legs and squeezing my ass with just the right amount of roughness. Meanwhile, I'd half-unbuttoned his shirt and was sliding my palms over his pecs, delighting in the hard curves of him, the warm, muscled solidness of him. We'd missed out on this stage, in the fisherman's hut, and I was discovering how fun it was.

He pulled my clothes up over my bra and kissed my stomach, then kissed a line up over my breasts, along my throat and up to my lips. We kissed in slow rhythm, only breaking for him to pull my sweater and vest top off completely. He lay back on the bed and pulled me full-length atop him, our faces almost touching. Then his hand snaked down between our bodies. There was a smooth little pop as a button opened and then...*oh God,* his hand was inside my jeans, his fingers brushing against me through my panties. He gave an experimental rub and watched as my eyes widened and my breathing tightened.

He began a slow circling, caressing my lips with the soft cotton of my panties. I sucked in my breath and unconsciously began to grind my hips. He looked down my body, grinning approvingly at the sight of my denim-clad rump drawing circles in the air. His fingers began to stroke in opposite directions, the middle one sliding forward as the outer two drew back, and I gave a quivering little breath and stared down into his green eyes, utterly helpless.

"God, you're gorgeous," he told me. "You know I'm crazy about you. *Crazy.*" His eyes were locked on mine as he touched me, *played* me, his breathing quickening along with mine as I became soaked. He brought the pleasure spiraling up and up until I was a panting, begging mess and then took me over the edge. I was full-length atop him and he could feel every twitch, every shudder, as I came: it was the most intimate experience I'd ever had with a man, more intimate than sex, somehow, but afterwards, things didn't feel awkward. They felt light and fun because I trusted him completely.

He rolled us onto our sides and we began kissing again, hands everywhere. He deftly unhooked my bra and pushed it out of the way, filling his hands with my breasts. My breathing went shaky as he squeezed them, then bent his head and began to lick, my nipples hardening under his tongue. Meanwhile, I finished unfastening his shirt. My hands roved over the ridges and valleys of his abs and slid under his shirt to climb the rugged mountains of his back. But mainly, they smoothed across the big, wonderful slabs of his chest. There was something about the size of him, there, the hard muscled bulk of him, that made me feel deliciously tiny and feminine.

We were rolling over and over on the big bed, now, unable to keep still. I heard the metal rasp of my zipper coming down and then my jeans and soaked panties were being pushed down past my knees. They got stuck around my ankles and then, with some twisting and prying, my sneakers slid off and the whole bundle of jeans, sneakers and socks hit the floor and I was naked below the shoulders. A moment later, he stripped off my bra and then I was nude in the middle of the bed, the sheets gloriously soft against my skin. I looked up at the four poster bed's drapes and the canopy overhead, and it was like being a princess in one of my fantasy books.

Danny pushed his pants and jockey shorts down his hips and off and started to knee-walk towards me. I scooched back to give him room, my eyes glued to his cock as it slapped against his stomach. I leaned back against the pillows and then flushed as I realized I'd unconsciously opened my legs for him. Danny gave a filthy smirk and I flushed harder, but a hot throb rolled through my body. He rolled on a condom, brandished himself in one hand and—

I groaned, my mouth opening in a wide *O* as he entered me. It was utterly different, in a bed. For one thing, I was under him, this time, feeling the weight and power of him as he pushed into me. In the fisherman's hut, riding him, I'd felt small and fragile, clinging onto all that muscled power. But now, looking up at that wide chest and strong shoulders, feeling his hips spread me as they slid up between my thighs... It lit something dark and primitive inside me, sending waves of heat trembling outward from my groin.

He planted his hands either side of my head, looked deep into my eyes and then started a slow pumping of his hips that sent him deeper. I rocked my head back on the pillow, chin to the ceiling, and bit my lip at how good it felt, at the fluttering in my belly as he filled me, *stretched* me. The weight of him settled between my legs, pinning me, and another wave of dark heat fireworked out and then contracted into a glowing, pulsing center.

He took his weight on his elbows so that he could cup my face in his hands, fingertips toying with my hair as we stared into each other's eyes. His thrusts were slow at first, tender little kisses of his groin against mine, as if he was afraid of hurting me. I felt his whole body going hard with the tension of holding back. But I didn't want him to hold back, and when my hands crept down his back and pulled lightly at the small of his back, he growled and let loose.

My breath shook as he began to pump hard into me: the silken friction of him, the heat of him so deep inside. I glanced down the bed and saw his ass rising and falling between my thighs, and a wave of heat rippled through me. I grabbed at the sheet with both hands, scrunching it in my fists, the pleasure tightening and concentrating with every hard thrust.

He pounded me and I began to writhe and buck beneath him, tilting my hips to meet him. He ducked his head and licked at my nipples, then lowered himself more, letting his chest rub against the hardened peaks as he fucked me. The pleasure was folding in on itself, now, growing as heavy and dense as the core of a star. I could feel the climax thundering towards me, unstoppable, and I lost control. I lifted my feet off the bed and stroked at the backs of his thighs and his ass with the soles, urging him on. My mouth opened but I didn't know what I was going to say until I said it. *"Don't stop."* The voice didn't sound like my own. *"Don't stop, don't stop."*

He growled again, as if hearing me say that turned him on even more. He went harder, faster, and I reached up and grabbed two fistfuls of the pillow, crushing it in my fists as the pleasure became incandescent, my whole body strumming with its power. I was on the very edge. Nothing else existed, just Danny and me and the feeling of him taking me. *"Don't stop, don't—"*

And then it arrived, a wave of pleasure that started at my toes and rippled all the way up to my head before racing back down. I arched, going stiff. My hips lifted under him and he grunted and groaned as I spasmed around him, sending him over the edge. His hips hammered me back down into the bed for three more thrusts and then he hilted himself and shot inside me in long, shuddering streams. I wrapped my arms around him and clung to him and he clung to me as we rode the pleasure on and on.

61

ERIN

THE WIND HOWLED OUTSIDE, blasting snow past the windows at ferocious speed. But in the bed we were cozy and snug. Danny's body was deliciously warm and solid and I decided I'd be happy if I never moved again.

I had my head on his chest and after a while, I could feel him watching me. I craned my head back and looked up into those incredible green eyes. There was a look on his face I couldn't decipher. "What?" I asked. Then, when he didn't respond, my voice went tight with worry. "*What?*"

He shook his head as if it was nothing to worry about. "Just sorting stuff out in my head," he muttered. "I wasn't planning on this."

I slid on top of him so that I could look up at him properly. "You're worried about JD?"

He shook his head again. "We can deal with that, we've just got to do it right. No I just—" He scowled, trying to find the words. "I wasn't planning on falling for someone." His voice dropped. "Didn't think I *could.*"

I said nothing: I'm not great with people but we'd spent so much time together, in the last week, that even my malfunctioning social radar had gotten dialed in to Danny's wavelength. And right now, the right thing to do was just listen.

He looked up at the ceiling, frowning and uncertain. I'd never seen him be uncertain about anything before. It felt like he was discovering something new, testing out its limits. "I thought...." he said at last, "I thought that bit of me was...broke, or something."

He huffed a little, as if angry with himself for saying anything. His chest filled, lifting me...but when I didn't laugh at him, when I just gazed tenderly down at him, he relaxed. He went to speak again once, twice, but kept biting it back. "The scars on my back," he blurted at last. "They're not from Iraq."

I nodded. There'd been a cold ache in my chest, before I even saw the scars for the first time. Ever since that moment when he'd sheltered me from the wind and I'd seen the pain in his eyes. I'd known someone had hurt him.

He stared up at me, those sexy lips pressed together in a tight, hard line. He could charm any woman out of her panties but he couldn't talk about *this*. Not while he looked me in the eye.

I knew what I had to do. I sank down on his chest and turned my head to the side, using his pec as a pillow. I felt him relax. A second later, his big, warm hand stroked my head and that seemed to help, too. And eventually, the words came.

"We were poor," he told me. "But so was everyone, in our neighborhood. My dad had a temper but we were happy enough. Then one night when I was eight, him and my mum had this huge fight: real shake-the-walls stuff. My dad marched into my room, he looked down at me...and he took his belt off for the first time." I felt Danny shake his head. "It wasn't seeing him take his belt off that scared me, though. It wasn't even thinking about what he was going to do with it. It was the look in his eyes. *Absolute, fucking hatred.* I sat there on my bed, with these Pokémon cards all around me, and I thought: *but I haven't done anything.*" Danny swallowed. "And then he started."

I had my arms draped around his sides. I wrapped them tight around him and hugged him hard, pressing my body to him.

"After that, he beat me whenever he saw me," said Danny, his voice numb. "Sometimes, it was worse when he *didn't* beat me. 'Cos once he did it, it was done for a few hours. But when I was waiting for it, waiting for him to notice that I was in the house...." He went quiet. "People think the worst part is the pain. And it did hurt, it hurt a lot. Part of why I flunked so much of school was because the teachers kept sending me out because I couldn't sit still: the back of my chair used to dig into my back, right where he strapped me. But the pain wasn't the worst part. The worst part was what he said, when he was strapping me. That I was a piece of shit."

Danny gave an embarrassed little chuckle. "Stupid, innit? I mean, it's just words, it's nothing. But they kind of soak into you, they get right down inside you. And that look in his eyes, every time. He *hated* me. He'd loved me, and then he *hated* me, like he wanted to just..." Danny twisted his thumb against the bed, as if squashing an insect.

I hugged him tighter. Hugged him with my legs, too. I wanted to have fourteen arms, so I could hug every part of him at once. I understood now. He'd loved, like any child loves their parents. And in return he'd been detested, told he was worthless. Of course he'd shut down that part of himself. Of course he'd never loved again. "No one did anything?" I asked.

"I forgot to mention," said Danny bitterly. "My old man was the local police sergeant. Everyone loved him. And my mum...she'd started drinking, by this point. She'd just disappear into another room with a bottle." He sighed. "Took me a while, but when I was ten, I worked it out. My dad yelled at my mum every day, but he never raised a hand to her. And this thing had all started with that big fight between them." He took a deep breath. "My mum had blue eyes. My dad had brown eyes. But I had these very particular green eyes. And there was a bloke who hung around the neighborhood, a crook, a bit of a charmer, who had the exact same green eyes." His voice went tight. "My dad still loved my mum. But me? I had no connection to him at all. I was just evidence of what she'd done, staring him in the face every day."

I said nothing, just clung to him, silent tears trickling down my cheeks. He stroked my head in silence for a while and when he spoke again, his voice was calmer. "The older I got, the more I looked like my real dad. The beatings got worse. I had to get out of the house so I started hanging around with one of the local gangs." I felt him shrug. "They didn't want me at first 'cos I was a cop's kid. But I was a tough little fucker. Cocky. Wasn't intimidated by anyone, 'cos nothing they could do to me was as bad as what I'd get at home. That got me in. The girls liked it, too, even at fifteen. But it was always just quick flings, never anything real. I couldn't feel anything deep, couldn't fall for anyone." I felt him look down at me. "Not until I met you."

I lifted my head and met his eyes. Then I threw my arms around his neck and pressed my cheek to his, feeling the wetness of my tears. "*You,*" I told him, "are a *good man.* And you deserve to be loved, you deserve every bit of love I can give you and—" I couldn't put any more of it into words so I just hugged him as tight as I could and he hugged me back just as tight.

When we finally let each other go and I looked up at him, the pain in his eyes was still there—I knew it wouldn't ever go completely. But he looked more at peace with himself, like he'd excised something poisonous and now the wound could start to heal.

We cuddled up together with me on top, both of us still naked. "How are we going to tell JD?" I asked at last.

"Gently," said Danny. "Look: we'll get out of this, get back home, then I'll sit him down and—"

The door creaked open. I sat up, startled, and turned towards it.

JD was standing in the doorway, his mouth open in shock.

62

DANNY

THE BOTTOM DROPPED out of my world. I saw JD's face change from shock and embarrassment to raw, burning anger and then to something I'd never imagined seeing: betrayal.

He turned and stalked away down the hall.

"Aw, Christ," I muttered, jumping out of the bed and grabbing for my jockey shorts. *Where the fuck are my pants?* "JD!" I yelled. "JD, wait!" But he didn't stop. I gave up on my pants and ran after him in just my jockey shorts. I had to fix this *now*, before it got any worse.

I could see how pissed he was. His shoulders were set, his feet slamming down like he was crushing me underfoot. But I wanted to believe I could fix it, if I just got to him quickly enough. "JD, mate—" I grabbed his shoulder, wrenched him around to face me...

He shoved me up against the wall. "*How could you?!*" he bellowed. "*How could you, she's my SISTER!*"

I'd never seen him so mad. I'd miscalculated: I should have let him cool off. But it was too late now. "It's not like that," I told him. "I swear, mate, Erin means—"

JD slammed his fist against the wall, as if it was either that or hit *me*. "I trusted you! I *told* you! You *promised!*"

My mouth worked but nothing came out. Because all those things were true. And in his eyes, that meant I was just a horndog who cared more about getting his dick wet than his best friend.

People started to arrive, drawn by the shouting. First Vasiliy's security, guns drawn. Then the rest of the team, pulling up short when they saw what was going on. Then Luka and Arianna, hand in hand. *Great.* The whole world was there to see our friendship disintegrate. Erin arrived, breathless, her feet bare and her sweater inside out. I saw Colton, Cal, and Bradan do a simultaneous *oh shit* as they realized what had happened. Gabriel and Gina just winced.

"JD," I began, "look, it's not..." I stared at him helplessly. If I said I loved her, he wouldn't believe me. For years, he'd known me as the guy who *never* fell in love.

He pointed a finger at my chest like a gun. "If we get out of this," he told me. "I want you off the team."

I felt myself crumble. *No! Not JD. Don't take JD from me, please!*

"JD," said Erin, her eyes full of tears. "You can't just—I'm not a kid anymore, I can make my own decisions."

JD shook his head at her, fuming. In his eyes, she'd betrayed him, as well.

Gina stepped forward. "I hate to interrupt, but don't we have more important things to think about? Like the fact we're utterly screwed? Becker has the nuke and he's going to sell it. We've got no way to clear our names."

Erin hung her head. She obviously blamed herself for losing the nuke, even though she'd done it to save me. She must have been pushing it out of her mind but now it was hitting her: everyone but me could have been free and clear and on their way home, if she'd made a different decision. I walked over to her and put my hands on her shoulders, feeling JD's eyes burning into me. "It'll be okay," I told her.

"I could have got the nuke on the train," she whispered.

"If you had, I wouldn't be standing here now," I told her firmly. "We'll figure something out."

She shook her head. "It's not just us, though," she said. "Once

Becker sells it, someone's going to use it. They're going to set it off, in some city." Her voice cracked. *"That's on me."*

I wrapped my arms around her. I didn't have an answer to that. I knew it wasn't her fault but I also knew that, when that nuke went off, she'd never, ever get over it. We all stood there, silent and helpless.

Then Erin suddenly straightened and she pushed out of my arms. "It has a key!" she said breathlessly. "The nuke has a key! A weird, circular one, I saw the keyhole when we opened the case!"

"Couldn't Becker work around that?" asked Gabriel.

Erin shook her head. "No, the whole point of having a key is to stop someone setting it off who isn't authorized. The mechanism will be built right into the heart of the thing. It's useless without the key."

"Well then Becker'll be going after the key," said Bradan. "Where would it be?"

"The General would have had it," said Gabriel. "So—"

"Oh God!" Erin went sheet-white and grabbed my arm. "The General's son and daughter. Becker'll go right to their house. He'll tear the place apart looking for that key. They have their grandkids there! You have to stop him!"

JD drew in a deep breath. "Everyone grab their stuff." He scowled at me. *"You,* get some clothes on. We've got to protect those people."

Erin ran over to Vasiliy. "I need to borrow a car, too," she told him.

JD turned to her. "What? Why?"

"Because I think I know where the key is," she said. "And it's not at the house."

63

DANNY

LESS THAN FIVE MINUTES LATER, we were tearing through the streets of Berlin in the two borrowed Mercedes, with me and Gabriel at the wheels.

"We've done entirely too much racing around in cars this week," grumbled Gina from the backseat. I wondered if this was the longest she'd ever been on the ground.

I slowed as we turned into the street where the General's son and daughter lived. JD used a rifle scope to check the building out from a distance. "One guy outside, keeping watch," he reported. "Bradan, you're up."

I pulled over and Bradan climbed out. We watched as he strolled down the street, head down, the hood of his hoodie hiding his face. There was something about the way he walked that made him look like a local: he just blended into the scene. No one so much as glanced at him.

"I should have gone with Erin," I muttered, my eyes fixed on Bradan.

"I need you with me," said JD from the passenger seat. Which was bullshit: he was just determined to keep us apart. I'd argued and argued with him but he wouldn't listen. He was so mad at me, he wasn't thinking straight: he might even be putting Erin in danger. But I didn't blame him, I blamed myself. If I'd just buried my feelings for Erin, we'd still be friends.

Bradan walked straight past the guard, who ignored him. Then there was a flurry of movement, too quick to follow, and Bradan was dragging the guard's unconscious body into an alley. *Christ.* He seemed so normal, when we were watching a football match or sinking beers. Then I saw something like this and remembered that his past wasn't normal at all.

We flooded out of the cars and across the street, guns hidden under our clothes. Fortunately, the General's kids lived on the ground floor so we could peek in through the windows. Four of Becker's men were tearing the place apart, stabbing knives into couch cushions, emptying drawers on the floor and smashing vases in search of anything hidden inside. The daughter was sitting in a chair in the living room, pleading with one of the men. He had his gun pointed at the two grandchildren, who were huddled sobbing in a corner. All of our faces grew dark when we saw that.

We formed up outside the front door and Gabriel quietly picked the lock. I went first, since I was the only one who'd been there before. My job would be to get the kids to safety, while the others dealt with the men. As we crept to the living room, I could hear my heart crashing against my ribs. I remembered looking at the grandkids' model house, being a dog and a giraffe. One stray shot, that's all it would take. *Don't think like that.*

I nodded to Colton and launched myself forward. He kicked the door open and—

Time became syrupy slow. Becker's men turned to face me, guns rising. *Good.* That meant they weren't aiming at the kids.

Two gunshots rang out. I flinched but didn't look, focused on the children. In two big strides, I was close enough that I could see the tears glistening on their cheeks. I hooked an arm around each one, scooped them up and—

More shots. A scream. The stink of cordite. Then a female cry, and not the daughter. *Gina.* She was hurt. *Ignore it. Ignore everything.*

I reached the door to the kitchen and barreled through. I had to get the kids behind something but there were no corners or kitchen islands. I tipped the table onto its side and crouched behind that, the kids clutched to my chest.

Two more shots from the living room. Then silence. "*Clear,*" I heard Gabriel yell. Then *clear, clear, clear* from other rooms.

I peeked out from behind the table and saw JD coming into the kitchen with the daughter. I let the kids go and they ran to her. As they embraced, JD and I looked at each other. This is when I'd normally make a joke, and he'd pat my arm and say *good job* and I'd feel that lift, the one I can't put into words.

JD turned away. And I knew the friendship was gone. I hadn't realized how much I'd miss those little lifts, or how much I'd needed them.

I moved through to the living room. All of Becker's men were down. I spotted Gina across the room. "You okay?" I asked urgently.

She scowled, going red. "I tripped over a fucking coffee table."

Behind her, Gabriel and Colton were trying not to laugh. I quickly turned away. I was in that momentary adrenaline high you get when the shooting stops and everyone's safe and, despite everything happening with JD, if I kept looking at Gabriel and Colton, *I* was going to start laughing, and I didn't want Gina to kick me in the balls.

Then I frowned. Someone was missing. "Where's Becker?" I asked. No one had seen him.

I ran back into the kitchen and talked to the daughter, who was sitting on the floor hugging her grandchildren. "Was there an older guy here?" I asked. "Fifties. Silver beard."

She nodded, hugging the children protectively to her chest. "He said he'd kill them both, if we didn't tell him where the key was. We don't know about any key! He left, just before you got here."

I crouched down. "Where did he go?"

The woman sniffed. And then she said the words I didn't want to hear. "He went to find my brother," she told me. "At the church."

I jumped to my feet. "*JD!*"

Erin was at the church.

64

ERIN

VASILIY HAD LENT ME A CAR: not one of the big, bulletproof Mercedes but a modest—or at least, modest for their family—BMW that blended in a little more. "I use it when I want to meet with someone discreetly," he'd told me with a wink. I remembered what Arianna had said about his American girlfriend, and wondered who she was.

Some quick internet searching had revealed that the General's son worked at St. Hedwig's Cathedral. I found a place to park, jumped out and hurried along the street. It was late morning by now, I'd been up all night and I was running on raw adrenaline. It was only when I glanced up and saw a German street sign that it hit me: I was on my own in a foreign country, on the run from the police, chasing down a lead. A week ago, I'd been scared to leave my apartment in Vegas.

I ran up the steps of the cathedral. The place was a towering mass of gray stone topped with a huge, copper dome that age had turned turquoise. I ran from room to room, my footsteps echoing around the vaulted ceilings, until a nun pointed me in the right direction.

I found the General's son dressed in his priest's robes, about to begin mass. When I explained about the nuke, he crossed himself. "But what has that got to do with me?" he asked.

"The bomb can't be activated without a key," I told him. "And I think your father hid that key in a very safe place. Can I see your crucifix?"

He carefully took it from around his neck and handed it over. I examined it, feeling the weight. Too heavy to be wood. I'd been right.

"Sorry," I told the priest. And snapped the crucifix in two.

He let out a strangled cry...which turned to a choked gasp when he saw the cylindrical metal key inside. "I thought he was giving me a gift," he said, fingering it. His voice turned bitter. "I thought he'd made his peace with me." The poor man was crushed.

I took his hand and squeezed it. "Your father hid it there because he knew you'd never abandon your faith," I told him.

A shoe squeaked on the tiles behind me. I whipped around and my stomach dropped when I saw Becker standing there.

"Very clever," he said coldly. And he held his hand out for the key.

He was between me and the exit. I backed away towards the only other door.

Becker moved closer. The General's son moved to block his path.

"Get out of my way," Becker snapped. "Or do you think I won't shoot a man of God?"

The priest drew himself up to his full, impressive height. "I think my father gave me that key to keep it away from people like you," he told Becker. Then he looked at me. "*Run!*" he commanded.

I turned and fled deeper into the building. Behind me, I heard a tussle, then a gunshot. I ran on, not daring to look back.

65

DANNY

WE BLASTED out of an underpass and despite weighing over two tons, the car actually got air for a second as we crested the top of the hill. I spun the wheel and we turned into the plaza in front of the cathedral, sending pedestrians running. We slewed to a stop in front of the massive building and jumped out.

From inside, we heard a gunshot. JD glanced at me, looking sick: it was sinking in that his anger had put Erin in danger. But it was myself I was mad at. *This is all my fault.*

A few cops who'd been on patrol nearby were running towards us, shouting into their radios when they saw our guns. In a couple of minutes, the entire Berlin police force was going to descend on this place. But we couldn't worry about that now: we had to save Erin.

We ran inside and spread out, searching. I asked everyone I saw, wishing I spoke German. I eventually started miming Erin's long hair, and finally a nun pointed to a door. "That way? She went that way?"

I ran through the door and found the General's son lying on the floor, a sobbing nun tending to him. He'd been shot in the stomach. I fell to my knees beside him and got pressure on the wound, like Olivia taught us. "Is an ambulance coming?" I asked the nun. She understood well enough that she nodded.

The priest reached up weakly and pointed to a door at the back of the room. I nodded my thanks, grabbed the nun's hand and pressed it to the wound, and ran.

66

ERIN

I POUNDED down another flight of stairs, my lungs burning. Becker was old but he was far fitter than me. I could hear him steadily gaining.

Every room I'd run through had led me further into the building and all the stairs had led down. I was somewhere deep under the cathedral, now. The walls were bare stone and the rooms were filled with huge stone tombs covered in inscriptions. I stumbled on, my legs starting to go rubbery. There had to be an exit *somewhere!*

Then, at last, I saw a flight of steep stone steps leading up. It looked like it went all the way up to ground level. There was a door at the top and—*yes!*—I could see a sliver of sunlight beneath it.

I started up the stairs, panting and wheezing. They were incredibly steep, and there was no handrail. I had to go up them almost on all fours, using my hands. Behind me, I could hear Becker reach the bottom of the stairs. *Move!*

I reached the top and, with my chest feeling like it was going to explode, I fell against the door and turned the handle—

Nothing happened. The door was locked.

No! No, how can it be locked?! I threw myself against the door but it held firm. I rattled the handle, almost hysterical, but it wouldn't open.

Becker started to climb the stairs, his steps unhurried. "They had to lock it years ago," he told me. "Junkies kept getting in and stealing things."

I spun to face him, my chest heaving. He was smiling the smile of a man who knows he's won.

The stairs were steep. Maybe if I sprang at him, I could knock him over and run past him. As he reached me, I tensed my legs and—

He drove his fist into my stomach and I doubled over. He knocked the air out of me so completely that I couldn't even cry out in pain. He grabbed the key from my hand and pocketed it, then wrenched my arms up behind me, folding me over completely. A zip tie cinched tight around my wrists. "You're going to tell me everything your friends know," he told me. "And everyone *they've* told, so I can kill them, too."

He set off down the stairs with me in front of him. He held my bound wrists cruelly high behind my back, so I had to stagger along, bent over, still barely able to breathe.

67

DANNY

WHERE IS SHE?

I'd run through what felt like the entire bloody cathedral but there was no sign of Erin or Becker. I slowed as I saw Gabriel ahead of me. "Anything?"

He shook his head. Cal emerged from a different doorway, then Gina, Bradan and JD. No one had seen her.

Sirens had been growing gradually louder as we searched. As we looked at each other, they reached a peak and stopped. The police were here. I peeked out of a window and saw at least twenty armed officers swarming towards the cathedral.

"We could fight," said Colton. "Fall back room by room, try to find another way out."

JD shook his head. "They're cops. We're not going to start shooting them." He looked around at us. "Everybody put your guns down."

We could hear booted feet racing up the cathedral's steps. Reluctantly, we tossed our guns on the floor. None of us wanted to give up: Erin was in danger. But JD was right, we couldn't get into a firefight with innocent cops.

When the police burst through the door, we were on our knees, our hands laced behind our heads. The cops weren't gentle, as they cuffed us and led us outside to a van, but at least no one got shot.

We were nearly at the van when I saw Erin. Becker was guiding her towards a car, keeping her cruelly bent over by her bound wrists. I exchanged a panicked look with JD. Becker was going to take her off somewhere and interrogate her. Then he'd kill her.

The police bundled us into the van and slammed the doors. I sat there staring at the bare metal wall in defeat.

Erin was going to die. JD hated me. We had no way to clear our names and were all heading to jail. And once Becker sold the nuke, it would kill tens of thousands of people.

We'd lost.

68

ERIN

As soon as we were out of the city, Becker pulled over on a quiet side road. He hauled me out of the backseat, pushed me around to the back of the car and opened the trunk. "In."

I froze. Just being his prisoner was terrifying. Being locked in that tiny, dark box as we drove God-knows-where....

Becker leaned close. "You can get in now, or I can hit you again. I'll make sure to break a few ribs, this time, and the broken ends will grind together every time we hit a pothole."

I stiffly climbed in and lay down on my side, trying not to cry. He slammed the trunk and it was worse, much worse, than I'd thought. I'd known it would be dark but it was pitch black: I couldn't even see the walls. But I could feel them, so close to my face that I had to fight not to panic.

We moved off and, immediately, I was thrown to the back of the trunk. With my hands behind me, I couldn't brace myself or hang on. I was just dead weight, hurled around every time we went around a corner and soon my whole body was throbbing with bruises. I lay there sobbing, terrified and helpless. No one was coming to save me. I kept seeing JD, Danny and the others being led towards the police van in cuffs. They were going to jail for years.

And I was on my own.

I lost all sense of time. By the time the car stopped, I didn't know if I'd been in there for half an hour or three hours. Becker opened the trunk and I shrank back, a sobbing, bruised wreck.

He hauled me out by the collar and thumped me down on my feet. A shockwave went up my legs and set off a violent wave of cramps: my legs hadn't been straight in hours. I nearly fell but I was so scared that he'd hit me again that I breathed through the pain and managed to stay standing. As my eyes adjusted to the light, I looked around...

Where the hell are we?

We were at the top of a steep hill, exposed to a bitterly cold wind. The land dropped away dramatically, the slopes covered in thick, snow-dusted forest. Beyond the forest were towering blue mountains. And right in front of me, forcing me to crane my neck right back to see its top—

My brain rebelled for a second. Was I seeing things? I blinked a couple of times but it was still there.

It was a castle straight out of a fairytale, with white walls, a slate gray roof and pointed turrets that reached high into the sky. It was beautiful...and *huge*: it had forty or fifty windows just in one wing. How far had we driven? Was this still Germany? Switzerland? I didn't even know which country I was in!

Becker picked up the nuke in its leather case from the passenger seat—even he grunted with effort, lifting it—and loaded it onto a two wheeled mover's cart. Then he took the key from his pocket and attached it to the handle of the case with a zip tie. My stomach knotted. Whoever bought the thing would have everything they needed to set it off.

"Stay with me," Becker warned. "Try to run and I'll break a leg so you don't try again."

I swallowed and nodded. We walked together to a massive door, guarded by two men with machine guns around their necks. Becker handed one of them something that looked like an ice cube. He held it up to the light, examining it, while the other guy kept his gun pointed at us. Then the man nodded and spoke into a radio, and the door swung open. "She's waiting for you in the main hall," he told Becker in English.

We started down a long hallway hung with tapestries, our footsteps echoing. I looked around in wonder. *This* was where he was going to sell a nuclear bomb to terrorists?! I'd imagined those things happening in graffiti-covered, abandoned buildings. Two hundred million dollars, Vasiliy had said. "What are you going to do with the money?" I asked in a small voice. "You can't spend it. Your bosses will ask questions."

Becker frowned at me, surprised. "You think I want to buy houses and cars? Retire to a desert island?" He shook his head at me. "Money buys much more than things. It buys influence."

I stopped walking. I suddenly saw his plan. Katharina had told us about how merciless he'd been in his career, doing whatever it took to rise through the ranks. Then he'd collected blackmail information on politicians to ensure he *kept* getting promoted, right up to the top levels of Germany's intelligence agency. But, stupidly, we'd assumed that was as far as his ambitions went. "You want to *rule*," I breathed. "You want to be Chancellor."

"This country needs a strong leader," he explained, and pushed me forward.

My mind was spinning. He could already blackmail most of the country's politicians. Now he was going to have millions of dollars to bribe the rest, and to spend on a huge election campaign. *He could actually do it.* And the thought of someone like him running a country... *Oh God.*

I'd let him have the bomb. I'd failed to keep the key away from him. This was all on me.

We entered a huge room, the ceiling thirty feet high. Four huge windows, each the size of a semi truck stood on its end, allowed the freezing winter light to flood inside in four diagonal shafts. Standing in one of those shafts, as if soaking up the winter, was a woman in her forties in a cream business suit. She had those curves that make men crazy, her cleavage smoothly tanned and perfectly presented by a low-cut black blouse. And she was beautiful, with black hair in a glossy, shoulder-length bob and the palest blue eyes I'd ever seen. But there was something about being in her presence that was deeply unsettling. She stared at me as we approached and I felt like a mouse being watched by a snake.

"Who's she?" asked the woman. Her accent was British but nothing like Danny's. This was an upper-class drawl, a razor wrapped in silk.

"No one," Becker told her.

The woman arched an eyebrow suspiciously and then mercifully moved her gaze to Becker. "Your buyers should be here in a few hours," she told him.

"Please let me know when they arrive," said Becker. I'd never known him to be so deferential to anyone. Who *was* this woman? "Is there a room we can use?"

"The east tower bedroom." She pointed to a door. Becker handed over the mover's cart and led me towards the door. As we walked away, the woman raised her hands in the air and clapped twice. Two men hurried in from another room, took the cart from her and wheeled it away: apparently, she didn't sully herself with such things.

The door led to a stone staircase that corkscrewed upwards for what felt like forever. When we finally reached the top, a door opened into a suite with a bedroom, living room and bathroom, all with curved walls. We were right at the top of one of the towers, the trees tiny and toy-like far below.

Becker took me into the bedroom. "Now," he said. "Who knows about me? Who knows about the bomb? People at the CIA?"

We hadn't told the CIA. The only people who knew, other than the team, were Vasiliy and Luka. If I told him, he'd kill them. Probably Arianna, too.

I shook my head.

"If you won't tell me," he said calmly, "I'll *make* you tell me."

My chest closed up tight. *I don't want to do this!* But then I thought of the Russians. They'd helped us. I couldn't just let them die. I shook my head.

Becker gave a tired little sigh and stalked towards me.

And it began.

69

DANNY

I SAT STARING at the floor of the prisoner transport van, brooding. The frustration was boiling up from deep inside, expanding outward like storm clouds, pushing me to leap up, to hit something, to *do* something. That bastard had Erin and I had to help her. But we were locked in a metal box with no weapons and our hands cuffed behind our backs and fastened to the truck's walls.

Then I realized there was one thing I *could* do.

I didn't want to do it here, with everyone listening, but if they split us up and sent us to different prisons until our trial, it might be months or years before I saw JD again so I had to suck it up and start talking.

I leaned forward towards JD. "Look, me and Erin—"

"This ain't the time," said JD, looking away.

"It's the only fucking time!" I snapped. "After this, I don't know if I'll see you again. If any of us'll see each other again! Now will you just listen to me?"

If there'd been a way JD could have walked away, I think he would have. But we were stuck there. He glowered at me, but listened.

I took a deep breath. "I know...that I've got a bit of a reputation."

Everyone stared at me and I felt myself flush. "More than a bit.

But that isn't how it is with Erin." I groped around, trying to find the words. How was it that I could chat about nothing for hours with a woman in a bar, but when it came to talking about something important, with someone I really cared about, I was tongue-tied?

JD shook his head. He thought it was just words, Danny the charmer trying to talk my way out of trouble. Right in front of my eyes, I was losing him.

And then I took a deep breath, stopped trying to find the right words and just said how I felt. "The first time I met her, I thought the color of her eyes was like something you'd see on a butterfly's wing. So delicate. She was just this adorable little thing. I wanted to take care of her...." I shook my head at JD, helpless. "I know you want to protect her, mate, but you don't have to protect her from me because *I feel the same way.*"

JD stared at me silently. If he was softening at all, he wasn't showing it.

"She's just this little thing," I said, "but God, she's brave. And she's special, JD. She's different to you and me. Her mind, all that electronics stuff...she's on a whole different level. She makes me want to learn stuff. She's got me reading this fantasy book and I'm loving it! And I know we're different: sometimes I wonder what she sees in an idiot like me but we work together, JD. I like fixing things and she likes fixing things and when we talk, it's like I've known her for years. I'm going to this electronics show with her and we're going to go camping in Scotland and she's going to take me running around twatting people with a rubber sword...."

I'd never heard myself sound like this before. I was breathless, just talking about her. I glanced up and saw Gina staring at me, her scowl gone for once. Then she quickly looked away. I turned back to JD...and saw the hardness in his eyes flicker.

I took a deep breath. "I need her in my life. I love you, mate, but I love her, too." I leaned forward even more. "And if we're going to save her, you and me better get our shit together."

JD's big, soulful blue eyes looked right into my soul. I gazed steadily back at him, letting him know I had nothing to hide. At last, he looked away. He didn't exactly hug me and give me his blessing, but his tone softened a little and that was a start. "First thing we've got to do is get out of this goddamn truck," he rumbled.

The world suddenly shot sideways. The metal wall behind me slammed into my back. Meanwhile, everyone on the far side of the truck shot out of their seats and would have wound up in our laps if their handcuffs hadn't been bolted to the wall. Then the wall behind me became the ceiling and I was dangling from my cuffs, the metal cutting painfully into my wrists. The truck twisted and shook and there was a metal scraping that made my teeth hurt.

Everything stopped and for a second, there was total silence. We all looked at each other, panting. *What the fuck?*

The rear doors swung open. A man in a leather jacket, jeans and a black balaclava ran over to me with a pair of bolt cutters and cut the chain of my handcuffs. I fell in a heap to the floor and he threw me the bolt cutters, then ran back outside.

Who the hell's that? Then I decided I didn't care: free was better than jail. I quickly cut everyone's handcuff chains. Our guns were in a separate locker at the back of the truck. I cut the padlock on that, too, and we grabbed them.

Outside, we saw a cement truck with its front grill crumpled: now we knew what had rammed into the side of our truck. The guy in a balaclava was holding off the German police, firing over their heads to make them duck down behind their cars. When he saw us, he ran towards a parked van and nodded me towards the driver's seat. I jumped in, he got into the passenger seat and everyone else piled into the back.

I crushed the gas pedal and we tore off down the street in a cloud of tire smoke. The guy next to me finally pulled off his balaclava and we all stared at him in shock.

"Well don't all feckin' thank me at once," said Kian.

Bradan threw his arms around his brother and hugged him tight from behind. Everyone else pressed in close and started slapping his shoulders in thanks. I had to make do with blindly reaching across

and ruffling his hair because I was blasting us through the center of
Berlin at sixty miles an hour.

"What about the Secret Service?" asked JD. "Does Emily know
you're here?"

"She helped me give 'em the slip," Kian said fondly. "As soon as it
all went south for you lot, she understood."

I screeched around a corner, threw the van into reverse and
slotted it into an alley. Five seconds later, the police tore past. We
waited as their sirens faded into the distance, then relaxed.

"Tell me everything," said Kian.

We caught him up, finishing with how Becker had taken Erin.
"We've got to get her back," I said, my voice tight. I felt JD look at me,
but he didn't say anything.

Kian glanced between JD and me, sensing the tension. Then he
shook his head: *later.* "We will," he told us.

It was good to have him there. But my stomach was a tight, cold
knot of worry. How were we going to save her when we had no idea
where she was?

70

ERIN

I SCREAMED. The sound filled the room, bounced off the stone walls and pounded at my ears but I couldn't stop, I had to let the pain out. My throat went raw. My body arched like a bow in the chair and my fingers clawed at the air. The pain reached a peak...went *higher,* higher than I'd thought was possible. There was a final, tearing *pull*—

And then the pain dropped away, becoming a throbbing, steady burn. I descended into a limp, blubbering mess, tears pouring down my cheeks. "*Please stop!*" I managed between heaving sobs.

Becker held up the pliers and showed me my big toenail. His voice was sharp and cold as a scalpel. "Tell me who knows about the bomb."

I panted for air, trying not to look at my foot. If I told him about Vasiliy, Luka and Arianna, he'd kill them. And he'd kill me, once he had no more use for me. My only chance was to hold on. *But for what?* No one was coming to rescue me. Danny and the others were in jail and no one knew where I was.

"You have nine more," said Becker. "Then the fingernails. Then the teeth."

I took a big panic breath of air and he leaned forward, thinking I was going to talk.

"Nu-nu-*No*," I got out between sobs. I'd let him have the bomb, at the metro station. Tens of thousands of deaths were going to be on me. I wasn't going to be responsible for any more.

He stood and, without a word, he left. I sat slumped and panting. My foot throbbed and my wrists burned where the cord tying them to the chair's arms had rubbed them raw.

Becker returned, pushing someone ahead of him. She was a year or two younger than me and she wore a dark blue knee-length dress. She had a duster and a can of spray polish in her hands. A maid.

Becker closed the door and shoved the woman to her knees in front of me. He pulled out his gun and the woman shrieked as he pressed the muzzle to the side of her head. "Tell me who knows about the bomb," he said again.

"*Nein! Nein bitte!*" The woman started to sob, pleading for her life. I collapsed inside. I knew he'd do it. And if I didn't talk, he'd find someone else and keep doing it and doing it until I *did* talk.

I nodded. Becker hauled the woman roughly to her feet and shoved her out the door.

I told him about the Malakovs. I told him the CIA didn't know. I didn't try to hold anything back because I knew he'd be able to spot a lie in a heartbeat. Interrogating people is what he *did*.

When I'd finished, he took out his gun again. I'd been right: I was no more use to him, now. I closed my eyes and thought of Danny's garage and the feel of his arms around me as we'd danced.

"What the *hell* are you doing?"

My eyes snapped open and I saw the woman with the British accent from before standing in the doorway. "I've just found one of the maids in tears. What did you do to her? Now I'm going to have to pay her off! And what's *this?!*" She scowled at Becker. "We have rules at these events, Mr. Becker! If you need to kill her, do it after you leave here!"

Becker glowered at her but the woman just stared coldly back at him and, eventually, he dropped his eyes. Whoever this woman was, she had serious power.

"I'll lock her in here until the deal is complete," said Becker. "Acceptable?"

"Don't leave her tied to a chair," snapped the woman. "You've already got blood on the carpet, I don't want her pissing herself, too."

She stalked out. Becker moved around the suite, checking there was no way for me to escape. He checked there was only one door. He tried the windows: they didn't open. Besides, we were a hundred feet up.

Then I saw the phone. A landline one, on a side table in the corner, almost hidden by a houseplant. If he didn't notice it...

Becker bent and untied my wrists, then my ankles. He dug in his bag and pulled out a first aid kit, then tossed it on my lap. "I don't want you bleeding out while I'm away."

I nodded meekly. *Please don't see the phone, please, please—*

He put his hand on the doorknob, ready to leave. Then he turned and took a last look around the room. Suddenly, his face soured. *Shit.*

He marched across the room, grabbed the landline phone and wrenched, snapping the cable. Then he left, taking the phone with him and locking the door behind him.

I put my head in my hands and wept slow, silent tears, feeling myself sink down and down into absolute despair. I didn't even bandage my foot. What was the point? In a few hours, when Becker's deal was done, I'd be put in the trunk of his car again and driven off to a shallow grave.

I stayed like that for a long time, sinking lower and lower, until I was where it's black and cold. And right down there, in the darkest pit, I felt something. Green eyes, glittering. This sort of situation was where Danny flourished, where he lived. Because when you don't have anything left, when all's lost...the only thing you can do *is* to be cockily confident, to grin and give Death the middle finger.

He wouldn't give up. And if he wouldn't, I wouldn't. I *wasn't* on my own. Danny and the team wouldn't let themselves be sent to jail. They'd find a way out. I just had to believe in them. And find a way to let them know where I was.

I opened my eyes. Dug into the first aid kit and bandaged my foot. There were painkillers in the kit, too, and I dry-swallowed some so I could think.

I checked the door but it was solid wood and firmly locked. I limped around the whole suite just in case Becker had missed anything, but he hadn't. I stood in the center of the bedroom, thinking furiously. *If only he hadn't taken the phone!* I stared at the ragged ends of the phone cable that hung from the wall. Down that wire, somewhere on the other end of the network, was Danny. All I needed was a $10 phone from any electronics store and I could just call him!

Then my eyes narrowed. I didn't have to *call* him. I just had to *dial* him.

These days, phone calls are mostly just streams of data: your voice goes over the internet like everything else. But before *that,* numbers were dialed with tones: *beep boop beep* as you pressed the buttons. And before *that,* you dialed with clicks. That's how old rotary dial phones worked: you turned the dial to four and released it, and it made four little clicks as it sprang back. And that system's still there, it's just barely used anymore.

I sat down next to the broken cable. I didn't have wire strippers, but the first aid kit had scissors. I didn't have electrical tape, but I had sticking plasters. And I found a pen in a drawer that had a springy metal pocket clip. It took me about half an hour, but I managed to wire the pen to the phone cable. By pressing down on the metal pocket clip, I could complete the circuit and make a *click. In theory,* I could dial out.

But who to dial? I didn't have the number of the burner phone Danny was using. Or any of the team, or the base back in Mount Mercy. But there was one number I had written down...

I pulled out Luka Malakov's business card. *Better than nothing.* I took a deep breath, then carefully tapped the pen clip ten times: that was a zero. Then a pause, then seven taps to dial a seven. It took forever but, finally, I tapped out the last digit. And then I waited. Somewhere, hopefully, a phone was ringing.

The problem was that there was no way to know if it had worked. I counted off thirty seconds, then dialed again. I'd just have to pray that Luka understood.

71

DANNY

I WAS PACING up and down Vasiliy's living room. The rest of the team were scattered around the couches and armchairs, all of us stewing in silence. It was eerily quiet except for the ringing of a cell phone, off in another room, and the quiet was driving me crazy. I needed to be out there, finding her. She was all alone with that psycho—

"Could we try the Sisters of Invidia again?" I demanded.

"They've been through the satellite feeds a hundred times," said Kian gently. "We know Becker went south from Berlin but then they lost him. He's probably gone to meet the buyer. He could be anywhere by now."

I kept pacing. "We could go to the police."

"They'd never believe us," said Bradan. "We're fugitives, accusing one of their top spies."

JD didn't say a word. He just stood by the fireplace, staring at the flames and going through the same hell I was going through.

The cellphone rang again, coming closer. Luka walked into the room in a bathrobe, stabbing angrily at the screen to reject the call. He watched me pace for a few seconds. "You wear out rug," he said, not unkindly.

I spun to face the room. "There's got to be some way to find her!" My stomach was churning with cold, sick fear. I could feel her slipping away with every second. I looked desperately around the room but everyone just looked back at me helplessly.

Luka's phone began to ring again. He cursed in Russian and stabbed at the screen again to reject it.

"Who keeps calling you?" asked Gina.

Luka shrugged his massive shoulders. "Salesman, maybe. But their machine broken. No one there when I answer. They keep calling and calling." He gestured at his bathrobe. "Even in sauna!" He scowled. "I keep number private to *avoid* this!"

I froze. "Wait. Wait, wait, wait. *Erin* has your number!" I snatched the phone from him before he could stop me and brought up the last caller, then called Lily, one of The Sisters of Invidia. "Can you locate a phone number?" I read it out to her.

"Southern Germany," she said a few seconds later. "Private estate. Wait, is this right? It's a *castle!*" She sent me a photo and a map.

JD and the others crowded around to look. "We're going to need a chopper," said JD.

"*Finally!*" breathed Gina.

~

A little over an hour later, we were crouched in thick forest, looking in disbelief at the white-painted castle. "Who's buying the bomb?" asked Kian. "Cinderella?"

"I don't think this is just about selling the bomb," said Gabriel slowly. "Look how many guards there are. He pointed to a whole row of expensive cars parked next to the castle. More were approaching up the winding road. "This is something bigger."

"I'll go slip in and find Erin," I said, checking my gun, "while the rest of you secure the nuke."

"*I'll* get Erin," said JD firmly.

I turned to him. "We need you to lead the team. You've got to trust me, mate. I'll get her back, I *promise.*"

He stared at me for a long time. I could still see anger burning in his eyes: things weren't resolved, between us. But at last, he nodded.

"I'll go with you," Kian told me.

And we moved out.

72

ERIN

I DROPPED my homemade dialer to the floor and clutched my hand to my stomach, nursing my cramped fingers. *Enough.* I couldn't reliably dial the numbers anymore. If it hadn't worked by now, it never would.

The roar of an engine made me limp over to the turret's window. Far below, a black snake of cars was crawling up the mountain road towards the castle. A tiny, toy-like figure in a suit was walking out to meet them. Even from this distance, there was no mistaking the way he walked, his back ramrod straight, or the silver of his beard. *Becker.* That meant that the approaching cars must be his buyers.

He was about to sell the bomb. And then, as soon as he left, he'd kill me.

73

DANNY

THERE WERE plenty of guards patrolling but the castle was vast, far too big for them to watch everywhere at once. Kian gave me a boost up onto the top of a narrow, ice-crusted wall and I heaved him up after me. On the other side, we found a darkened annex that looked like it hadn't been used in a while, but it connected to the main castle. Kian duct-taped a pane of glass and then smashed it out almost silently. I blinked at him. I'd always thought of him as the guy behind the desk.

"Not my first time breaking into somewhere," he told me.

Inside, we stayed low, creeping along passageways and flattening ourselves into doorways whenever we heard people approaching. There seemed to be multiple groups strolling around the castle, talking in a whole mixture of languages. Mostly men but some women, too, all in expensive clothes. We could hear lively discussions going on in some of the rooms and waiters were carrying trays of drinks and canapés back and forth. *What the hell is going on?* Was this business? A party? Both?

We crept on, deeper and deeper into the castle. The size of the place was working against us, now. It would take hours to search the whole thing and we didn't have that long: sooner or later, someone was going to see us and raise the alarm.

A door opened right beside me and a woman in a maid's uniform stifled a scream as she saw me. I put a finger to my lips, "*Sh! Shh! Bitte!*" *Please* was one of the few German words I knew.

The woman looked at us uncertainly, but she kept quiet. Her eyes were red from crying. I tentatively put my hand on her shoulder. "It's okay," I told her, praying she spoke English. I pointed at Kian and me. "Good guys," I explained.

She looked at our guns and swallowed nervously, far from convinced.

"I need to find a woman," I told her. I put my hand down low. "Small." The woman looked blank—maybe her English wasn't that good. In desperation, I put my hands to the back of my head and mimed Erin's braid.

The woman's face lit up with recognition and, for some reason, she relaxed. She beckoned us and led the way down the hallway, almost to the far side of the castle. Then she pointed us up a spiral stone staircase. "Up there?" I asked.

She nodded firmly, then hurried away.

Kian and I slunk up the staircase, backs pressed against the wall and guns raised. At the very top was a heavy wooden door. I peeked through the keyhole and drew in a deep, shuddering breath.

"Is it her?" asked Kian. "Is she—"

I didn't waste time answering. I backed up to the far wall, ran at the door and shoulder-charged it. There was a crack of splintering wood, I staggered inside....

And there she was, standing by the bed, her eyes wide with disbelief.

The relief was like nothing I'd ever felt. I grabbed Erin by the waist, picked her up and crushed her to me. Then I saw the chair with cord tied to the arms and the blood on the carpet, and my arms tightened even more. "I'm here now," I told her in a choking gasp. "I'm here now."

74

JD

GABRIEL'S LOCKPICKING skills had got us into one of the garages and then down into the cellars. We were creeping through a wide, vaulted tunnel that seemed to twist on forever. So far, it was all quiet and that was good. But it meant my mind was free to race non-stop.

Erin. She'd been right, at Katharina's apartment: she wasn't a kid anymore. And she'd been brave as hell, coming all the way to Siberia to help rescue me, and then doing everything since. But she was still my little sister and if something happened to her...

And then there was her and Danny. At first, it had felt like betrayal. He'd lied to me, lied right to my face. My *best friend.* Now, that was beginning to fade. I could see he was serious: he really cared about her. But did he really *love* her? This was Danny: I wasn't sure he'd ever been in love. And if he was wrong, Erin was going to get her heart broken all over again. I couldn't let that happen.

Bradan was leading the way, since he was the stealthiest. He suddenly stopped and we all froze where we were, weapons up. But after a moment, he waved us forward and pointed to something leaning up against a wall. I played a flashlight over it and saw a gold frame, then an image of a man. There were more next to it. "Oil paintings?" I muttered.

Gabriel moved up alongside me and gave a half-groan, half-sob. "That's *Portrait of a Young Man!*" He looked around at our blank expressions. "By *Raphael,* you philistines! This has been missing for nearly eighty years! It'd sell for millions. And *God,* that's *Harlequin Head,* by Picasso, everybody thought this was destroyed!" He reached out and touched the frame lovingly. "Do you know how much money we could make, if we just grabbed one of these?"

I drew him gently away. Gabriel was reformed...but not *all the way* reformed.

Around the next corner, we found dust-covered bottles of wine nestled in boxes of straw. Then, at the bottom of a ramp that led up to ground level, the gleaming curves of cars: a Lamborghini, two Ferraris and a Nissan GTR. Piled next to them were about twenty long, olive-green metal cases. We opened one and found a shoulder-mounted missile launcher. Gabriel cursed. "I know what this place is."

A footstep echoed from around the next bend. We immediately backed into the shadows, crouching behind the piles of military gear. Seconds later, a woman in a cream suit stalked past us, her heels click-clacking on the stone floor. She was issuing orders to a couple of armed guards at a ferocious pace. "Make sure the Chinese have refreshments and show them into the Great Hall. Then use the library for Mr. Becker and his buyers."

When the group had passed, Gabriel turned to the rest of us. "That's Selina Kirk-Hughes! This must be one of her fairs." He looked wistful. "I sold a Dali and a sapphire necklace at one of these." He indicated the castle above us. "She organizes these events. Hires a big place, out in the country, brings lots of buyers and sellers together. Stolen art, cars, arms, information...it all gets traded in one place, in one day. You have to be invited and the invitations are little cubes of glass, etched by laser, impossible to tamper with."

There was a sound right next to us and everyone spun, raising their guns. I swept my flashlight back and forth and found the source: a metal cage. All I could see inside was brown fluff. Then it turned around and I saw its face. A baby brown bear, about the size of a big puppy.

Colton moved closer, reached through the bars and stroked the bear, and it pressed its head into his hand. "A *bear*? Why's someone selling a *bear*? For some rich guy's zoo?"

Cal looked at me. I looked at Bradan. Bradan looked at Gabriel. None of us wanted to be the one to tell him. "It'll be going to China," I said at last. "For traditional medicine. They keep it in a cage and they, uh..." I swallowed. "They put a tube in it. To collect bile from its gallbladder. They can keep it alive for about ten years."

Colton stared at me in disbelief. Then his expression changed to anger. He stroked the bear again and it made the most pathetic, keening yowl I'd ever heard. I could see the rage spreading through Colton's body as he stroked the little thing, his shoulders and back tensing. When he stepped away from the cage, he was shaking. I'd never seen him so mad.

We found stairs leading up into the castle. We knew Becker would be meeting his buyers in the library, but where was *that*? The place was huge and there were no signposts.

Then we heard the squeak of a wheel, around the next corner. Bradan crept forward and peeked, then waved us to him. A guard was pushing a moving cart and on it was the brown leather case of the bomb.

The guard disappeared through a doorway. We formed up beside it and I counted us in: *one, two three—*

We burst in, guns up. We'd found the library, a cavernous space with towering shelves of leather-bound books and a staircase leading up to a second floor. Becker was there, setting up a laptop, probably to arrange his payment. Two blond-haired men in expensive suits were inspecting the bomb. I could only see one guard, the one who'd pushed the cart, and he raised his hands as soon as we pointed our guns at him. We'd got the drop on them.

I marched forward, keeping my sights right in the center of Becker's face. "Where's Erin?" I yelled. "Where's my sister?"

Becker's lips twitched into a sad little smile. And suddenly the room exploded into noise and chaos.

There was a balcony, directly over the door we'd come through. Three more guards were there, firing down at us with assault rifles, the bullets chewing up carpet, furniture and books as they sprayed us, filling the air with splinters and shredded paper. I cried out as something slashed across my arm. I'd run in too fast, without checking the room, and now we were completely exposed.

Cal grabbed me and hauled me behind a desk in the corner of the room. There was barely room for the five of us to huddle there. We ducked down as bullets chewed away at the edges.

We were pinned down, with no way out.

75

ERIN

I CLUTCHED DANNY TEDDY-BEAR TIGHT, so tight it must have hurt, but he didn't complain. He was breathing hard in my ear, whispering that it was okay now, each breath shaky with emotion. But I needed a different level of reassurance: I pressed my body as hard as I could against his, feeling every hard contour of him, filling my nostrils with his scent, until my soul accepted that he was really real, really alive, really there. Behind Danny, Kian was checking the other rooms of the suite, making sure we were alone. Then he relaxed a little and watched us, smiling.

At last, Danny reluctantly put me down, but he immediately cupped my cheek in one hand as if he couldn't bear to fully break contact. He looked down at the bandages wrapped around my foot. Blood was soaking through them. Danny's voice went so tight with anger that he could barely get the words out. "What did he...do to you?"

"I'll be okay," I told him. "He wants to be Chancellor. That's why he's selling the bomb, he's going to bribe and blackmail his way to running the country."

Kian and Danny both grimaced. "It's okay," said Kian. "JD and the others are getting the bomb."

"We're getting you out of here," Danny told me. "Can you walk?" He was already stooping to pick me up again, ready to carry me.

I nodded quickly. I could limp along and he needed to be able to hold his gun.

Danny went first, with me right behind him, a hand on his back, and Kian watching our rear. We spiraled down the stairs and Danny led us through the castle's ornate hallways. For the first few minutes, it was quiet. Then we heard gunfire from behind a set of wooden doors. We all looked at each other. If the guards were fighting someone, it had to be the team.

Danny gestured for us to stay back, then crept to the door and silently cracked it open a half inch so he could peek. He crept back to us, his face grim. "It's the others. They're pinned down, downstairs."

"We've got to help them!" I said immediately. Why was he even hesitating?

"Our job's to get you out." I could see the battle going on in his eyes. Protect me or save the team?

I put my hand on his chest. "It's my decision too. We have to help them."

Danny cocked his head to one side and stared at me, then slowly shook his head in wonder. "Stay at the door," he told me firmly. Then he and Kian pushed open the door and crept in.

I peeked around the edge. A hallway led to a balcony overlooking a library. Two guards on the balcony were firing down at a big wooden desk. I saw JD pop his head out from behind it for an instant, then duck back as more bullets hit.

Between us and the guards were two pedestals, each topped with a stone bust. I watched, digging my nails into my palms, as Danny and Kian crouch-walked closer and closer to the guards until they could get a clear shot. Then there were two quick bursts of gunfire and the two guards dropped to the ground. I slumped against the wall in relief. *Whew.*

That's when the *third* guard, the one none of us had seen, ran out of the shadows and slammed his rifle into Kian's head. Kian sprawled on his back, not quite unconscious but not getting up, either. The guard raised his gun to shoot—

Danny dived at him and tackled him to the ground. Both of them lost their guns and rolled over and over, hands at each other's throats. Danny wound up on the bottom, his face turning scarlet as the guard choked him. The team were running to help, now that they weren't pinned down, but there was no direct way up to the balcony from where they were.

I limped towards Danny, adrenaline making everything bright and clear. I grabbed one of the stone busts and—

Oh God, it was much, *much* heavier than it looked. But I was committed now. I staggered on, the guard looked up as he heard me coming—

I pretty much fell on him. It wasn't elegant, but the stone bust hit him in the face and he fell off Danny, out cold.

I slumped on top of Danny and we lay there panting. A moment later, JD and the rest of the team arrived. "You okay?" JD asked me immediately.

I nodded shakily and pointed to his arm: he was bleeding.

He shook his head. "Got clipped by a chunk of wood. I'm fine."

Kian raised himself up on his forearms, groaning, and looked at the library below. "Where's Becker?"

Bradan ran to the balcony and looked over the railing. "Shit. The bomb's gone, too."

JD's radio squawked. "I've got him," said Gina, yelling over the rattle of helicopter blades. "He's tearing down the hill in a red Ferrari."

"A *Ferrari?*" Danny clambered to his feet and hauled me up, too. "Where'd he get *that?*"

"There were supercars in the cellar, being sold," Gabriel told him. "Becker must have grabbed one."

"He's really moving." Gina sounded worried. "Once he gets into the forest, I'll lose sight of him. He's going to get away."

"No he's fucking not," said Danny.

76

DANNY

WE BLASTED up out of the cellar and went airborne for a second as we reached the top of the ramp. Then we thumped down and shot forward across the castle's courtyard, already doing fifty and accelerating fast.

I ran my hands lovingly over the steering wheel of the Nissan GTR. It was so beautifully engineered, I could feel the ice crystals crunching under the tires and the texture of the asphalt beneath. I snapped in a gear change and we rocketed down the hill, hitting seventy before I had to brake for the first corner.

As we slid through the turn, I stole a glance at Erin. She had one hand on the grab-handle above her and one gripping the edge of her seat. The road hugged the side of the mountain, looping back and forth as it descended, so there was a sheer drop on one side of us and she gulped whenever she looked at it. She was scared, but she'd jumped into the car with me without a second thought. We were a team, now, bonded forever. But for us to have a future, I had to catch Becker. He had a fast car and a big head start.

Fortunately, this was *what I did*.

I fed the car through bend after bend, feathering the gas to make the back end swing out just so, missing the trees at the edge of the road by inches. And finally, I saw a flash of red up ahead. Every corner brought it a little closer, until we pulled alongside Becker's growling, snarling Ferrari.

Becker tried to use raw speed to get away, and together we went faster and faster, the scenery blurring. I heard Erin moan and I guessed she'd closed her eyes.

A corner raced towards us. I backed off, slowing, but Becker went in full speed. "No," I muttered aloud. "No, no, you'll never make it...."

Becker flicked the car into the turn. He wasn't a bad driver and any other time, he might have made it: the Ferrari designers had lovingly crafted the car to have perfect weight distribution and it handled beautifully.

But Becker had ruined all that by putting a huge lump of lead in the passenger seat. I saw the tires give up their grip and the car began to spin, slewing across the road. I braked but not fast enough. Becker's car hit ours and together, we went spinning towards the edge of the cliff.

77

ERIN

I WENT SILENT, too scared to scream. I was on an out-of-control carousel, spinning so fast my head was pressed hard against the side window. Through the windshield I caught glimpses of trees then cliff, trees then cliff, and every time I saw the cliff, it was closer....

There was a crunch of metal, then another one that jolted our car and stopped the spin. We straightened out heading straight for the cliff and now I *did* scream, crushing myself instinctively back into my seat.

The brakes squealed, there was a rattle of gravel and we slid to a stop a foot short of the cliff edge.

"You okay?" asked Danny.

I nodded weakly. I just wanted to slump there for a while but we couldn't. *Where was Becker?*

Danny was already climbing out and I followed, my legs shaky. The air stunk of hot metal and rubber and there were deep gouges in the snow where the Ferrari had slid. It had hit a tree and come to rest on the edge of the cliff, with the driver's side hanging over the edge. As we approached, we saw Becker climbing awkwardly over the bomb in the passenger seat and crawling out onto the ground. Just as

Danny reached him, Becker scrambled to his feet and punched Danny viciously in the kidneys, sending him stumbling.

Danny motioned for me to stay back and I did, watching as the two of them circled each other, Danny wincing and clutching his side. Danny was younger and probably fitter, but Becker had years of experience of hurting people. Danny pressed forward, swinging punches, but Becker dodged and weaved, then stamped down hard on the inside of Danny's shin. Danny let out a groan of pain and stumbled sideways, and I winced.

That's when I saw Becker's car move.

The ground sloped down towards the edge of the cliff and the car was slowly sliding, In another minute or two, enough of it would be over the edge that it would tip and go tumbling over. And the bomb was still in the passenger seat. I peeked over the edge: it was at least a hundred feet to the bottom and there was a village down there. Would the bomb go off, if it fell? Even if it didn't, if the casing cracked open, it could cover the village with radioactive debris. I had to get it out of there.

I limped over to the car and grabbed hold of the case. *God,* I'd forgotten how much the thing weighed. It didn't help that the car was tilting away from me, so I was trying to pull it uphill. I strained and pulled and eventually realized it was useless. If I wanted to get it out, I'd have to push, not pull. I'd have to climb over it, into the driver's seat, and *push* it out. The only problem was, the driver's seat was hanging over space.

I took a deep breath and scrambled in, slithering over the bomb's case and onto the soft leather of the driver's seat. I tried not to look at the drop through the driver's window, or think about how the car was rocking, as my weight shifted.

I hung onto the seat, got my feet against the bomb and pushed, but that didn't do it. I didn't have enough leverage. I scooched back and braced my back against the driver's door, then prepared to push again. If the door latch had been damaged in the crash, if it swung open when I pressed on it...

Don't think about that.

I braced myself against the door and *pushed.* The bomb shifted. Slowly at first, then faster. The leather seat was grippy on the leather case, but inch by inch, I was doing it.

Then I felt the car move under me. My weight in the driver's seat had changed the car's balance. It was sliding faster.

The car was going over the cliff with me in it.

78

DANNY

I was panting and wheezing, the sweat pouring down my face. One eye was swollen shut, my right leg wanted to collapse under me and my kidneys were a mass of pain. I was stronger but Becker was more skilled. He was smart and vicious and he was taking me apart piece by piece. I was a big dumb animal fighting a scorpion. And we were fighting only ten feet from the cliff edge. One mistake and he'd grapple me and throw me over it.

Then I saw Erin climb into Becker's car. *What? What the fuck is she doing?!* I looked at Becker and only just dodged an elbow that would have finished me. When I checked the car again, it was moving, rocking. *Oh Jesus.*

I had to finish this, *now*. But if I turned my back on Becker, he'd kill me and then kill Erin.

I glared at Becker and blinked back blood and sweat. He dropped into a fighting stance. All that training he'd had...he was ready for any martial arts move I could throw at him.

But maybe he wasn't ready for what I'd learned back in that working-class neighborhood in London.

I put my head down, bellowed, and charged him like a bull. My head rammed into his stomach and he grunted as I forced him back towards the very edge of the cliff. But then he punched me in the kidneys again and I had to let him go. I straightened up, wheezing in pain and holding my side. He grabbed my shoulders, ready to throw me over the cliff.

That's when I headbutted him as hard as I possibly could. My forehead smashed into his nose and he staggered back...and ran out of ground. I watched as he went over the edge and tumbled a hundred feet to the valley below. "That's what we call a Glasgow Kiss," I panted. "You wanker."

Then I stumbled over to Becker's car. Erin was wedged in the driver's seat, trying to push the bomb out with her feet. "Get out of there!" I snapped.

"Pull it!" she hissed through gritted teeth.

I cursed, got my arms around the thing and heaved and with her pushing, too, it slithered off the seat and fell to the ground, narrowly missing my foot. But now we had a new problem: the massive weight of the bomb had been helping to hold the car on the cliff. Now it was gone, the car started to tip even faster. "*Move!*" I yelled.

She started to scooch forward towards me but the car was tipping too fast. Even as her feet reached me, the seats turned almost vertical. I lunged in, grabbed her sneaker and—

There was a horrible second as the car fell away from her. If one of her fingers got caught, if a seatbelt snagged on her....

But then the car was gone, tumbling and spinning in space, and Erin was dangling from my hand. I managed to take a couple of stumbling steps backwards, enough to pull her back onto solid ground, and then I fell flat on my ass. We lay there in the snow, panting and utterly spent but together. Then she got to her hands and knees and crawled just far enough that she could collapse with her head on my chest.

I heard a chopper overhead but I couldn't be bothered to open my eyes. I just wrapped my arms around Erin and stroked her hair. Everything else could wait.

We lay cuddled there until a shadow fell across us. I looked up to see JD standing there, watching us.

I tightened my arms around Erin and stared back at him.

The emotions played across his face: anger, worry...and finally, hope. At last, he lifted his jaw and glared at me, but it was a glare I recognized, one I understood. *You better not break her heart.*

I nodded solemnly.

JD took two steps forward, crouched beside us and wrapped his arms around us, pulling us both to him in a three-way hug.

EPILOGUE
ERIN

THE GERMAN POLICE arrived and slapped cuffs on us. But we had the nuke, now, and that was the hard evidence we'd needed. The authorities started looking into Becker and, gradually, the mood changed. The charges against us were dropped one by one. We still had *a lot* of questions to answer, but the Germans started feeding us coffee and treating us as guests, not prisoners.

Then a guy from the US Embassy arrived and started yelling at us. He got right up in Kian's face, screaming that he was a *loose cannon*. Kian looked completely nonplussed, as if it wasn't the first time he'd been called that. But the embassy guy raged on, telling Kian he'd nearly started an international incident, that if he had his way, we'd all be in jail—

Then Roberta from the CIA burst through the door and pinned the embassy guy with a look. "Don't be a dick, Maurice," she told him in a withering voice. And Maurice slunk away with his tail between his legs.

Roberta looked around at us. "The State Department's pissed that you did all this on foreign soil but don't worry, I'll smooth things over. You're heroes, even if you may have bent a few laws. Just cooperate with the Germans." We heard footsteps in the hallway and she turned towards the door. "There's someone I've got to debrief…"

Vasiliy Malakov walked in, surrounded by lawyers. He was in good spirits, telling everyone who'd listen about how he'd helped to save the world. When he saw Roberta, he nodded politely. "Miss Geiss."

Roberta's voice was cool and calm. "Mr. Malakov."

And then, just for a fraction of a second, Vasiliy gave her this *look*. An *I want to bend you over the nearest table* look. And Roberta lifted her chin just a fraction of an inch as if to say, *well why don't you, then?*

Then it was gone, so fast that I wondered if I'd imagined it. "I'll handle your debriefing myself, Mr. Malakov," Roberta told him. "Is there a quiet interview room we could use?"

The German police led the two of them away and I stood there stunned. I was remembering what Arianna had said, about Vasiliy's American girlfriend.

~

The police had a doctor take a look at our injuries. Danny had broken two toes when he dropped the nuke on it, but they'd heal. And my toenail would grow back, given a year or so.

It felt like we told our story about six hundred times to twenty different German agencies, but none of us minded too much: we were warm and safe for the first time in a while and there was plenty of coffee. Most importantly, we weren't fugitives anymore. And they let Danny and I give our interviews together, sitting hand in hand, which was good because neither of us was allowing the other one out of their sight.

When it was finally over, we were released. And just a few hours later, we were standing in the snow at a private airfield, watching as a crew fueled the plane that would take us home. "I could have flown us, y'know," said Gina grumpily.

"Not by yourself," Kian told her. "It's way too far. It's not a bad idea, though: maybe we should get you a co-pilot. Then you could do longer flights. You could handle bigger aircraft, too."

"Whoah, whoah, whoah," Gina told him. "Fine, I'll be a good passenger. But I'm not sharing my cockpit with anyone."

Danny looked around. "Where's Colton?"

"He said he had to run an errand," said JD. Then he nodded across the tarmac. "Looks like someone else is here, though."

An Audi with a police light on the dash was pulling up. Katharina jumped out, elegant and sophisticated in a long black coat. She ran over to us. "I managed to get away for a minute," she told us breathlessly. "Didn't want you to leave without saying goodbye."

Danny put his hand on her arm. "Everything okay?" The last time we'd seen her, she'd been in cuffs.

She nodded, smiling. "They dropped the charges against me. And now they know I'm the one BND officer who definitely *wasn't* working with Becker, they've put me in charge of rooting out any other corrupt officers." She shrugged. "I might even get a promotion out of it."

"You deserve it." Danny put his arms around her and hugged her close and I didn't get even an echo of jealousy. We were friends now. "I'll never forget what you did for us. We owe you."

She hugged him tight. "I might call that in, one day."

She released him and the rest of the team moved in to embrace her. Finally, it was my turn. As we squeezed each other close, she spoke into my ear, "Take care of him, okay?" Her voice was level and calm but I could hear the pain lurking like jagged rocks just beneath the surface.

I nodded. "I will," I said firmly. My chest ached for her. *She needs to find somebody, too.*

Just as we were getting worried, a taxi pulled up and out climbed Colton, holding something wrapped in a blanket against his chest. We all crowded around curiously.

The blanket twitched...and then something brown and fluffy poked out and my heart swelled in such an overload of *cute* that I had to grab hold of Danny's waist.

We were looking into the face of a little baby bear.

"I was worried he'd wind up being sold to China," Colton told us. "So I asked the cops if I could take him. They said it was the least they could do."

"Colton...you can't take him home with you—" started JD.

Colton looked him right in the eye, his jaw set. He was *not* giving up that bear.

Gina sighed. "He'll get big."

"I don't care," Colton told her. And at that point, the baby bear yawned and rubbed at its eyes with its paw, and my brain just went *fzzt* and stopped working, overloaded with cute.

"Fine," said JD, and petted the bear. "Let's go home."

It was two in the morning when we arrived back in Mount Mercy. Danny was at the wheel of the huge black SUV as we drove around dropping everyone off. I was in the passenger seat, watching him as he guided us carefully through the snow. Every now and again, he'd lift one hand from the wheel, reach over and brush my cheek with his knuckles. Outside it was dark and cold and the snow was falling in heavy, silent flurries but as long as he was at the wheel, I knew we were completely safe. And sitting there cozied up, watching him drive, it felt like I'd found a new favorite place.

We went to the edge of town first, to drop off Cal. I hadn't seen their cabin before and I stared at it, amazed: *they built that themselves?!* With the roof covered in snow and lights glowing inside, it looked like something on a Christmas Card. Before Cal had even reached the door, it swung open and Rufus came racing out, bounding through snow drifts that were up to the top of his legs and showering Cal in snow as he leapt up at him, ecstatic. Bethany ran out in a dressing gown, the legs of her PJs getting soaked as she waded through the snow. Then she and Cal were embracing, with Rufus leaping and woofing in the tent their bodies made, his tail smacking their legs.

Next up was Colton, who had a trailer not far from town. He

climbed out carefully, cradling the bear. "C'mon, little guy," I heard him murmur. "Lemme show you where you're gonna live."

Then we sped into town, to where Bradan and Stacey had an apartment. Stacey was waiting outside the apartment block when we turned into the street: Bethany must have called to let her know we were on our way. She was in a slinky robe and, from the silhouette, very little underneath. She must have been freezing but she toughed it out, standing there shivering while we drove up and parked. She slumped in relief when she saw Bradan climb out. He hurried over and picked her up, wrapping his arms around her and crushing her to his chest, and I heard her sigh as if instantly, cozily warm.

Then it was over to Kian and Emily's place, a townhouse on one of the older streets. Two Secret Service agents came over and checked who was in the car before radioing that it was safe for Emily to come out. She and Kian met on the steps of their house and Kian picked her up and spun her around. Emily limpeted onto him and refused to be put down. It hit me that Emily hadn't ever had this before. She'd seen the other girlfriends worry about their men, she'd comforted them, but she'd always had Kian safely beside her. "Don't do that again," I heard her say into his chest. "At least not for a while."

JD was the last one to be dropped off. We pulled up outside the apartment block and I walked in with him to pick up my bags. Inside, he didn't switch the light on straightaway and we stood there in the darkness for a moment with the snow falling outside the window. JD looked at me and gave a long sigh. "Thank you for getting me out." He shook his head in wonder. "What you went through, with no training... That was pretty incredible."

I looked at the floor, embarrassed. "I'm tougher than I look."

JD nodded. "Yeah. Guess I'm figuring that out."

A swell of pride filled my chest. I tentatively lifted my eyes. "We okay about...the other thing?"

JD gave another long sigh, then looked at the ceiling. "It's gonna take some getting used to. And if he hurts you—"

"He won't."

JD's face softened. "No. No, I don't think he will." He looked down at me for a moment, proud but sad, the same look he'd given me the day he dropped me off at my college dorm. Then he pulled me into a hug.

"What about you?" I asked, my voice muffled by his body. "Will you be okay?" Over his shoulder, I was looking at the barely-furnished apartment, the stark emptiness of his life.

"Always," he told me, rubbing my back. "Now go on, *git!*" That made me laugh: I hadn't heard him say *git* for years. "Your guy's waiting for you."

I grabbed my bags and hurried back down the stairs to Danny. But as we drove off towards his garage, I kept looking back at JD's apartment. He needed to find someone who could heal that big, broken heart of his.

As we stepped inside Danny's garage, I closed my eyes for a second and inhaled, feeling my body relax at the scent of oil and metal. I'd only spent a day here, but it felt like home.

When I opened my eyes, Danny was standing in front of me. God, he looked glorious: black overcoat, black suit with that crisp white shirt stretched over the broad swells of his pecs…. Snowflakes were melting in his hair and he was gazing right at me with those glittering, absinthe-green eyes. But for once, he wasn't grinning that cocky grin. He looked serious. Nervous, even. "What is it?" I asked, worried.

He didn't answer for a moment. He took hold of a chain that hung from a pulley above, running the links through his fingers. When he finally spoke, his voice was slow and gentle, as if he was trying not to spook me. "I want you to stay."

I smiled and nodded, a little confused. *Well, good.* I mean, I'd kind of assumed I was staying the night. Had I been wrong, to just assume? We were together now, right?

Then I saw the way he was looking at me and—*Oh. OH!* "Stay in *Mount Mercy*?" I thought aloud. "For good?"

He nodded and I saw the fear in his eyes. It was so rare to see Danny afraid of anything and that made it hit me even harder: he was scared I'd say *no*.

I grabbed his hands. "Of course I want to stay. But I don't know if I can find a job here. What I do is pretty specialist and it's a tiny little town. The work is all in cities with tech firms—"

"Work for *us*," Danny told me. "Work for Stormfinch. You've seen us, we don't even know how to hook up a screen. The whole base needs fitting out. And *we* need fitting out: better communications gear. And gadgets. Colton told me he's already asked you for something."

I nodded. Colton had asked if I could make a tracker for bounty hunting. Something small he could secretly attach to a bail-jumper he was transporting, so that if they escaped, Colton could track them down.

"I've spoken to Kian," Danny told me. "He's ready to bring you on board as our tech specialist. Just say the word."

I stared up at him, tears filling my eyes. My whole life, I'd been searching for the right burrow. I'd finally found it. "Yes," I told him. "*Yes!* Of course yes!"

He grabbed me around the waist, picked me up and spun me around with a whoop of joy. We pinwheeled across the garage, his chest shaking with delighted laughter. When he eventually put me down, I was lightheaded and giggly. Something was deliciously warm against my ass. I looked down and realized he'd set me down on the hood of the Jag.

Danny glanced around the garage, excited. "I'll clear out a rack for your tools."

With other women, it would be *I'll clear out a drawer for your clothes.* He knew me well. "We should celebrate. Do you want to go out? A bar?"

Danny gave a filthy chuckle and pushed me down on the hood. "I can think of a better way to celebrate."

The next evening, we finally had the party that had been on hold ever since the team came home without JD. It was too cold for a barbecue so the main room of the base had been transformed into a cozy space. The building's aging furnace had been cranked up to max, making it toasty warm, the leather couches had been covered in soft throws and strings of fairy lights hung overhead.

Bethany had cooked up an entire vat of venison stew, hot and full of meaty, salty flavor, and it paired well with pints of the Irish stout Kian had provided. Emily had baked an apple pie fully two feet across—I couldn't figure out how she'd got it in the oven—the crust sugary crisp and the fruit luxuriantly soft and tangy. Stacey had set up a hot chocolate table, blending steaming milk with chunks of Belgian chocolate to make the smoothest, richest hot chocolate I'd ever tasted, and she was offering it with marshmallows, whipped cream, chocolate sprinkles and optional shots of liquor to really chase the cold away. Olivia brought out the tin of cookies she'd made and we all grabbed one before Colton saw them and snarfled the lot.

After Siberia and the freezing streets of Berlin, the warmth and comfort food was exactly what we needed. As I snuggled up against Danny, I could feel the chill finally starting to leave my bones.

The highlight of the party, though, was the bear cub. It didn't seem to have seen snow before and we all watched as it stared at the falling flakes from the back door of the base. Then it slowly ventured outdoors, gazing in wonder as a snowflake drifted down, down...and landed smack on its wet nose. The cub gave a kind of sneeze and fell on its rump, looking confused, and then started to gambol around in the drifts. Rufus showed up and Cal made him stay back at first, not wanting to scare the bear. But Rufus was surprisingly gentle, nudging the cub with his nose as if he was a puppy, and within minutes the two were playing in the snow together.

Back inside, we all collapsed in the couches, sipping hot chocolate. I found myself sitting across from Emily and, at first, I was intimidated. But she turned out to be chatty and down-to-earth and we hit it off immediately: having a shared Texan background helped. It sounded like she was enjoying the small-town life in Mount Mercy:

now that her dad had won the Presidency again, every paparazzi in Washington had declared it open season on the First Family. "If I wear the same dress twice, I'm *saving the pennies,*" she told me. "If I buy a new dress, I'm *throwing daddy's money around.* If I put on an ounce of weight, I'm either *letting myself go* or I'm *secretly pregnant.*" She shuddered, then looked out of the window at the lights of Mount Mercy and smiled in relief. "Here," she told me, "I can just be *me.*"

Olivia and Gabriel came over to join us but there was only one seat. Gabriel immediately sat down, glanced at his lap and then looked up at Olivia with a cocky grin. Olivia flushed, wide-eyed, and shook her head.

"C'mon, doc," Gabriel told her, his voice teasing and warm and as intoxicating as neat whiskey. "Live a little."

Olivia bit her lip, blew a stray lock of hair back from her face... and sat on his knee. Carefully, as if she worried she might be too heavy. But as soon as her ass touched his knee, Gabriel wrapped his arms around her waist, leaned back and lifted his knee. Olivia yelped in surprise as she slid into his embrace. Then, as her back pressed against his strong chest and he dipped his head and kissed her neck, she giggled: a light, musical sound that I wouldn't have expected to come from her. She was so serious, most of the time...and I realized that that's why those two were so good for each other.

Bethany was sitting with Rufus between her knees and the massive Cal leaning over the back of the couch, his hands on her shoulders. Rufus looked up at her while Cal looked down, both faces equally doting. "How's Mount Mercy hospital?" she asked Olivia.

"Really, really good," Olivia told her with feeling. "Big enough and busy enough to be exciting, small enough that you can get to know everybody. And the staff are really friendly. They didn't have anyone in the ER who specialized in toxicology so I filled a gap. And I think they wanted someone...."—she flushed—"serious. There's an ER doc who's known for getting in trouble and the theory is, I can balance him out."

"I'm going to need to restart my residency to get my license in Colorado," Bethany told her. "Think they'd take me on as a student?"

She looked up at Cal. "It'd be amazing to be in Mount Mercy full time."

Olivia nodded. "I don't see why not. We have med students there." And the two of them launched into a deep discussion of departments and rotations. I relaxed back into the couch's cushions, sipping the last of my hot chocolate, and looked around at everyone. We made a weird little family. But it was one I really, really liked.

My eyes stopped on one of the windows. I could see down the hill to where Mount Mercy lay, the shops and houses spilling amber light from their windows as snow fell silently on their roofs. It was a fantastic view, but it wasn't what got my attention. The darker parts of the window acted almost like a mirror and I could see Stacey, standing in the corner. She was out of direct sight of everyone and she looked different to the energized, organized woman I'd met before. She looked exhausted. Worried.

Was it possible that she'd just been putting on a mask, all this time?

Someone needed to talk to her. Someone who was good with people. *Bethany*. But Bethany was deep in conversation with Olivia. And just as I was about to say something to Emily, Kian came over and led her away to talk to Danny. That only left—

I looked at the window again, seeing my own face looking back at me. *No. I can't.* When they'd been giving out people skills, Bethany had gotten a double scoop and I'd gotten none.

But there was no one else.

I took a deep breath, got up and went over. As soon as she saw me approaching, Stacey straightened her already-perfect dress, smiled a wide smile and lifted the milk ladle. "Refill?"

I had that feeling, like I always do when I talk to people, of trying to maneuver a gigantic barge in a narrow river without scraping the sides or colliding with any fragile rowing boats. The safe thing was to just smile and get another hot chocolate. But something was wrong. "You okay?" I asked at last.

She froze and the mask slipped again. Then she tried to cover it, smiling even wider and nodding: *don't be silly*. But the nod was jerky, like a motor that's not getting enough power. I kept looking at her, concerned....

And she just crumbled. Her face fell and she beckoned me into the empty briefing room. She leaned back against the door, pushing it closed, and put her face in her hands. Not crying, just...*defeated.* "I'm sorry," she said, shaking her head. "I'm sorry, I barely even know you...."

I reached out tentatively and touched her shoulder. "It's okay. What is it?"

She took a long, shaky breath. "It's Bradan."

I held her shoulder and waited. Danny had shared with me how Bradan had been taken by his mother into a cult when he was just fifteen. How Kian and his other brothers had reunited after years apart to find the cult and find out if their long-lost brother was alive or dead. They'd found Bradan brainwashed and being used by the cult as an assassin. They'd broken him free and smashed the cult, but....

"I thought he was fine," said Stacey, her voice almost a whisper. "He had *gaps,* things we all take for granted that he just didn't do because those bastards treated him like a machine. He'd never been in love. He'd never had friends. They'd even made him forget he had a family. But we got through all that, I reintroduced him to the world. He was doing great. And then he joined *this*—" She spread her hands, indicating Stormfinch. "And since he first went on a mission...."

I wasn't good at this. My weird brain was trying to reduce the problem down to concrete practicalities, so I could offer solutions. But I knew that wasn't what she needed. I tried to think like Danny, or Gabriel. They were good at this stuff. They'd just...*listen.*

I listened.

"I'm glad he's doing this," Stacey told me. "He needed this. He needed to...make amends, I guess. But since Ecuador, he's been getting these nightmares. He wakes up soaked in sweat. When I ask him about it, he says it's nothing. He's embarrassed. So now I just lie there, pretending to be asleep but I can hear him panic-breathing and I just want to turn around and put my arms around him!" And now her chest *did* jerk with a half-sob. "I just—Jesus, I just feel so helpless! I just want to help him and there's nothing I can do! And I shouldn't even be telling you this, it's private—"

"Oh, Stacey...." I used my hand on her shoulder to lever her forward into my arms and wrapped her into a hug. She was taller than me and her towering heels made her taller still, so she had to awkwardly hunch over me, and I wasn't really sure what to do with my hands because I'd never had a friend cry on me before, but....

But it worked. She nestled into me and I rubbed her back. My brain was still trying to adjust. This was *Stacey,* the super-organized, super-efficient one. I'd kind of thought problems just didn't dare happen to her. And maybe that was why she'd been bottling this up, because she was so used to succeeding. "You didn't need to go through this on your own," I told her. "You don't anymore."

She slumped against me and I relaxed, too. It felt like I'd just made a friend.

Danny

We'd left the women to talk because it was nearly time. We'd cleared an area for the guy to work: there was a table and a couple of chairs and, most importantly, a couple of good, powerful desk lamps because he'd said he needed good light. JD, Kian, Colton and Bradan were already standing around waiting, and Colton was telling everyone how this corner was where we could put a boxing ring.

"Is he here yet?" I asked as I walked over.

JD took a slug of his longneck beer and shook his head. "Any minute."

We studied each other, both still trying to adjust. He'd been my mate for so many years, now suddenly he was *Erin's brother.* And I'd been just Danny for so many years and suddenly, I was *Erin's boyfriend* with potential to transition into *Erin's scummy deadbeat bastard ex-boyfriend.* If it went wrong, I'd lose them both.

But that thought didn't come with the payload of dread it had back in Siberia. Nothing was going to go wrong. Because I loved her. I knew it, she knew it and JD knew it, too.

JD held my gaze for another few seconds, then reached behind him and passed me a cold beer. "Saved you one," he told me.

We clinked bottles and in that magical little sound of glass on glass there was more emotion than in any long, drawn-out conversation about our feelings. That *clink* said everything was okay. I finally relaxed. *Best friends again.*

"Been thinking," JD told me. "I might take a trip. I know this little bar south of the border where they serve margaritas *just right.* Figured I might drop by there and just sit in the sun for a few days."

I blinked. "A vacation? You *never* take a vacation."

"But now I know there's someone I can leave running things, while I'm gone," said JD. He looked me right in the eye as he said it and I felt such a sudden rush of pride, I had to turn away for a second. Maybe he was right: I was different, now. More responsible. But the fact he'd noticed made me—

"Yeah," I managed to choke out, punching his shoulder. "Yeah, 'course, mate. I'll keep an eye on things." I was happy. Happier than I'd ever been. The future rolled out before me, a blank page Erin and I could write together. Books in bed. Long drives. That computer show she wanted to go to. And sex. A *lot* of hot, filthy sex.

I had Erin in my life *and* I still had JD. I felt like I'd won the lottery twice. I frowned as something hit me: if things went well with Erin, JD and I could wind up brothers.

Steady, I told myself. One thing at a time.

The door opened and a man walked in, accompanied by a swirl of snow. "Frickin' *arctic*, out there," he told us, shaking off his coat. He had a long, black beard and a neck covered in tattoos. "Had to keep my stuff next to the heater or the ink would have frozen."

We showed him over to the table and chairs and put a hot chocolate in his hands to thaw him out. Kian showed him the design: a small, black and white bird. A stormfinch. "On all of you?" the man asked, looking from the piece of paper to us.

"On all of us," I confirmed as Cal and Gabriel joined us. We were a family, now.

Across the room, I saw Erin talking to Stacey and I raised my eyebrows questioningly: *you could get one.* She'd been on the mission with us, after all, and she was joining the team.

Erin took one look at the tattoo gun and shook her head, eyes wide. I chuckled.

"Okay," the tattoo artist asked. "Who's—" He broke off. "Wait, is that....?"

I followed his gaze. Colton's bear cub was scampering through the room, chased by Emily. "Yes," I told him.

The guy rubbed his beard. "Okay. Who's first?"

Everyone looked at Kian. He nodded and unbuttoned his shirt, and it began.

Erin

When the party was over and we'd all said goodbye—saying goodbye to Colton's baby bear in the parking lot took a full ten minutes of petting and fur-ruffling—I set out hand-in-hand with Danny for the walk down into the town.

Ahead of us were Kian and Emily, flanked at a polite distance by Secret Service agents. I saw Kian glance at one of them. "Thank you for letting me go to Berlin," he told her solemnly. "One thing I'm curious about, though: how *did* you distract Miller and the rest of the agents, so I could slip away?"

Emily stopped and turned to him. "Well, I—"

And then she just *dropped,* a puppet with its strings cut, her eyes rolled back in her head. Kian lunged forward and caught her before she hit the ground. "Emily? *Emily!*" Danny and I darted forward to help.

Then Emily opened one eye, a sly grin spreading across her face.

Kian's jaw dropped. Then he shook his head, awed. "You faked fainting?"

"Miller was *not* happy when he realized," she told him. "I felt really bad. I bought him socks, and promised to never do it again. I think he's forgiven me."

We all walked on in silence for a moment. Then I heard Kian mutter, "You were *worryingly* convincing..."

Emily stretched up on tiptoe and kissed his cheek. "Don't worry. I never need to fake anything with you."

I grinned, then looked back at Stacey and Bradan. They were walking slowly behind us, arms around each others' waists, their heads touching. I'd have to talk to JD about figuring out a way to help Bradan. And I was going to make sure to check in with Stacey regularly, to make sure she was doing okay. At least she knew she wasn't on her own, now.

We stopped for a second and looked at the town spread out below. It was late and most of the houses had their lights off but the moon was out, turning the crust of snow on their roofs silvery-blue. It was a beautiful little town, especially in the snow. Which was good because I'd heard it sometimes snowed *a lot.*

It's funny: I used to hate the cold. But after everything we'd been through, I was starting to realize that the cold can be a good thing. When you're unprepared, in a hostile place, it can make everything harsh and painful. But in a place like this, where there were warm places to cuddle up, the cold just made those cozy burrows snugglier. Every foot-numbing step we scrunched through the snow just built the anticipation because it took us a step closer to the garage, where I could tinker and fiddle to my heart's content without anyone judging me, where Danny could bring me coffee and I could bring him tea, where we could dance to the jukebox and kiss and fumble our way up the stairs and fall into the bed and then spend the next morning cuddled up reading.

I'd finally found my burrow.

I squeezed Danny's hand. He looked down, saw what was in my eyes and gave me one of those cocky grins. Then he slid his big, warm hand along my cold cheek and brought his lips down on mine, a slow kiss that gradually moved and changed, our tongues teasing and then dancing, faster and faster—

I broke the kiss, breathless, and tugged on his hand. "Come on," I told him. "Let's go home."

The End

Thank you for reading! If you enjoyed *Off Limits,* please consider leaving a review so other readers can find it.

JD's story will be next.

Want more of Danny and the other *Stormfinch* guys? For the team's first mission, and how roguish thief Gabriel fell in love with Olivia and became a hero again to save her, read *No Angel.*

The story of how Kian came to protect—and fall in love with—Emily, the President's daughter, is told in *Saving Liberty.*

The story of how Bethany saved Rufus and in turn was saved by Cal is told in *Deep Woods.*

The story of how shy languages expert Arianna was sent by the CIA to seduce Luka and wound up falling for him is told in *Lying and Kissing.*

Finally, the story of Kian and his brothers rescuing Bradan from the cult is told in *Brothers* (but you should read the four O'Harra brothers' books first. They are: *Punching and Kissing, Bad For Me, Saving Liberty* and *Outlaw's Promise*).

You can find details of all my books on my website at helenanewbury.com. All of them are available in paperback from Amazon or can be ordered from any bookstore.

Join my newsletter to hear about new releases and exclusive reader giveaways: https://list.helenanewbury.com

Made in the USA
Monee, IL
12 October 2023

44484856R00208